USA TODAY BESTSELLING AUTHOR
KRISTA SANDOR

The Nanny and the Hothead

Copyright © 2021 by Krista Sandor

All rights reserved.

No part of this book may be reproduced in any form or by any electronic or mechanical means, including information storage and retrieval systems, without written permission from the author, except for the use of brief quotations in a book review.

This is a work of fiction. Names, characters, places, and incidents either are the product of the author's imagination or are used fictitiously. Any resemblance to actual events, locales, or persons, living or dead, is entirely coincidental.

Copyright © 2021 by Krista Sandor

Candy Castle Books

Cover Design: Qamber Designs

All rights reserved.
ISBN: 978-1-954140-09-7
Visit www.kristasandor.com

ONE

CHARLOTTE

"NINE DOLLARS AND ELEVEN CENTS!"

9-1-1, this is an emergency—of the near-bankrupt kind.

Charlotte Ames stared at her account balance in horror. "That can't be right," she said, her voice rising a panicked octave. She refreshed the screen, then gasped. "This can't be right either."

Holy nonexistent savings! The charge for her morning coffee had rolled in.

"Five dollars and twenty-three cents!" she exclaimed. Could the decimal be in the wrong place? It had to be a glitch. An error. But no, her eyes weren't deceiving her. She was broke.

She dropped her phone onto her lap, sank onto the bench, and observed Denver's posh Crystal Creek shopping district.

At least it was a gorgeous day—not that the weather could alter her dire financial predicament. But it was better than being broke and pelted with hail or battered with rain.

Birds were singing. Bees were buzzing. And the hum of conversation hung in the air as patrons strolled by. Dotted with bistros, boutiques, and galleries, there was a good chance that the people frequenting the stylish neighborhood had a heck of a lot more than five bucks to their name. And these ritzy folks probably didn't sit on park benches muttering to themselves either.

Stupid fancy coffee!

She shouldn't have purchased the latte this morning! But it was so good, and the little shop had a sign posted that said it donated a portion of each sale to a local homeless shelter. Her latte helped the city, right? She blew out a frustrated breath. She'd be living in that shelter if she didn't get her act together.

She stared up at the sky. "I'm twenty-five years old, and I have less than ten bucks to my name. That's it! I'm putting myself on a latte lockdown," she mumbled, her shoulders slumping as an older gentleman stopped in front of her. Dressed in khakis and a navy polo shirt with an emblem of a heart made of tiny multi-colored handprints, she recognized the image from somewhere. But before she could rack her brain, she glanced up to see the gentleman frowning, concern clouding his gaze.

Why would he be staring at her?

Oh yeah—because she was a crazy lady camped out on a bench staring up at the sky and talking to herself!

"Are you all right, miss? Do you need help?" he asked gently.

Okay, those were, actually, excellent questions.

Let's break it down.

Was she *all right?*

That would be a hell no!

Almost every facet of her life was a hot flaming mess.

Her landlord had decided to convert her apartment building into condos, and there was no way she could afford to buy her place. She could barely pay the rent as is!

And her cash flow had recently been reduced by more than half!

Not only was she a twenty-five-year-old with five dollars to her name, who was about to get kicked out of her apartment. She was also a broke-ass twenty-five-year-old who had lost her steady waitressing gig due to an incident with a tomato, cucumber, and avocado salad.

What kind of vegetable clash could cause a gal to lose her job?

The kind of clash where that gal hurled vegetables at the back of her ex-boss's head. An ex-boss who just happened to be a hothead chef and the owner of the Crystal Cricket Bistro.

And she was not a vegetable hurler!

She was a good person. She went out of her way to be kind. She respected vegetables—even the ones that asshat of a chef had assembled into a beautiful salad. But the man was a tyrant. The absolute worst!

She might be Miss Goody Two Shoes. But even she had a limit.

Now, her sole income came from working part-time as a photography assistant.

Moment of truth—describing what she did in this position as actual *photography assisting* was a bit of a stretch.

Still, she was making her way in the industry. She had her foot in the door.

Rah, rah! Go, team, go!

Who was she kidding? The job was the pits!

She stared at her camera bag, and a soothing warmth settled in her chest, edging out the angst and disappointment. She set her gaze on her prized possession—her Nikon camera. She'd scrimped, saved, and even pawned a few things to purchase it. It was a camera that could take her to the next level if only she had the chance.

And she'd be wise to remember that chance may very well come today.

Her pulse quickened. But then she caught sight of a gaudy seashell hair clip tucked beside the camera and frowned.

Do not let that hold you back!

She shook her head and wiped the pout right off her face. She could not let that part of her job get her down. She checked her watch. In less than twenty minutes, she had an appointment at the gallery across the street. She was cutting it close. It was a busy day. She was assisting at an event in less than an hour. But this was the only time she was able to get an appointment at the gallery. And it was a connection worth maintaining. One of her old college professors, Janine Tran, had opened the trendy spot for local artists to showcase their work. And this place attracted buyers—real buyers, ready to throw down cold hard cash. She'd been emailing Professor Tran's assistant for months, and he'd finally gotten back to her yesterday. The professor had a few minutes free to chat today.

Take it or leave it.

Oh, Charlotte Ames will take it!

This was a big deal. A word from this woman could open doors. And Charlotte had a doozy of a door—a huge opportunity of sorts—she wanted to discuss.

Her life would change today. She could feel it in her bones.

And it wasn't just her career.

She looked up as an airplane sailed across the sky, and a rush of warmth flooded her body.

An airplane! It was a sign—a silly sign she'd held on to since she was thirteen—but a sign, no less!

Things were looking up in her love life, too. Fine, maybe looking up was pushing it. But it was on a steady trajectory. She'd gone on a lovely date six days ago with a handsome man named Cliff, *and* she'd signed up for a speed dating event tonight.

Don't get the wrong idea. The speed dating thing was a backup.

Yep, she was simply waiting on Cliff to reply to her text. And he would. Surely, he would! She'd listened to him go on and on about BASE jumping. She'd even pretended to enjoy the activity as well. Had she ever BASE jumped before? Heck no! What type of crazy person climbs to the top of a building only to leap off with nothing but a parachute? But she could play the part and tell the guy it was on her bucket list. That comment seemed to have made him happy. Granted, that's all they'd talked about. But relationships had to start somewhere, right?

Charlotte Ames might not have two nickels to rub together, but she was ready for love. Forget the string of awful exes. Inhale the positive and exhale the negative. That's what her yoga teaching best friend Libby would say. And it wasn't just Libby cheering her on. Her friends Penny and Harper were always in her corner.

Her girl squad had her back!

With a fresh surge of resolve, or perhaps it was some residual caffeine from her city-supporting latte, she straightened her shoulders. She studied the kindly gentleman standing in front of her, again noticing the embroidery on his shirt pocket. But she couldn't let her mind wander. She was a woman on a mission. "I'm going to make things happen today, sir. I'm in control of my destiny. Love will find me. Success is within my grasp!" she affirmed—to the dismay of the man.

"Do you need to take some medication?" he asked, enunciating his words.

Charlotte tucked a lock of auburn hair behind her ear as her cheeks burned. She'd gone full tomato—the terrible predicament of what happened when a redhead was well and truly mortified. "I don't usually recite affirmations to strangers in public," she explained, giving the nice man what she hoped wasn't a serial killer smile.

"Is there someone I can call for you? A friend? Your boyfriend?" the man questioned, looking more concerned by the second.

A boyfriend?

Just as the thought crossed her mind, her phone pinged an incoming text.

That had to be Cliff!

Her positivity was already making things happen.

She shot up to her feet, and the man sprang back.

"Sorry, I didn't mean to scare you," she apologized. "You see, first, an airplane flew over, then you mentioned a boyfriend, and now my phone pinged. It's got to mean something! I went on a date six days ago, and I think it went well. I texted him to tell him that I had a great time. And—"

"You texted him first?" the man pressed as a frown tipped the corners of his mouth.

She amplified her *hopefully-not-a-serial-killer* smile. "Yes, I texted him."

"And he hasn't responded?"

She wasn't expecting to have a whole Dr. Phil session with a random old man on the street—but whatever—she'd go with it.

"Not yet. But people get busy. You blink, and it's been a week," she answered with a touch too much enthusiasm. She had to tamp down the rah-rah factor.

The man shook his head. "Listen, honey, I'm eighty years old. I'm not sure what airplanes have to do with it, but even I know that it's a bad sign if the guy waits that long to text you back."

She lifted her chin. *Project determination!* "I could be the exception."

Her heart sank, but she had to keep the faith.

"As long as you're okay and not in need of medical help, I'll be on my way," he said with a friendly nod. But his comment about Cliff percolated in her mind.

How could an octogenarian know more about modern love than she did?

"For your information, sir," she called after him. "While I appreciate your concern, I'm great, I'm superb, and I'm not in need of medical attention." She slipped her camera bag over her shoulder. "In fact, I have an appointment at the gallery across the street. I'm a photographer."

Girl power! Be bold!

It wasn't a lie—exactly. She held a bachelor's degree in fine arts with a concentration in photography. She just wasn't practicing her craft in a traditional sense...yet.

Yes, that's it! Her career situation was temporarily nontraditional.

Her best friend Penny Fennimore, a gifted writer, would surely approve of that description. Did it border on fiction? Possibly! But it was true, more or less.

"You take care, young lady. Good luck with your fella," he replied over his shoulder as he continued down the sidewalk.

Her fella.

That's more like it!

Electricity zinged through her body.

The text!

She stared at her phone and grimaced at the bank statement before closing the window and tapping the text icon.

Here goes everything! She had a new text from...

Not Cliff!

It was from Madelyn Malone—again.

The second text in two days.

MADELYN MALONE: This is Madelyn Malone again. I sent you a message yesterday regarding an opportunity. The position needs to be filled immediately, and I believe you'd be the perfect fit.

Charlotte pursed her lips, index finger hovering over the keypad. She hammered out a reply.

CHARLOTTE AMES: I'm sorry, but I'm not interested.

She stared at the message, then deleted the response as an odd sensation washed over her—a strange, topsy-turvy reaction like when you've woken up from a wild dream, and you're caught between two worlds.

You see, while she wasn't more than an acquaintance of Madelyn Malone, she knew plenty about the lady. The woman was a regular at the Crystal Cricket Bistro. Before the whole vegetable incident, she'd waited on the chic senior citizen a time or two. Stunning with tumbling locks of dark hair with a lone silver streak highlighting the woman's high cheekbones, the lady oozed class and sophistication. Her vibe was part worldly witch, part Gucci-clad fairy godmother. She ran an exclusive specialty nanny service that matched nannies with wealthy, prominent single men.

And how did she know so much about the woman?

Her friend Penny had been recruited a few months ago to nanny for the tech guru, Rowen Gale, who was raising his six-year-old niece, a spunky little thing named Phoebe.

And how's the nanny gig going for good old Penny?

Pretty freaking amazing! She's engaged to the guy and has that *I-live-on-orgasms* glow twenty-four seven. And not the kind of glow that comes from a battery-operated device. Nope, Penny's getting the real deal. Between her hot nerd fiancé and killing it in her writing career, Penny was living the dream.

Of course, she was happy for her bestie. She loved Penny like a sister. The Penny, Rowen, Phoebe trio was about as cute as you can get. The guy owned a wildly successful video gaming company, and now they work together—Rowen does the techie stuff while Penny crafts the narratives for his games. It's a dream come true for her writer friend. But becoming a nanny wasn't in the cards for Charlotte Ames—no matter how well it paid. And it paid well, like really well, which honestly, might not be such a bad thing. Her bank account wouldn't turn away two thousand dollars a week and free room and board to boot.

But she had one problem. And that problem was time.

Here's how the nanny match worked. The first sixty days were a trial period. Both parties, the nanny and the employer, committed to staying together through this transition. But on that sixtieth day, the contract could be broken by either the employee or the employer.

No questions asked.

After the first Madelyn Malone text rolled in, she messaged Penny and asked if she knew what was going on. But Penny was clueless.

And now, the nanny match maven seemed to have moved on to her.

Charlotte twisted a lock of auburn hair between her fingers and peered across the street at Professor Tran's gallery. Here's where the time part comes in. If she played her cards right, with her teacher's help, in sixty days, she could be in London as part of an intensive photography workshop at the Royal College of Art—the top institution for art and design in the entire world. Here, she could hone her craft with the best of the best. The intensive lasted two weeks. But it could be the two weeks that changed her life. Mind you, they didn't accept just anyone. She had to submit a photograph, and she had to pray she'd qualify for a scholarship. That whole five bucks in her bank account wasn't enough to cover the Uber to the airport.

And that's why today was so important.

She checked the time. She had fourteen minutes until her appointment with Professor Tran. Fourteen minutes until she could ask her teacher which image she should submit. Her mouth grew dry as a chill danced down her spine.

Breathe.

She smoothed her skirt, then adjusted her camera bag as she set her sights on the gallery.

It wouldn't hurt to arrive a few minutes early, would it?

The thought had barely crossed her mind before a woman waving her cell phone in the air jogged toward her.

"Excuse me? Would you mind taking a picture of me and my boyfriend?" she asked through a cascade of bouncing blond curls.

Charlotte checked the time. Thirteen minutes. Plenty of time to snap a shot. She nodded, accepting the phone. "What would you like in the background?" she asked as a man—presumably the boyfriend—joined them. The guy pulled at his collar, then adjusted his sport coat.

Maybe he was camera shy.

"Anywhere on this block will do," the woman answered, all smiles.

Charlotte gestured for the couple to move close together, but the guy looked ready to lose his lunch. Luckily, she knew what to do.

"Instead of posing, how about, I ask you a few questions? It'll make the shot look more natural. Let's start with the basics. What are your names?" she began, snapping a picture as the woman leaned into the man.

"I'm Larissa, and this is my boyfriend of exactly one year, Royce."

"One year—that's a big anniversary. What's special about this place?" Charlotte asked, doing her best *not* to think about the fact that she hadn't come close to making a relationship last a month, let alone a year.

Larissa gazed up at Royce with puppy-dog eyes. "This is where Royce told me he loved me for the first time."

"Oh, wow!" Charlotte breathed, her envious heart tightening in her chest.

What must that be like?

From Larissa's expression, it looked pretty freaking amazing.

Charlotte glanced at the time. She had twelve minutes. It was time to combat her love-envy monster with kindness. She had time to do something nice for these two. She snapped another picture on Larissa's phone, then closed the photo app. "I'm a photographer. Would you like me to take a few shots with my camera? I could email them to you."

Larissa clapped as her beaming smile widened. "Royce, isn't that so kind? Yes, we'd love it! Being a photographer must be so exciting. I bet your family is proud of you."

Charlotte's lips parted as a knot twisted in her belly. "Yeah, absolutely," she lied.

Pushing thoughts of her family aside, Charlotte handed Larissa her phone, then removed her Nikon from the camera bag. "Now look at each other and tell me the story of how you met," she said, framing the shot. Royce still looked a little shaky. But as he stared into Larissa's eyes, his shoulders relaxed.

"It's quite a story," he said as the couple laughed. No, it wasn't a laugh exactly. It was one of those exchanges she'd seen thousands of times between people in love. That moment when a couple looked as if they were the only two human beings on the planet. That easy intimacy, like they'd wished upon a star and their dream had come true.

"We met at a speed dating night at some bar not far from here," Larissa answered, and Charlotte almost fell over.

Speed dating?

"I'm signed up to do one tonight, here in Crystal Creek. I wasn't sure if I should go," she replied.

Larissa did her happy clap again. "You should totally do it! Royce and I did it as a joke—not expecting to find our soul mate."

"And there were the free margaritas," Royce added playfully as he wrapped his arms around Larissa's waist.

Charlotte captured the moment as the man gazed down at his petite girlfriend with such tenderness.

A blush graced Larissa's cheeks. "Royce had gone with his friends for the booze. And I went with my friends for—"

"The booze," Royce finished with the sweetest grin as he brushed a lock of hair from his girlfriend's forehead. The camera clicked, then clicked again when Larissa teasingly tapped her boyfriend's chin.

"And life hasn't been the same since," Royce answered, now entirely at ease.

Charlotte stared at the viewfinder, taking in two people who were simply enamored with each other.

Would she ever find that?

It was absolutely intoxicating.

She was about to take another shot when a shrill voice cut through the air.

"Oh, look, Esther! Royce hired a photographer."

Charlotte peered over her shoulder, and her eyes went wide as a horde of people closed in on them.

"What's going on?" Larissa asked, confusion marring her sunny features. "Why are our entire families here, Royce?"

The man swallowed hard, the muscles in his throat

constricting. "I invited them to meet us at the restaurant down the block to celebrate."

"Celebrate what?" the woman pressed.

"That depends on your answer," the man replied as he reached into his breast pocket, then dropped to his knee.

His knee!

Charlotte froze. Royce was popping the question! No wonder he looked as if he'd eaten eight-day-old egg salad.

She basked in the swoony display. And then it hit her. This was a scene right out of a romance movie. And who was she?

The bit part.

Woman with a camera.

"Well, keep snapping, honey!" a lady who looked a heck of a lot like a middle-aged Larissa barked.

Charlotte shook off her angst-ridden haze, then glanced from the couple to the camera in her hands. "I'm not actually *their* photographer."

"You're holding a camera and taking pictures, aren't you?" a man, who looked a heck of a lot like a middle-aged Royce, tossed back.

What was she supposed to do?

She checked her watch. She had four minutes until her appointment with Professor Tran! Where had the time gone? And then she had to book it to the event she was working tonight.

Hello, dry mouth! Hello, wave of overwhelming anxiety! Why didn't she bring a bottle of water?

And she couldn't forget about her date with destiny tonight.

She had to make it to the speed dating thing right after she worked the photography gig. Meeting Royce and Larissa was a sign. The universe was dangling the possibility of love and unlimited margaritas right before her eyes.

Who knows! Within a year or less, she could be a Larissa—

the leading lady, the object of someone's complete adoration. Isn't that what she'd always wanted? That spark. That click. The ability to share that look with someone—the look that said, you're my person, and you always will be.

"Hey, photographer lady! He's holding the ring. Snap some pictures," the older version of Royce called.

Earth to Charlotte!

"Yes, I'm on it!" she exclaimed, moving in to get a shot of their hands.

"Can you get a picture of the whole family, too? I'd love to put a framed photo on my bookcase in the living room," a little elderly woman rasped from somewhere inside the horde of Royce and Larissa's family members clambering around the couple.

Charlotte looked at her watch. She had one minute. "I'm sorry, ma'am, but I really must be going."

At least twenty pairs of eyes stared her down.

"You're not going to say no to my great-great granny, are you?" Larissa asked, crestfallen, as the entire group watched her like a hawk.

Oh crap!

"What kind of photographer would deny a great-great granny?" the middle-aged Larissa lookalike lamented.

Hello, people, the kind of photographer who has a date with destiny!

But Charlotte couldn't say that.

Her gaze bounced between the teeny-tiny granny and the newly engaged couple. "Of course, I'll take a picture of the entire family. Please, gather in," she directed, her heart pounding as she captured a few shots. "That should do it. Now, I need to be on my way. Congratulations on your engagement!"

"Did you get my good side?" a woman dressed in orange asked, patting her gray bob.

Charlotte's mouth had become the Sahara Desert.

Stupid nervous reaction!

"I got everyone's good side. All good sides! All the time! But I have an appointment and—"

Larissa stepped forward, now rocking a giant, sparkling rock. "I need to give you my email address so you know where to send the pictures. It's Larissa with three S's at—"

"Larissa, sweetheart, have the photographer send the pictures to me. I can get them printed and framed," the Larissa lookalike crooned.

Larissa hugged her mother. "Thank you, Mom!"

Charlotte nodded, needing to get out of Dodge. "I can send the pictures anywhere. I just need an email address."

"Mom, what's your email?" Larissa questioned.

The woman scratched her chin. "You know, I have two email addresses. Bob, honey, which email is the email I should use?" she mused as precious seconds spiraled down the drain of time.

Charlotte checked her watch, and her belly did a flip-flop.

She was three minutes late for the most critical meeting of her life!

She grabbed a business card from her bag. Her best friends had made them for her. She hadn't given out one yet. But this was the perfect time to start. "Here, this has my information on it. Send me an email when you know where you'd like the pictures sent."

Larissa took the card and skimmed it. "You're the best, Charlotte Ames! Good luck with the speed date."

"Thank you," she answered, putting her camera away and zipping the bag closed.

Three minutes late couldn't be that bad!

She looked again.

Okay, four minutes late was within the acceptable range of lateness, wasn't it?

It had to be!

She inhaled a breath, working to calm her frayed nerves, when she glanced across the street, and a disorienting dizziness struck like a kick to the head.

"*No!*" she cried.

The open sign hanging in the gallery's window had been replaced with one that read, *Sorry, we're closed.*

TWO

CHARLOTTE

"WAIT! I'm within the acceptable range of lateness!" Charlotte cried, booking it across the street like an insane toddler—without checking for traffic. Tires screeched, and horns blared as she stopped dead in her tracks and stared down a shiny Mercedes Benz. The vehicle purred mere inches from her body as the scent of burnt rubber hung in the air.

"Are you insane, lady?" a man called through a cacophony of honking.

She took a shaky step back. No, she wasn't insane. She was simply a woman on a mission. A gal chasing her dreams.

"Get off the road," the angry luxury car driver griped, leaning out the window.

Charlotte blew out a shaky breath. "Yes, sorry," she panted, adrenaline coursing through her veins as she took a step and...

Crack!

She pitched forward as the spike on her left heel busted.

Could this get any worse?

"Are you all right?" the man called.

She pushed up onto her tiptoe, then took a tentative teetering step. "Yes, I'm okay. Thanks for asking."

"Then get the hell out of the way!" he bellowed.

"Good grief! Give me a second." She scooped up the broken remnant of her shoe, then did a graceless wobble-hop across the street as the honking died down and the traffic resumed.

"You're not dead," she whispered—at least she had that going for her. But death might have been a better alternative. She glanced at the gallery and saw none other than Professor Tran standing at the door, wide-eyed, with her mouth hanging open.

What a way to make an entrance, Charlotte!

The woman opened the door. "I heard the ruckus," she said, her gaze dropping to the ground and the unfortunate shoe situation.

Charlotte held up the broken heel. "Yes, that was me."

"Are you okay?" the woman pressed.

People seemed to be asking her that question a decent amount today.

Charlotte gathered her resolve, unzipped her camera bag, tossed in the heel, then removed her portfolio. It was showtime!

"I'm fine and so grateful to speak with you." She checked her watch. "I'm sorry I'm late, Professor Tran. I hope you still have a minute to spare for me."

Please, please, please!

It was hard enough to beg the professor's assistant to schedule this appointment. And she didn't want to email her teacher. Professor Tran probably got a boatload of messages a day. She couldn't risk being forgotten in the mix.

The woman slipped her cell from her purse. "I have a few minutes, Charlotte. My car should be here any moment. I'm headed to Chicago to lecture at the Museum of Contemporary Photography."

"That's exciting," Charlotte replied, wondering if her photography career would ever take her to prominent galleries.

"It's a quick trip. I'm there for one night. I have to get back to Denver. I recently purchased a building in an up-and-coming part of the city to open a second gallery." She glanced at her watch. "My assistant told me you had a quick question. Why don't we chat inside until my car arrives?" the woman offered smoothly, opening the door.

Charlotte nodded, catching her breath as she entered the bright space. What she wouldn't give to have the poise and confidence of Janine Tran! The woman was a celebrated photographer, gallery owner, and lecturer. Charlotte took in the spacious room. Enlarged photographs dotted the crisp white walls. Immediately, a portrait caught her eye. She studied the composition of a young boy holding a bowl of rice. The child sported a wide grin—a grin that lit up his face. The joy coming from this child stood in stark contrast to the tents and piles of trash burning in the background.

"This print is one of yours, isn't it?" Charlotte asked, spellbound, as she stared at the engaging image.

Janine Tran came to her side. "It is. I was invited to photograph a refugee camp in Cambodia. It's a hard life for those children, but we can learn quite a bit from them. They find happiness in difficult times. It's important to share their stories—the good and the bad."

"It had to be difficult to witness," Charlotte commented, but Janine shook her head.

"Our job isn't to judge a situation. Our job as photographers is to allow the story to unfold and find that sentient moment. Yes, it's important to employ empathy. But we're after the truth—whatever that truth may be."

And this is why Janine Tran was *the* Janine Tran.

Charlotte nodded, unable to look away from the boy. When you engaged with a Janine Tran photograph, it was as if the layers of the moment had peeled back, exposing the very essence of her subject.

"Are you freelancing?" Professor Tran asked.

Charlotte studied the floor. "Something like that. I'm assisting a photographer."

"And how are you finding the experience? Are you able to hone your craft?" the woman continued.

Honing her craft?

The one hundred percent honest answer—a big fat no! But she couldn't admit that. She had to spin it.

Her current position didn't afford her an opportunity to use an actual camera—yet.

She worked for the photographer Sutton Bryan. The guy's real name was Bryan Sutton, but he made her call him Sutton Bryan. Not Bryan. Not Sutton. Sutton Bryan. The four-syllables grated in her brain just picturing the man. She'd been with him for almost a year. Every time she'd broached the subject of taking on more photographer duties, he'd tell her it was only a matter of time—that she was working her way up.

That line was starting to ring hollow.

She met Professor Tran's expectant gaze. "My duties are slightly non-traditional. But yes, I'm assisting at events several times a week. In fact," she peered at her watch, "we've got an event coming up in..."

In thirty minutes!

Crap! She'd have to change her clothes in her car again.

"You were saying you have an event," Janine prompted.

Gah! She could not zone out.

"Sorry, we're shooting a private event at the Crystal Creek Country Club—a party," she finished, praying Professor Tran wouldn't ask what type of party.

The woman nodded. "Parties give a photographer time to absorb the environment and observe. Start there."

Charlotte cocked her head to the side. "Start by absorbing?"

"Look beyond what's right in front of you and capture the heart of what's there. A party, a rock, a leaf fluttering to the ground—it's the photographer's job to tell that story through her lens," Professor Tran explained.

Charlotte nodded.

"Now, did you have a question for me? My assistant said you'd like my opinion for a submission."

Charlotte swallowed hard—which was some feat, with a mouth devoid of liquid. "I'd like to apply for a workshop at the Royal College of Art. I was hoping you could help me choose a submission photograph," she finished, handing over her portfolio. "I think the first two photographs are the strongest, but I'd appreciate your insight."

Professor Tran opened the book and examined the images. "Do you have any more?"

Charlotte's stomach dropped. That wasn't a good sign! Plus, she was sure those shots of the city were two of her best. "Yes, I've got more images on my iPad."

"Could I see them?" the professor prompted.

She slid the device from her bag, opened it to her digital portfolio, then handed it over.

Janine Tran scanned photo after photo as frown lines pulled at the corners of her mouth. Charlotte steadied herself, wobbling a fraction thanks to her precarious shoe predicament. Now she was the one who must look as if she'd eaten eight-day-old egg salad.

"When is the submission due for the workshop?" the professor asked.

"It's a few days away," she rasped, working to keep her voice steady, when a car stopped in front of the gallery.

Time was up!

Professor Tran nodded to the driver, then handed back the iPad.

Charlotte couldn't speak as she observed the woman whose opinion she valued above all else.

"When I look at your work, it's sound photography. Perspective is good. You understand how to work with the light," the professor began.

"Thank you," Charlotte answered. Okay, this wasn't as bad as she thought.

"But I don't see you," the professor finished.

The hope in Charlotte's heart withered away. "I don't like to have my picture taken," she confessed.

Janine Tran shook her head. "That's not what I mean. What do you want? What's your vision?"

Charlotte swallowed hard. "My vision?" she parroted back.

"Yes."

Vision?

Charlotte shifted her stance. Did the woman mean the visual components of a composition or something else?

"I'm not sure I understand the question. When I take a picture, I'm mindful of what the client wants—what shots they'll be expecting. How is that wrong?" she replied, and not a second had passed before she knew her answer wasn't the answer Janine Tran was looking for.

"Anyone can point a camera at something," the woman began, reaching for the door. "When you call yourself a photographer, you become part of the equation. Think of the shot like it's your family. You're a part of it even if you're not in the frame."

Charlotte mustered a weak smile. While she understood the analogy, not every family fit the bill. When it came to her family, she wasn't included in the frame. "I see," she answered, her voice barely a whisper.

"I suggest you go back to the beginning, Charlotte."

The beginning?

She frowned. "What do you mean by that?"

"Why did you choose to study photography?" Professor Tran pressed.

That wasn't a hard question to answer.

"Because it's what I love."

"Why do you love it?" the professor continued. "Boil it down to one reason."

Charlotte's mind raced. "I can't think of just one reason."

Shoot!

Janine opened the door and gestured for Charlotte to follow her out. "I'll be honest with you. I didn't see any image worthy of submitting to the Royal College of Art."

"Oh," she breathed, barely able to form the syllable.

"You have a little time, Charlotte. And the talent is there. You need to tap into it."

"I still don't understand, Professor Tran. What should I do?" she asked, trying to keep the soul-crushing disappointment from her tone.

"Extend beyond your comfort zone. The next time you pick up your camera, ask yourself what truth are you looking to reveal? Scratch beneath the surface. Show the world what Charlotte Ames sees," the professor replied as the driver opened the door to the town car, and the woman settled herself inside.

Charlotte nodded, putting on a brave face as the car disappeared into traffic and tears welled in her eyes.

※

HER TIRES SCREECHED as she pulled into the Crystal Creek Country Club's parking lot like a bat out of hell.

She was late.

Again.

Tardiness seemed to be the template for today.

"Do not cry! You do not have time to cry," she whispered to herself as she pulled into a parking space in an isolated corner of the lot.

Saying that the visit with Janine Tran had not gone as expected was an understatement. But all was not lost. She might have struck out with the professor, but she still had a shot at finding love. Once she finished working the event with Sutton Bryan, she had a date with destiny.

That's how she had to frame it in her mind.

After she met Mr. Happily Ever After, she could replay her conversation with Professor Tran and figure out what going back to the beginning meant for her.

She cut the ignition, then pulled the lever to recline her seat. She'd become good at changing her clothes in the car. She twisted out of her skirt and pulled the first part of her event wardrobe from her tote. Wiggling her hips, she shimmied into the formfitting aquamarine lower portion of her costume. Next, she plucked the top part from the bag, then grimaced at the ridiculous thing.

What kind of ridiculous thing?

A shell brassiere—that's right, a freaking shell bra—with gaudy aquamarine rhinestones hot-glued around the edges. Putting on this contraption without giving everyone within eyesight a glimpse at her breasts was no small accomplishment. Obviously, this wasn't a skill one would list on a résumé. But she'd mastered the art of whipping off her regular bra and switching into the shell garment beneath her shirt.

A little boobalicious switcheroo in the parking lot!

With nimble fingers, she unclasped her bra, pulled it out of her sleeve, then went to work donning the most uncomfortable undergarment known to man.

Scratch that—known to women!

Men had it so easy in the clothing department.

She shifted in the seat and adjusted the shells to cover as much as possible—which wasn't much. And ouch! The stupid thing cut into the sides of her boobs, something fierce.

Bra in place, she pulled her long auburn hair over her shoulder, started braiding, then caught her reflection in the rearview mirror. She froze, staring at herself as a heaviness set in. This was her life. A life where, in exchange for money, she dressed like a mermaid hooker! Her phone buzzed, and she tied off the braid, then glanced at the text. It was from the text chain between herself, Libby, Harper, and Penny.

LIBBY LAMB: How did it go with your professor, Char? Your energy is off. How much caffeine have you had today?

Charlotte rested her head on the steering wheel and released a weary chuckle. She loved her friends. And Libby, their resident Zen diva, was a riot. But the peacefulness that came with seeing Libby's name pop up on her phone was replaced with dread. What was she supposed to tell Libbs? The professor basically said she'd never taken a picture worthy of the Royal College of Art. Charlotte swallowed past the lump in her throat.

No! She couldn't tell Libby that.

CHARLOTTE AMES: She gave me some good feedback.

LIBBY LAMB: Which image did she suggest you submit? That great shot of the city skyline or the one of the kids playing in the fountain outside the museum or one of your night sky shots?

Charlotte blew out a slow breath.

**CHARLOTTE AMES: Neither. She told me to go

back to the beginning and remember why I chose to study photography.

Immediately, three dots flashed.

HARPER PRESLEY: WTF? Do I need to go kick some academic ass?

Charlotte shook her head as a happy tear ran down her cheek and she brushed it away.

What would she do without her girls?

LIBBY LAMB: Harper, take a breath! That reaction will not balance your chi.

HARPER PRESLEY: Screw the chi, the fee, the fie, the foe, and the fum! Charlotte's pictures are amazing! Definitely worth throwing down for.

Charlotte had met her girl squad way back in kindergarten. And while they'd grown up, some things remained the same. Case in point, not even the bullies in fifth grade messed with the badass kindergartener version of Harper Presley.

The dots appeared again, and Penny joined in.

PENNY FENNIMORE: I'm reading through the text string. Harper, how many piano lessons have you taught today? I sense some 'roid rage—I mean Rachmaninoff rage.

LIBBY LAMB: Good one, Penn! Using that writer's brain.

HARPER PRESLEY: Ha! Ha! And FYI, that would be eight back-to-back lessons—and I have two more to go.

LIBBY LAMB: Breathe, girl! I'm sending positive energy.

CHARLOTTE AMES: I'll need those good vibes, too. I've got an event with Sutton Bryan now.

**HARPER PRESLEY: I know it sucks, Char. But

you're a crazy hot mermaid! You will always have that.

Charlotte scoffed.

CHARLOTTE AMES: F you, H!

HARPER PRESLEY: That's more like it, Char! Embrace your inner redhead. Get fired up! You don't always have to be nice. Know your worth, girl!

PENNY FENNIMORE: We love you, Char!

LIBBY LAMB: You're my favorite mermaid and a talented photographer. Don't ever forget it!

HARPER PRESLEY: And if you need me to kick some ass—I've got a narrow window between lessons.

Charlotte chuckled.

CHARLOTTE AMES: Love you, H! Let's hold off on the ass-kicking for now.

LIBBY LAMB: OK, now that we've established that we're not resorting to violence tonight, I gotta go! I have three yoga classes to teach. I'm sorry I can't meet you for the speed date thing, Char.

HARPER PRESLEY: Why are you doing that, Charlotte????

Charlotte stared at the screen. The answer? Because for as long as she could remember, she'd longed to have a man wrap his arms around her and tell her that she held the key to his heart.

Cheesy?

Yes.

Did she care?

No way! Pile on the love cheese—the more, the better.

She'd longed for that sweet security. The bliss she'd antici-pated would hit her like a Mack truck the minute she locked eyes with Mr. Cheesy Forever. She was about to float away imagining meeting Mr. Right when thoughts of her parents bubbled to the surface. An unwelcome, sickening sensation passed over her. But she couldn't go down that road. Not now! Tonight was not the night for that.

CHARLOTTE AMES: I'm going for the margaritas, of course.

She stared at the screen. Another half-truth. How many more would she tell today?

PENNY FENNIMORE: Be careful! And only have one. I hear the margs at that place pack a real

BANG! BANG! BANG!

Charlotte gasped, dropping her phone before reading Penny's entire text. Her heart hammering in her chest, she met her boss's angry gaze.

"What are you doing? The party started ten minutes ago. And why aren't you dressed? Where's the hair clip?" the man hissed, glaring at her through the windshield, his orange spray tan highlighting the whites of his bulging eyes.

Charlotte reached into her camera bag, wishing she could remove her camera instead of the gaudy hot-glued-to-hell hair clip.

"I'm sorry, Sutton Bryan. It's been a busy day," she answered, sliding the clip into her hair. She opened the car door, then swung her legs out in a well-practiced maneuver as the flared tail swooshed in the air. Moving around in this getup was a nightmare! With no help from her asshat of a boss, she arched her back, then flung herself out of the vehicle. She was no Lady Grace, but there was no other way to do it. She peered down at her shirt, hiding the shell cleavage. "How about I keep this on and let the shells peek through?" she asked, knowing what Sutton Bryan would say. Still, it was worth a shot.

The man huffed. "Charlotte, this is my art. You are a part of the process. That is what an assistant does. They assist the professional in his process."

She'd hit a brick wall with him—again!

She gifted him with her most placating smile. "I hoped that I could assist in human being clothing at some point. It would certainly be more comfortable," she replied, wincing as the left shell cut into her boob.

The man's eyes nearly popped out of his head. With his fake tan, broad forehead, and bulgy eyes, he'd make a great bronzed bullfrog. "Do mermaids wear human being clothing?" he croaked in reply.

Her nerves started to get the best of her—a deluge of verbal vomit was surely on its way. She twisted the tail of her braid. "Sort of. They do wear bras."

Sutton Bryan's shiny white eyeballs might have detached from his retina as his perma-tan took on a decidedly rosier hue, and he went full bullfrog.

"Shell bras," he countered. "Ocean bras!"

"I think an ocean bra would technically be a bikini top," she corrected—and just as the words passed her lips, she'd regretted it.

"Do you know how much work went into the construction of that shell bra?" he squawked.

Charlotte unbuttoned her blouse, then peered down at the gaudy thing. "I don't know."

The boob torture device looked like something a drunk toddler made at a preschool arts and crafts fair.

Somehow, the man's eyes bulged even more. "My mommy made it! She put hours into planning and flawlessly executing my vision."

Wait, what?

Charlotte had to physically keep her jaw from dropping.

Mommy?

What grown man calls his mom *mommy?*

She'd have to tell the girls.

But before she could feel too high and mighty, a depressing realization hit. She worked for a grown-ass man who called his mother mommy.

"Oh my God!" she uttered under her breath.

"Charlotte?" he chided as a muscle ticked in his orangey-red jaw. "This event was booked as a mermaid birthday party. There has to be a mermaid."

She needed to make one more attempt to change the man's mind. It most likely would fall on his deaf bullfrog ears, but something inside of her needed to try. If Professor Tran wanted her to go back to the beginning, she had to start acting like an actual photographer—not a hooker mermaid!

"How about this? I was thinking..." she began.

"I don't pay you to think," he barked, cutting her off. "I pay you to wear the damned costume and smile."

That's all she was—a convenient redhead who fit into his mommy-made costume.

Her lips parted, but nothing came out.

Sutton Bryan pasted on a syrupy smile. "And what about the kids, Charlotte? Do you want me to tell them that there's no mermaid? Imagine how disappointed they'll be—all because of you."

Dammit! The kids!

Her shoulders slumped a fraction, and she caught a glimpse of herself in the car window's reflection. "Okay, fine, I'll do it. But I need to cut out a little early. I have a...prior commitment," she added.

She wasn't about to tell him it was to attend a speed dating night at a bar.

"Shirt," the man growled, holding out his hand. Did he even hear that she couldn't work the entire event?

She handed it over, and the guy set off at a breakneck pace. She could barely move her legs three inches, thanks to the rubbery, formfitting hell that was the mermaid tail. Crossing her arms to keep her shell-clad boobs from popping out, she tittered behind the asshat photographer. On the bright side, at least she could go barefoot.

Wait...she was barefoot, chasing after her creep of a boss through a parking lot toward an event where she would get no practice honing her photography skills while wearing a slutty mermaid costume.

This must be rock-bottom.

Even so, her situation would improve. There was no way to sink any lower.

Reframe! Reframe! Reframe!

The universe might have broken her heel and tried to mow her down with a Mercedes. But she had gotten to talk to Professor Tran. She just had to figure out what kind of photograph would be good enough to impress the Royal College of Art.

What did they want?

Whatever it was, she could do it.

She'd *be* what they wanted.

And she had speed dating! Meeting Larissa and Royce couldn't have been a fluke. She had to make it through the next hour.

Goodbye, rock-bottom! Hello, life filled with love!

Toddling along like a five-foot-six penguin, Sutton Bryan ushered her through a side gate—not into the shiny clubhouse.

"It's an outdoor party?" she asked as a large pool came into view. It was late spring. Most outdoor recreation spots didn't open until after school was out at the end of May—a little more than two months away.

"No, it's the backdrop for the mermaid photos. The party is inside."

"Okay," she answered warily as a terrifying thought tore through her.

He wouldn't want her to go in the pool, would he? This was their first gig at a location with an actual pool.

"I don't think I can swim in this costume, Sutton." Maybe she could—honestly, she wasn't sure. But she couldn't show up to the speed date event soaked.

He glared at her. "Sutton..."

Ah, yes! The jackass had two names.

"Sutton Bryan, I'm not a real mermaid!" she exclaimed when a chorus of horrified gasps peppered the air.

"She's not a real mermaid?" a child whimpered.

Charlotte looked past a stack of deck chairs. There had to have been fifty, no, more like one hundred people staring at her. A bunch of little boys that looked to be eight or possibly nine years old gathered in front of the group while a cluster of frowning adults looked on.

"You said you'd have a real mermaid, Declan! That's the only reason the boys in our class came. Mermaids are for girls," a beefy kid with a bowl cut snapped.

The birthday boy stared at her expectantly, bottom lip trembling.

Sutton Bryan turned to her, eyeballs ready to explode. "Fix this, or you're not getting paid," he hissed between clenched teeth.

Oh crap!

Charlotte waddled forward. "How do you know that I'm *not* a real mermaid?"

"You just said it, lady," the loud-mouthed boy shot back.

"How do you know I don't say that to throw people off?

Imagine how many children would want to keep a real mermaid in their pool. I have to be careful."

The birthday boy smiled up at her. "You are a mermaid!"

Crisis averted!

Charlotte's hammering pulse slowed.

"She's just some lady pretending," the beefy boy replied before swiping a lollipop from a snack table.

Hopefully, that would shut him up!

She shrugged, playing it cool—or at least as cool as one can be with dozens upon dozens of pairs of eyes boring into them. "Maybe, maybe not! Declan is the only one who knows the truth," she finished.

The birthday boy lifted his chin as the corners of his mouth gently tipped. "Yeah, I'm the only one who knows," he answered, playing along. Thank God!

She tossed the kid a conspiratorial wink.

"Who'd like their picture with Charlotte the Mermaid? Go on and stand by the edge of the pool, Charlotte," Sutton Bryan directed, sounding as smarmy as a used car salesman.

"Me first," the bully called, dropping the candy to the ground, then charging toward her.

Heart hammering, she stared down at the kid and tried to muster some empathy. He was a kid. A little boy—nothing more.

"Grover, smile for the camera," a woman crooned.

"Your name is Grover?" Charlotte asked.

The kid scrunched up his face. "Yeah, it's Grover. Grover Cleveland Schulte. You got a problem with it?"

Oh no! The hostile bully was back!

"No, it's a unique name," Charlotte said, trying to connect with this pint-sized pest.

"Say cheese!" Sutton Bryan crooned, but the kid didn't utter a word.

She caught the boy's gaze, glittering with mischief, as he looked from her to the pool.

She should have known Grover Cleveland Schulte was up to no good.

"Cheese, fake mermaid!" the boy belted, then shoved her in the stomach. She didn't have a fighting chance to remain upright in that stupid, body-hugging mermaid tail. And for the second time today, she teetered, swaying side to side before gravity took over. Reflexively, she reached out and grabbed onto the only thing she could.

Grover Cleveland Schulte.

Splash!

Their bodies hit the ice-cold water like two cement slabs.

"My baby! My sweet Grover!"

Charlotte thrashed around as the gaudy decorations on her shell bra came loose—like rhinestone sailors abandoning ship. Luckily, they'd fallen into the shallow end. Okay, not luckily. There was nothing fortunate about her situation besides the fact that she wasn't in danger of drowning. Soaking wet, she stood and looked on as Grover Cleveland Schulte's parents pulled him out of the water like a beached whale.

"Everyone, let's head inside for cake," a red-faced woman called with her arm around a crying Declan.

Poor thing!

She'd tried to make it right! Surely, her boss would understand. She searched the patio and found Sutton Bryan looking the exact opposite of understanding.

She scooped a few floating rhinestones into her hand and sloshed toward him. "Sutton Bryan, I'm so sorry."

An orange vein pulsed in his neck, and his protruding eyeballs looked ready to burst out of his head. "You're sorry? No, you don't get to be sorry. You're fired!"

Panic—no, complete and total terror rippled through her.

She had five dollars to her name and no job!

"Fired?" she repeated, her voice barely a rasp. "But it wasn't my fault! And look! I found a few stones. I can fix the shell bra."

"Fix it? You've ruined the mermaid costume! Mommy will be overcome with despair," the man lamented.

Charlotte stared down at the crusted remnants of hot glue where the awful rhinestones once sat. "The only despair I harbor is that I actually wore this hideous thing," she said, holding the man's gaze.

And *oh no*! Did she say that?

Sutton Bryan's jaw dropped. "I'm docking your pay for the costume, and I'm not paying you a dime for today," the man bit out before turning on his heel and stomping off toward the clubhouse.

Charlotte released a slow breath as rivulets of water trailed down her face. "Did I tell off my boss?" she whispered, brushing a few wisps of wet hair from her cheek.

"Yes, that's exactly what you did," answered a voice—a vaguely familiar woman's voice.

Charlotte froze—and not because she was still immersed in four feet of frigid chlorinated water. She recognized the rich voice with a distinct cadence—a European accent she couldn't quite place.

No, it couldn't be!

Slowly, she looked over her shoulder and caught a flutter of red in her peripheral vision—the flutter of a red silk scarf.

Madelyn Malone's signature red scarf.

She'd never seen the woman without it.

"I've got a towel for you, dear. You'll catch a chill if you stay in there."

Charlotte mermaid-walked over to the steps, fumbled her way up, then accepted the towel. "What are you doing here?"

"I'm a member of the country club," Madelyn answered smoothly.

Of course, she was! The pricey Birkin bag on her arm cost as much as ten of her old Hondas. The nanny match maven probably belonged to every country club in the city.

"And you happened to be here to witness this unfortunate event?" Charlotte replied.

Calling this an unfortunate event wasn't quite right. It was more like her complete and total humiliation. But at this point, it didn't really matter how she labeled it. She was screwed.

Madelyn waved her off. "A little water never hurt anyone. Now, you haven't answered my texts."

That's right! She hadn't.

Charlotte accepted the towel and pressed the soft fabric to her face. "I'm sorry about that. I've been..."

"You haven't been waitressing. That's for sure," Madelyn supplied.

Charlotte shivered, then wrapped the towel around her shoulders. "I don't work at the Crystal Cricket. There was an incident with a salad."

"Yes, I know. I was there," the woman answered with the ghost of a grin.

Charlotte gasped. "You were?"

"The chef was yelling at a busboy," Madelyn continued.

She nodded. "Yeah, he was."

"And you didn't approve?" Madelyn continued, watching her closely.

Charlotte glanced away. "The kid didn't mean to break a glass. He didn't deserve to be berated."

"So, you threw a salad at your boss—Chef Elliott?" Madelyn supplied.

More like the hothead super-prick Chef Mitch Elliott!

She hadn't meant to assault the man with leafy greens—it just happened.

"I did. Then I walked out. But I want you to know I don't usually react like that. I'm a nice person ninety-nine point nine, nine, nine percent of the time."

Madelyn nodded, then surveyed the mermaid tail. "You're not waitressing, and it appears that you aren't employed as a professional mermaid any longer."

Charlotte released a resigned sigh. "I'm supposed to be an assistant to a photographer."

"Perhaps you're supposed to be a nanny," the woman slipped in, raising an eyebrow.

It wasn't the worst job offer in the world. But what about London?

She adjusted the towel. "There's a chance I may be accepted into a photography workshop in London."

A tiny, infinitesimal chance—but still, a chance.

"When?" the woman probed.

"Two months from now—again, only if I get accepted. It's a two-week intensive workshop."

Charlotte expected the woman to change her tune and rescind the offer, but Madelyn's eyes sparkled as a wide grin stretched across her face.

"Then you have the time to participate in the nanny trial period. You're friends with Penny Fennimore. Did she share with you how the sixty-day trial period worked?"

Sixty days. Live-in nanny position. Two thousand dollars a week. At the end of that time, either party could choose to end the contract—no questions asked.

Charlotte nodded. "How many children would I be looking after—if hypothetically, I got the job?"

She had to ask. This might be her only way to pay the bills. It was that or run after Sutton Bryan and sink to her knees and beg the blathering orange bullfrog to give her back her job, which she was not about to do. Plus, there was an excellent chance she'd fall on her ass if she tried to kneel in the mermaid getup.

"One. A little boy. He's six," Madelyn replied.

Charlotte held the woman's gaze. "The same age as Phoebe."

"That's right."

Charlotte twisted the wet tail of her braid. Was she doing this? Was she considering it? Before she fell down the rabbit hole of questioning what she was supposed to do, Madelyn plucked a small, velvet pouch from her zillion-dollar purse.

"I'm structuring your nanny/employer introduction a bit differently." The woman opened the pouch and removed a necklace. "Turn around, dear."

As if she were under a spell, Charlotte complied.

"I'd like you to wear this necklace," the woman finished.

The clasp clicked, and Charlotte peered down at a golden key dangling between her shell-clad breasts. Madelyn then removed a card from her bag.

"Take this," she said.

Charlotte's fingers trembled as she accepted it—and it wasn't from the chill. This felt like a crossroads. And then she turned the card over and read the address, and the breath caught in her throat. "I know this place," she answered, astonishment coating her words.

What were the chances?

It was the same location as the speed date event.

Madelyn maintained a neutral expression. "It's a bar. A public place in the Crystal Creek business district. I've instructed my client to meet you there. He'll find you with that," the woman said, gesturing to the key.

A public place was a safe place to meet. But unease twisted

in her belly. "I'm not sure if nannying is for me. I know how things worked out for Penny, but I—"

"You have dreams of becoming a famous photographer," Madelyn interjected.

Charlotte weighed the question, then lifted her chin. "I do."

"Here's what I've learned about dreams, Charlotte," Madelyn continued. "You see, I've been around quite a while, and I've helped many people. I think of myself as a facilitator of fate."

"Fate?" Charlotte echoed. The word hung in the late spring air like a wish upon a star.

"Sometimes, the future needs a nudge in the right direction. That's where I come in."

Charlotte stared down at the key, resting against her skin as if it had been there—as if it belonged with her, to her. And a seed of hope bloomed in her chest. Could tonight be the night she got a cushy job making bank *and* found her Mr. Cheesy Forever?

She met Madelyn's gaze. "Why me? Why do you think I'm the right fit?"

"The little boy you'll be caring for has an artist's spirit."

"What's his name?"

"Oscar," Madelyn replied.

Charlotte smiled. She couldn't help it. She'd always loved the name. "Oscar is interested in art?"

"Let's say that I see that as his calling."

This woman could sure say a lot without saying anything!

"His calling?" Charlotte questioned.

"Yes, dear. You see, you're nice ninety-nine percent of the time, and that will benefit the child. My client, however, could use a bit of your not-so-nice one percent."

Madelyn Malone was a walking book of presumptions, riddles, and veiled assertions.

"Again, Madelyn, I don't understand," she replied, searching the woman's expression.

The nanny match maven smoothed her scarf. "Luckily, I do understand. I understand completely. That's my gift. And that's why I believe that you're a match for this placement."

Charlotte held the key as she stared at the starry sky, searching for answers.

"What are you waiting for, Charlotte? You've got the key," Madelyn said with a curious lilt to her rich vibrato voice. "It's up to you to figure out if it opens the right door."

THREE

MITCH

MITCH ELLIOTT SCOWLED as he swiped a tasting spoon from the counter. He stared hard at his sous chef's version of tonight's special—a dish he usually only prepared for one person.

Truffle risotto.

He slid the spoon into the creamy concoction and scooped up a bite.

But he wasn't happy—far from it.

He could already tell something was off before the risotto even hit his tongue. Like a toddler not wanting to eat his vegetables, Mitch forced the spoon into his mouth. The problem presented itself like a four-alarm fire.

There was too much parmesan cheese!

Such an egregious overuse that the whole dish was thrown off. Jesus! He might as well run down to the corner market, snap up a canister of the cheap dried-out shit, and serve that on a platter. It would be better than the catastrophe his sous chef threw together.

Was he the only person in this restaurant who cared about quality?

He swallowed the crap risotto, then scrutinized the young sous chef cowering before him. Could he go easy on the kid and tell him to dial it back on the parm?

Yeah.

Would the old version of himself have done that?

Absolutely! He probably would have patted the guy on the back, too.

But he wasn't that guy anymore—and hadn't been for quite some time.

Seven years, to be exact.

Oh, and by the way, the old Mitch Elliott was a real sucker. A true chump! He'd been played in the very worst of ways. At the thought of the old version of himself, heat rose to his cheeks, and his pulse quickened.

There was no Mr. Nice Chef at the Crystal Cricket. His restaurant. He was the owner and executive chef. He didn't have to be nice. His pedigree spoke for itself. His résumé was littered with culinary awards and prestigious honors. Despite his fiery temper, line cooks clamored to work for him. Sous chefs happily took his shit, lowered their heads, and got to work executing his menu. The front of the house was booked for weeks on end. The waitstaff endured his outbursts because, thanks to his rep and the positive buzz about the Crystal Cricket, they made decent tips.

Was he easy to work for?

Hell no!

Did he fire whole shifts of waitstaff for making minor errors?

Yeah, that happened.

It was no picnic working for him, but it didn't have to be. Being employed by Mitch Elliott was a privilege, and they all knew it.

Well, perhaps not *all* of them.

One person had dared to defy him. She'd done it with a

salad while calling him a *stupid hothead*. He could still feel the plate crashing into his back. A vegetable carnage of lettuce, avocado slices, diced cucumbers, and tomato wedges scattered around his feet. When he'd finally gathered his wits, he'd caught a flash of the salad-hurling bandit hightailing it out the back door.

Who was the culprit?

It was the quiet redhead with emerald-green eyes!

The one he had to pretend to ignore. She smelled like strawberry sunshine. He could barely avert his gaze when she'd breeze into the kitchen to pick up her orders. He didn't even have to see her to know she was there. She'd always pulled her auburn locks into a ponytail. It swished and swayed with her every move, tempting him, taunting him as if it were calling out to him.

Come and get me if you can!

He'd be a liar if he said that he hadn't imagined twisting the locks of hair in his hand and pulling hard as he took her from behind.

He'd played out that fantasy more times than he could count.

But that's as far as it could go.

Charlotte. That was her name. He didn't learn the names of any of the waitstaff. But he knew hers. And now she was gone. After branding him a stupid hothead and littering his floor with produce, she'd bolted out of the kitchen. And he hadn't seen her since.

A damned good thing!

She'd been a distraction. And he'd cut distractions out of his life. That's how it had to be. But this one, this Charlotte, she was different. The other employees not only feared him, but they also accepted his crap willingly. Not Charlotte. She wasn't scared of him. The few times he'd caught her eye, he'd found her steady and unflappable. And her observant eyes spoke volumes. She might appear meek, but a strength dwelled beneath the surface. A strength she might not even know she possessed. Not to mention, she clearly wasn't impressed with the second reason people put up with his bullshit.

What's reason number two?

He was rich and famous.

He was a who's who in the food world, thanks to breaking out as a reality TV chef in his early twenties. And things snowballed from there. He'd become a staple on morning TV programs and starred in shows on various food networks. Scratch that. He *was* basking in the limelight, raking in high TV ratings, putting out cookbooks, getting paid bank to speak at events, and being flown around the globe to cook for royalty until he'd dropped off the radar three years ago when the shit hit the fan.

When he learned a truth that rocked him to his core.

His throat thickened as he recalled the past. But he swallowed it down like a poison pill. Emotions in check, he glanced around the bustling kitchen. His kitchen. Running the way he demanded.

Forget about the past and focus on the food.

Unfortunately, that was a lot harder these days.

He tossed the tasting spoon into a tub containing dirty dishes, then focused his rage on the subpar truffle risotto. He glared at the man who'd screwed with his recipe. "Why the hell did you add extra parmesan?" he snarled as the sous chef shrank.

He'd tasted the imbalance immediately. That was part of his gift, part of what propelled him to stardom in the culinary world. He knew what components went together to create the perfect bite, dish, sandwich, soup. You name it. He could rock the hell out of it. Akin to that damned mouse in *Ratatouille,* his sense of taste and smell was heightened. He was probably a bloodhound in a past life. But whatever you wanted to call it, he had it in spades.

Was it a curse, or was it a blessing? He wasn't sure. What he did know was that he exacted excellence in the kitchen, and he knew what that tasted like.

News flash: it wasn't this parmesan massacred slop.

"Sorry, Chef, I'll remake it," the sous chef stuttered, anxiously fidgeting with the tie on his apron. The kid looked like he had ants in his pants. But it was Mitch who was truly itching to get out of his skin. Every cell in his body vibrated as the muscles at the base of his neck tightened. And surprisingly, it had nothing to do with the shitty risotto.

No, there was another distraction coming his way. A distraction as innocuous as the detonation of an atom bomb.

He gritted his teeth, suppressing the urge to break every damned plate in the restaurant to work out this maddening energy. But he held it together. Blowing out a frustrated breath, he leaned toward the kid, lowering his voice. "It's a delicate balance," he began, schooling the young chef. "The fats—like in the parmesan—bring out the flavor. The dish's rice complements the truffles. There's a goddamned order to it! A symmetry, a balance," he hissed. "Follow the recipe to the T. Do it my way or see yourself out."

"Yes, Chef, thank you, Chef," the kid replied like an obedient foot soldier.

Mitch eyed the young man. He couldn't be much older than twenty-one—the age he was when he got his big break, and his name became a household staple. It was eleven years ago, but it felt like a thousand lifetimes had passed between then and now.

He shook off the sappy sentiment. He had no use for it anymore.

"What's the one rule in my kitchen?" he asked, holding the

kid's gaze as he morphed back into asshole chef mode. He ran a tight ship. He had to. Discipline meant strict adherence to the rule. The culinary world attracted many with colorful backgrounds. That was a nice way of saying that some real screwups graced the back of the house. And once upon a time, he'd been one of them. His first time in a commercial kitchen had been an unmitigated disaster. Discipline saved him. Now, he relied on it in every facet of his life.

And it was about to be put to the test.

"Well?" he prompted, crossing his arms.

"Do whatever the hell Chef Elliott tells you to do. And do it right. Or get out," the sous chef replied, his words popping in sharp staccato breaths.

He nodded to the kid. "Now do it right," he demanded.

"Chef?" came another timid voice.

Jesus Christ! Did he have to hold everyone's hand around here?

"What?" he hissed.

It was his manager—his new manager. He'd been burning through them lately.

"There's an issue with an order."

Mitch glowered. "What order?"

The manager fiddled with his collar. "It appears that some special ingredients for a sandwich that's not currently on the menu were purchased from our vendors. It may have had something to do with the new online accounting software. Maybe a glitch."

"Maybe a glitch?" he barked back. "We don't have glitches at the Crystal Cricket. We follow protocols. We keep our heads down, and we do our jobs. Take care of it!" he growled when the back door swung open, and a woman's voice cut through the grinding clatter.

"My goodness, Mitch, I thought you ran a kitchen, not a platoon."

He scrubbed his hands down his face, then released a weary breath. Still, he couldn't help but find a bit of comfort in the voice.

"Why are you here, Ines?" he replied, meeting his publicist's eye.

Barely five feet tall, one would be a fool to write off Ines Gordon as a pushover. While she looked like a sweet granny who set out plates of cookies and mustered up spoonfuls of marmalade, the pint-sized PR wiz was one hell of a powerhouse. She'd been with him since his big break over a decade ago. And she knew everything—one of only a handful of people who had the goods on Mitch Elliott.

She looked over her shoulder toward his office, tucked away in the back of the sprawling kitchen. "We had an appointment to chat after the Friday night dinner rush. And we need to talk, Mitch. You're about to fuck up royally, young man."

Oh yeah! In addition to being a cutthroat PR professional, Ines had a mouth on her and got to the point faster than it took for a snowball to melt in hell.

And dammit, she was right. He remembered seeing the meeting on his schedule. A meeting he'd been dreading. A wave of nausea nearly had him losing that awful bite of parmed-to-the-max risotto.

The jig was up.

He barked orders to his trio of sous chefs, then met Ines's eye and gestured toward his office. Was the dinner rush already waning? He checked his watch. It was! It was easy to lose track of real time. Culinary time took over his brain when he was working. Order in. Order out. He'd surrendered to the rhythm of the kitchen. Once, this had given him a high like no other. Cooking and observing as people oohed and aahed over his creations had sustained him. It drove him to succeed and fed the part of him that grew intoxicated with the adulation. But for the last three years, he'd simply been going through the motions.

And that shit had caught up with him.

Ines stepped aside as he entered a code on a keypad next to his door. The lock clicked as the bolt disengaged. And Christ, he hated that sound. The opening. The vulnerability.

The weakness.

"You and those locks, Mitch," Ines remarked. "I don't think any of your employees would dare steal from you, let alone want to step foot in here," she finished as he held the door open for her.

"The lock is for everyone. It doesn't give anyone the chance to screw me over," he answered, about to close the door behind them when Ines stopped him.

"Leave it open, Mitch. I like to hear the sound of the kitchen in the background."

He stared at the half-open door, and the agitation that prickled through him earlier dialed up a few clicks. She was doing this on purpose. He'd known her long enough to catch on when she was trying to help him, trying to nudge him out of the prison he'd designed for himself. But she should know better than anyone that he was well beyond help at this point. In fact, now he was more screwed than ever.

"It's a door, Mitch. Leave it open," she quipped.

"Yep, a damned door," he muttered, taking a seat behind his desk as Ines settled herself across from him in a club chair.

"Do you know what I hate, Mitch?" she said, removing a file from her bag.

He ran his hands through his cropped hair as the knots at the base of his neck tightened. "I assume you're going to tell me."

She schooled her features. "I hate when publishers hound me night and day."

He glanced away. "Me too. That's why I stopped responding to their emails and calls."

Ines huffed an exaggerated breath.

Here's the deal. He was under contract to put out another book. Thanks to his rigid discipline, knocking out a best seller used to come easy.

But not this time.

That safety net had slipped.

And he wasn't just responsible for himself anymore.

The muscles in his stomach twisted. "Listen, Ines," he began, but she cut him off.

"I need you to hear everything I'm about to say to you, Mitch."

"I'm listening," he answered, looking away and wishing like hell he could tune her out.

"Your career is in the damned toilet. And not even a nice toilet, like the kind at the Four Seasons. I'm talking about a port-a-potty toilet after a chili eating contest," the woman finished, not mincing words as she painted one of the most disgusting metaphors he'd ever heard.

"Jesus, Ines!" he exclaimed, making a mental note never to put chili on the menu.

"I needed to put it into terms you'd understand, Mitch. I know that you've got a lot on your plate. But this book deal is your chance to reinvent yourself. And might I remind you of the hefty advance they forked your way," the woman continued.

"I've got plenty of cash. If they want their money back, I can write a goddamned check now," he mumbled.

She slid her phone from her bag and began hammering away on the keyboard.

"What are you doing?" he asked as his phone chimed an incoming text.

"Reminding you of the mess we've got to clean up," she answered, stone-faced.

He pulled his phone from his pocket, opened the text, and tapped play on the video as his blood ran cold. He didn't turn on the sound. He didn't need to. He knew the sound of his roaring voice. He scowled at the madman on the screen, tearing apart the studio kitchen. He absorbed the rage written across his face. He flicked his gaze to Ines. "I'm familiar with this. Obviously!"

"We're lucky that only a few people have seen this. Do you know how many favors I had to call in to keep this footage from being plastered across the internet?"

He didn't answer. She knew that he was aware he'd pissed away a rock-solid career. A muscle ticked in his jaw as the vice clamped around his heart tightened. The blurred memories of the day when he'd exploded on set three years ago flashed through his mind. The moment he'd become untouchable—a loose cannon. The world hadn't seen his breakdown. But those in the know, the ones who green light television shows and ad campaigns, they'd heard the whispers. What they hadn't heard was the phone call he'd received minutes before that video was taken.

Ines picked up an old spatula on his desk. It was the one sentimental item he kept in his office. The only piece of his past that brought him any sense of comfort. The hint of a grin bloomed on her lips as she took in the scuffed piece of his former life. "The money isn't what makes you happy, Mitch. The money comes second for you. It always has."

"How do you know what makes me happy?" he asked as a heaviness set in.

Ines cocked an eyebrow. An eyebrow that said *I am no one*

to mess with. And she wasn't. The truth is, she'd seen him at the top of his game. But it broke him to recall that time.

Except now—in mere hours, he'd be face-to-face with that reality.

"What do you suggest I do? How the hell do I meet the publisher's deadline? They want the rough version in sixty days. I haven't even decided on a concept yet," he grumbled, leaning forward with his head in his hands.

"I've taken care of that," Ines purred.

Mitch looked up as the woman stood, then waved for someone to enter the office.

And he could barely believe his eyes when two people he hadn't seen in ages sauntered in.

His jaw dropped. "What the hell are you two doing here? Don't you have your own restaurant and bakery to run in Kansas City?" He came around his desk, hardly able to believe Gabe Sinclair and Monica Brandt-Sinclair were standing in front of him.

They'd met a few years ago at a food and wine event up in Aspen, Colorado, and had instantly hit it off. Gabe and Monica had their own show, a restaurant in Langley Park, a small town not far from Kansas City. And it wasn't just the similarities in their success that allowed them to form a professional connection. Gabe and Monica shared a dedication to craft and a reliance on discipline in the kitchen that mirrored his approach.

And Ines was good friends with the couple's PR guy, Corbyn Howell.

"Dire times require your publicist to act, Mitch," Ines said.

"Ines talked us into spending some time in Denver as guest chefs at your shitty restaurant," Gabe answered with a smirk as the men shook hands.

"Oh, stop, Gabe," Monica chided, swatting her husband on

his shoulder. The woman was a former supermodel turned baking phenomenon. She and Gabe were thriving in their careers.

But Mitch had to look away. It was almost too much to take the unmistakable bond between Gabe and Monica. Just the way Gabe looked at his wife was how he used to look at...

STOP!

"Mitch, your restaurant is wonderful. But the risotto—" Monica added with a cringe.

"I know! I know!" he answered, embracing the woman. "I've got a new sous chef I'm breaking in."

Monica nodded, her dark hair tumbling at her shoulders as her expression grew serious. "And what about Oscar? Is he living with you in Denver now?"

Mitch's eyes widened at the sound of those two syllables.

Oscar.

His son's name.

Son.

A lump formed in his throat. He could barely wrap his head around the fact that he was Oscar's father. You'd think after three years, it would have sunk in. But circumstances were beyond messed up. Since learning the truth, he'd seen the kid a handful of times. And this kid—*his kid*—this six-year-old boy he barely knew was going to live with him—would grow up in his care.

What the hell was the universe thinking?

He turned to Ines. "You told them?" he asked, his voice a thick rasp.

Ines's features softened. "Yes, because Oscar will be an enormous part of your life, Mitch. You're the only person left to care for him now. You're his father."

The words hit like a wrecking ball. He was literally the last person on the planet who should raise a kid. He'd been a hellion as a child and a terror as a teen. It was no surprise he'd turned out like that. That's what happened when a grandfather who didn't give two shits was put in charge of raising an unruly boy.

That might be all he and his son had in common. Life had thrown them for a loop at a young age and had supplied each of them with the worst possible caregiver.

But Ines was correct. And he had to look at life in black and white now. Truth be told, he owed Ines a debt of gratitude. Personally and professionally, he was in a world of shit—spiraling, angry at everything and everyone. Like it or not, this was his life—and he needed to get back on track.

As much as he hated relinquishing control of his restaurant, Gabe and Monica were the only two people he'd even consider allowing to grace the back of the house. Ines was also the one who'd connected him to Madelyn Malone's nanny services. The nanny lady might employ unusual tactics—like, for example, making him hang out with other single guys who'd found they'd soon be caring for a kid. Rowen Gale, a tech genius, had been the first in this curious quartet to be assigned a nanny. And Christ Almighty, that guy had been put through the wringer during the sixty-day trial period. But now, the nerd seemed to be walking on goddamned sunshine. And he was engaged to his nanny.

That sure as hell wouldn't be the case for Mitch Elliott. No way! When it came to love, he'd been fooled once, and he sure as hell wasn't about to be fooled for a second time.

"Mitch," Gabe began, cutting into his wild train of thought.

He gathered himself. "Yeah."

"It would be a privilege to look after the Crystal Cricket while you take some time off," Gabe offered.

Monica nodded. "You don't have to worry, Mitch. You know

I keep Gabe in line. What's another restaurant on my plate? Remember, I was raised by my strict German grandmother, and Oma doesn't put up with any shenanigans, and neither do I," the woman added with a twinkle in her eye.

"How is Oma?" he asked, grateful for the distraction.

"Scary as ever, dude! She might be a card-carrying member of the American Association of Retired Persons, but you do not want to cross Oma," Gabe replied.

The couple was keeping it light—for him.

"Then it's settled," Ines said, relief coating her words as she shared a look with Gabe and Monica.

"What would have happened if I'd said no?" Mitch asked, eyeing the trio.

"You don't want to go there," Gabe replied with a cheeky grin.

"Oma's on standby, Mitch. She's ready to kick your ass halfway across Denver if she has to," Monica answered.

Mitch nodded as a comforting warmth settled over him. Monica's grandmother made him think of another no-nonsense, elderly woman who had busted his teenage ass into gear and the remarkable chain of events that the crotchety angel from his past had set into motion.

He'd most likely be rotting away in jail if it hadn't been for her.

"There's one last thing," Ines said, checking her watch, then turned to Gabe and Monica. "Would you mind giving Mitch and me a minute?"

"No problem! We'll check out the kitchen and say hello to the staff," Gabe answered before he and Monica slipped out of the office.

"It looks like you've got everything figured out," Mitch said, dropping to the club chair next to Ines.

"This is a good thing, Mitch. You can take care of getting

Oscar settled and get the rough draft of your next book pulled together. This is a critical time in your life and in your career," she answered, pinning him with her gaze.

He sank back into the chair as the totality of what was to come weighed heavy on his heart. Sure, he was Oscar's biological father. But now he had to be a dad—and he didn't have any idea what the hell he was supposed to do. Growing up without a mother and a father can do that to a person.

He released a weary breath. "Yeah, I get it."

"I don't think you do, not entirely, Mitch."

He sat up ramrod straight.

What the hell did that mean?

"How much more is there to get?" he asked as a prickle traveled down his spine.

Ines took off her glasses and pinched the bridge of her nose. "This book is it. I haven't been able to book anything for you in almost a year. No speaking engagements, no endorsements. Nothing."

That hit like a punch to the gut. But there had to be more to it. There was a time when he was inundated with a barrage of offers and requests.

"It's no secret that I opened the Crystal Cricket. I'm running a restaurant. I'm busy. That's got to be the reason," he shot back. But deep down, his words rang hollow.

"Nobody gives a damn if you're busy, Mitch. If they want you, they want you," she countered, then leaned forward, concern marring her features. "It's my job to keep the revenue avenues open, to keep the feelers out there for you. But something else is going on. Something far worse than business opportunities drying up."

He hardened his expression. "Just say it, Ines. You know you don't have to sugarcoat it."

"You've lost it, Mitch. I haven't seen it in your eyes in ages," she answered with, Christ, was that pity in her eyes?

The muscles at the base of his neck, the same muscles that had been clenched for what seemed like seven years, tensed within an inch of snapping. He was a man on the edge, ready to explode. "Lost what?" he barked. But he wasn't an idiot. He knew the answer. He just hadn't acknowledged it.

"Your passion, Mitch," she replied, then rested her hand on top of his. "Remember that twenty-one-year-old kid—the one with so much zest for life? He was electric on the screen and magnetic in print. People couldn't look away. They'd watch you cook for hours. You need to go back to the beginning and find that spark, or it's over for you."

The urge to flip his desk and trash his office in an all-consuming rage burned inside of him

"That kid was an idiot," he seethed through grated teeth as it came back to him. The humiliation, the soul annihilating crush of anger and a sense of loss so profound it was as if, although he walked among the living, he'd died on the inside. Trust and love, which had once been cornerstones of not just his life but his business, shattered into a million tiny pieces in the blink of an eye.

And now, in a mere matter of hours, he'd be reminded of that old life every single day from here on out.

"No!" Ines scolded. "That kid wasn't an idiot."

He crossed his arms, holding it in—the pain, the anguish. "You know damned well what happened," he said when a flash of red caught his eye.

Who was here now? Another damned visitor?

He turned. It was a visitor, but it wasn't just any visitor.

It was Madelyn Malone.

She smoothed her scarf as she entered the office and shared a look with Ines.

"Is he ready?" the nanny matchmaker asked his publicist.

"Ready for what?" he interrupted.

How many more surprises would he have to endure tonight?

Madelyn procured an envelope from her satchel, then placed it on his desk. "The match is made. It's time to meet your nanny."

FOUR

MITCH

"I HAVE to meet the nanny now?" he blathered as his gaze bounced between the women.

Could he have a second to breathe—or cry out in frustration?

Ines nodded. "You're due to pick up Oscar tomorrow, Mitch. There's no time to lose."

"This is a critical moment," Madelyn added, observing him closely. "Your case has presented a few challenges. But I'm happy to report that I've found the perfect nanny candidate for you and for Oscar."

A sense of panic tore through him. "Who is she? Is she here? Did you bring her to the restaurant?"

"No, I've set up a meeting for you at a nearby establishment. Open the envelope. The answers are inside," the matchmaker directed.

He lifted the flap and emptied the contents onto the desk. What was this? He stared down at a set of car keys, a blank card, a smaller envelope with *Whitmore Country Day School registration papers* printed across the top, and a vintage lock.

He held up the rusty hunk of metal in the shape of a heart.

A little larger than a silver dollar, it fit perfectly in the palm of his hand. "What's this for, Madelyn?"

"It's an antique lock," she answered matter-of-factly.

Shit! He knew that! Why was she giving him an old lock?

"I know. Why are you giving it to me? Is it for Oscar? Is it a toy?" he asked, his voice cracking on his son's name. It still felt foreign to speak the two syllables. Despite not knowing him well, the kid was never far from his thoughts. But to say his name aloud added another layer of permanence to this situation.

A sly grin pulled at the corners of her lips. "The lock is part of the process."

This woman and her crazy methods!

As a chef, he was all for following a regimen—all for order and discipline. But how the hell did a rusty lock fit into the nanny selection? He scanned the rest of the items. She'd given him an old lock, but the keys on the desk were too large and modern to work on it. There had to be another key somewhere. "How do I open it?"

Madelyn raised an eyebrow. "That's an excellent question."

Holy hell! It appeared this process was comprised of ambiguous answers and a bullshit trail of bizarro clues. He shoved the lock into his pocket, then moved on to the next item. "Is this the school stuff?"

"Yes, Oscar is registered for first grade," Madelyn answered. "My dear friend's granddaughter-in-law teaches at Whitmore Country Day. I believe Oscar's been placed in her first-grade classroom. I think he'll be quite happy there. My friend tells me there's an end-of-the-year activity coming up where the class gets to stay in cabins in the mountains for the last week of school. They call it Outdoor Laboratory."

"Okay," he answered as it sank in. This was happening. School schedules. End of year activities. This would be his life. And he didn't know a damned thing about being a parent.

Hopefully, the nanny could take charge of this. The only thing he remembered about school was being sent to the principal's office.

"My people have finished up at your house," Madelyn continued. "They set up Oscar's room and added a few items to the nanny suite."

He was going from a party of one to a party of three!

How would this work?

Before his world imploded, he'd thrived on human contact. But that piece of him died seven years ago. Now, he could barely stand being around others. Yes, the back of the house was a busy, crowded place. But everyone had a task, a purpose. There was no small talk in his kitchen. His employees kept their heads down and got their work done. What the hell was he going to do when he bumped into the nanny in his house—his refuge, his escape? His thoughts ricocheted through his mind. How the hell was he supposed to get his career back on track in that environment? Pulse thrumming, he had to slow down, or he'd give himself a heart attack. He scanned the remaining items on his desk. "What are the car keys for? I have plenty of vehicles," he asked, needing to focus on something to hold it together.

"The camper van, of course," Madelyn replied with a flick of her wrist like everyone had camper vans lying around.

"Why are you giving me keys to a camper van?" he shot back.

"This is why you've hired me, Mitch. I provide the framework to facilitate an effective transition."

"And that includes renting a camper van?" he pressed.

Dressed to the nines, Madelyn Malone didn't come off as a wilderness warrior. Connecting him with childcare made sense —setting up the school stuff, too. But hooking him up with a recreational vehicle seemed way out of the nanny match lady's wheelhouse.

"Yes, it does," Madelyn replied. "It's an integral piece for your passage into parenthood, Mitch."

His face must have said he didn't know what the hell that meant.

Madelyn crossed her arms and zeroed in on him. Shit! He'd known her long enough to recognize that she'd crossed over into the no-nonsense nanny match maven mode. "Here's how your next few days are going to go, young man. You and the nanny will drive in the camper van to retrieve your son. Then you'll spend Saturday night camping before returning to Denver on Sunday. Come with me," she said, breezing out of the office like she didn't suggest the most utterly insane idea he'd ever heard.

This was flat-out nuts! She wanted him to camp with the nanny he'd never met and the son he hardly knew? It wasn't that he was against camping. He used to do it quite a bit back when...

"Mitchell," Madelyn called over her shoulder as she charged out of his office.

Mitchell? No one had called him that in years.

And he had to leave now—like this very second?

He shoved the items back into the envelope, grabbed his bag and roll of chef's knives, then froze as he stared at the old spatula on his desk. For whatever reason, he swiped it off the table and tucked it into his bag, then met Ines's gaze. "Did you know about this?"

"Not entirely," she answered, coming to her feet. "Madelyn's in charge of this part of your life. You need to do exactly as she tells you. She's the best, Mitch. And you need as much help as you can get."

It was true. He hated it—hated needing help, hated feeling vulnerable. He studied the kitchen before finding Monica and

Gabe chatting with his manager. He knew exactly what they were doing. The pair was getting the lay of the land. Monica was taking notes while Gabe gestured to the different workstations. It's what he'd do if he were in their shoes. Still, releasing his iron grip—even if it was to professionals like Gabe and Monica—set his nerves on edge.

"It's under control, Mitch," Ines assured him, then ushered him out the back door. He'd barely taken two steps outside before he gawked at what he saw. The camper van was enormous and currently blocking the entire alleyway. He didn't even have time to blurt out an expletive. If anything deserved a *holy shit*, it was this! The horn blared with two sharp blasts, and he nearly pissed himself.

"What the hell is that?" he cried.

"That's the horn," Ines answered.

Did everyone think he was a complete idiot?

"Get in. You're driving," Madelyn called from the passenger seat.

"Is this for real?" he asked on a bewildered breath. Was he talking to the universe, himself, the damned monstrosity of a camper van? At this point, he didn't know.

"It's as real as it gets, honey. Life is about to move fast for you. And it would be a fuck ton easier if you could muster up a little trust and go with the flow," Ines replied as gently as one can when inserting *fuck ton* into a sentence.

"I don't do trust, Ines. You know that," he answered as another defensive, bitter layer went up around his battered heart.

Madelyn leaned over and opened the driver's side door. "Get in, Mitchell! There's no time to lose."

He gave Ines one last look before climbing into the camper van. He set his bag behind the seat, slammed the door shut, then took in the dash. With a bunch of buttons, multiple screens, and a battery of switches, it was like the space shuttle in there.

"I'm told this model contains every bell and whistle one could desire. Now drive," she directed, not messing around as she took the envelope from him, then handed him the keys.

"Where are we going?" he asked, firing up the ignition. Was this her plan? Was she attempting to make him so scatter-brained he'd accept any nanny she presented?

He couldn't lie. The damned strategy wasn't a bad one. If she pulled out papers and asked him to sign over half the Crystal Cricket to her at this discombobulating moment, he'd probably do it. He was half out of his mind.

Madelyn settled herself into the plush seat. "Take a right, then take your next left. We don't have far to go. And I need you to listen closely. I have a lot to say and not much time to say it."

He stopped at a red light. "I'm listening."

"I've packed a few things for you. They're in the back."

"Okay."

"You'll have to leave quite early. You have a decent drive ahead of you."

He tightened his grip on the steering wheel. "I know."

Since finding out that he was Oscar's father, he'd done the drive a total of four times. Should he have gone to see the kid more often? Jesus, that was a hard one! Of course, once he learned the boy was his, he'd insisted on providing financially for Oscar. The first time he'd laid eyes on his son, he'd felt something pop in his chest—like a part of him he'd never known was there had come to life. But he'd pushed that emotion aside as an equally powerful realization hit. He had nothing besides money to offer anyone. The kid was better off without him. He was better off with Holly.

Holly.

The muscles in his chest tightened as a rush of heat flushed his cheeks.

"Oscar has lost his mother," Madelyn said, her tone softening. "He's losing the life he's always known. Be prepared for some push-back. He is your son, and from what I understand, you were quite a rabble-rouser when you were younger."

Mitch swallowed hard. "Something like that."

Madelyn folded her hands and rested them in her lap. "These sixty days will be your time to bond. Don't expect to get it right off the bat. There will be bumps in the road. This time is a gift, but you need to use it wisely. Ines shared with me that you also have a book to write."

"The publisher wants a rough draft in sixty days," he answered, keeping his eyes glued to the road.

"Then it's good I've found the perfect nanny for your situation," she remarked.

He glanced at the woman. "What if it's not a match? What if I meet the nanny candidate, and I decide it won't work?"

"Oh, it's a match," she answered, patting his arm—which wasn't a real answer.

He had to change tack if he wanted to get anything out of her.

"When Rowen met Penny, she dropped by his office. Can you tell me about my nanny candidate? Her name? Her age? Has she cared for children before?" he rattled off.

Madelyn pointed out the window. "Park in the lot. We're here."

So much for getting any answers!

He parked the behemoth, taking up a few spots, then stared at the row of shops and restaurants.

He cut the ignition. "Where is here?"

"You'll meet the nanny at that little bar on the end of the block," she answered.

"A bar?" he exclaimed. "Why couldn't you send her to the Crystal Cricket?"

Madelyn smoothed her scarlet scarf. "This match requires a neutral setting."

He stared at the bar's green awning as a group entered. "What does that even mean—a neutral setting?"

Madelyn unclasped her seatbelt. "It means what it means. And one last thing—a crucial element."

He perked up. Now she was talking! He needed important information. "What is it?"

She frowned. "What did you do to the risotto tonight? The flavors were off."

Shit! That was not the crucial information he'd wanted.

He ran his hands through his hair. "It was a new sous chef. Now, help me out, Madelyn. What's the nanny's name? How will I find her?"

"I took care of that, too," she said, plucking the card out of the envelope and handing it to him.

But it wasn't a business card. It was a picture of a necklace with a gold key hanging from a chain.

"Will the nanny candidate be wearing this?" he asked. It was like a Nancy Drew mystery trying to decipher what the hell was going on!

"Yes," Madelyn answered with a smirk.

"This feels like a wild goose chase," he muttered.

"Nothing wrong with a wild goose chase every now and then," she tossed back.

He threw his hands into the air. "Does she know that I'm the employer? Will she be looking for me?"

A whisper of a grin bloomed on Madelyn's lips. "No."

His jaw dropped. "No?"

"You like control, Mitch," she replied.

That would be a duh! Clearly, he craved control.

"You'd be hard-pressed to find a chef who didn't. It's who I am. It's how I live."

She clucked her tongue. "Not anymore."

Damn! His brain could explode at any minute!

"Madelyn," he began, working to keep his tone even. "I get that you have your ways. But how will I find the nanny? I can't go up to every female in the place and stare at their chest. That'll get me thrown in jail."

"I have a distinct feeling you'll be drawn to each other," she answered, exiting the RV as a sleek town car pulled up.

"You're leaving?" he blurted, then climbed out of the RV.

"That's my ride, dear. Now, hurry inside. I'll caution you not to drink, Mitch. You've got quite a few busy days ahead of you, and I hear the margaritas at this place are quite potent."

His career and impending parenthood were on the line, and this woman gives him a camper van and sends him on a nanny treasure hunt!

He glanced around wildly. This had to be a joke. "That's it? That's the plan? I go in and hope I find this nanny?"

"Have a little faith, Mitch," she replied as the driver helped her into the car.

Faith. Trust. That shit was for the birds.

With his mouth hanging open as if he wanted to catch every fly in Denver, he watched the nanny match lady's vehicle disappear into traffic.

"Unbelievable!" he whispered.

Not knowing what else to do, he set his sights on the little bar, then scrubbed his hands down his face. This was it.

It was nanny or bust time.

FIVE

MITCH

HE JOGGED across the street toward the bar. With his senses heightened, he scanned the area. He had to be ready. He needed to appear stable and levelheaded. But a rush of topsy-turvy energy pulsed through his veins. And it wasn't just him. The crisp evening air held an expectancy as if Mother Nature knew something was coming—a change, a transformation. He shook his head, pushing away the bullshit metaphysical musings.

"Go in the bar and find the nanny. It's as easy as that," he whispered—and excellent! He'd become one of those nuts who mutter to themselves.

He stared at the bar's tarnished door handle. There was no turning back now.

He opened the door, and the buzz of conversation over Classic Rock drifted outdoors. He spied a seat at the bar when a guy popped out of nowhere and slapped a sticker on his chest.

"What the hell!" he exclaimed.

"Are you ready to meet your soul mate?" the man asked with a wide grin.

What kind of damned bar was this?

"Sorry, buddy, you're not my type," he answered, removing the sticker and tossing it into a trash can.

The dude laughed. "Aren't you here for the speed dating event? It's a relationship kick-starter—an event that lubricates the wheels of love."

Where the hell did Madelyn send him?

Mitch took a step back. "What are you talking about?"

"Speed dating," the man answered, then waggled his eyebrows like a psychopath. "It's about to begin. Here, take a Jell-O shot and a margarita. But there's a two-margarita limit here. These potent drinks are the perfect social lubricant."

Mitch pegged the guy with his gaze and went into scary chef mode. "I'm not here for that. And if you say *lubricant* again, I will be punching your lights out. So why don't you step aside," he bit back. Nobody, not even this asshat, could mistake that he wasn't playing around.

"Sorry, man! No speed dating for you," the guy answered, holding up his hands defensively.

Mitch headed for the bar, but not before surveying the room. It was jam-packed. And not only that. It looked like the alcoholic version of a kindergarten classroom. Tables were set out in rows with pitchers of margaritas, along with little baskets in the center. A line of women sat on one side, crossing then recrossing their legs, while a trail of men, looking like the dudes who didn't get picked for kickball, sat on the other side. He shook his head at the saps out there so desperate for love they'd subject themselves to this.

"What can I get you, man?" a bartender asked as he settled himself on a stool.

"Club soda," he answered, trying not to look like a total pervert as he peered down the line of women, checking for necklaces with a golden key. He scoffed. He couldn't see shit. And this was ridiculous! He pulled his cell from his pocket. He should call Madelyn and demand she give him the nanny info. He was in no mood for games. If anything, he should be working to come up with a concept for his book. He opened the contacts app on his phone when the door swung open and a red blur bolted into the room.

"I'm not late, am I? I can't be late!" a woman exclaimed, and his eyes almost popped out of his head as his pulse skyrocketed.

He recognized that voice.

It couldn't be her, could it?

"Are you in need of help?" the man at the door asked. The guy had lost his mega-watt smile and frowned at the late arrival. And for a good reason. To say that this woman had chosen an interesting outfit for the speed dating event would be the understatement of the century. She brushed a tangle of hair from her face.

"No, I don't need help! I don't know why everyone keeps asking me that. My name is Charlotte Ames. I should be on your list for the event," she replied, her words coming out in a frantic jumble.

The breath caught in his throat. Charlotte Ames! It was her! His vegetable bandit.

The bartender set his club soda on the counter, but Mitch couldn't look away from the absolute train wreck of a beauty that had blown in like a hurricane.

The door guy looked her up and down. "The costume contest is next week, lady. Come back then."

He could see why the guy thought she'd mixed up the dates. The woman had rolled in with a towel draped around her shoulders. He couldn't quite make out what was underneath it. It kind of looked like she had nothing on under it. But the bottom part of her outfit was most definitely a fishtail.

And was she barefoot?

He couldn't tell from where he sat. He tossed a twenty onto

the bar, paying for the untouched club soda, then got up and weaved his way through the mass of people. Thanks to a well-placed pinball machine, he'd found a spot where he could observe her, but she couldn't see him.

Panic marred her features. Now that he'd gotten closer, he could tell that her hair was wet. She tucked a damp auburn strand behind her ear.

Who traipsed around town soaking wet, sporting a towel and a fishtail?

Still, in her state of dishevelment, with her hair in wild damp waves and those green eyes flashing, she was as beautiful as ever. She'd been so quiet as a waitress. That is until she called him a hothead and hurled a salad at him. He'd wondered if he would ever see her again. Not that he was complaining, but this was the last place he'd expected to run into her—and to find her dressed like a soggy fish lady to boot!

"This isn't a costume," she replied, then glanced down and grimaced. "Okay, it might look like a mermaid costume. It's my work clothing. I wasn't able to change into my normal clothes. You see, my boss, well, I guess he's my ex-boss now. He has my shirt. I didn't have a good opportunity to ask for it back. He'd already fired me." She took a breath. "I'm dressed like this for a party. I stand there in my grand mermaid-ness, and children take pictures with me. But Grover Cleveland Schulte pushed me into the pool, and then I lost that job. Yes, that's how it happened, and now I'm here," she finished with a weak grin.

"You lost your job as a professional mermaid because a dead president pushed you into a pool?" the guy asked, looking half-ready to call security and have her removed.

She shrugged, and the towel opened, revealing shells. Shells! That's all she had on under that towel. He noticed a glint of gold around her neck that trailed into her hair. The woman was the walking definition of a hot aquatic mess.

She pulled the towel around her body. "No, Grover Cleveland Schulte—he's not a dead president. He's a little boy. And I'm not a professional mermaid. I'm a photographer. No, I'm a photographer's assistant. Well, I was a photographer's assistant," she rattled, then plucked a margarita from the guy's tray. "Hold on! After the day I've had, I need this. I haven't had anything but a latte today. I'm totally parched." She downed one margarita, then tossed the empty plastic cup into a trash can before downing another.

This woman did not mess around with the margs!

"You should only have two max," the guy advised as she lifted a third cup to her lips and knocked it back.

Part of him was half impressed. The other part was a little afraid of this badass boozehound.

She wiped the back of her wrist across her lips as she shifted a tote bag to her other hand. "Listen, sir, I have to attend this speed dating event. Everything in my life has pointed me to this one moment and to this one place. Tonight, I'll find the man of my dreams. I just know it."

Was she serious? What on God's green earth would make her think she'd meet the man of her dreams at a cheesy event like this?

The door guy nodded. "Fine, I'll let you in. But the minute you pull any Disney mermaid princess bullshit, you're out."

Charlotte swayed, then pressed her hand to the wall to get her balance.

Could she already be feeling the effects of the alcohol? She did mention she'd only had a latte today.

This could be bad! He had a sneaking suspicion that a petite redhead plus no food plus downing three potent drinks in under thirty seconds, like some idiot eighteen-year-old kid on Spring Break, would not be a winning combination for the recently sacked mermaid.

She stared into the door guy's eyes. "I promise, sir, no funny business. I may look like a human being, but I'm a mermaid."

The guy cocked his head to the side.

"Wait!" she crooned, then reached for a fourth margarita and tossed it back.

Mitch cringed. That was a lot of tequila for such a tiny person.

"I may look like a *mermaid*, but I'm really a *human being*," she restated before gifting the door guy with a wide boozy grin.

"Don't make me regret this," the guy answered warily, clearly not one hundred percent sold, but he handed her a sticker with a number on it.

"Thank you! Thank you!" she gushed. "You've played a pivotal role in changing my life."

Again, with this life-fate bullshit! Was she seeing the same thing he was? This place looked like the location where true love went to fucking die. From what he could tell, the majority of people came for the booze.

"Here's how it works," the door guy said, ignoring her over-the-top enthusiasm. "This is lightning speed dating. One minute in each round. You'll pull a question from the basket on the table. Write your answer on a pink slip of paper while the guy writes his on one of the blue slips. At the end of the night, you write down the number of your three top choices, and we'll see if you've made a match."

"Okay, got it!" Charlotte replied, smiling like the guy had given her the world.

"Oh, and I almost forgot," the door guy added, "when I ring the bell to switch, everyone has to do a Jell-O shot."

A different kind of bell went off in Mitch's head—alarm bells. The last thing Charlotte needed after pounding four margaritas was an onslaught of Jell-O shots. But what was he supposed to do? Jump out from behind the pinball machine and shout, *Surprise, it's your old boss! You know, the guy you called a stupid hothead. You might want to take it easy on the hard liquor.*

No, he had to hang back. Still, panic prickled through him as he watched the waitstaff place the small paper cups filled with the gelatinous red substance on each table.

Here's the thing. It wasn't his business if she decided to guzzle a pitcher of margaritas, hoover a tray of Jell-O shots, then jump on the table, rip off that towel, then belt out the complete soundtrack to *The Little Mermaid* in nothing but a fishtail and a shell bra. He should be scouring the joint for the nanny with a gold key on her necklace. But something inside of him couldn't abandon this total wreck of a woman, who most likely hated his damned guts.

"You can sit there—at that spot near the corner," the guy directed. Charlotte wobbled over to the table. The fish skirt didn't allow for much movement. And sweet Christ! It hugged her curves in all the right places, revealing one hell of an ass. It swayed from side to side as she moved through the crowd. And, unable to stop himself, another Charlotte fantasy took hold. His fingertips tingled as he played out the delicious scenario of gripping those perfect orbs of prime ass and—

Ding, ding, ding, ding!

"Gentlemen, find your first table. We start in ten, nine, eight, seven, six..."

Mitch watched in horror as some lanky douche with his hat on backward plopped down in front of Charlotte. She couldn't think this was her Prince Charming, could she? And he couldn't help himself from watching over her. Luckily, now that she was seated, he could get a little closer. Plenty of the bar patrons were getting a kick out of watching the spectacle and had huddled around the perimeter of the speed dating tables. He slid in next to a group of men talking sports, allowing him to position himself a few feet behind the tipsy mermaid.

"Five, four, three, two, one! Speed date!" the jackass from the door called, counting down again, then dinged the stupid bell.

Charlotte reached into the basket and opened the first question. From his vantage point, he could see it, too.

She folded, then unfolded the paper.

"What's with the outfit?" the guy across from her barked.

"It's a long story," she answered, shifting in her seat. "How about I read the question, and we can get started?"

"Whatever," the dude answered, checking out a busty brunette a few tables down.

"What's your favorite sandwich?" Charlotte read. She set the question down, then scribbled her answer on the pink scrap of paper.

Grilled cheese.

Holy shit! Mitch stared at her answer.

The douche scribbled something, then held it up. "I'm a BLT guy."

Charlotte set her pink square down on the table and covered it with her hand. "What are the chances? BLTs are my favorite, too."

That was a lie! He freaking saw her write grilled cheese. Why the hell was he so interested? Again, what did it matter? But oddly, it did.

Ding!

Charlotte's shoulders slumped beneath the towel as she popped a Jell-O shot into her mouth, and a new guy slid in across from her. Looking more like he had a piece of brown shag carpet stapled to his chest, the guy had undone five, no, six buttons on his shirt. Who did he think he was, Don Juan? This dude was worse than the last one!

The hairy speed date guy plucked a question from the basket with meaty fingers. "What's your dream vacation?"

"That's a good one!" Charlotte replied.

Mitch looked on as she wrote.

A secluded mountain retreat.

He raised an eyebrow. That would have been his answer, too.

The meaty chest hair guy held out his response. "I'm all about Cabo. Bring on the drinks! Where's the beach? What do you say, Red?" the leisure suit Larry wannabe cooed in a syrupy voice as he stared at Charlotte's chest.

What a pig!

He was half-ready to drag the weasel out of the bar and toss him into the gutter.

"Yeah, that's my idea of a great vacation, too," she lied—again.

What was she doing? He could see her answers. Why did she agree with these total ass clowns?

"Any chance you wanna give me a peek under the towel?" the guy pressed, taking her hand into his as Charlotte gasped.

Mitch took a step forward as his body tensed, ready to pounce on this tool.

"So nice of you to ask, but I have to decline," she replied, her words beginning to slur.

Okay, she was probably halfway to *Hammeredville* by now. But at least she didn't seem into this creep.

Ding!

Mitch breathed a sigh of relief as the stupid bell rang, and the poster-dude for how *not* to wear a button-up moved to the next table. His racing pulse slowed a fraction when Charlotte blessedly didn't take another Jell-O shot. Instead, she adjusted her towel and muttered something under her breath that sounded like, *where are you, Mr. Cheesy Forever?*

No, she couldn't have said that. Or if she did, it was the alcohol talking.

The next guy in the speed date trail of losers walked over, then grimaced. But he didn't take a seat.

"Oh shit," the guy whispered, looking ready to bolt when Charlotte glanced up.

"What are you *cliffing* here, *do*?" she said, then shook her head. "What are you *doing* here, *Cliff*?" she replied with a distinct shake to her voice.

"Why are you dressed like that, Charlotte?" he replied, still not taking a seat.

Mitch edged closer. This guy knew her. He knew her name.

She straightened in her seat. "It's a long story. But I have to ask. Did you lose your phone, Cliff?"

"No, why?" the guy answered, slipping his hands in his pockets, looking visibly uncomfortable.

"I ask because you never texted me back. And we went on that date—that date that I thought went really well. You talked and talked all night."

Heat rose to Mitch's cheeks as anger set in toward speed date asshole number three. It made no sense why he cared. He wasn't invested in this chick. He barely knew her. But for whatever reason, he inched forward, needing to get closer to her.

The dude, this Cliff, shifted from foot to foot but didn't answer.

"It's a sign, Cliff! You're here, and I'm here. You're supposed to be my Mr. Cheesy Forever," Charlotte said with such boozy hope in her voice it was almost painful.

"Are you okay?" Cliff asked, his grimace turning to a look of irritation.

Charlotte blew out a frustrated breath. "Yes, I'm not sure I can feel my toes. But besides that, I'm *stupor*." She shook her head. "No, I'm *slooper*." Her shoulders rose and fell as she took another breath. "I'm super!" she jabbered on the third try.

The dude glanced down a few tables and caught the eye of a

blonde. "Listen, Charlotte, I'm here with my girlfriend. We got back together."

"But this is speed dating," Charlotte replied, her voice raising an octave. "Why would you bring your girlfriend to a speed dating night?"

Cliff gestured to the speed date tables. "Look around. Only total losers come here to find love. Normal people do this for the free margaritas."

"Oh," Charlotte breathed, her slender shoulders caving forward.

A muscle ticked in Mitch's jaw. He was ready to throttle this guy into next week.

"Actually, I should thank you, Charlotte," Cliff the douche said as his irritation gave way to a wide grin.

"For what?" she replied with that damned heart-wrenching hope in her tone.

"Our date was so bad, I knew I should get back together with Kimberly," the guy—no, the total asshole—answered, then blew a kiss, an actual air kiss, toward the blonde.

He couldn't see Charlotte's face, but he could feel the waves of humiliation rolling off of her. The sting of her rejection opened a wound in his heart, and he clenched his fists. He hadn't gotten into a brawl since he was seventeen. He blew out a slow breath. He couldn't get into a fight. He'd put that life behind him. But he'd happily resurrect that part of him to deal with this fool. Unfortunately, or perhaps, fortunately, he didn't get the chance. In a burst of drunken fishy movement, Charlotte stood. Mere inches away from him, he inhaled her strawberry sunshine and unclenched his hands.

"I'm glad I could help," she said through a tight sob, then grabbed her bag and tottered away toward a hallway with the word *restrooms* painted on the wall.

Mitch ran his hands down his face. He knew why this hit

him hard. He knew the utter devastation of betrayal, of thinking you were on cloud nine only to have your hopes and dreams busted to hell. He blew out a tight breath when he caught a glimpse of Mr. Chest Hair scurrying through the crowd toward —yep, the hallway leading to the restrooms.

She's not your problem. Don't concern yourself. You're picking up Oscar tomorrow. Find the nanny so you can get your damned life under control.

Dammit!

Despite all the reasons he should leave Charlotte Ames alone, he moved through the crowd. He'd simply walk by and make sure she'd made it to the ladies' room. It didn't hurt anyone. The chest hair Casanova probably had to take a piss. Yeah, that had to be it.

But it wasn't.

He froze when he saw the beefy guy's back and, on the floor, a swish of an aquamarine mermaid tale. The ape had backed Charlotte into a corner and had pinned her against the wall.

What a prick!

Without giving it a second thought, he charged down the hall. "Step back, man. Give the lady some space," he growled, placing his hand on the dude's shoulder.

The man craned his neck, not moving an inch. "There's no problem here, buddy. I'm getting acquainted with the little mermaid."

"Wrong answer," Mitch hissed. He grabbed the guy by the collar and twisted the polyester fabric. "If you want to leave this place in one piece, I suggest you get the hell out of here."

"Jesus!" the guy huffed. He was big, but he sure as hell wasn't strong.

Mitch watched as the tool disappeared, then turned to find Charlotte staring up at him, wide-eyed.

"Hothead!" she exclaimed. Her mouth opened and closed a few times like...well, like a fish. "I mean, asshat chef. I mean, stupid tyrant."

He raised an eyebrow in amusement. Looks like she had quite a few names for him.

"It's Mitch," he said, holding her emerald gaze.

"Mitch," she repeated, and God help him, the syllable never sounded sweeter.

"Are you okay? Did he hurt you?" he asked, suddenly feeling quite vulnerable himself.

She pulled the towel around her shoulders. "No, but I could use some air."

So could he. But he couldn't let her walk around Crystal Creek like that.

"Hold on," he said, unbuttoning his shirt.

Her jaw dropped. "What are you doing?"

Dammit! She probably thought he was no better than the chest hair jerk.

"I have a T-shirt on under this. I think you could use a real shirt—even one that's ten sizes too big," he said, handing over his button-up.

She stared at the garment and touched one of the pearl white buttons. "Thank you," she whispered, then turned those emerald eyes on him, and the breath caught in his throat. A man could lose himself in those deep pools of green. "Could you turn around, hothead?" She gasped. "I mean, Mitch. Sorry, I shouldn't call you that. I don't know if you recognize me. We've never really talked. I'm—"

"I know who you are, Charlotte," he replied, his voice a low rumble as he spoke her name. And in that hallway, the ding of the stupid bell and the buzz of music and conversation faded away. All that existed was this spellbinding woman.

"You do?" she asked on a shaky exhale.

"I'll turn around, so you can..." he blathered, then gestured to his shirt in her hands. He stared at the wall, searching the scuffs for some sort of message. What was going on? What was he doing? Why did he feel as if he were about to combust into a million tiny pieces? He should go. Charlotte was fine—well, as fine as a drunk chick dressed like a mermaid could be.

"I'm ready," she said, then took a wobbly step and tripped on the damned fishtail. Reflexively, he lunged forward and caught her by the elbows. She pressed her hands to his chest, gathering the fabric of his T-shirt into her fists.

"That fishtail is a real piece of work," he said because he didn't know what the hell else to say with her tequila-infused breath warm against his lips.

Charlotte nodded, then captured him again with her emerald eyes. "Will you wait for me?"

He'd damn near wait his entire life for her.

He blinked.

Pull yourself together!

"Sure," he replied as he released her from his grip, and she disappeared into the ladies' room. He'd barely waited a minute before she emerged—*tail-less.* He drank in her bare legs. His button-up was long enough to cover her ass and hung about mid-thigh. A strange primal sense of victory washed over him. This woman, in his shirt with her tangle of red hair and toned thighs on display, had to be the sexiest thing he'd ever seen.

"Look, I'm a human being. I have legs," she replied, doing a little twirl that did a number on his cock.

He glanced away. "I can see that."

"Can you break the heel off this sucker? I tried in the bathroom, but I wasn't strong enough," she said, then handed him a high heel.

He frowned. "Why do you want me to break your shoe?"

She pulled a broken shoe from her tote. "My heel broke

today in the middle of the road. And I almost got run over by a Mercedes. I stopped traffic and everything. If you break that one," she said, touching the heel in his hand. "I'll have a pair of flats. Pretty awesome, right?"

Hello, alcohol buzz!

He shrugged. It was her damned shoe. With a flick of his wrist, he removed the slender heel.

"Great!" she exclaimed, slipping on the jacked-up heel-less heels when her stomach gave one hell of a growl.

She gasped, looking adorably embarrassed as her cheeks turned scarlet. "Was that me?"

He bit back a grin. "It wasn't me."

She pressed her hand to her belly. "What does that mean?"

Again, he nearly smiled. It was the first time in God knows how long he'd felt the inclination. "It means you're hungry, Charlotte."

"I'm hungry," she repeated as if he'd just shared the secrets of the universe with her.

"Let's get out of here. And let me carry that for you," he said, taking her giant-ass tote bag as she took his arm.

"Do you mind if I hold on to you? Everything is a little off-balance," she said, tightening her grip on his bicep.

Did he mind?

He should!

He wasn't that guy anymore. He didn't hold hands, and he certainly didn't parade around town with a woman on his arm like he'd bounced back into the Victorian age. But he couldn't say no to her.

"It's fine," he answered. But it was more than fine. It was grounding. In a world where he saw darkness, her touch lifted the veil and gave him a glimpse of the light.

"I remember seeing something!" she exclaimed, pulling him

down the hall, her broken shoes clomping along the hardwood floor.

"Where are we going?" he asked.

She leaned against him as she charged forward—without the mermaid tail, this spitfire of a woman could move.

"To heaven!" she declared.

He stared down at her. He didn't have a clue as to what she was talking about. But he now knew what four super-potent margaritas did to this chick.

With a bit of bumping around and several apologies, they worked their way through the crowd and made it out onto the sidewalk. She stopped and took a deep breath, then grinned up at him. "Heaven's not far!" she exclaimed.

He inhaled. And holy shit! She wasn't wrong. Heaven was close by. But she wasn't talking about the place with pearly white gates and winged saints in robes. No, she was talking about pizza.

"See, hothead! I told you. I drove by it on my way to the bar," she said, pointing at the Heavenly Pizza food truck.

He nodded. It was the only thing he could do.

"I love, love, love food trucks!" she gushed, then frowned. "You probably hate them. They're probably not fancy enough for Denver's top chef."

He did hate them. But not for the reason she'd thought.

"How about this? To thank you for lending me your shirt, I'll buy you a slice," she offered, leaning into him as they descended upon the truck.

The muscles in his chest tightened as he took in the scene. A cluster of people stood waiting to order as groups sat on the edge of a nearby fountain, chatting and laughing, sharing a simple meal in good company. That's what a food truck could do—pull up to an empty corner, and like magic, it sparked conversation and camaraderie in a once desolate location.

"Mitch," Charlotte whisper-shouted with absolute terror in her eyes.

He startled. Was she having another mermaid emergency, or was she feeling the effect of the copious amount of liquor she'd consumed? "What is it? Do you feel sick?"

"I can't buy you pizza. I just remembered—a latte broke me," she confessed with tears in her eyes.

Note to self—if he ever saw this woman in a bar again, he'd make sure to cut her off after one drink.

"A latte hurt you?" he questioned.

She shook her head. "No, I bought a latte this morning that cost a small fortune because the shop donates part of their proceeds to the Helping Hands Shelter."

A lump formed in his throat. "What did you say?"

"Handy Helper Shelter," she repeated, then scratched her chin. "I think that's what it's called."

"What about it?" he pressed as the memories flooded back.

"I spent most of my money at a coffee shop that donates to them. And now I have five dollars to my name."

That couldn't be everything she had.

"What do you have in savings?"

She waved him down, then leaned in. Her lips brushed against the shell of his ear. "Nothing," she whispered, then giggled. He doubted she'd be laughing about being broke as hell when she sobered up.

"I'll buy the pizza. It's not a big deal."

"Thank you, hothead," she beamed as the people in line in front of them got their slices, and he and Charlotte stepped up to the counter.

"I'll have a slice of cheese. I adore cheese," she chimed.

This woman and cheese!

"We'll take two slices of cheese," he said, removing a twenty from his wallet. "And keep the change," he added, handing over the cash as he peered in the window to get a peek at the inner workings of the mobile operation. They'd rigged the truck with a wood-fired pizza oven. But that wasn't the only modification. He observed a man in a wheelchair, sweat on his brow as he slid pies into the fire, and a woman working furiously to prep the pizza toppings.

Two guys and one gal busting their asses in a sweltering metal box to put out delicious food.

A knot twisted in his gut.

"Hold on a second!" the guy who took his order exclaimed wide-eyed. He turned to the pair in the back. "It's Mitch Elliott!"

He should have known this would happen.

The man grinned ear to ear as he handed over the two slices. "You're the reason we went to culinary school—the reason we refurbished this old delivery truck," the guy explained.

"That's nice of you to say. Good luck," he mumbled, ushering Charlotte away from the truck.

"I forgot, you're a big-time celebrity chef," Charlotte said, tapping his chin.

"Here, eat," he grouched, handing her a slice.

She held it up, went in for a bite, and fucking missed.

"Oops!" she cried, turning the slice around in her hands like she was an alien from a pizza-less planet. "I never realized how tricky it was to walk and eat."

"Those four super-charged margaritas might have some-thing to do with it," he said under his breath.

"Super-charged?" she echoed.

"Yeah, that place has a rep for their margaritas. They tell people to limit themselves to two."

Her jaw dropped. "I had three."

"You had four," he corrected, then pointed to a bench.

She plopped down and inhaled a gargantuan bite. Thank

Christ she was able to eat while sitting because he sure as hell wasn't going to cut up her food into tiny bites.

"I'm not usually a lush." She folded the pizza in half, then hoovered the rest of it.

Impressive!

"When I'm nervous, my mouth gets dry. See," she said, opening her mouth.

He raised his hand to shield his face. "All I see is chewed-up pizza."

"Below the pizza, it's super dry," she garbled with a mouthful of food.

If his life wasn't in shambles, this entire evening might be funny.

They sat there, in the dim glow of a streetlight, and ate their pizza side by side. Well, he ate his pizza like a human being while she absolutely devoured her slice and his crust like a starving animal.

"I started my day on a bench," she mused, her words coming out in a dreamy slur.

A bench! Was she homeless?

"Please don't tell me you spent the night in a park, Charlotte."

She sighed. "No, I still have a few more nights in my apartment before I get booted."

Jesus! She was broke and on the cusp of losing her home!

"Sitting on a park bench was where I met a couple that made me think I would meet my Mr. Cheesy Forever today," she said, then pointed up in the air.

"What is it?" he quipped, looking for...for what? He didn't know what the hell a Mr. Cheesy Forever even looked like.

"A plane! Do you see the blinking lights?"

He watched the plane as it headed west toward the darkened outline of the Rocky Mountains. "Yeah, I see it."

"There could be a Mr. Cheesy Forever waiting for it to land," she mused, making no damned sense. She slumped forward. "I guess I have to go back to the beginning for that, too," she finished, then released a resigned groan.

Back to the beginning!

Ines had given him the same advice. Not to mention, that was the second time she'd mentioned finding her Mr. Cheesy Forever. Charlotte popped the last bite of pizza crust into her mouth, then shifted on the bench.

"Look at me, Mitch," she said gently.

He complied, and she cupped his face in her hands.

"You're a hothead, and I know why," she whispered.

His pulse quickened. Mere inches away, he'd only need to lean forward to press his lips to hers.

"What do you think happened to me?" he asked, mesmerized by this hot mess of a woman.

"The same thing that happened to me. Somebody broke your heart," she whispered, her wise, drunken words insulating them from the cruel world.

His heart nearly stopped beating as she ran her fingertips down his jawline. And suddenly, he had the urge to lift her onto his lap and kiss her until he couldn't remember how to poach an egg.

"What makes you say that?" he asked, his voice a low rasp as he fought the impulse.

"Pass me my bag, please," she replied, not answering his question.

Regaining his bearings, he did as she asked. The woman went to work, pulling out the mermaid tail and the broken heels before removing a camera.

She held it up and framed a shot—a shot of him. "Don't move. It's hazy, but this light is perfect, and I can get the truck in the background. Hothead in Heaven."

He didn't like being filmed or photographed anymore. Once upon a time, he'd lived for it. But not anymore. His first impulse was to tell her to put the camera away. But he didn't.

Click.

"I got it," she chimed.

"What did you get?" he asked.

She met his gaze in the misty darkness. "The man behind the hothead."

With the scent of pizza and her strawberry sunshine scrambling his senses, he felt as if he'd hoovered those four margaritas. "Who do you think that is?" he asked. It was an honest question—he truly didn't know the answer.

"It's—" she began, then hiccupped and bent over.

Here it comes! Tiny woman versus tequila! They were bound to get to this portion of the night where she parted ways with the boatload of alcohol she'd ingested.

He rested his hand on her back. "Are you going to be sick?"

"No, but I need to lie down," she replied, curling up on the bench and resting her head in his lap. She shifted, pulling her arms out of the sleeves. She twisted, this way and that, before shooting her arm out of the left sleeve. He cocked his head to the side. There was something clenched in her fist. "Hold this, would you?" she asked.

He took the item and held it to the light. "Is this the shell bra?"

She cuddled into him. "Yeah, I'm good at taking off my bra under my shirt. What time is it?" she asked, her voice sounding far-off.

He swallowed hard. "It's almost eleven."

"PM?" she pressed.

He chuckled. "It's usually light out at eleven a.m. So yes, it's eleven p.m."

"I missed it. I screwed up again," she mumbled.

He brushed the hair from her face. "What did you miss?"

"The lock guy," she replied with a yawn.

Immediately, he pictured the lock Madelyn had given him—the lock still tucked away in his pocket.

"A locksmith?" he asked on a shaky breath.

She rolled onto her back, stared up at him, then undid the top button on her shirt, well, his shirt, and slipped a chain from beneath the fabric.

No way!

Thanks to the towel she'd wrapped around her shoulder, he hadn't noticed what had been hanging from the gold chain around her neck.

"No, I don't need a locksmith. I was supposed to wear this key necklace to meet my new boss," she finished, holding a gold key—the gold key from the picture—between her fingers.

Blood pounded in his ears, whooshing and thumping like a roaring river.

Charlotte was the nanny candidate!

"I think I could have been a good nanny. It was for a little boy—Oscar. I've always liked that name. It rolls off the tongue and just makes you smile."

That's what Holly had said when he'd asked her why she'd chosen that name.

Emotion rose in his chest, but he held it at bay. "It's a fine name," he stammered as the image of the boy, a boy with his eyes and crooked smile, flashed through his mind.

"But I screwed up and lost another job," she lamented. "No, not lost—I don't even know if I was going to get hired to be his nanny."

"Do you need a job?" he asked, staring down at her. She'd closed her eyes. She looked like an angel—an angel with a golden key.

"I need a job. I need a Mr. Cheesy Forever. I need to go

back to the beginning, hothead," she replied, followed by one last yawn before drifting off to sleep.

He traced the curve of her neck with the tip of his index finger. "I don't know a damn thing about a Mr. Cheesy Forever, but I can give you something, Charlotte."

She didn't reply. The air hung heavy around them, and he thought of his son. Releasing a weary breath, he froze when his phone buzzed. Without disturbing Charlotte, he retrieved his cell from his pocket, then read the incoming text.

It was from Madelyn.

Madelyn Malone: Did the nanny accept the position?

His gaze flicked from the glow of his cell to the woman wearing his shirt asleep on his lap. He had two options, and both would most likely end in disaster.

He tapped the keys and hammered out a one-word reply.

SIX

CHARLOTTE

CHARLOTTE SIGHED as a rhythmic hum surrounded her in a gentle, rumbling symphony of sound and inhaled a deep breath. And was that coffee in the air—fresh-roasted ambrosia? It sure smelled like it.

But her moment of pre-wake-up bliss didn't last long.

She turned her head, and immediately, her sleep cocoon gave way to a thunderbolt to her brain—at least, that's what it felt like. She cracked her eyes open, only to have the thunderbolt transform into a cataclysmic lightning storm inside her skull. And it wasn't just her head that was hellbent on putting her through the post-margarita ringer. Her body felt as if she'd brawled with a steamroller. She rubbed the muscles at the base of her neck and brushed her fingertips against the collar of her shirt. This wasn't her pajama top. Shaking off the clothing conundrum because her brain couldn't handle that level of scrutiny yet, she ran her tongue across the seam of her dry lips. She swallowed the teensy-tiny amount of saliva in her mouth. The Sahara Desert was a water park compared to her dehydrated state!

"Water, aspirin, then go back to bed," she muttered as she

pushed up onto her elbow. She peeled open her eyes a fraction wider, then clapped her hand over her mouth to restrain a scream.

Where the heck was she?

She blinked once, then twice.

This was not her crappy apartment. No, this wasn't even an apartment.

She studied her current setting, which looked a heck of a lot like the inside of a luxury RV.

How on earth did she get here?

Then it hit her. She was inside a freaking recreational vehicle headed to God knows where!

And that wasn't the worst of it.

Someone had to be driving this portable palace on wheels. Another scream threatened to escape. She slapped her other hand over the hand currently covering her mouth as the pieces of the puzzle came together.

She'd been flipping kidnapped!

Kidnapped!

In her twenty-five years, she'd always played the bit part, the reassuring friend, the forgettable extra. Not now! No, she'd landed her ass straight onto one of those posters with *MISSING* scrawled across the top in bold lettering.

She bolted upright—a terrible freaking idea—then cradled her head in her hands.

Stupid margaritas! Of course, she'd get kidnapped after enduring the most craptastic day.

"Think, think, think," she whispered, scanning her prison, which was, honestly, pretty spectacular. She took in the stainless-steel appliances, big screen TV, and a plush seating area, then turned her attention to the front of the vehicle and gasped.

There he was!

Her abductor!

She needed to come up with a plan to get out of there in one piece. And for that, she required a weapon. Slowly, she rose to her feet, and the fabric of her clothing billowed around her. What was she wearing? She stared down at a man's button-up shirt in a shade of pale blue. Where did she get it?

The answer to that question hit like another anvil strike to the brain.

She'd run into the hothead, Mitch Elliott, and he'd given her his shirt last night at the speed date event.

No, the speed date catastrophe!

She had not had the Larissa meets Royce evening she'd expected. A wave of humiliation passed over her as she replayed the reel of last night. Cliff was there—the creep! Then there was the hairy guy who'd followed her down the hall. He'd cornered her—the jackass! The guy wouldn't budge, and in her boozy haze, she'd wished for a white knight—a gallant, chivalrous hero to send Mr. Meaty Hands packing.

The universe answered, but boy, oh boy, did it have a screwed-up sense of humor.

Mr. Meaty Hand's breath was nearly too much to bear when Mitch Elliott appeared. He'd come out of nowhere and sent the hairy creeper running. She racked her brain. What happened next?

"Pizza!" she whispered.

Yes, they'd gotten pizza from the food truck. And then what? Did she blackout? Did she hit her head? Her pulse skyrocketed. Her poor moisture-less mouth felt as if it were made of sandpaper. Where did she go after they ate pizza?

It went blank after that.

But one thing was crystal clear.

Somewhere between sharing a slice with Mitch and this very moment, she'd been abducted.

Wasn't this just her luck! With no mermaid gig and eviction

on the horizon, she'd mucked up her one decent job prospect and had totally stood up Madelyn's client. And now she'd been kidnapped! She reached for the key at her neck and glared at the little thing. So much for opening the right door.

But there was no time to lament her cluster of a life. She had to act.

She craned her head and got a look at the back of her captor's head. The set of her abductor's shoulders told her it was a man—a man wearing a ball cap—a blue ball cap! She'd have to remember that. The police would need to know this information. She took a steadying breath, lowered herself to the RV's shiny tiled floor, then crawled over to the kitchenette area. Carefully, she opened a drawer. And bingo! She'd hit the utensil motherlode. Euphoria tingled through her body, or maybe that was adrenaline or even the remnants of the margaritas. Whatever it was, it triggered her drive to survive! Moving as carefully as a dehydrated, hung-over woman trapped inside a luxury vehicle traveling at forty miles an hour could, she swiped a spatula and a pair of metal tongs from the drawer. Exhaling a shaky breath, she set her sights on the driver—the depraved beast who thought he could take advantage of her.

Had she been drugged? Whatever circumstances brought her here, she'd have to hit this bastard hard enough to knock him out, then she could slam on the brakes and make a run for it. Her hands trembled, but she willed herself forward. "You can do this," she whispered. She had the element of surprise, and she needed to use it to her advantage. And she also needed to get him off-balance. Gathering her wits, she inhaled a deep breath, then screamed her head off as she charged toward the driver, waving the utensils like a wild-eyed, blood-thirsty, incredibly dehydrated lunatic.

She could not hold back. It was fight-or-flight time, baby, and she was fixing for a fight.

"You kidnapped the wrong redhead, asshole!" she exclaimed, hurling the spatula at the back of the criminal's head.

The RV swerved violently from left to right, then corrected its course. Excellent! She'd gotten her abductor good and discombobulated. But before she could blink, the vehicle screeched to a stop on the side of the road.

This was it! She zeroed in on the exit, then took off like a shot toward the door.

"Are you crazy?" the kidnapper called, springing to his feet and cutting off her escape route.

Undeterred, Charlotte widened her stance and raised the metal tongs like a battle-ax. Her heart hammered in her chest, ready to throw down when she made eye contact with her capturer. And it was no stranger! "You!" she exclaimed, addressing the hothead. "Mitch Elliott?" she cried on an astonished breath. He looked different. Sure, he was angry. But she'd seen him angry and spitting fire more times than she could count. Whatever level of angry this was, the emotion went deeper and appeared to cut closer to the bone.

"Of course, it's me!" Mitch snarled, glaring at her from beneath the ball cap. "Jesus, Charlotte, put the tongs down. Are you trying to get us killed?"

Like he had any right to glare at her!

She scoffed. The gall—the absolute gall of this stupid hotheaded chef.

"Let me out of here! You're not kidnapping me. Not today!" she cried, wishing she could amend that statement. She'd prefer never to be kidnapped—today or any day. But she could not show weakness. No, sir! She was the un-kidnappable Charlotte Ames—whatever the hell that was!

"Go ahead! Who's stopping you?" he barked, then pointed to the door.

"I will! I'm leaving! I will not be kidnapped today!" And crap! She'd said it again.

"I know! You've made that perfectly clear," he answered, then pressed a button on the RV's insanely high-tech dashboard, causing the door to swing open. The fresh mountain air whooshed inside as she got a peek at the evergreen-encased mountainous terrain.

But this wasn't over! She wasn't out yet. And this could be a trick.

She held the tongs like a sword. Then, moving stealthily, she slid past him and sailed out the RV door before sprinting toward a cluster of Aspen trees swaying in the breeze.

"We're in the mountains!" she exclaimed, gesturing to...well, the mountains surrounding them on every side.

"Where the hell did you think we'd be? Bora Bora?" Mitch answered on an exasperated breath as he leaned against the camper.

She surveyed her surroundings, looking for any signs of civilization—a gas station, a roadside rest stop. But there were none to be had. "Is this an abandoned road? Is this where you take your victims?" she shrieked when, as if on cue, a minivan cruised past them, taking the wind out of her sails.

"Are you still drunk?" he asked, taking a step toward her.

She waved the tongs at him. "Not one more move! I'm flagging down the next car and calling the police."

Mitch removed his cap and ran a hand through his hair. Pale with circles under his eyes, he looked terrible. "Charlotte, let me explain what's going on."

"Explain why you kidnapped me?" And eureka! She figured it out! She snapped her fingers. "It was the salad, wasn't it? I became a mark after I hurled those vegetables at you."

Confusion marred his expression. "A mark?"

"Yes, a potential victim. That's what they're called in the

movies and in spy novels. You can look it up," she shot back, smoothing her shirt—no, his shirt. Ugh! This was probably the part in her abduction where she should start running. Dissecting the inner workings of why she'd made an excellent kidnapping candidate could happen at a later date without the kidnapper staring her down.

"Charlotte, you're not my potential victim. You're my kid's nanny," he cried.

And O.M.G! This abduction kept getting weirder and weirder!

Mitch was a dad? That couldn't be true, could it? No, this must be part of the act.

She shook her head. "Liar! You don't have a child. I worked for you long enough to know the only thing you love is making people's lives a living hell."

He winced, and she almost felt bad about hurling the cruel words at him.

He paced along the side of the road. "Think, Charlotte! Did you talk to Madelyn Malone? Were you supposed to go to that bar to meet your new employer?"

She lowered the tongs a fraction. Okay, despite being a crafty, deceitful kidnapper, he wasn't completely wrong. But he'd omitted one crucial fact. And she wasn't sold that he could actually be Madelyn's client. She raised the tongs. "The person I was supposed to meet regarding the nanny position never found me."

"Yes, he did," Mitch replied, exasperation coating the words. "Madelyn rented this RV for the nanny and me to pick up my son and then camp for the night. And she gave me this," he finished, then removed an item from his pocket and held it out for her to see.

It was an old, rusty lock—a heart-shaped lock—but a creepy old lock just the same.

She held the tongs at the ready—still not convinced. "Is that the lock you were going to use to keep me trapped inside? You were always big on locks. You have that security lock in your office. Penny and I used to joke that's where you kept the managers you fired. And, oh my gosh! Are they in there? Is there a secret door to a scary cellar under the Crystal Cricket?"

"For Christ's sake, Charlotte! Do you really believe that I have a basement dungeon?"

"You're the hothead holding a lock," she replied, ready to chuck those salad tongs at his head and hightail it the hell out of there.

"You haven't been kidnapped. I doubt you noticed, but your tote bag was next to the pullout bed on the floor. I even stopped and got you a latte. Didn't you see it in the cupholder? It was next to a bottle of water and a packet of aspirin. I figured you'd have one hell of a hangover. I had no idea tequila turned you into a raving lunatic."

"I'm not a raving lunatic!" she shrieked, sounding an awful lot like...a raving lunatic.

"I've explained to you why we're here. Plus, you're barefoot on the side of the road in nothing but my shirt, screaming about being kidnapped when, in fact, you have not been kidnapped. That's the very definition of a raving lunatic!" he shot back, then stared up at the sky. "Penny knows you're here," he added on an exhausted exhale.

What the heck!

"Penny, my friend, Penny Fennimore?" she pressed.

Mitch nodded, liked she'd hit the idiot jackpot. "Rowen's Penny, yes. I saw them last night."

Last night?

When? Where? How? Charlotte pinched the bridge of her nose, sifting through the barrage of spiraling questions. "How does Penny know that I'm here?" she asked. And Holy moly!

Ordering one's thoughts post tequila bender wasn't the easiest of feats!

"Penny has an extra key to your apartment. She and Rowen met me at your place, so I could pack a bag for you," he answered, holding out his hands defensively as if he knew that the revelation would set her off—which, yeah, it sure as hell did.

"Where was I the whole time?" she shouted. And she should stop doing that ASAP. Her pounding brain couldn't take much more abuse.

He released another weary sigh. "You passed out in the RV. And by the way, you talk in your sleep."

Who did this man think he was?

"I do not," she shot back indignantly.

"You do," he corrected. "You were telling off someone—a Sutton Bryan."

Stupid drunk sleep-talking!

This was absolutely insane! Okay, she'd cop to the talking in her sleep, but she needed more proof that Penny and Rowen knew where she was. She lifted her chin, challenging the hothead chef. "Call Rowen this very minute and put him on speakerphone," she demanded.

"Really?" he asked. "Because we're basically at our destination."

"Yes, really!" she exclaimed. "And hello! As of right now, this whole situation still looks like an abduction to me."

"All right," he grumped, like the crotchety hothead he was. Sliding his phone from his pocket, he tapped the screen, then held it up.

"Hey, Mitch, what's going on?" Rowen said, picking up the call. But before Mitch could say one word, she lunged forward and grabbed onto her captor's wrist just below where he held the cellphone.

"Rowen, it's Charlotte," she blurted into the phone. "Mitch

Elliott has kidnapped me and brought me to the middle of nowhere!"

"Hey, Charlotte," the guy answered casually as if he'd completely glossed over the severity of her dire situation. "To clarify a point," he continued. "If you've got cell service, you're not in the middle of nowhere. In fact, I could tell you how many apps are currently tracking Mitch's phone if you're interested. I could probably hack in myself."

Charlotte screeched an animalistic, frustrated sound of a woman who'd had enough. Penny's billionaire tech nerd fiancé didn't get it!

"Char, is that you screaming?" Penny asked, her voice joining the line.

Thank God!

"Penn!" she said, gasping as she tightened her hold on Mitch's wrist. "What is going on, Penny? Mitch said you met him last night at my place and packed a bag for me."

She watched the chef—inches apart, the guy was...Ugh! Stupidly handsome!

"Yes, that's what happened," Penny confirmed. "Mitch called Rowen last night and said you'd accepted the nanny position—which OMG, yay! But then he told us that you'd overdone it on margaritas and had totally passed out. He didn't want to go through your things to get your keys, so he called to see if I could help. And, Char?"

"Yeah?"

"I tried to tell you about that bar, girl," her friend chided. "They've got a rep for super-strong margaritas. One or two can mess a person up."

Charlotte felt heat rush to her cheeks. She wasn't a lush—far from it. But she'd be laying off the margaritas for the foreseeable future. With her friend seemingly confirming Mitch's story, she studied the enigma of a man. While the guy's story checked out, the man hadn't said a thing about a nanny position—not one word the entire time they were together. Granted, she was crazy tipsy, but she would have remembered that. "What else did Mitch say last night?" she pressed, holding the man's gaze, searching his eyes for some clue about why he'd omitted this critical information.

"Let's see," Penny mused. "He was surprised to learn that Madelyn had chosen you. And he mentioned that the two of you had to leave right away to pick up his son. Not much more than that. He was pretty quiet. And, hello, Mitch, it sounds like you and Char are off to a great start."

"I'm not sure great is the correct way to describe it," he answered.

No kidding!

Charlotte shook her head, clearing the hangover cobwebs. She could barely believe it. But Penny wouldn't lie to her.

This was happening! She'd gotten hammered and woke up a nanny.

Her gaze softened as she took in the chef—the chef who had a secret son. This had to be the child Madelyn had told her about—Oscar, the six-year-old, who could use ninety-nine percent of her kindness, while the client, *Mitch,* would benefit from the one percent of her that didn't give an inch. Well, she was living up to her end of the bargain. Still, she couldn't help but wonder if there could be more to this hotheaded chef? And while that might be true, she wasn't ready to let him off the hook yet. He hadn't outright lied. But he hadn't told her the entire truth either.

"And just so you know," Rowen chimed, back on the phone. "You haven't been kidnapped, Charlotte. Not even close! I hacked into your phone. I hope you don't mind. I was able to do it through Penny's phone. As far as pinpointing your current location, you're in southwest Colorado, not far from Telluride."

"Rowen, babe," Penny exclaimed. "Just because you *can* use your super-nerd brain to hack into a phone doesn't mean you *should*." But Charlotte wasn't paying attention to the couple on the phone anymore. All she could do was stare into Mitch's blue eyes. She'd never noticed the color before. They were a deep shade of blue—almost navy. And they were hauntingly lovely, like the sky seconds before storm clouds exploded into a fury of rain and hail.

"I think we're good here. Thanks for your help, guys. I'm hanging up now," Mitch said, tapping the end-call icon while holding her gaze as if he, too, had fallen into a trance.

The line went quiet, and then it was the two of them. Her bottom lip trembled—actually trembled as her breathing grew ragged. What was wrong with her? She didn't like this guy—not like that. This had to be part of the hangover, right? The result of severe dehydration and skyrocketing amounts of adrenaline. But before she could even process her body's treacherous response to the hothead chef, Mitch looked away. He stared at her hand as she clutched his wrist in a white-knuckled death grip. She stared at it, too. Strangely, she couldn't bring herself to let go when a dizzying current zinged through her body. From the top of her head to the tips of her toes, electricity pulsed from his body to hers. And hello, Tingle City! The man looked at her as if he wanted to devour her in one bite. His laser-focused intensity could melt a gal into a pool of goo.

"Do you remember what happened when we were in the hallway after I took care of that jerk who had you cornered?" he asked, his voice low and gravelly, barely a whisper.

"Yes," she got out, lucky to even form the word as her nipples tightened into pebbled peaks.

"You went to change out of your mermaid tail, and then you asked if I'd wait for you. And I did, Charlotte. I waited," he said, his voice taking on a gentler tone.

She swallowed hard, recalling the shock as well as the utter relief when he'd appeared out of nowhere, then sent the hairy beast of a man packing. And while she'd been surprised, something inside her knew that, although he was a hotheaded chef, she was safe with him. Suddenly, with her hand wrapped around his wrist, she was painfully aware of his warm skin and muscled forearm. Her heart hammering, she steadied herself. "I remember asking you to stay," she conceded.

"After you changed," he went on, "you said you were hungry and that you wanted food truck pizza. And then—"

Heaven! She'd told him she wanted heaven. It all came back to her.

"And then we each ate a slice from the Heavenly Pizza food truck. And the cooks in the food truck knew you, right?" she interrupted.

He nodded as a blush graced his cheeks.

"And I took your picture," she continued as her thoughts fluttered back to that moment—back to sitting on the bench with him. And while she'd been pretty wasted, she couldn't deny that when she'd taken his picture, she'd done it without worrying about what he'd think or what he expected. She'd simply done it because she had to do it. Because, in that sweet snippet of time, she'd witnessed the truth. And as a photographer, it was her job to capture it.

"You fell asleep on the bench after that," he finished. But he'd failed to mention the part about how she'd curled up in his lap or how he'd brushed the hair from her eyes—that she could never forget.

"I know I owe you for getting rid of that creep in the bar, but you still lied to me, Mitch."

"I didn't," he replied on a pained breath.

"You didn't mention a thing about the nanny position."

"I didn't know you were the nanny candidate until you

showed me your necklace. And before I could figure out how to tell you who I was, you were telling me you'd lost your job and didn't find your Prince Charming. You called him Mr. Cheesy Something."

Mr. Cheesy Forever.

"I said that?" she squeaked.

"Yeah, and if we're throwing around the title of liar, you did your fair share of lying last night," he bit back.

She released his wrist and stared him down. "I did no such thing!"

"Grilled cheese," he growled—like that meant anything!

She scoffed at the man. "What are you talking about?"

"I was right behind you during the speed date bullshit. I could see your answers. You lied and agreed to whatever the douche bags across from you said," he snapped, all smug and self-righteous.

She could feel herself turning full-on redheaded tomato. "That wasn't lying. I had a very good feeling that I was supposed to meet—"

"I know! You were supposed to find your Mr. Cheesy Forever last night. You think the way to do that is by lying?" he snarled.

Searing indignation burned in her chest as she narrowed her gaze. "It's not lying. It's called being flexible."

Mitch donned his asshole chef expression. "It's acting like a doormat, Charlotte."

"I am not a doormat!" she threw back. But the shake in her voice begged to differ. *Dammit!*

Mitch sneered, clearly not swayed. "So, you'd be cool jetting off to Cabo with that hairy jackass?"

This infuriating man!

"No, I would not," she answered through a clenched jaw.

"How do you know that he wasn't your Mr. Cheesy Forever?" the chef tossed back, using her words against her—the creep!

She had to turn the tables and fast.

"How do you know that I want to nanny for you?" she countered. She might be out of options when it came to paying her bills. But he wasn't without vulnerabilities either.

A muscle twitched in his jaw—she'd landed a verbal punch. "Because you've lost your job, and you're about to get kicked out of your apartment. I'm your only option."

Dammit! In her tipsy state, she'd shared her woes with the man. She parted her lips to unload on him when his fiery expression cooled and gave way to a tenderness she'd never observed in the man's eyes.

"And when you said my son's name last night," Mitch began, his voice cracking. "There was such warmth to the word. It made me think—"

"What? What did you think when I said *Oscar?*" she asked, the name falling from her lips like a lullaby or a mystical incantation. Instantly, the humiliation and the fury churning in her belly quieted as she waited, breathless, for his answer. And holy heated exchange! Did she get a reaction! Her heart fluttered in her chest. If she wasn't glaring at him, she would have missed it —the slight upturn in his lips—the ghost of a sad, sweet grin.

"I just knew that you'd be good for Oscar because, despite chucking a salad at me and getting blitzed out of your mind on margaritas, you care about people, Charlotte. All a person has to do is look in your eyes, and they know it."

No words. She had no words.

The muscles in Mitch's throat constricted as he swallowed hard. "The truth is, you're better suited to be with Oscar than I am. I don't know the first thing about being a good parent," he confessed, running his hands down the scruff of his jawline. "I'm in a world of shit. I'm under contract to write a damned book to save my career, and I recently became the sole caregiver for my kid. What do you say, Charlotte? Can you give me sixty days and help me figure this out?"

Wide-eyed, she stared at the man. His uncharacteristically earnest words went straight to her heart. She had no idea his career was on the rocks. Then again, he was a TV chef who'd completely bucked the limelight three years ago to cook at a small bistro in Denver, far from the likes of the television food meccas of Los Angeles and New York.

"You learned about Oscar three years ago, didn't you? That's when you found out that you had a son," she said, unable to stop herself. It was a hunch, a strange premonition, but she had to be right—she felt it, the truth of it.

His lips parted as pain clouded his expression. But just as he began to answer, something hard hit her square in the back as an out-of-place mechanical sound purred. "Ouch!" she cried, reaching to rub the tender spot as a barrage of pebbles rained down on them.

Mitch grabbed her hand, and the two of them sprinted toward the RV, running for cover as a voice rang out.

"Gotcha suckers!" a boy called from way up in a tree.

How long had he been there?

The child stuffed something into a worn backpack, then zoomed down, springing back and forth, limb by limb, like he was part boy and part ape. The child flashed a wicked, toothy grin, and Charlotte could barely believe her eyes.

Barefoot and barely four feet tall, the boy looked like a mini-Mitch with his cropped dark hair and the same strong jawline. But before she could even greet the tiny heathen child, the kid disappeared into a cloud of dust.

She leaned against the RV and caught her breath. "That was—"

"That was my son. If it's not already completely obvious

from the welcome he just gave us, it's safe to say that I've been a shit father. The boy and I barely know each other." Mitch pinned her with his gaze. "Please, Charlotte, give me sixty days. I'm not the type of guy who likes to depend on anyone. But I'm not an idiot—and I know you see that I need you."

"You need me?" she echoed, hating how much she liked the sound of that. She glanced down at their joined hands, but Mitch was quick to release his grip.

He shifted his stance. *Was the man nervous?* "I need a nanny for Oscar. What do you say, Charlotte? Are you in? Can you put up with a hothead and his kid for the next two months?"

She twisted the cuff of her shirt—no, his shirt.

"I'll be upfront with you from here on out," he continued, his words tumbling from his lips. "No surprises. I hope I can ask the same of you. I don't do well when things catch me off guard. That's probably pretty apparent," he finished.

The raw vulnerability of the man drew her in. And that was dangerous. If she said yes, she'd have to keep it professional. She couldn't give in to the tingle monster this man ignited inside of her. And speaking of being *upfront*—this was the point where she should mention the possibility of going to London for the photography workshop. Reflexively, she reached for the key, and Madelyn's words came back to her.

You've got the key. It's up to you to figure out if it opens the right door.

Was this the right door, or was this opportunity her only door, her last resort? There was only one way to find out.

"Charlotte?" Mitch said, his voice barely a whisper.

She swallowed past the lump in her throat. "I'm in. You've got yourself a nanny."

SEVEN

CHARLOTTE

"I DON'T CARE *if you're my dad! I'm not living in your house!*"

"Oscar, we talked about this a few days ago. You're coming to Denver with me, and that's the end of it."

"You're the worst dad in the whole world!"

Charlotte lifted the mug of coffee to her lips and took a sip as the father versus son battle waged on down the hall.

"I can make another pot if you'd like more, Charlotte."

She swallowed the last sip of her fourth, okay, fifth, steaming cup of coffee, then set the mug on the table as Oscar called his father a *super-duper jerk,* or maybe it was *super-duper-pooper-scooper-jerk.* Either way, in the hothead department, the apple hadn't fallen far from the tree. Charlotte pasted a grin to her lips. "No, thank you, Amy. I'm good."

A lie.

She wasn't good. She was in over her head—big-time!

After Oscar's roadside, rock-fueled ambush, she'd barely had time to dash into the RV and change her clothes before Mitch pulled up in front of a picturesque cabin perched between a sea of majestic evergreens that bordered an equally picturesque creek. When she'd emerged from the fancy camper, the view had taken her breath away. Had she not landed ass over elbow into Mitch's family drama, she would have taken out her camera and started snapping away. This place, this rustic escape, was her definition of Shangri-la.

Unfortunately, the circumstances of their visit dashed any hopes of making this a light and breezy photo op.

She was twisting her wild mane of red hair into a ponytail as Mitch knocked on the door. In those brief seconds, he'd given her the world's fastest recap of why they were there.

Here was the takeaway. Oscar's mother had passed away suddenly a few weeks ago from an intracerebral hemorrhage. It was similar to a stroke, he'd explained, barking out the information as if he were reading off an order ticket at the Crystal Cricket. Her death was a freak occurrence. She was thirty-two years old. The only saving grace was that her younger sister, Amy, had been visiting at the time. And it was Amy who'd been watching Oscar since Oscar's mother's death. But her work as a flight attendant precluded her from caring for the boy full time. Charlotte didn't even have a second to ask what Oscar's mother's name was before Amy opened the door and ushered them inside.

Mitch had barely said hello to the woman before heading down a hallway, presumably to the room where a child called out, over and over, that there was no way he was leaving. Describing the situation as awkward was an understatement. Amy had wrung her hands and led her to the kitchen. And for the better part of the last twenty minutes, the women had made small talk, the way people did when something monumental had occurred, and all one could do was lean on social graces and put on a brave face.

Charlotte glanced around the cozy, rustic space, then took in a row of framed photographs lining the windowsill. The vast majority were of Oscar and a smiling woman with chestnut-colored hair—most likely, Oscar's mother. But there was one photo without Oscar that had caught her eye. A photo of Oscar's mother, another man, and Mitch, crowded together, leaning through an open window. She could barely believe her eyes. Mitch looked like a different person—and then she realized why. He was smiling. She'd never seen the man don a wide grin. She'd seen him smirk and sneer and frown. He had those down pat. But she'd never seen him like this. It transformed his entire demeanor.

"That's a shot of Holly, Mitch, and Seth from the old days," Amy said, picking up the framed photo as sadness clouded her gaze. "You should take it. Mitch won't want it, but Oscar loved it when his mom used to tell him stories about this time in her life," the woman finished, handing it over.

Charlotte stole another glance at the image, then slipped the framed photo into the side pocket of her tote.

"Holly? That was Oscar's mom's name?" she asked. She didn't want to pry, but this might be the only time to get some information about Oscar's life from someone other than the tight-lipped hothead.

Amy took the seat across from her, and the sadness in her eyes changed to confusion. "Yeah, her name was Holly Abrams. Mitch didn't tell you?"

The man didn't even tell me I was his nanny until half an hour ago.

No, she couldn't say that.

Charlotte shifted in her seat. "He hasn't shared much information with me yet. But I was recently hired. I'm sure Mitch, I mean, Mr. Elliott," she fumbled, not sure how to navigate the conversation or what she was supposed to even call Mitch now that he was her boss...*again!*

At the Crystal Cricket, it was Chef, and she wasn't about to call him that now. She twisted a lock of hair that had broken free from her ponytail. She'd been in awkward situations before, but this one took the cake! Still, she had to remember that Amy had lost a sister, and Oscar had lost his mother. And Mitch? While the man clearly had a past she knew nothing about, it didn't take a genius to see that he was in a world of pain as well.

"How long have you been a nanny?" Amy asked.

Crap! She hadn't even thought of how to answer this question.

She straightened in her seat. "This is my first official nanny position. But I've worked with kids extensively in my old job."

It wasn't a lie!

One of the only perks to being a child's party mermaid was that it schooled her in the art of charming children—well, most children. Grover Cleveland Schulte had been the exception, not the norm. And the truth was, she loved kids. She wanted children—lots of children—and a family of her own. A family that went on trips and shared meals at the kitchen table. A family that laughed and loved each other.

A family that didn't ignore her. A family that saw her—really saw her.

The muscles in her chest tightened as she ignored the unwelcome memories.

"And you understand the situation with Oscar?" Amy continued.

Charlotte blinked as Amy's question snapped her back from her gloomy walk down family memory lane. She had to put all that baggage aside and focus on the task at hand.

"I understand that Mitch is Oscar's father. But there's some friction between them," she answered as a clunk and a bang came from the other side of the cabin, followed by the sound of a door slamming.

"Friction is a good way to describe it," Amy agreed as the

raised voices continued on the other side of the house. "Will you be coming back to the cabin, or do you think you'll stay in Denver?"

That seemed like an odd question.

Charlotte scanned the kitchen. "I'm not sure. Isn't this Oscar's mother's place? Won't it go to you?"

Amy cocked her head to the side. "No, Mitch bought this place for Holly and Oscar. It belongs to him."

That was new information. Mitch had left that out of his rapid-fire recap.

Charlotte sighed. "I'll level with you, Amy. I'm sorry, I don't have more answers. And I'm so sorry for your loss. This has got to be a hard time for you and for Oscar. But I'll promise you this; I'll do everything I can to make this transition easier on Oscar."

"I appreciate that," Amy said on a relieved breath. "And I wish I could help more, but I'm a flight attendant based out of Paris. There's no way I could care for Oscar full time, and Mitch is his dad. I remember when we found that out three years ago," the woman finished, and the breath caught in Charlotte's throat as Amy confirmed her premonition.

They sat quietly as silence engulfed the kitchen when, over the chorus of Oscar telling Mitch he wasn't leaving, Charlotte heard the same mechanical hum that accompanied Oscar's rocky welcome. And instantly, she placed the sound.

"This might be an odd question," she began, breaking the bubble of silence. "But does Oscar have one of those instant Polaroid cameras?"

A grin pulled at the corners of the woman's mouth. "Yes, he does. He won it in some school raffle not long ago. What made you ask that?"

"I heard him take a picture with it. I heard the same sound when Mitch and I had pulled over onto the side of the road so we could…" she trailed off. Oh boy! How should she put this without sounding insane? There was no way she was about to disclose that until about an hour ago, she'd assumed she'd been kidnapped by a psychopathic chef with a basement dungeon. "We stopped so we could tie up a few loose ends," she finished, going for vague. "And while we were talking, like normal people do on the side of the road, I thought I'd heard the sound of one of those instant Polaroid cameras," she finished, knowing she should have left out the *normal people* part.

Normal people never called themselves normal people.

Luckily, Amy didn't seem to notice, and her expression brightened. "That would be Oscar," she answered through a little laugh. "He's obsessed with that camera. He brings it everywhere and wants to take a picture of everything he sees. When the woman who owns the nanny service called to ask about his interests, I told her about his new hobby."

Madelyn knew Oscar was into photography.

"Take a look," Amy continued, then opened a wooden box on the table and removed a stack of instant Polaroid prints.

Charlotte flipped through the images and couldn't help but smile as she admired pictures of trees, toy cars, and food. Lots of pictures of food—specifically grilled cheese sandwiches.

"Grilled cheese is my favorite, too," Charlotte mused, staring at picture after picture of gooey, cheesy deliciousness.

"He's an amazing kid—smart as a whip—and he likes to cook. But you probably knew that already," Amy added.

Charlotte looked up from Oscar's photos. "Did Mitch teach him?" she asked.

Amy narrowed her gaze. "No, Holly did. She was a chef, too. But she stopped working after Oscar was born. She, Mitch, and Seth started—"

"We're ready to go," Mitch interrupted, red-faced, as he strode into the kitchen with two suitcases under his arms.

Amy checked her watch. "I'm late! I didn't realize the time. I have to get to the airport. My crew is working a flight to Dubai." She stood and surveyed the kitchen. "Can you lock up here, Mitch?"

"Yeah, I can. Thanks for everything," he answered, exhaustion coating the words.

Amy patted his arm. "Take care of yourself, Mitch. I know that Holly would be grateful for what you're doing."

Mitch grunted something as he studied the floor.

"I'm going to say goodbye to Oscar. It was nice to meet you, Charlotte. I hope we meet again soon," Amy added, then left the kitchen, her heels clicking against the rustic wooden floor.

As soon as they were alone, Mitch released a weary sigh, then set the suitcases down.

What now?

Charlotte searched for the right words, but nothing came to her. Needing to do something with herself, she rose to her feet. "Is there anything else to pack up?"

"I don't know," the man answered, looking as if he'd been mauled by a pack of wild dogs.

This was certainly off to a rocky start!

"How about I bring these along?" she offered, gathering the stack of Oscar's Polaroids.

Mitch stared at the top image—a shot of a grilled cheese sandwich—and the man's expression darkened. "Do whatever you want," he griped as Amy returned.

"I'm off, and Oscar asked for you, Charlotte," the woman added.

"Me?" Charlotte questioned as a jolt of anxiety prickled through her body. The boy didn't even know who she was.

"Yes, he was adamant that he needed to speak to you."

"Okay, I'll go say hello," she answered, resurrecting that brave awkward situation expression.

"Oscar's room is down the hall. It's the second door on the left. You can't miss it. He's got a keep-out sign taped to it," Mitch said, then turned to Amy. "I'll walk you out."

The pair disappeared, and then it was just her, alone in an unfamiliar kitchen, smack-dab in the middle of a family tragedy. She'd felt woefully out of place. Her entry into the field of child-care had been the very definition of baptism by fire. And it seemed she was about to encounter her first obstacle: the meet and greet.

She picked up her tote, placed the stack of Oscar's Polaroids inside, then tiptoed down the hall like a cat burglar.

"He's a boy who requires a little kindness," she whispered, giving herself her first nanny pep talk.

She stopped in front of the door, took a steadying breath, then knocked twice.

"Who is it?" Oscar called, his growly tone matching Mitch's surly manner.

"It's Charlotte. Your aunt said you wanted to talk to me."

"Yeah, I did! Why are you here? Why did my dad bring you to my house?" the boy barked.

Yep, he was Mitch's son.

"I'm your nanny," she answered.

A series of squeaks and creaks emanated from the room. "I don't need a nanny. I can tie my shoes in double knots, and my mom taught me how to make a grilled cheese sandwich on the stove. I want to live here by myself. You can leave," the boy shot back.

Charlotte sat down and stared at the door. "I don't blame you, Oscar. This seems like a great place to live."

The squeaking stopped with a hard thud. The boy must have been jumping on the bed. It wasn't long before the pat of cautious footsteps grew louder, and she heard him move closer.

"You like it here?" the child replied, his curious tone softening. He wasn't expecting her to agree.

This was progress. Step one: find something you have in common with the kid. When she worked those mermaid parties, she always made sure to amp up the enthusiasm.

"Sure, this place looks awesome. You have your own creek, and who wouldn't want to eat grilled cheese sandwiches every day? By the way," she added, slipping one of Oscar's pictures from her tote. "I see you like to make your grilled cheese sandwiches super-cheesy," she finished, sliding the Polaroid under the door.

Little fingers snapped it up. "I can make peanut butter and banana sandwiches, too. And I get to use the big knife to cut it into triangles."

"That's pretty impressive," she answered, catching a glimpse of his sneakers through the gap between the floor and the door.

"So, I can stay at my house?" Oscar pressed, his voice losing the hothead edge.

"Sorry, buddy, that's not my call," she answered gently.

"But you don't like my dad, either," the child exclaimed, sliding a photo facedown under the door. She picked it up and gasped. It was the picture he'd taken from the tree of her and Mitch. From the bird's-eye view, with their bodies less than an inch apart, it looked as if they were about to kiss. And then the moment came back to her—Mitch's vulnerability and her inability to resist the man.

"I don't dislike your dad. But he sure can be a hothead when he wants to," she added.

The boy giggled. "A hothead?"

"Yes, it's a funny word, isn't it?"

"I like it! Hothead, hothead, hothead," the boy repeated, and she could hear the smile in his voice. "Do you want to see something, Charlotte?"

"I'd love to," she answered, listening as Oscar disengaged the lock on the bedroom door, then peeked out.

"I took a picture of my dad when he was a super-duper hothead," he said, handing her a Polaroid as he came out of his room wearing a worn army-green backpack, then plopped down onto the floor beside her. She pressed her lips together to suppress a laugh as she studied the photo. Mitch stood in the center of the room, red-cheeked and squeezing the bridge of his nose. She'd seen this version of the man more times than she could count in the Crystal Cricket kitchen.

She set the photo on the floor, then turned to Oscar. It was her first chance to get a good look at the boy. And even without the child's temper, the resemblance to Mitch was uncanny. They shared the same stormy blue eyes and the same strong, stubborn set of their jaw.

"I'm calling that picture *the hothead,*" Oscar announced

"Did you take it with a Polaroid?" she asked, knowing he did but wanting to give him the chance to share.

"Yep," the boy replied, slipping off his worn pack, then removed the camera. He held it up as if he were presenting the Crown Jewels.

"You have a good eye. You captured the moment," she replied, remembering that she also had a picture of Mitch. She reached into her bag. "Would you like to see one of my pictures?"

"You have a Polaroid camera, too?" he asked. "I like the noise it makes when the picture comes out," the boy finished, then emitted a grinding, guttural sound mimicking the camera.

"No, I have a Nikon," she answered, handing it to the child.

"It's nice and all, but it doesn't print a picture right there in like two seconds," Oscar commented.

She chuckled. "It doesn't. But I can see every shot I take here," she replied, turning on the camera and activating the LCD screen. Then gasped as the last picture she'd taken appeared.

"Is that my dad?" the child asked.

The glow of the food truck blurred behind the image of a man—Mitch—whose expression held an intense honesty that mesmerized her. The darkness dotted with hazy light surrounded him, giving the picture an ethereal quality. But it wasn't the background that left her speechless. It was the subject. Mitch stared into the camera as if he'd wanted to show her his soul. There was nothing wooden or hollow about the photo. It held a beautiful melancholy quality that broke her heart while simultaneously igniting a kernel of hope deep in her chest. Shaking her head, she could hardly believe she'd taken the photo.

"Yes, that's him," she answered.

"He looks like the opposite of a hothead," the boy remarked as the two of them stared at the image.

Wasn't that the truth!

"He does," she answered, assessing the composition. It was a good shot—an exceptionally good shot.

A shot worthy of the Royal College of Art.

"Do you mind if I do something with my camera real quick?" she asked, her pulse racing.

The boy handed it over. With trembling fingers, she pulled up the menu, then transferred the image to her phone. It was as if she wasn't quite acting on her own volition—like a force within had taken over. She removed her phone from her bag and opened the digital application for the London intensive work-shop. She stared at the button with *attach image* written in bold type. Not giving herself a moment to second-guess, she attached the photo of Mitch and hit send. The *whoosh* of the sent email sound washed over her.

She'd done it!

"What did you do with the picture?" Oscar asked.

"Just something for a photography class," she answered, trying to keep her tone even as she willed her heart not to beat out of her chest.

"What about a photography class?" came a gruff voice.

She whipped her head toward the source of the sound and found Mitch, arms crossed, as he filled the small hallway with his large, brooding body.

"Oscar and I were comparing cameras," she replied, not answering his question. And especially not disclosing that she'd submitted a picture of him as part of the application for the workshop. A tiny knot formed in her belly, but she ignored it. What were the chances they'd accept her? It was a pipe dream. The longest of long shots. Still, she had to do it. She owed it to herself to try.

Mitch blew out a heavy breath, then checked his watch. "It's time. We need to leave now if we want to make it to the campsite by dusk."

She nodded, then felt a tug on her shirt. She looked over to find Oscar frowning.

"Do I have to go, Charlotte?" the boy asked.

"Yes, Oscar, it's not a choice," Mitch barked, answering for her.

The boy crossed his arms and pouted, looking like the mini version of his father.

She glanced between the glowering pair. "Oscar and I will meet you at the camper in a minute," she said to the fuming chef.

"One minute," he said, holding her gaze, and that's when she saw it—the agony and the confusion. He was trying to keep up a stone-faced front. But his hothead chef facade didn't fool her. Not anymore. This man was terrified.

"We'll be right there, Mitch."

Oscar's shoulders slumped. "I've never been to Denver. I don't know what my dad's house looks like. He always came here."

The child's words went right to her heart. She patted his leg. "I don't know what it looks like either. We're both getting a new home."

The child perked up. "You're going to live with us?"

"Yes."

"I have to go to a new school, too," Oscar added, twisting his shoelace. "Aunt Amy said it was called Whitmore."

Whitmore!

"Oscar, I know that school," she exclaimed. "My friend's soon-to-be step-niece goes there. Her name is Phoebe. She's in the first grade."

"I'm in the first grade!" the boy chimed.

"Look at that! You'll already know someone."

Oscar nodded, but his initial enthusiasm faded. "I don't think my dad wants me to live with him."

This poor boy had lost his mother, and now, he had to live with a father he barely knew. She understood what it felt like to feel alone in this world. She understood what she had to do. Come hell or high water, she'd do everything in her power to show him that he wasn't alone—that someone believed in him.

"I think your dad isn't sure what to do. But I know that he's trying. And I know that he loves you," she said, working to keep the emotion from her voice.

"That's what my mom used to say," the boy replied, twisting a loose thread on the strap of his backpack.

"Your mom sounds like she was a smart lady."

Oscar met her gaze. "She also told me I shouldn't call my dad names. But I'd get so mad, I couldn't help it."

She waved him in and lowered her voice. "I have something you can do whenever you get frustrated. It's something my friend Penny showed me when I was your age. And it works like magic."

"What is it?"

"Do you want to call your dad a super-duper hothead?" she asked, raising an eyebrow.

It was time to lighten the mood.

The boy's demeanor brightened. "Yeah."

"Watch my foot," she said, then tapped out the six syllables for super-duper hothead. "Super-duper hothead," she said, doing it again. "Only you know what the taps mean," she whispered conspiratorially.

Oscar's lips twisted in a wicked toothy grin as the RV's horn blasted. He came to his feet, then glanced into his room.

"Try the taps," she encouraged, rising to stand next to him.

He stared at the floor, and she held her breath. A beat passed, then two.

This had to work!

The boy needed a way to work through all the emotions that had to be trapped inside of him. She wasn't a child psychology expert, but the taps had sure come in handy when she was his age.

Tap-tap-tap-tap-tap-tap.

He smiled up at her.

"You got it," she said softly.

She picked up his backpack, helped him put it on, then offered the boy her hand.

He gave his room one last look, then rested his hand in hers. She gave it a squeeze. "Here we go, Oscar. This is where our adventure begins."

EIGHT

MITCH

MITCH POUNDED a tent stake into the hardened, pine needle-covered ground, then stood and walked to the next corner. Over the last several hours, as they'd made their way across the state to the campsite, he'd maintained his stony, muted countenance—his silent facade of control. But even now, as they set up camp under the setting sun, he couldn't deny the truth. It was an act. His body vibrated with nervous energy as he hammered the next stake into place. Usually, the crisp late spring mountain air cleared his head. But after the last twenty-four hours, it would take a hell of a lot more than a fragrant mountain breeze to calm his frayed nerves.

It had been one hell of a day!

This time yesterday, he'd learned that Gabe and Monica were stepping in to run his restaurant and that Madelyn had matched him with a nanny. He thought things seemed out of control then! Jesus, look where he was now—setting up camp with the son he barely knew along with the woman who'd hurled a salad at him. He was so out of his element, so absolutely oblivious. In the kitchen, he was in control of every minute detail. He ran the show and called the shots. He knew what to expect, and he knew what was expected of himself.

Who was he now?

Who was this new, off-balance version of Mitch Elliott?

For Christ's sake! He'd spilled his guts to Charlotte on the side of the road. He'd stared into her emerald eyes and couldn't hold back. His jaw had nearly hit the ground when she'd put together the timeline. She now knew that he'd learned that Oscar was his son three years ago. He'd have to watch himself and be more careful about what he disclosed. Despite his best efforts, she'd penetrated his defenses. If she were anyone else, he'd cast her aside and block her out. But she wasn't just anyone.

She was his nanny match. And under the circumstances, he was damned lucky she hadn't slapped him in the face and quit, right on the spot after waking up in a moving vehicle. Yeah, he could have played it differently. He could have picked up Oscar on his own and left her with Penny and Rowen. But he didn't—because he wanted her with him. Still, she didn't exactly hold all the cards. The only saving grace was, in her tipsy tequila-clouded state, she'd let a few pertinent, private details fly as well. She was broke, jobless, and looking to find her Mr. Cheesy Forever. He couldn't help her in the cheese-covered, soul mate department. What he had left of his battered heart wasn't worth giving. But he did have plenty of cash and desperately required a nanny.

Like it or not, they needed each other—which introduced the next complication.

He was her boss...again!

Here's the problem.

When their eyes locked, and he met her fiery gaze, she didn't feel like an employee. She was his equal, standing her ground and not giving an inch. It was utterly intoxicating. Not to mention, her scent and that damned ponytail were making him crazy. Every time he saw it, it ignited the dirty fantasies that begged for one touch, one lick, one bite of her strawberry sunshine sweetness.

When he'd confided that he was in a world of shit with his career and didn't have a damned clue about being a good father, it was as if he were under her spell. As the words fell from his lips, all he wanted to do was wrap his arms around her and anchor himself to her goodness. He craved to hold on to this aura of kindness that followed her wherever she went. Standing inches apart, he'd been a breath away from claiming her mouth in a kiss so intense and so agonizingly sinful, it threatened to cost him everything.

He could not have her—not like that. There was too much on the line.

But the dogged impulse to claim her lips in a searing kiss had been damned near impossible to ignore. With his broken heart exposed and raw, the urge to disappear into this woman had nearly overtaken him. Had it not been for Oscar's pebble storm of a welcome, he wouldn't have been able to hold back. And it wasn't just him—it couldn't be. He'd seen the ferocity in her and sensed the energy pulsing between them. She felt something, too.

Dammit! Again, it didn't matter. He couldn't hook up with the damned alluring nanny.

Releasing a heavy sigh, he played the events of last night over in his head. He'd watched her sleep on that bench for far longer than he should have. Wearing his shirt with her head in his lap and the golden key glinting in the glow of the street-lamp, she nuzzled into him as if she'd spent a lifetime falling asleep while he caressed her cheek. And like a sucker, he'd held the key between his fingers and couldn't help but wonder if this was the key that unshackled him from the myriad of locks he'd fashioned around his heart. It was a stupid wish—a pathetic momentary yearning he shouldn't entertain. It was dangerous to believe that someone was the answer to his prayers. He knew better than anyone how foolish it was to hand your heart over to another on a silver platter, then trust that they'll protect it.

It was dangerous to trust, period.

He'd made that mistake before, and he wasn't about to make it again.

No, his focus had to be on jumpstarting his career and figuring out how *not* to screw up his son. He loved the kid. It was impossible not to. The boy was smart and crafty—just like he was as a kid. It was like looking into a mirror. Except, it wasn't exactly an even match. Oscar had twice the will—and twice the smarts—as he did. But they were on the same level with one Elliott trademark characteristic: a complete allegiance to bullheadedness. A willful drive that egged on others with a cunning smirk that said *you'll regret the day you messed with me.*

He could ask the kid to jump, and the boy would nail his shoes to the floor. He had to find a way to reach him, a commonality to bond over. The connection was there. Unfortunately, at this juncture in their unconventional father and son journey, the relationship appeared to hinge on a decent amount of head-butting and mutual surliness.

How the hell would they move forward?

The last thing he wanted was to be like the man who raised him. But there wasn't a perfect recipe for parenting. And what he thought might be the ingredients shifted from minute to minute,

A rocky crash cut into his thoughts. He looked over his shoulder to where Oscar was building a rock tower. Without a word to anyone, the kid had filled his pack with stones he'd pulled from the bank of a nearby stream. One by one, the boy stacked the smooth rocks, only to have them wobble and tip over before he started again—going back to the beginning.

Back to the beginning.

That was what Ines suggested he do. Go back to the beginning and unearth the spark he'd lost when the two people he loved the most had betrayed him in the worst possible way. How could he do that? Why would she even ask that of him? It was damned near impossible to catch lightning in a bottle once— Ines wanted him to do it twice!

He kept his focus on Oscar and watched as his son carefully placed a thin onyx-colored stone atop the pile. The stack teetered as the kid slowly lifted his hand. He could almost hear Oscar's thoughts, silently commanding the pile to remain upright. That was another trait they shared. Both father and son tried to control the uncontrollable.

But he knew what was coming. He pounded the final stake and listened as Oscar's rock tower tumbled to the ground in a burst of crackling thuds for what must have been the hundredth time. He felt a lot like that rock tower. He tried to stand firm, believing he had a handle on the situation, only to have another weight added to the load that sent it toppling. He dropped the hammer, rubbed his neck, then rolled his head from side to side, working out the kinks and knots when the door to the RV swung open, and Charlotte stomped out of the vehicle. Her ponytail brushed the nape of her neck in a fierce left to right swish as she scanned the campsite and frowned. This didn't look good! She strode to the space between himself and Oscar, surveyed the scene with a crease to her brow, then pressed her fists to her hips.

"The silent treatment ends now, gentlemen," she announced.

What had gotten into her?

Then again, to her point, he couldn't remember the last time he'd spoken. He'd been in his head as he'd driven the RV. And dammit, he couldn't remember hearing a peep out of Oscar during the hours-long drive either.

His son looked up from the pile of stones and shrugged in response to Charlotte's outburst.

She was upset. He should do something. But for the life of him, he didn't know what to do. And he didn't have a second longer to formulate a response. Time was up!

Charlotte huffed an angry breathy sound. "Does anyone here have anything to say?"

This felt like a trick question.

He caught Oscar's eye. The kid shrugged again. It seemed like an appropriate response. He turned to Charlotte and duplicated Oscar's move.

In retrospect, he should have taken into account her flushed cheeks and flashing eyes. He was acquainted with this *take-no-shit* version of Charlotte. He had to figure out what had set her off. Honestly, under the circumstances, she had a decent amount to be peeved about. But siphoning it down to one thing was damned near impossible.

"This is not happening! You two can't simply pretend to be busy and ignore each other. That's not the point of camping. You camp to connect," she announced, then proceeded to remove her shoes.

"It's a good idea to keep those on," he said, watching her closely. Had the woman lost it completely?

"Yeah, my dad's right, Charlotte! You need to protect your feet outdoors," Oscar added. And holy shit! That might have been the first time his son had agreed with him on something. It wasn't much, but it was a start.

She chucked her shoes into the air like a maniac. "Well, look at that. They speak!" she remarked as her sneakers clunked to the ground.

Yep, she'd lost it! But he sure as hell wasn't about to blurt that out.

"Have you spent much time in the wilderness?" he asked gently, not wanting to poke the auburn-haired beast, but he needed to know if she was utterly clueless when it came to roughing it.

Defiance flashed in the woman's eyes. "While I did grow up in Colorado, I can't say that I spent much time in the mountains. But I like being outside, and the scenery is beautiful," she added, gesturing to the landscape like a game show hostess. "Also, my friend Libby, who is a very Zen yoga instructor, often tells me that she takes off her shoes to feel connected to the earth." Charlotte lifted her foot and brushed a few pine needles away. "On that note, we are going to bond with the land and find some wood to make a campfire."

"There's a bag with—" Oscar began, but Charlotte lifted her hand and silenced the boy. A damned good trick! He'd have to try it out next time he and his son went head-to-head.

"This is a group activity. No excuses! We're doing this together," she continued.

Oscar scratched his head. "Is she serious, Dad?"

"I am serious, Oscar," Charlotte answered for him. "This will be great! We can forage for wood, then build a fire."

"But, Charlotte, we don't need to—" Oscar tried again. And *again*, Charlotte used the hand thing.

Sweet Jesus, it was genius! It turned the volume on the kid right off.

Oscar raised his hand in the air as if he were in school.

"Yes, Oscar?" Charlotte answered.

"May I keep my shoes on, ma'am?"

Mitch's eyebrows shot up. *Ma'am!* His kid had some manners when he wanted to use them!

"You may, Oscar. The shoeless part is optional." She

trudged over to her bag, stopping every few yards to flick dirt and dry needles from her feet, then removed her camera. "We're also going to document the experience," she added, holding up her camera like exhibit A in a courtroom before taking a shot of the RV.

Oscar caught his eye and shrugged. He shrugged right back. Was he still concerned his nanny had gone off the deep end? Yeah, he was. But this was the first time it felt like he and Oscar were on the same side.

"And when we return triumphant in our quest for wood, it's only proper that we also make a fire—like the cavemen did—after they figured out how to make fire with flint or lightning," she continued. She waved her hands like someone who had no idea how cavemen came upon fire but wanted to sound knowledgeable.

Oscar raised his hand again. "Um...Charlotte?"

"Yes, Oscar? Do you have something to add?"

The kid kicked at a mound of dirt. "It would be easier with a match. I saw some in the—"

"All right, then," Charlotte conceded. "We can use a match unless someone has some flint."

"Do you know how to start a fire with flint?" the boy pressed with a crease to his brow.

Mitch cemented his lips to suppress a laugh. The kid was just as confused as he was.

Charlotte twisted her camera strap. "No, I don't know *exactly* how to start a fire with flint."

"It's not easy," Oscar said under his breath, with another kick to the dirt mound.

"Okay, we'll use a match. But we can scavenge around for wood like the cave people did. And as previously stated, shoes are optional," she finished with a resounding nod.

He peered at her tote. "You don't have any to-go margaritas in there, do you?" he asked, unable to stop himself.

Her jaw dropped. "Of course, not! Why would you even ask that?"

He dusted off his hands. "Because you sound a little out of it."

As soon as the statement passed his lips, he instantly regretted it.

"I'm not *out of it*. This is an important trip for you and for Oscar—for your family, Mitch," she answered, her voice cracking as she said the word *family*.

Family?

As odd as it sounds, he hadn't put together that this was his first family trip with his son. He'd written off the notion of having a family—at least in the Norman Rockwell white picket fence traditional sense. But Charlotte was right. Oscar was his family. And besides Holly's sister, he was all the kid had. A heaviness set in, but there was no time to dwell on it as Charlotte continued barking orders.

"Oscar, you should bring your Polaroid camera. We can take some shots of our wood gathering adventure. Mitch, you're in charge of..." She tapped her chin. "Carrying the heavy pieces," she instructed. He had to give it to her. He'd never seen anyone try harder to make gathering sticks sound like a good time.

Oscar removed his camera from his pack and looped the strap around his neck. "Oscar Elliott is ready to go, ma'am!" the kid called.

He glanced at his son. He'd never seen the boy so eager to please.

Wood foraging it was!

But he needed to let her know she didn't have to act like a cruise ship activities director. He walked over, then lowered his voice. "You don't have to do this, Charlotte," he said, trying to read her, trying to understand why she was so adamant about finding a few sticks to burn.

"Do what?" she asked, flinching as she shifted her stance. That whole *F.U. to shoes* wasn't working out so great for her. But he was smart enough not to mention it.

"You don't have to organize a whole list of activities. We just have to get through the night," he replied, thinking his words would make her feel better.

They didn't.

She shook her head, eyes blazing. "You're wrong! This isn't some pit stop. And I do need to do this for Oscar—and for you."

For him?

"Why?" he asked, dumbfounded.

"Because a happy family enjoys doing things together," she replied, again employing the word family.

"Is that how it is in your family? Do you enjoy being with them?" he pressed, then watched as the muscles in her throat contracted as she swallowed hard.

"This is what we're doing now," she replied with a shake to her voice—not answering his question. And her non-answer answer spoke volumes. He knew a thing or two about glossing over the painful parts of life.

"Charlotte," he began, but she cut him off with that hand thing.

"We'll trek across the forest to find wood for a fire. And we're doing this *together*," she said, heading off into the woods—barefoot.

He met his son's gaze. "Are you in?"

"I don't think we can say no, Dad," the kid answered with a weary look in his eyes.

The kid had smarts.

"I don't think she knows where she's going," Oscar continued. "And she'll probably get splinters in her feet."

Another excellent observation!

They started walking, and he fell into step with his son as Charlotte's form disappeared behind a row of evergreens.

"Do you like camping?" he began, surprised he'd never asked before. But they never really conversed. Their visits over the last couple of years had been strained at best. The kid had mostly stayed in his room from the minute he'd stepped foot in the cabin. Once or twice, Holly had gotten him to come out to play a board game, but they hadn't spoken much. Sure, part of it had to do with his age. Oscar was three when he'd started visiting. But it hadn't gotten easier. In fact, the kid seemed to like him less and less the older he got.

The boy kicked a rock along as they walked. "Mom used to let me put up my tent outside the back door. She'd make me a hot chocolate, and for dinner, I'd get to eat my favorite sandwich."

"Grilled cheese?" he answered, knowing he was right.

"Yeah, and they're Charlotte's favorite, too. She told me," the boy replied, focusing on the rock.

Mitch nodded, then bent down to swipe a stick from the ground. He'd expected that to be the extent of their conversation. It had been their first real exchange that hadn't dissolved into yelling or resorting to ignoring each other. But Oscar abandoned the rock and glanced up at him as they continued.

"Charlotte taught me a trick," the boy offered.

Okay! This had to be good. They were conversing.

"Did she?"

Oscar stopped, tapped his foot twice, then smiled up at him with a mischievous glint in his eyes.

He knew about this foot business!

Rowen had mentioned this foot-tapping trick to him. His niece did it. Penny taught her to use it instead of saying one particular bad word. "Did you tap out *butthead?*" he asked his son.

Maybe this bonding session wasn't going as well as he thought it was.

Oscar gasped. "You know the trick?" the boy asked, his jaw nearly hitting the ground.

"Yeah, I've heard about it. And you can't go around calling your old man a *butthead,*" he answered.

A sly smile bloomed on Oscar's lips. "I didn't tap *butthead.* I tapped *hothead.* That's what Charlotte says she calls you. It's a funny word. I like it! *Hothead Dad,*" the boy said, tapping out the three syllables.

God help him! He was starting to like it, too. He was ready to cop to it when a bloodcurdling scream echoed through the mountainous terrain.

"Dad!" Oscar exclaimed. "What is that?"

Oh no!

Mitch scanned the desolate landscape as adrenaline surged through his veins. He turned to his son. "It's Charlotte!"

NINE

MITCH

MITCH'S PULSE QUICKENED.

Where the hell was Charlotte? And how did she get so far ahead of them? For Christ's sake, she wasn't even wearing any shoes!

He and Oscar shared a worried look, then picked up their pace, sprinting in the direction of Charlotte's voice.

"There she is, Dad!" Oscar cried as Charlotte came into view.

They headed toward her. She'd stopped in the middle of a small clearing and stared at something on the ground past a trio of boulders. He breathed a sigh of relief. She wasn't hurt. But as they got closer, the woman waved her hands. Except she wasn't gesturing for them to come to her. No, she was telling them to stop.

Why would she do that?

"What is it? Are you hurt?" he called.

She was standing and seemed to be able to move her arms just fine. He didn't see any cuts or bruises. But she remained frozen in place. She raised her finger to her lips and shushed him—an odd reaction since she was the one screaming her head off ten seconds ago.

"Dad, look," Oscar whispered, pointing to a spot on the ground not ten feet from the woman.

Now he understood the screaming—and why it had stopped.

Mitch hung his head. This is why it was a bad idea to go frolicking around the woods near nightfall.

"It doesn't look like a regular skunk. But I still think it's a skunk," Charlotte whisper-shouted across the clearing.

She was right about that!

"Leave it alone, and you'll be fine," he answered, keeping an eye on the spotted skunk, who, at least at the moment, didn't seem that concerned with a terrified, shoeless redhead.

"But it's not moving," she called back.

He shrugged. "It's a skunk. It'll do what it wants."

"It's a spotted skunk, Charlotte," Oscar chimed with a wide grin. "I should take a picture of it," the boy finished, raising his camera.

Mitch assessed the situation, then patted Oscar's shoulder. "Hold off on taking a picture for now," he said as he took a few cautious steps forward. The hum of the Polaroid's printer might be enough to spook the animal.

"Are spotted skunks dangerous? Do they spray people?" Charlotte asked, her words coming out in an anxious tumble of sound. And even in the dim light of dusk, he could see that she'd turned completely white.

"They won't bother you if you don't bother them," he assured her. He needed to keep her calm.

"Unless it's a rabid skunk," Oscar added.

"What?" Charlotte croaked.

Oscar nodded. "Yeah, a ranger came to talk to my class, and

he said rabid skunks sometimes go crazy and like to chase people and even bite them."

Mitch blew out a tight breath. That mouthful of factoids wasn't going to help.

"How can you tell if it's a rabid skunk? Is this one rabid?" she replied, her voice rising to an uneasy octave.

He took another step forward. "Rabid or not, the plan remains the same. Stay calm and move slowly."

Charlotte's head whipped from side to side. "I feel like I should run."

"Don't make any sudden moves. That would scare the animal," he cautioned.

"Don't run, Charlotte! The ranger also said that he saw a rabid skunk chase a guy back to his car. And then the skunk started clawing on the door like a bloodthirsty zombie skunk," Oscar added.

Shit!

"This thing is going to follow me back to the RV?" Charlotte exclaimed.

Mitch met his son's eye. "Let's cool the rabid zombie skunk talk," he said, lowering his voice.

"Sure thing, Dad," the boy agreed.

"Charlotte," he said, keeping his tone calm and even.

"Yes?" she answered, looking ready to bolt.

"It's not rabid," he lied. Well, it wasn't exactly a lie. Honestly, he had no idea. The damned thing hadn't gone after her yet, so he was eighty percent sure it was your run-of-the-mill skunk out foraging in the woods at dusk.

"How can you tell it's not rabid?" she pressed.

Double shit!

"It would have come after you by now if it was," he said, leveling with her. What else could he do?

She held his gaze across the clearing, and it was as if she

could see every part of him. A shiver ricocheted down his spine. He couldn't keep entertaining these thoughts. He broke their connection and focused his attention on the docile spotted skunk when a quick burst of movement caught his eye.

And it wasn't Charlotte.

"It's a great horned owl!" Oscar exclaimed, holding up his camera as the giant bird of prey swooped in out of nowhere and snatched the skunk right off the ground. "He's picking up his dinner!" the boy cried in a bout of excitement.

And holy skunk snatcher, the scene unfolded like a slow-motion car crash.

Charlotte belted out another frantic scream, then took off like a shot. Forget the slow and steady plan. He wasn't sticking around either.

"Come on, Oscar!" he called as the mechanical hum of the Polaroid printing the image cut through the screech of the owl and the high-pitched shrieks of its prey as a real-life episode of *National Geographic the Predator Edition* played out in front of them.

"That was awesome!" the kid called, holding up the photo as they ran toward camp.

Sure, it was exciting for a six-year-old boy, but clearly terrifying for a shoeless woman.

He and Oscar made it back to the RV and found Charlotte leaning against the side of the camper, dusting off her feet. He slowed his pace to a jog as the lantern he'd hung on the RV cast their camp in a dim orange glow. But there was enough light to see that she'd made it back in one piece. Besides being breathless and shoeless, she looked no worse for wear. He scanned the ground, then gathered her shoes and held them up. "Want these back?"

"I have so much adrenaline pumping through my body, I

can't even feel my feet," she answered on a breathy sigh, but she accepted the footwear.

"Check this out, Charlotte!" Oscar said, handing her the Polaroid. "You can move fast."

She released a shaky breath. "You captured the moment. I wasn't expecting the skunk or the owl."

"Yeah, I can tell! Look at your face," Oscar added, tapping the corner of the print.

"That's quite a shot," she replied through a relieved chuckle, sounding more like herself.

"Take a look, Dad," the boy beamed.

He leaned in. Charlotte wasn't wrong. It was one hell of a shot.

The flash gave Charlotte red demon eyes which complemented the look of sheer terror on her contorted face. The blur of the owl with the skunk in its clutches rounded out the hilarious image. And before he knew it, he'd busted out laughing. And sweet Christ, he couldn't recall the last time he'd felt like this. But his body remembered. His cheeks warmed as an ear-to-ear grin stretched across his face like an old friend returning after an extended absence. He couldn't help but admit that the foreign sound of his laughter was a welcomed improvement to the angry grumbles and irritated grunts he'd relied upon for the last handful of years.

"So, you think it's funny that I was almost sprayed by a skunk, then attacked by a giant owl?" Charlotte teased, the panic in her voice subsiding.

Mitch caught his son's eye, and the boy joined him in a bout of giggles.

"You were so scared, Charlotte. And your face got twisty. How did you even do that with your mouth?" the boy asked through a rollicking belly laugh as he worked to contort his features to mimic Charlotte's petrified expression.

Charlotte pressed her hand to her belly, joining the giggle-fest. "I don't know! But I never want to make that face again," she answered, then turned her attention from Oscar. "Thanks for coming after me, Mitch. And sorry about all that. I wasn't planning on having your son witness a skunk kidnapping," she said in her teasing tone when a look of awe came over her as she studied his face.

He stilled, unable to look away. He liked having her eyes trained on him. It was the first time in ages he enjoyed the atten-tion. He observed her mouth and those damned lips that looked so inviting and so irresistibly kissable. For what seemed like an eternity, the two of them stared at each other. Her presence woke the dormant part of him—the part he'd written off, the part he'd hidden under layer upon layer of defenses. It was almost too much to take when the mechanical hum of the Polaroid jolted him back.

"Gotcha!" Oscar cried, holding up the Polaroid.

He and Charlotte shared one last glance before she lifted her camera to her eye. "Two can play at that! Let's see what you look like when a wild animal attacks," she said in a mock-menacing tone.

"Where's the wild animal?" Oscar asked, scanning the area.

"It's me! *Roar!*" she cried, chasing the boy around the tent as she snapped pictures. And the kid was game for it. Hooting and hollering, he darted this way and that as Charlotte followed in hot pursuit.

She was good with Oscar. That he couldn't deny.

He shook his head and chuckled, watching the mayhem when Charlotte called a timeout and waved Oscar over. She kneeled and whispered something in his ear. The two looked thick as thieves as they whispered back and forth. Oscar nodded, then pointed in the air. "Dad, look out! It's another great horned owl. And it's headed straight for you!"

What the hell?

He was no fool. He ducked, flailing his arms as he ran in circles. The *click, click, click* of Charlotte's camera peppered the air, and the camera's flash went off in dizzying bursts of light.

What was she doing? Photographing the owl?

He ignored the sound and shielded his eyes from the bright pulses of light. He was more concerned with the giant bird that may or may not be making a beeline for his head. He waved his arms, batting at the air when Oscar's laugh cut through the commotion. "Just like that, Dad! Keep going!" the child called as the hum of the Polaroid added to the *click, click, clickity-clack* party of sound.

He stopped hopping around like he had ants in his pants. He'd been duped by his child and the nanny. He put on his best cranky chef expression. "There's no great horned owl, is there?" he asked in his best growly voice. But it didn't seem to have the same effect on Charlotte and Oscar. The pair's laughter intensified.

"Attack, Oscar! Attack the hothead!" she cried.

The boy swung the Polaroid strap over his head, handed Charlotte his camera, then sprinted toward him. Oscar's knobby knees blurred as the boy emitted a mixture of loud primal calls, punctuated with uncontrollable giggling. Only a few feet away, the kid sprang from the ground and jumped into his arms.

"Easy, now," he bit out, his voice cracking, as Oscar wrapped his arms around his neck. He held the boy, tightening his grip. The *click, click, clicks,* and pops of flash resumed as Charlotte snapped pictures, capturing the moment. He should tell her to give the photography a rest. But he couldn't. His throat had thickened with emotion.

And he knew why.

This was his first hug from his son.

"I think we got him, Oscar," Charlotte said, taking one last shot before lowering the camera.

"Did we get you, Dad?" the boy asked through a toothy grin.

Mitch nodded, pulling himself together as his gaze flicked from his son to Charlotte. "Yeah, you got me. You both got me," he answered, giving the kid one final squeeze before setting him down.

Charlotte sighed, then looked up at the full moon. "I'm no camping expert, but I think we missed the window to forage for wood."

"We don't need to. We've got a whole big bag of wood. Want me to show you?" Oscar asked.

"Hold on a second," Charlotte blurted with a crease to her brow. "We already have wood? Where is it? How did it get here?"

All good questions!

Mitch turned to his son. "What are you talking about, Oscar?"

"I found it when I was exploring the RV," the child explained. "It's in a big canvas bag next to a box of chocolate bars in a storage bin near the back."

"We have chocolate?" Charlotte exclaimed, and Mitch took note. He figured she might be a bit peeved about the wood supply. But the mention of chocolate seemed to wipe her mind of the animal adventures that had derailed her plan.

Oscar nodded. "There's a whole box of full-sized candy bars," the kid answered like he was sharing the secrets of the world with her.

Good to know! Charlotte and Oscar were mega-chocolate fans.

He hadn't tried his hand at desserts in ages. But if chocolate made these two grin like a couple of cocoa-obsessed super freaks, he could dust off his sweets skills. And just like that—like back in the old days—the ideas started flowing. Soufflés, fudge, tarts. The list went on and on.

"I'll help you with the wood in a second, Oscar. I could use a minute to catch my breath before we start a fire," she answered. Her body coming off the hit of adrenaline, she leaned against the side of the RV.

He clapped his son on his shoulder. "Why don't you go inside the camper and see what else we have in there. If there are chocolate bars, I bet there are also marshmallows and graham crackers. You can see if we have the ingredients to make s'mores," he added, then turned his attention to the nanny. "I'll stay out here with Charlotte."

"You got it!" the boy exclaimed.

"Would you mind taking my camera inside with you?" Charlotte asked.

Oscar straightened his shoulders. "I'll be real careful with it," he answered, cautiously accepting the item, then grabbing her tote bag before disappearing inside the RV.

Once the boy was gone, Charlotte cradled her head in her hands. "I hope the owl versus skunk situation doesn't scar Oscar."

What was she talking about? How could she not see it?

He tipped her chin to meet his gaze, and damn, the pull of the invisible thread between them intensified. "Charlotte, this is the happiest I've ever seen him," he confided as the urge to sweep her into his arms nearly overtook him. That's exactly what he'd done last night after she'd fallen asleep on the bench. He'd carried her to the RV and gently set her down on the plush sofa bed. And then he'd watched her sleep and listened as she quietly murmured. He wasn't a sentimental guy anymore. In Charlotte-speak, he was no *Mr. Cheesy Forever*. But seeing her in his shirt with the key around her neck glinting in the light almost made him think that the man he used to be hadn't completely disappeared.

Almost—but he knew better.

She looked up at him with such tenderness. And despite knowing damned well who he was and what he was and *wasn't* capable of when it came to matters of the heart, he couldn't ignore the dizzying current pulsing through his body. Even in the misty darkness lit only by the moon and the RV's dim outdoor light, everything was brighter when she was there. The sheer power of it took his breath away.

A shiver traveled through her body, and he felt it—that energy that danced between them. Her chest heaved as she inhaled a shaky breath, then looked away, breaking their connection. He should be grateful that she could exercise some semblance of control. He dropped his hand to his side, but that didn't stop the pads of his fingers from tingling.

"My plan for a fun family activity went about as well as I assume it's going for that skunk. You don't have to try to make me feel better, Mitch," she said, her eyes trained on the ground.

Heat rose to his cheeks. He couldn't let this stand. He couldn't let her think for another second that she'd done something wrong. He pressed his hands against the RV—one on either side of Charlotte's head—then leaned in, going into alpha-chef mode. And this *alpha-chef* required her full attention. "I'm not trying to make you feel better. I thought you knew better than that. I don't go out of my way to be nice to anyone."

"That's not true," she replied. The strong-willed salad-hurler had returned. She pressed onto her tiptoes, and her warm breath caressed his lips as her words floated in the air that sizzled with anticipation. "I thought that about you once. But I don't believe it anymore."

Every cell in his body called out to her. He shouldn't want her like this. He was an asshole, a brick wall, a tyrant in the kitchen, and a sourpuss anywhere else he went. He'd become a jerk—by design. Nobody wanted to get close to a jerk. He'd hidden behind his gruff demeanor. It was easy to maintain the simmering rage when he was only responsible for himself, and he could spend his free time focusing on his painful past. Before he learned Oscar was his, he was content to live a life yelling at the kitchen staff, then holing up alone at his home to wage another war—a war with his demons.

But he wasn't alone anymore.

"I'm not a nice guy," he warned, tucking a lock of hair that had broken free of her ponytail behind her ear. Unable to stop himself, he allowed his hand to linger. His thumb brushed past her earlobe, and she inhaled a tight breath.

"Is that what you tell yourself?" she replied.

Her sweet scent and the heat of her body drew him in like a siren's song. His breathing grew ragged as she rested the palms of her hands against his chest. What was this between them? The angry, skeptical, untrusting part of him would want to write it off as a reaction to extreme stress and the topsy-turviness of his out-of-control life. But those clawing, negative voices quieted when Charlotte was near. It was intoxicating to come out from under the angry, seething weight he carried each day.

"Mitch?" she whispered.

"Yeah?" he rasped, under her spell, ready to give her whatever she wanted.

She gathered the fabric of his shirt into her tiny fists, and he leaned in another inch. His heart pounding, he twisted her ponytail around his hand. His fantasies couldn't hold a candle to the reality of touching her.

"We should..." she breathed, arching into him as he tugged the locks, tightening his grip. Her lips parted as she gasped, and the alluring sound went straight to his rock-hard cock.

He could kiss her right now. One kiss. That's all he'd need—

one little taste, and then he'd put on the blinders, go back to being an epic asshole, and treat her like anyone else. She was his kid's nanny. That's it. Nothing more.

Dammit! Who was he kidding? Her mere presence pushed those thoughts to the back burner.

"What should we do, Charlotte?" he said instead, coming in close enough to whisper against the shell of her ear.

"We should check on Oscar," she finished, releasing his shirt.

And *pop*—no, more like *wham!* The bubble around them didn't pop. It burst.

One kiss? What kind of bullshit was that? There could be no kissing this woman.

He stepped back and dropped his hands to his sides.

What was he thinking?

Were they going to make out like horny teenagers against the side of the RV with his son inside? He inhaled a steadying breath, then caught a whiff of chocolate in the air—his damned canine-strength nose, homing in on the scent.

Get ahold of yourself!

He cleared his throat and started toward the door. He had to get her out of his head. "I think Oscar started without us."

"Started what?" she asked, following him into the RV where the smell intensified—and for a good reason.

"Oh, my gosh! So much for a whole box of chocolate," she said softly, but there was a nervous lilt to her tone. They were back to square one, dancing around each other like they each had two left feet.

Maybe it was better this way.

They took in the cocoa-infused crime scene. Oscar's chocolate binge gave them something to focus on besides the insane attraction that sparked between them. He folded his arms. The kid had outdone himself in the junk food department. Oscar had made a nest of cushions on the pullout bed where Charlotte had slept last night. He'd cuddled in with a Halloween-haul amount of chocolate at his disposal. Surrounded by a sea of pillows and a ton of empty wrappers, the boy slept peacefully with half a candy bar clutched in his hand.

Charlotte removed the chocolate from his grip, then smoothed Oscar's hair. "He might wake up with a tummy ache," she said, leaving Oscar's side and heading to the kitchenette. She wet the corner of a hand towel in the sink, then gently wiped the chocolate residue from the corners of the boy's mouth. "I'm not surprised you fell asleep, Oscar. It's been quite a day," she finished, setting the towel aside.

Mitch shifted his stance. He should do something. He should busy himself as well. But he didn't. He simply watched as she went to work removing Oscar's shoes. She looked around the RV, then plucked a blanket off one of the chairs and tucked the boy in on the sleeper couch.

Oscar curled into a ball, then yawned a heavy sigh. "Good night, Charlotte. I'm glad the owl took the skunk and not you," the boy commented in a dreamy slur before dozing off.

Mitch stared at his son as a lump formed in his throat.

"Sleep well, Oscar," she whispered with such gentle kindness it went straight to his battered heart like a salve. She lifted the corner of one of the pillows and removed a Polaroid shot. "Wow," she breathed, staring at the picture.

"What is it?" he asked.

"It's us." She passed him the photo. It was the shot that had pulled him from his Charlotte-induced stupor. The camera had caught them staring at each other. He was smiling at her—there was no doubting the slight curve to his lips. He gritted his teeth. Dammit! He couldn't keep entertaining this bullshit. It was too much. This picture could be the damned definition of a Mr.

Cheesy Forever. No, more like a *Mr. Sucker Who Should Know Better*.

"Let's call it a night. I'll take down the tent. I can bunk next to Oscar on the other pullout couch, and you can have the bed in the back," he barked, not waiting for her reply. It was time to act like the damned hothead she'd labeled him. And he could use some fresh air to help get his head on straight—both heads. The strain in his pants wasn't because his trousers were too small. Nope, that reaction happened thanks to the raw, undeniable attraction that he had to get under control. He strode outside, stood next to the tent, and closed his eyes, listening to the forest landscape come alive at night. But his pulse kicked up when the door opened and shut behind him.

It was her.

Charlotte walked past him, then ran her hand down one of the tent poles. And heaven help him, his tent pole took notice.

"You went to the trouble to put up the tent. We should go inside once," she finished, unzipping the opening, then crawling inside.

He stared at the tent as his pulse kicked up.

He shouldn't go in. He should let her sit there for a minute to get her fill of tent camping. Then he'd take the thing down and get some shut-eye—alone on the sleeper bed across from Oscar.

Yes, that's exactly what he should do.

But he didn't. He couldn't! He bent down and entered the snug, enclosed space.

"This is cozy," she remarked, stretching out her legs and leaning back onto her elbows. The dim outdoor light on the camper van allowed him to see the dark outline of her body. But that was enough to keep his heart thumping. The muscles in his chest tightened as he drank in the curves of her breasts and the lines of her hips.

He cleared his throat. "I'm sorry that Oscar and I laughed about the skunk. You seemed pretty freaked out."

Why the hell did he apologize? He didn't do that. The nearness of the nanny scrambled his brain.

She sat up, and their arms brushed as she maneuvered her body to sit in front of him. "You don't have to apologize. It was worth it."

The darkness masked her features, but that didn't stop him from searching her face. "What do you mean by that?"

She touched his cheek, then slid her index finger to the corner of his mouth. And like the last time, his skin tingled beneath her touch.

"I got to see you smile, Mitch. I've never seen one of those on your face. You should do it more. It suits you."

"It's been a long time since I had anything to smile about," he admitted, the broken words slipping past his tongue. The darkness made it easy, and the words came effortlessly. He took her hand in his and slid her palm against his lips, listening as she inhaled an audible breath. With his resolve dwindling by the second, he pressed a kiss to her hand. Her skin was soft, so soft. She tensed, but she didn't pull away. Drunk on her scent and the frenzy of heat surging through his body, he parted his lips and licked a hot line from her palm to her wrist. And as he'd imagined, she tasted like strawberries and sunshine. No, not as he'd imagined. It was better. He'd sampled some of the best dishes ever created. Hell, he'd cooked most of them. But nothing could have prepared him for this. It was as if he'd found himself in the Garden of Eden and had taken the first bite of forbidden fruit.

And he wanted more, and he wanted it now!

He gathered her onto his lap and held her flush against him. Nothing had felt so right in ages. Again, he waited for her to protest. But she didn't. Quite the opposite happened. Silently, she tangled her fingers in the hair at the nape of his neck. With the sound of their heated breaths, their bodies molded into place as if they'd done this a million times before. He wrapped his arms around her, cementing their bodies together. His hard lines met her soft curves as she rocked her hips in a deliciously slow, rhythmic song. And he heard it, too. It wasn't exactly music. It was energy. They'd tapped into the buzz that pulsed around them, through them, and inside of them.

The steady rock of their bodies and the sensual friction between them had him breathing hard as he gripped her hips, setting the pace that had his cock weeping. Still moving to their silent song, she cupped his face in her hands. "I want to try something," she whispered, her breath warm against his lips.

He couldn't help it. He smiled.

"There it is. How does that feel?" she asked, touching the corners of his mouth.

How did it feel?

It felt like a goddamned exorcism. It was like tearing off the locks and chains he'd fashioned around his heart and grinding the iron shackles to dust.

"Let me show you," he answered, erasing the space between them. His lips met hers, and he devoured her softness as the chaos in his life dissolved. His world narrowed to include this moment in this tent with this woman. Her touch and her scent took center stage as the sensations washed over him. His clawing thoughts silenced until all that existed was Charlotte and the sweetness of her kisses. Their tongues met in a slow burn of desire, tasting and caressing as their hands roamed freely in the darkness. Without giving it a second thought, he flipped her onto her back. He needed complete and total access to every part of her.

Her skirt bunched around her waist as he settled himself between her thighs. She pulled at his shirt, untucking it. Her nimble hands skimmed across his stomach. She traced the ridges of his abdominal muscles before sliding her hands south and undoing the top button on his pants.

She wanted this, too.

He cupped her face in his hand. Time seemed to stand still while moving at light speed. He brushed his thumb across her cheek, slowing himself down. "Charlotte, is this okay?" He could barely get the words out.

"Yes," she breathed, wrapping her legs around him.

Their bodies moved together in a frenzied symphony of hands and lips and teeth and thrusts. Jesus! Every muscle in his body vibrated in anticipation. He was never a fan of dry humping. But the heat sparking between them as they made out like this was their only chance at human contact before the world ended was better than any sex he'd ever had. He tasted the delicate skin beneath her earlobe. "Do we need—"

She released a dirty little moan. "I'm on the pill," she finished, again reading his mind. A good thing because he seemed to have no control over his.

He undid his pants and shrugged them down far enough to free his cock. He studied the woman beneath him. He couldn't see her face, but he saw her. Like one of Oscar's Polaroids, her image and her beauty were locked in his mind. Still, it was like watching someone else's life play out before his eyes—like he was an imposter, a voyeur.

But no! This was happening!

She reached between them and took his hard length into her hand. Her touch was velvety soft until she tightened her grip. He gritted his teeth as raw need tore through his body. Slipping his hand between her thighs, he pushed her panties aside and found her wet. The satin of the silky fabric was drenched in her desire. And a rush of carnal victory brought the hint of a grin to his lips.

Christ, it felt good to tear off the mask and let go!

She positioned his cock at her slick entrance as two competing impulses battled within him. He wanted to take it slow, to nip, to bite, and to taste every inch of her body while fighting the growing desire to drive in hard, hold her tight, and piston his hips, faster and faster until he disappeared into their lovemaking and lost himself with each fierce thrust.

"I want you now, Mitch," Charlotte whispered in a dirty little moan.

A devious smile stretched across his lips.

Hard and fast, it was!

He hadn't expected her to make the choice for him. He'd expected to be in control. Then again, after the last twenty-four hours, he'd become well acquainted with the fiery, headstrong redhead. The woman could turn up the heat as fast as she could turn on her sweet, demure nanny side. "And I want *it* now," she finished, in full-on fiery redhead mode.

It was one hell of a turn-on!

"I can do that," he growled, holding her wrists above her head.

The air inside the tent positively hummed with the heat of their ragged breaths. He slid his cock inside, and her sweet heat threatened to take him over the edge with one damned thrust.

There was no way he'd allow that to happen!

He held back, tightening his hold on her wrists as her body welcomed him, opening and stretching to accommodate his hard length. He closed his eyes and drank in the sensations, not able to understand how something could feel both completely new and utterly familiar. But that's what this was. He abandoned her wrists and entwined their fingers, holding her hands —no, anchoring himself to her—before pulling back, then driving in hard.

She bucked her hips as they moved together, two becoming

one. And he was no longer in control. He wasn't in charge. He should be terrified, but he wasn't. Their union drove each kiss, each lick, and each breathy sigh. An understanding that required no words set the pace. He rolled his hips, finding her sweet spot as a coil took shape around them, encircling them, squeezing them tighter and tighter. And she was there, hovering on the edge of ecstasy, her body trembling beneath him. He covered her mouth with his, swallowing her cries of pleasure as they disintegrated into oblivion, awash in a sea of sweet release.

She ran her fingertips along his jawline, breathing hard as they wound down, coming back to their bodies. Neither said a word. They didn't need to. He lowered his head and kissed the corner of her mouth, and she released a dreamy sigh.

"You're doing it again," she whispered into the darkness.

"What's that?" he asked, pressing a kiss to the opposite corner.

"Grinning," she answered, and he could hear the smile in her voice.

He was. He couldn't deny it. "How do you know that I'm smiling? It's dark," he countered, twisting a lock of her hair between his fingers.

She traced his lips with the tip of her tongue. A sexy little move that had him ready for round two. "I can feel it when you kiss me," she breathed against his upturned lips.

Yep, he was smiling like a goddamned fool!

He dipped his head, ready to grin his heart out some more and kiss her until he couldn't see straight. But he stilled when the creak of the RV door opening stopped him dead in his tracks. Charlotte tensed beneath him. She heard it, too.

"Dad? Charlotte? Are you out here?"

Oscar!

They remained stock-still as the cocoon of darkness gave

way to a blast of cold, hard reality. Balls-deep inside of his son's nanny, he wanted to punch himself square in the jaw.

Shit! What had he done?

That was easy to answer. The nanny! Against knowing better, he'd slept with the nanny.

How could he have allowed himself to slip and screw up so badly? She was dangerous. She made him feel things—the same damn things—that landed him in a world of shit seven years ago. Hastily, he pulled out, and with clumsy hands, he zipped up his pants as Charlotte adjusted her skirt. The two of them scrambled to get themselves presentable and *not* appear like a pair of raging hornballs, who'd knocked out one hell of a quickie.

"We're here, Oscar," Charlotte called as she fixed her ponytail. "We're taking down the tent. Why don't you head back inside the RV? We'll be right in. We're almost done."

They were done all right. They had to be!

"Okay," the boy answered through a yawn. Thank Christ he hadn't crawled into the tent!

The door banged shut, and the sound ricocheted through his body as a searing bitterness torched his soul. He was an idiot! A damned idiot! He had his son and his shit career to contend with. The last thing he should be doing was getting googly-eyed over a woman—any woman.

"Mitch," Charlotte whispered, and he could hear it in the syllable. That one word, his name, held such hope and such sweetness he could barely stand it.

Another woman had spoken his name with the same warmth blanketed around the syllable. And what he thought was the start of something good—*something really good*—had burned him hard. Hard enough to make him the angry ass of a hothead he was today. And no matter how much his stupid heart wanted Charlotte, he couldn't make that mistake again.

"Go inside, Charlotte," he said, his voice void of tenderness.

"I...I can help you with the tent," she offered, touching his arm.

There was no use in drawing this out, in having her think that anything could come of what they'd done. She needed a job that paid well, and he needed a nanny. That's how it had to be, period. He ignored the sap inside him who would have killed for another kiss and let the jerk take over.

"No, go inside and check on Oscar," he bit out. She gasped at his stern tone. But he had to be harsh. He had to play the part of the hothead. He didn't know any other way.

"What do you need from me, Mitch?" she asked with near-palpable concern in her tone.

He hardened his features, holding his emotions at bay.

He had to make this hurt.

Shrugging off her hand, he lowered his voice. "The only thing I need you to do for me, Charlotte, is your job."

TEN

CHARLOTTE

DENVER 7 MILES

The RV cruised past the sign, and Charlotte released the breath she hadn't realized she'd been holding. They were almost back. She checked on Oscar. The boy had nestled himself into the sea of pillows where he'd slept last night. He'd slid on a pair of headphones and was tapping away on a handheld gaming device.

And then she chanced a look at Mitch and damn her treacherous heart for skipping a stupid beat. She was only eight feet away from him. But they might as well have been separated by the Grand Canyon. While the guy hadn't exactly been rude or his gruff hothead self today, the man had barely said a word to her since...

A rush of heat burned her cheeks.

He'd hardly said a word to her since they'd had crazy amazing tent sex.

She'd never even slept in a tent—not that they'd done any sleeping.

She still couldn't believe what had happened. But holy hot sex, they'd done it! That was for sure. The excruciatingly delicious soreness between her thighs wasn't from some pony ride. Oh no! The sweet ache came from none other than the hothead chef, who she'd learned was as focused and obsessive in the sack as he was in the kitchen.

No, that wasn't it.

She'd sampled his food plenty of times. It was truly out of this world. The guy was a pain in the ass to waitress for, but the man could cook. There was no doubting that. But somehow, he was even better in the *getting-down-and-dirty* department.

She exhaled a slow breath as her nipples hardened into tight peaks at the very thought of Mitch Elliott flipping her onto her back and lacing their fingers together. He'd worked her body like he'd been born to do it. They hadn't even undressed. The sex was gloriously frantic and uncontrollably urgent. It was the *I-can't-fight-this-feeling* kind of lovemaking that she'd never experienced.

It was like something out of a dream—or perhaps a nightmare.

The hothead's silent treatment seemed to indicate the latter. Everything had come crashing down the moment Oscar called out to them. And instantly, while it had felt so right to let this man ravage her body, hearing the boy's voice had jolted her back to reality. It was like walking into a glass door or falling off a cliff into an icy sea of *what-the-hell-did-you-just do!* A reality where, despite the man's crooked, beautiful smile that could melt the panties right off of her, sleeping with her boss was about the dumbest thing she could do. But the events of the last two days had turned her life upside down.

If someone had asked her a week ago if she thought there was the teensy-tiniest chance she'd end up beneath the growly Mitch Elliott, she would have laughed her butt off. But in her case, reality was stranger than fiction. With her skirt bunched around her waist, she'd writhed in utter ecstasy as the man rocked her world with his perfect cock, strong hands, and a mouth—that mouth! He'd kissed her with such dogged intensity the heat they'd generated could have powered this gargantuan RV for the next ten zillion years. Her lips tingled at the very thought of him smiling as he pressed kiss after kiss against her neck, her cheeks, and the shell of her ear.

And then there was the titillating power that sent a current of confidence through her body. She'd made the grump of a chef grin. It was for her. It happened because of her.

Or maybe not.

Maybe he smiled at every woman he'd slept with.

She honestly had no idea!

And here she was, sitting across from the man's son as they headed toward home. Her new home. Mitch's home. Her boss's home!

And then it hit her like a punch to the gut. She'd barely been a nanny for two days, and she'd already slept with her employer.

Could she chalk it up to extreme duress?

Could being thrown into a completely foreign environment cause a normal, level-headed woman to briefly lose her mind and engage in mind-blowing tent sex?

There were many, many stressors!

The skunk versus owl escapade had thoroughly freaked her out. And Oscar had taken the photo to prove it. But when Mitch and Oscar started laughing, and that laughter manifested into an all-out giggle party between father and son, she'd thought of Professor Tran. And while she wasn't embedded in a refugee camp, she'd found herself in a slice of time that needed to be documented.

When Oscar leaped into Mitch's arms, she'd caught it in a series of shots. It was as if she'd disappeared. No, not disappeared. She'd allowed herself to become absorbed in the totality of the moment. She'd become one with her camera. The shutter opened and closed in rapid succession as the man she'd once pegged as a heartless hothead wrapped his arms around his son. A picture said a thousand words. These images were no different. But when she'd looked at the pictures alone, listening to the rise and fall of Oscar and Mitch's sleeping breaths, one phrase rang out over and over.

Go back to the beginning.

She'd captured Mitch and Oscar's new beginning.

The photos documented a profound shift. With a crinkle to the corners of his eyes, Mitch's entire demeanor transformed from unease to surprise to a sense of wondrous awe. And she'd caught it, frame by frame.

She'd stared at that smile—Mitch's smile. God help her! The thought of it made her core clench. And hello, Tingle City! The curve of that man's lips was something to behold—something that made her pulse race. And she couldn't forget the man's intensity. He radiated masculine energy. When he'd caged her in with muscled arms, pinning her in place, she hadn't felt trapped.

Quite the opposite.

She'd felt protected just as she had when Mitch sent the hairy speed date creep packing. Mitch had tried to play the asshole chef card. He'd attempted to hide behind the hotheaded mask. But it was too late. She'd seen him—the real him. Kisses like that couldn't lie.

Or could they?

Her stomach twisted at the thought of Mitch's harsh words.

The only thing I need you to do for me, Charlotte, is your job.

She couldn't even get angry. He was right. Still, a part of her couldn't believe that she'd read him so wrong. Reaching into her tote, she removed her cell. She'd sent the images from her camera to her phone and had fallen asleep scrolling through them. She was about to tap the camera icon when her phone rang. And her jaw dropped.

It was her mom!

Gloria Ames never called. Charlotte swallowed past the lump in her throat. She wouldn't allow herself to get excited—not yet. "Hi, Mom!" she said brightly, but no one was there. The line was dead.

She opened the text box.

Charlotte: I saw you called, Mom. Are you ok? Everything good in Florida?

She waited, her heart pounding as a kernel of hope sparked in her chest. Three dots flashed across the screen as her mother replied. Charlotte embraced this momentary happiness. Her mother had made the first move and reached out.

Mom: Sorry, Charlotte! I must have accidentally dialed you. I was trying to call my boyfriend. I'm at the salon. I'm going blond!

She stared at the message. Blond? She and her mom shared the same auburn locks. It was the one thing they had in common.

Charlotte: Why are you doing that? I thought you liked your hair.

Mom: Phil suggested it.

The kernel of hope fizzled.

Charlotte: Who's Phil?

She didn't have to ask. It didn't matter what the guy's name was. He'd always rank higher in her mother's heart than she ever could.

Mom: Phil's my boyfriend, of course! Didn't I tell you? I must have forgotten.

Charlotte's shoulders sagged as old wounds opened.

Charlotte: What happened to Marty?

**Mom: Marty is old news! I've got to go. Phil's

here. He dropped by to say hello! He's such a sweetheart! I'm so lucky.

Charlotte stared at the text bubble. There was no use in sending another message. She returned to the main screen and scanned the list of sent texts. She shouldn't do this. It never brought her anything but heartache. But she couldn't help herself. She stopped scrolling and scrutinized one word.

Dad

With a shaky hand, she tapped the screen and reread the last text she'd sent the man two months ago.

Charlotte: Happy birthday, Dad! Did my card make it to you?

He hadn't answered. All he'd done was mark her text with a thumbs-up. She scrolled through the chain of messages.

Charlotte: How are Julia and the boys?

Thumbs-up.

Charlotte: I saw the weather. Looks like there are tornados in Kentucky. Are you guys ok?

Thumbs-up.

Charlotte: Merry Christmas!

Thumbs-up.

It was like texting a digital appendage—not a parent.

There were more texts from her—so many more. And none of them had garnered an actual reply from the man. She swallowed past the tightness in her throat, ready to bury her phone in the bottom of her bag when the text alert chimed. Blinking back tears, she beamed at the screen as the haze of parental gloom lifted.

Harper: Hey, Char! Just checking in. If you're reading this, there's an excellent chance that you have not been kidnapped. I repeat, NOT KIDNAPPED! But if you were kidnapped and you

were still in your mermaid costume, would that be a mer-napping? I know! I'm hilarious!

Charlotte chuckled as the sting of disappointment that followed any reminder of her parents dulled. She couldn't help but smile as she observed the string of emojis when another text on the Charlotte, Penny, Harper, Libby text string appeared.

Sweet girl-power relief! She'd never been so grateful to hear from her best friends.

Harper: FYI, you aren't on any milk cartons yet. But on the off chance that you have been kidnapped, I'll be sure to give the police a good picture of you to pass around to the news stations. Definitely not the picture from sixth grade when you tried cutting your own bangs at recess.

Penny's name appeared.

Penny: Sorry, Char! I hope you don't mind. I told H and Libbs about your situation. Also, if you were kidnapped, we'd have to go with your eighth-grade class pic when you gave yourself that home perm. #FriendsDontLetFriendsCutBangsByThemselves #NoHomePerm

Harper: Yeah, lightweight! Penn tells us you got hammered with your boss—THE HOTHEAD CHEF —Mitch! That's crazy that you're working for him! And kudos! You are breaking out of the nice girl mold! Did you get your nanny credit card and car yet? OMG! The last thing I ever want to be is a nanny—but sweet mega-bucks limit, I'd take some rich dude's Visa in a heartbeat.

Charlotte inhaled a slow breath. This was becoming very real.

Charlotte: I'm not sure about the car and the credit card. We've been busy.

Harper: Penny got a freaking Lamborghini when she started as Phoebe's nanny, so I'd ask for one of those if you have any say.

Penny: H! I didn't ask for a Lamborghini.

Harper: We know Penn Fenn! But Charlotte totally deserves a Lamborghini, too. I mean, we all do. Me, especially! Do you know the hell that is listening to a dozen five-year-olds banging out Chop Sticks?! I deserve noise-canceling head-phones, two Lamborghinis, and spa treatments for the next thousand years.

Libby: Hey, Char! Spiritual check-in time! I'm getting a very non-kidnapped vibe. Actually, I'm getting a weird Charlotte vibe! Are you okay, or are you still hungover?

Charlotte groaned. She needed to set the record straight.

Charlotte: I didn't get hammered with Mitch. I accidentally drank a bunch of those super-charged margaritas at the speed dating thing. He happened to be there.

Penny: Mitch went to a speed date event???

Charlotte touched the golden key.

Charlotte: No, he was just there.

Libby: OMG! The universe did this!

Harper: Or the tequila.

Libby: 80% Universe 20% Tequila.

Penny: No, it has to be Madelyn. That woman has a sixth sense. I think she's part witch! How's it going with Mitch? What's his son like? It's still hard to believe you got matched with him.

Penny had that right! Charlotte chewed her lip. She'd answer the easy part first.

Charlotte: Oscar is great! He did throw a bunch

of rocks at me when we first met. But he's into photography, so we have that in common. He'll be going to Whitmore. He's in first grade like Phoebe.

Penny: I'll let Phoebe know! She can show him the ropes!

Charlotte: And I also taught him the foot tap trick.

Penny: Excellent! The two of them can call the kids in class buttholes and not get in trouble!

Harper: The foot tap trick is a real gem. I tapped five times for you, Char! Su-per lush na-nny! 5 Taps!

Charlotte puckered her lips, then tapped her foot.

Charlotte: I tapped four times for you, H!

Harper: Four times for what?

Charlotte: Shut-your-pie-hole!

Harper: Look at our Charlotte! So feisty! 🔥

Libby: Tell us about Mitch. Are you getting along with him?

Harper: Yes! You threw a salad at the guy. It can't get much worse.

Charlotte glanced at the hothead, then pressed her thighs together to quell the treacherous tingling.

Charlotte: Define getting along?

Penny: That's easy! Not throwing vegetables at each other.

Charlotte did a quick check on Oscar. The boy was still consumed with his game—which was a good thing. She couldn't allow him to see what she was about to type. But she needed advice. And she needed it quick. Her thumbs hovered above the keyboard as she blew out a slow breath, then hammered out a question.

Charlotte: What do you guys know about tents?

Harper: You threw a tent at Mitch? WOWZA hotheadette! I've never even thrown a tent at a guy.

Gah! How was she supposed to word this?

Charlotte: I didn't throw a tent at him.

Penny: That's promising!

Charlotte: I was in a tent with Mitch.

Penny: What's wrong with that? There's nothing like bonding in the great outdoors to bring people together!

Charlotte's knee bounced nervously.

Just get it out!

Charlotte: Does tent sex count as real sex?

Boom! That was the question.

A flurry of dots flooded her screen.

Penny: You slept with Mitch?!?!?!?!

Charlotte cringed. Oh no! Here it comes!

Charlotte: Possibly, I'm looking for clarification.

Harper: If Mitch inserted Tab Cock into Charlotte's Slot Hoo-ha, that's sex!

She tapped her cell against her forehead! Yes, she knew they'd had sex! But there had to be a caveat—an exemption clause.

Charlotte: But does it count if it happened inside a tent?

Libby: Now I know what vibe I was getting from Char. That must have been quite an orgasm to put a psychic ripple into the cosmos.

Charlotte gasped, then crossed her legs, unable to stop from reveling in the delicious soreness that accompanied the best sex of her life. Then again, if anyone could help explain an act as some sort of metaphysical non-action, it was Libby.

Charlotte: Libbs, does it count, or could it have

been a one-time cosmic anomaly? That could be a thing!

Her heart hammered in her chest as she watched the dots cascade across the screen.

Libby: Hell no! It totally counts! Sex is sex!

Penny: OMG! Charlotte! I can't believe you did that!

Charlotte's jaw about hit the floor. Time out! Penny had no room to judge her!

Charlotte: You and Rowen got together when you were Phoebe's nanny!

Penny: Not on the second day! Pace yourself, sister! You've been Mitch's nanny for less than 48 hours! And it's Mitch! Hothead Mitch!

Charlotte scowled as a hot blush graced her cheeks. Penny had her there!

Harper: I thought you hated the guy. You called him a tyrant. You threw vegetables at him!

Libby: Do not doubt the power of hate sex. That's some crazy energy!

Harper: BTW, your good girl status got obliterated. You are now officially the sex pot! Also, SPILL! Was it any good? We need details!

Libby: It was good. Like good, good, OH MY GOD, DON'T STOP GOOD!

Her friend wasn't wrong.

Charlotte: How do you know, Libbs?

Libby: I know.

Charlotte sighed. If anyone could read her vibe—even over the phone—it was Libby.

Charlotte: From here on out, it'll be completely professional. I'm going to be a model employee for the remainder of the trial period or longer—who

knows! His tab will not be inserted into my slot again. Ever. Never, ever, ever, ever.

Charlotte winced. Yeah, that looked as weird as it sounded.

Penny: What about London? Are you still going to apply for that photography workshop?

Charlotte's stomach dropped.

Penny: If you are, you should talk to Mitch about the possibility of being gone for 2 weeks. Remember, back when we were both working the lunch shift at the Crystal Cricket, Mitch blew his top when one of the waiters asked for the weekend off to attend his sister's wedding. The guy is strung pretty tightly. I'd give him a heads-up if I were you.

Crap! She'd forgotten what she'd done.

Charlotte: I kind of already sent in the application.

Harper: Kind of? Like you kind of had sex with Mitch?

She was never going to live this down!

Charlotte: I applied using a picture I took of Mitch. But in my defense, I was drunk!

Penny: You were drunk when you applied?

So much for gaining clarity! When did her life become such a train wreck?

Charlotte: No, I was pretty tipsy when I took the picture but totally sober when I sent it in with the application.

A picture she hadn't been granted permission to use. She chewed her lip. Breathe! Nothing terrible has happened. Getting accepted was a long shot at best. There was a good chance nothing would come of it, right?

She opened and closed her desert of a mouth, then chugged down the last of the water bottle. It was the water Mitch had set out for her the day she'd woken up and assumed she'd been kidnapped. She cringed for what seemed like the millionth time, recalling that over a relatively short period, she'd gotten drunk, failed at speed dating, and ended up working for her boss...who she'd screwed in a tent.

Every facet of her life had spun out of control!

Well, not every facet. At least she didn't have to dress like a mermaid anymore.

She sank into the seat. That was hitting one heck of a bottom.

"Charlotte, look!" Oscar cried, and she nearly fell to the floor.

Text time was over!

She tossed her phone into her bag and joined Oscar at the window as he pointed to a sign that read *Crystal Acres*.

"The houses here are so big!" Oscar added, pressing his nose against the glass.

That was an understatement!

Growing up in Denver, she knew about this glitzy part of town.

Crystal Acres was part of the Crystal Creek neighborhood not far from where Penny lived with Rowen and Phoebe in the uber-exclusive Crystal Hills. But there was one difference between the Hills and the Acres. The high-end homes in Crystal Acres came with a decent-sized plot of land—an insanely expensive extravagance in the densely packed Denver Metro area.

Former TV chefs must make bank!

"Do you know which one is ours?" Oscar asked softly.

Ours.

The word went straight to her heart, followed by a jolt of panic. She had absolutely no idea where they were going.

Zilch! Nothing!

What type of person didn't even know the address of where they'd be spending the next two months? She released a resigned sigh. That wasn't hard to answer. The kind of person who bangs their boss on the second day of work, apparently.

She straightened and lifted her chin. That was the past. It was time to move on.

There was one rule, and she couldn't break it...again.

No chef sex.

No toe-curlingly hot hanky-panky with the growly hard-bodied hothead.

None.

At all.

She closed her eyes, and her traitorous brain had to choose that very moment to recall the sweet slide of Mitch's hard length as he thrust inside her over and over and over—

"Should I ask my dad?" Oscar asked, cutting off her dirty-girl train of thought.

"How about we play a game and guess?" she offered, slightly breathless, as the RV turned down a winding road.

She fanned herself. It had gotten hot!

"Are you feeling all right, Charlotte? Your cheeks are real red," the boy observed.

She plastered on a grin. "I'm fine. It's a redhead thing. Now, do you think that's your new house?" she said, pointing to a sprawling Spanish-style home.

"Nope," Oscar answered as the RV passed by.

"What about..." Charlotte began as a mountain mansion appeared. Made of stone and exposed wood timbers, she knew that this was it. They turned onto the home's circular driveway, and Mitch cut the engine. She looked away from the stunning home and watched Mitch. She could see him in the rearview mirror. The man looked utterly lost. He rubbed his eyes, then glanced in the mirror and caught her staring. She froze, unable to look away. There it was—that flash of vulnerability, that glimpse of the man behind the angry facade.

"Who are those people over there, Dad?" Oscar asked, walking toward the front of the RV.

She scanned the property again. She hadn't noticed the two women sitting on a small bench beneath a leafy willow tree. But there they were. One waved while the other crossed her arms and sported a scowl.

Mitch peered at Oscar, then met her gaze in the mirror. And again, she was spellbound, unable to look away.

A muscle ticked in his jaw as his features hardened. "Those people are a big problem."

CHARLOTTE GRABBED her tote bag and hurried toward the front of the RV as a stone-faced Mitch exited the vehicle.

Whoever these women were, Mitch wasn't happy to see them.

"Do you know those ladies, Oscar?" she asked, helping the boy put on his backpack as she did that thing where one attempts to get an eyeful while appearing completely oblivious.

Oscar stared at her. "You're making a weird face, and your eyeballs are moving around like crazy," the boy added, crossing and uncrossing his eyes.

Yeah, she sucked at the eavesdropping game!

"Maybe those ladies are fancy lost grandmas?" he guessed, but she was certain it wasn't that.

The sharply dressed women looked to be in their late fifties or early sixties. And whoever they were, the taller of the two wasn't happy. Dressed in a tailored jet-black pantsuit with a slim briefcase and her hair in a severe French twist, the woman's seething scowl could probably be seen three states over.

She and Mitch must get along famously.

"Come on, Oscar," she said, taking the boy's hand as they

exited the camper. Her plan was to head up to the house. But they hadn't gotten two steps before Oscar knelt down.

"I gotta tie my shoes, Charlotte," the boy said, which gave her a second to listen in on the trio's conversation—not by choice, of course.

Oh, who was she kidding?

She knelt beside the boy and craned her neck. It wasn't exactly eavesdropping. Her focus was on Oscar's shoes. But from their location and the direction of the late afternoon breeze, the words simply floated right to her.

"Sorry to drop in on you like this, Mitch," the petite woman began. "I tried to let you know we were coming, but you didn't answer your phone or respond to my texts."

Charlotte caught a glimpse of the man shoving his hands into his pockets.

"I turned it off," he said in that peeved, sharp tone she heard over and over again coming from the kitchen of the Crystal Cricket.

The taller woman opened her slim case, whipped out a sheet of paper, then held it up. "That's unacceptable!"

"Excuse me?" Mitch bit back. And holy head-to-head hotheads! Perhaps Mitch and the frowning briefcase lady weren't bosom buddies.

"I need to be able to get in touch with you, Mitch. That's part of the arrangement. It's in your contract," she answered, her words popping and puncturing the air.

This might get ugly! Did this lady not know who she was dealing with?

"You are mistaken," Mitch shot back in a sharp whisper that sent a shiver down her spine.

What the heck? Now even his hothead moments turned her on? This had to stop!

"Here's the arrangement. My job is to come up with a

concept and write a book that will make your publishing house buckets of cash," the man shot back.

"And what concept have you decided on, may I ask?" the woman pressed. "Can you share the rough outline with me? What's the theme? Have you chosen any recipes?"

This was heating up fast!

Charlotte watched as Oscar tried and failed at his first shoe-tying attempt before beginning again. It gave her a second to process what she'd overheard. This was no joke! Despite Mitch going all *hothead,* it sure sounded as if he were in some serious *hot water* with his book deal.

She chanced a look at the group as Oscar crossed the loops and finished tying his shoes. Mitch blew out a tight breath and didn't say a word. Nothing—which wasn't like him. He really wasn't lying when he'd confessed on the side of the road that he was in a world of shit with his career.

"We're on a schedule, Mitch. We've got deadlines to meet," the woman added.

"Yeah, and I can't work with you barging in on me at my home. Remember who you're dealing with," he added with a decent helping of spite coating the words.

Heat rose to Charlotte's cheeks—but not because she was upset with the hothead chef. Surprisingly, it was quite the opposite. Who were these people? They'd ambushed the guy the second he returned home with his son. While she was usually on the side of whoever was on the receiving end of Mitch's wrath, she couldn't help but be in his corner on this one.

The petite woman raised her hands defensively. "Let's dial this conversation back a bit. Gwen was in town for her niece's wedding and wanted to see how you were progressing with the direction of the book. I suggested we drop by before she had to head to the airport to catch her flight back to New York. Coming here was a last-minute decision that I suggested."

Charlotte took note—this woman was the peacemaker.

"I've had a few things on my plate, Ines. You know that," Mitch answered as Oscar reared back, then sneezed one of the loudest *achoos* she'd ever heard. It caught her off guard. With a shriek, she pitched forward, losing her balance and landed flat on her ass. She hadn't realized how precariously she'd been perched in a squatting position on her tiptoes, no less. She brushed her hair out of her face, then looked up to find Mitch glaring at her and the women staring in her direction as if she were some painfully odd curiosity.

Get up! Act like a normal, non-eavesdropping human.

Every muscle in her body stiffened, but she mustered a grin, hoping desperately she didn't look like the biggest snoop on the planet.

"This must be what's been on your plate," the petite woman said with a sly grin.

Charlotte felt her cheeks heat as she came to her feet. "Everything okay with your shoes, Oscar?" she began, gesturing to the kid's laces like a game show hostess. "The shoes you were tying, right here on the ground, because they were untied."

Shut up! Shut up! Shut up! Could this be any more embarrassing?

She didn't look directly at Mitch, but she could feel his eyes on her. The question was, did he know she was listening? She parted her lips, but thankfully, Oscar spoke first.

"I'm Oscar Abrams Elliott! And I can tie my shoes by myself," the boy announced brightly, taking her hand and leading her to the group.

At the sight of the child, Ines's smirk smoothed into a smile. But the taller woman maintained an icy front while Mitch shifted his stance uncomfortably. His gaze bounced from them to the house to the women, as if he wasn't quite sure how he ended up here. Her heart twisted in her chest.

She wanted to reach out and squeeze his hand to let him know...

Know what?

That she was there for him?

That it would be okay?

That the tall lady with the briefcase deserved to have a salad hurled at her smug face?

No, she had to take a cue from the man and simply do her job.

"It's a pleasure to meet you, Oscar. I'm Ines. I've known your father for a very long time," the woman said, shaking the boy's hand. "And you must be the nanny," the woman continued with an odd glint in her eyes.

Who was this person?

The thought came and went before she felt all eyes fall on her...again. "Yes, I'm Charlotte Ames. I'm Oscar's nanny."

There! It was possible for her to act like a normal person!

Ines's sly smirk returned. "I hope Mitch has given you a warm welcome. He can be a little rough around the edges."

That was an understatement.

Charlotte cleared her throat as Mitch's gaze bored into her and the searing intensity of it made her core clench. No, no, no! This was not the time to take a walk down sexytimes memory lane.

She exhaled a slow breath.

Stick with normal! Say something normal!

"I assure you that Mitch has given me the warmest of welcomes—very, very warm. Scorching hot, in fact," she blathered. And OMG! She had to shut her mouth before something else insane slipped out. She pasted her lips together, but the damage was done. Even Oscar stared up at her like she had ten heads.

That muscle in Mitch's cheek ticked. "Ines is my publicist,

and Gwen is my publisher," he said, making the gruffest of gruff introductions.

"It's a pleasure to meet you both," she replied, knowing she'd gone full-on tomato redhead.

"Can I see my new room, Dad?" Oscar asked, blessedly shifting the conversation from her idiotic response.

Mitch turned to the women. "Give me a second," he said, then turned to her and Oscar. He pressed his hand to the small of her back, guiding them toward the house. And heaven help her, his touch was no less electric now than it had been last night. But she had to hold it together, if not for herself, for Oscar. So far, he seemed upbeat. But no matter his mood now, the kid was experiencing one heck of a shift in his little life.

Mitch lowered his voice. "Can you take Oscar inside so I can finish up with Ines and Gwen? I shouldn't be long."

She could do this. This was her job. She was the nanny—not some woman who enjoyed being ravaged by a hothead chef.

She shook her head to clear the lust-infused cobwebs.

No more thinking about being ravaged.

"Can I get your keys?" she asked, then reflexively, she felt for the key around her neck. Mitch's gaze drifted there. And for the space of a breath, they stilled.

"The keys, Dad?" Oscar pressed.

Mitch flicked his gaze from her neck. "You don't need a key," he explained. "The doors are equipped with a keypad entry. The code is one-one-two-four."

"Eleven twenty-four? That's my birthday!" Oscar chimed. "One-one is the same as eleven and two four is twenty-four."

Mitch nodded. "I thought that would be easy to remember," the man replied, and her stupid heart was at it again. It was a sweet gesture. But she didn't dare tell him that.

"Can we explore around the house, too? Please?" Oscar continued.

Mitch peered past the house toward another structure on the property. Constructed in the same rustic style as the house, it looked like a barn or an oversized garage. The man's already stiff posture tightened.

What could be in there?

Mitch exhaled a slow, weary breath. "Yes, you can look around. The code works on every exterior door on the property. The bedrooms are upstairs. Madelyn's people were supposed to prepare your rooms. They've had access to my house while we've been gone. Interior design's not really my thing," he finished, looking away, his voice barely a rasp.

Was he nervous? He wasn't the only one!

She adjusted the straps of her tote. "I'm sure they did a great job," she replied, wanting desperately to help this man who was so obviously struggling. No, that wasn't her job. But she would have sworn she'd seen a longing in his eyes—a sadness that cut bone-deep and a wish not to have to constantly go it alone.

"Come on, Charlotte," Oscar exclaimed, tugging on her hand. Mitch blinked, and the raw honesty disappeared behind a surly glare.

So much for trying to help!

She'd be wise to remember that as much as he needed it, he didn't want it. No, it was more than that. Besides caring for Oscar, he didn't want anything from her.

Why did that hurt?

A week ago, she couldn't have cared less what the man thought. But now...now she could barely discern which way was up.

Oscar dropped her hand and took the steps up to the porch two at a time as she followed close behind. But only a few seconds had passed when she felt a penetrating force at her back. She stopped. It was like being caught in a tingle tractor beam. And there was no second-guessing whose eyes were laser-focused on her. Being the object of Mitch Elliott's complete and unrelenting attention could not be mistaken. The breath caught in her throat as she glanced over her shoulder. And for a fraction of a second, she would have sworn the man was on the brink of smiling.

"We can wait for you, Mitch." She gestured with her chin toward a little bench on the property near the porch.

The hint of a curve graced his lips, and her stupid heart took notice. Was he about to gift her with a grin and ask her to stay close by? But before she could even blink, his countenance darkened.

"I'm fine. Stay with Oscar," he ordered as if he were calling out commands in the Crystal Cricket's kitchen before striding over to where Ines and Gwen were chatting.

Spitting mad one second, then drinking her in like she made up the entirety of his universe the next!

The guy was all over the place!

She exhaled, her heart hammering when an electronic chirp made her gasp.

Beep, beep, beep, beep!

She pressed her hand to her chest.

Get a grip, girl!

If she were any more tightly strung, she'd explode.

"I entered the door code," the boy chimed as a click punctuated the evening air, and he opened the door.

"Wow! It's empty," Oscar called, flicking on lights as he raced around the spacious, sparsely furnished house.

She walked past a grand staircase made of wrought iron and gleaming wood, then scanned what looked like it should be the great room. The cavernous space was void of furnishings, but the mountain mansion architecture still took her breath away. Exposed beams sailed into the air, creating steep peaks in the ceiling that framed a gleaming giant rock fireplace. She walked over to it and ran her hand over the cool stones that made up the majestic hearth.

"Charlotte! Come see the kitchen and check out this giant stove," Oscar cried, his voice echoing through the empty home.

She followed the pitter-patter of his footsteps, turned the corner, then stopped dead in her tracks. While the rest of the first floor barely contained a stick of furniture, the kitchen was like something out of a mountain home design magazine. In keeping with the style of the rest of the house, exposed wood timbers raised the ceiling. Large windows dotted the space between gleaming appliances and wooden cabinetry. She opened what she thought was a cabinet and found utensils hanging from a board like they were pieces of art: ladles, graters, and eight spatulas in different shapes and sizes.

Eight!

"Why would anyone need so many spatulas?" she mumbled.

"You use them for different things," Oscar answered, swooping in beside her. The child tapped the first row. "These are flippers. These are scrapers. And these are spreaders," he finished, schooling her in the art of spatulas, then started digging in his backpack.

"What are you doing, Oscar?" she asked, watching him closely.

"I've got one in my bag," he said, whipping out an actual spatula. With a pale, dried wooden handle and a flipper part that looked like it had seen better days a century ago, this spatula might very well be the most well-used cooking utensil in the entire state of Colorado.

"That's neat," she remarked—not sure what to think about the kid carrying around an old spatula. Maybe it wasn't that odd. Some kids had security blankets and teddy bears. Oscar must be a spatula enthusiast. She was about to ask him where he'd gotten it when he slid the old thing back into his pack before darting to the other side of the kitchen.

She returned her attention to the spatula museum of a cabinet, removed her camera from her tote, then took a few shots of the cooking implements.

"Charlotte, look! You could make like fifty grilled cheese sandwiches at one time on this gigantically enormous stove!" the boy exclaimed from the other side of the kitchen.

She raised her camera and framed Oscar in the shot. "Say cheese," she called.

"I love *cheeeeese*," the child exclaimed. The boy played along, pretending to cook on what truly was a gigantically enormous stove as she clicked away, recording Oscar's beginning in his new home. She was worried coming to Denver might be hard for the boy, but the kid had energy to boot. She kept him in her sights, capturing shot after shot. And there was plenty of room to move. He buzzed past, not one, but two sinks, and then, not one, but two industrial-sized refrigerators.

This place was a kitchen on steroids—the definition of gigantically enormous.

"There's a staircase hidden over here. Do you think it goes up to my new bedroom?" Oscar called from the far side of the kitchen.

She got a shot of him looking over his shoulder at her from the fourth step, then lowered the camera and raised an eyebrow. "There's one way to tell." She'd keep it light. If he could be upbeat and chipper, so could she.

Oscar bolted up the steps and disappeared from her view.

"I found my room!" he called. Then, five seconds later. "I found your room, Charlotte!" the boy added.

She made it to the second floor and peeked inside the first opened door. This had to be Oscar's room. Madelyn's people had given the boy a bunk bed and decked the room in mountain camping décor with a set of bean bag chairs and a real tent in the corner. Pictures of mountain maps and images of National Park postcards lined the walls. And film. A basket with several packets of Polaroid film sat on the nightstand across from a rustic wooden desk.

"You have a big bathtub," he announced as she exited the boy's room and found him next door—next door in her room. Her eyes widened. This couldn't be called a bedroom. No, it was a deluxe suite.

"There are boxes in the closet and a credit card with your name on it sitting right on the desk," Oscar said, opening the door to a—like everything else in this place—gigantically enormous closet.

Ah, the nanny match credit card! Harper would be pleased.

She studied the space. Madelyn's crew must have packed up her things. Penny probably let them into her old apartment.

A nervous buzz passed through her. This would be her home for at least the next fifty-eight days. She left the sizable closet and took in the rest of the room. A luxuriously rustic retreat didn't even begin to describe it. With the most enormous, fluffy bed she'd ever seen, the suite sported a cozy sitting area and a bathroom that could rival most spas.

"I bet you and my dad could fit inside that super-huge tub," Oscar commented.

She could feel the rush of heat to her cheeks.

Do not picture yourself in that gloriously oversized bathtub with Mitch...and his strong hands and magical mouth.

"Let's go see what's outside. I'll race you to that barn thingy. I saw a door that leads to it from the kitchen," he called—off again—running toward the stairs, which gave her a second to pull herself together.

"Just take showers," she whispered to herself, taking another peek at the tub. She rubbed her eyes, then checked her watch. It was nearly eight o'clock in the evening. How was Oscar not exhausted? That wasn't too hard to answer. For one, he actually slept last night. She, on the other hand, hadn't been able to stop her mind from playing and replaying what had happened in the tent. Something she had to stop doing.

"I'm coming, Oscar," she called, mustering up a second wind as she descended the stairs, then exited the house.

A gravel path led to the structure. She listened to the crunch of the rocks beneath her feet. Paired with the glow of the setting sun, she allowed the ethereal light and calming sound to soothe her ragged nerves. She lifted her camera and took a shot of Oscar's footprints on the ground, then snapped another of the structure with a door left wide open. "Oscar?" she called as she approached the building, then headed inside.

"You get a Lamborghini! It's like Christmas!" the boy cried, handing her an envelope with her name written on the outside.

She lifted the flap, then removed a key fob for—that's right—a freaking Lamborghini Urus. She shook her head, eyeing the sleek SUV. It was the same car Penny drove, except this one was candy apple red.

"It's a lot fancier than my old Honda," she replied, eyeing her vehicle parked on the other side of the garage next to Mitch's black beefy truck. But how did her car end up here? Had she given her keys to Mitch? Had Madelyn's people taken care of this, too? She searched her memories, cursing those potent margaritas. Stumped, she shook her head. At least it wasn't racking up parking tickets in the Crystal Creek business district.

"What do you think that is?" Oscar asked, pointing to what looked like a delivery truck under a large tarp.

"Another camper van?" she guessed.

"There's one way to tell," Oscar cried, borrowing her words with a mischievous twinkle in his eyes. Before she could tell him to stop, he sprinted to the covered vehicle and pulled the corner of the tarp, revealing...

Say Cheese, Louise?

"I know this truck! My mom showed me pictures of Louise," the boy exclaimed excitedly. He ran to the back of the vehicle and disappeared from her view. A metallic squeak and clang echoed through the garage. "Look at me, Charlotte! I'm making grilled cheese in a food truck," the boy called, popping up in a window on the side of the bright orange truck with the ancient spatula in his hand.

Charlotte stepped back and surveyed the food truck.

She'd seen it before too!

She opened her bag, then slid the framed photo Amy had given her from the side pocket. Her gaze bounced from the opening where Oscar sat with his elbows on a small shelf to the image of three people in that exact location.

"Come check it out!" Oscar called, waving her over with the spatula.

Slowly, she walked to the window and stared inside the truck. It was like a super-condensed version of the Crystal Cricket's kitchen with one glaring difference. Photographs of the food truck in different locations with the same three people standing together were plastered to the walls and to the windows. And Mitch was smiling ear to ear in each photo. It was such an easy, contagious expression. She found herself grinning at the enigma of a man. She touched one of the faded images tacked near the window that must serve as a place for patrons to order. "I recognize your dad and your mom in this picture. Who's the other person? Do you know his name, Oscar?"

Oscar stopped pretending to make sandwiches on the large stovetop, then came over and used the spatula to point to the other smiling man. "That's Seth! He used to visit my mom and me, but he stopped. I don't know where he is now," the boy answered with a shrug before returning to the stove to pretend to flip sandwiches. "The three of them started Say Cheese, Louise and got real, real famous. They were on TV and everything. But that was before I was born," he finished, then plucked a picture from the wall and passed it through the window. It was a shot of Mitch, Holly, and Seth standing in front of a camera crew. She turned it over. It was dated a decade ago. Mitch had to have been in his early twenties then.

She nodded to the boy and examined the image. She'd known that Mitch was a former TV chef, but that was about it. She wasn't sure where he'd gotten his start...until now! This food truck had to be it. She loved splurging on food truck delights, but she wasn't a foodie. It wasn't like she spent her free time watching television. No, ten years ago, she was fifteen. She bristled at the memories of her home life—if you could even call it a *home life*. Growing up, she'd spent as little time as possible at her house. Her life centered on her friends, school, and photography.

She took a few steps back and peered at the truck. The more she thought about it, the more she remembered hearing about an amazing food truck that made out-of-this-world grilled cheese sandwiches. It was featured on the news or in the paper—she couldn't quite remember. To the best of her knowledge, a major food network had signed on to follow the food truck chefs as they started out. It had to be Mitch and Say Cheese, Louise.

She stared at the picture of the hothead chef. Beaming with joy, the man didn't seem to possess an ounce of hotheadedness in any of the photos. "What happened to you?" she whispered as roaring music blared from the truck—a festive booming sound that startled the hell out of her.

"I don't know how to turn it off, Charlotte! I was playing

with some of the buttons up here by the steering wheel," Oscar shouted from the front of the truck.

When had he climbed into the driver's seat?

She ran over to the driver's side window, knocked a few times, then gestured for him to roll it down. "Tell me what you touched, and we'll figure out how to turn it off," she replied to the wide-eyed child when the passenger door to the vehicle swung open. She gasped as Mitch slid into the seat, red-cheeked, with a scowl pasted to his face.

Here comes the hothead!

He flicked a switch, and the music stopped. The garage grew dead quiet. "What are you doing in here?" he asked, eyes burning with anger—or was that agony. But she didn't have time to analyze the man's mood. Instead, she hurried to his side.

"You said we could look around, Dad," Oscar answered, lifting his little chin as he narrowed his gaze, going mini-hothead.

"And what are you doing with that?" Mitch pressed, pointing to the old spatula in Oscar's hand.

"I found it in a bag in the RV," the boy replied defiantly.

"That was my bag, Oscar. You had no right to be rifling through it. My knives are in there. You could have gotten hurt," the man growled.

"I know how to be careful with knives. My mom showed me," the boy shot back.

"Well, you shouldn't be in here. I said you could explore the house—not the garage!" he boomed.

"Stop being such a hothead, Dad," Oscar shot back.

She had to do something. That spatula totally set Mitch off and threw him for a loop. She touched his arm, and the man whipped around. Breathless, she studied his face. She'd expected to see anger in his eyes, but what she saw was the same broken expression he'd had on the side of the road. Again, this man was in pain.

"Mitch," she breathed when the door to the garage opened.

"I didn't know you still had her," Ines remarked, entering the space and looking absolutely gobsmacked with Gwen on her heels.

Charlotte glanced between father and son. With his little face scrunched up and Mitch going all hothead, these two were on the brink of another eruption. She couldn't have that—not in front of the stuffy publisher.

"I'm sorry, Mitch. We didn't mean to interrupt your meeting," she said, trying to defuse the situation.

The man didn't say a word, but his hardened expression spoke volumes. Whatever had transpired between the trio, it didn't appear to be good.

Gwen checked her watch, then cleared her throat. "Mitch, I don't have much time. I'll get to the point. I don't see a way forward for your book. Our lawyers will be in touch."

"Gwen," Ines pleaded. "Let's table the discussion and hash it out in a few days when tempers have cooled."

The publisher shook her head. "We don't have a few days to keep running in circles, Ines. Your client doesn't even have a rough idea for the book."

With the publisher ready to bolt and Mitch and Oscar about to break out into round two of father versus son regarding the curious case of the mysterious spatula, this was about as bad as it could get. Charlotte observed the chaotic scene, her heart hammering as Gwen set off for the door.

They needed a breather.

"Time out!" she called, not knowing why she'd chosen to act like a referee at this moment, but that's what came out. And all eyes fell on her. "Gwen, right?" she said, hustling over to the woman.

"Yes?" the lady barked, but she stopped. She hadn't left yet.

Charlotte smashed a giant, nervous grin on her face as she scanned the garage, then peered at the photo in her hand. "Did Mitch mention his back to the beginning idea to you?" she continued. Her mouth was a damned desert, but she couldn't stop the words from tumbling from her lips.

"Back to the beginning?" Gwen repeated with a sliver of interest woven into her reply.

Okay! This was better than the lady bolting.

"Yes, the back to the beginning idea for the book. This food truck was Mitch's beginning. What could be better than a book chronicling the reboot of Say Cheese, Louise?" she finished.

What was she doing? This was not her call.

"Keep talking," Gwen said, her icy demeanor defrosting a few degrees.

It was working! The stuffy publisher liked the idea.

A surge of confidence danced through her veins until she felt two eyes boring into the back of her head. She looked over her shoulder to find one very livid hothead.

She knew this look.

Hold on to your hats. The chef was about to blow.

TWELVE

MITCH

HE STARED AT CHARLOTTE. Had the woman lost her damned mind?

"Gwen, Ines, can you give us a minute?" he bit out through gritted teeth, then pressed his hand to the small of Charlotte's back and guided her away from the women. The muscles in his body tightened as he did his best to ignore the furious tingling in the pit of his stomach that erupted whenever he touched her.

Dammit, man!

This was not the time to untangle the tsunami of emotions that hit him like a Mack truck whenever he was close to this woman.

He had to put his maddening attraction to Charlotte on the back burner and focus—freaking focus! His reputation was on the line, for Christ's sake! But he couldn't cave to Gwen either. Forget the fact that she ran one of the top culinary publishing houses in the country. He wouldn't stand there and bend to her will and kowtow to her ridiculous demands.

But were they that ridiculous?

The tingling in his belly gave way to a gut-wrenching twist.

Shit! As a chef, he knew better than anyone the importance of following a set schedule and maximizing productivity. Every second in the kitchen counted. Structure and routine were paramount. Hell, he'd purchased software to increase the efficiency of ordering the staples for the restaurant. He lived and breathed timetables and agendas. But he'd screwed up. He'd allowed the shitstorm swirling around him to knock him off course. But this book catastrophe was his damned mess to clean up—not Charlotte's cross to bear. And her idea—this *back to the beginning* concept was crazy—complete lunacy, right?

Perhaps not.

The blurry red haze let up a fraction, and the measured part of him regained a thread of control. Maybe it wasn't a complete clusterfuck of a concept. If he removed the emotional scarring component that clawed in the darkest part of his mind anytime thoughts of Say Cheese, Louise crept up on him and considered Charlotte's idea objectively, it wasn't half bad. Millions of people across the globe watched his start into the culinary world via the Say Cheese, Louise reality TV show. Hell, the episodes were available to watch on-demand in the US, and there was talk of making them available in the UK. The buying power of that audience alone would sell a shit ton of books and catapult him back into the spotlight. Still, she shouldn't have dropped it like that in front of his publisher without even consulting him. The scorching heat surging through his veins was near-boiling.

"What the hell do you think you're doing, Charlotte?" he hissed.

She looked him dead in the eyes. "I'm saving your hothead ass," she whispered back with a thread of apprehension in her tone.

She was trying to hide it, trying to disappear behind those blazing emerald eyes, but she was completely bullshitting her way through this. He'd bet half his net worth she'd pulled this idea out of thin air!

The real question was why—why was she trying to save his hothead ass?

After what had happened in the tent and what he'd said after Oscar had called out to them, he figured she hated him. But he knew she needed the job—knew she wouldn't leave. A pang of disgust rippled through him. He was truly an ass! But she was a good person. Anyone with half a brain could see that. Case in point, she'd connected more with Oscar in three minutes than he had in three years! That was it—her blinding aura of compassion and the trustworthiness she emanated. Try as he may, he couldn't quash the reckless yearning in his heart to feel the sense of truly belonging to another. That's why he wasn't able to resist her in the tent.

The tent.

He stared at her lips, and he couldn't stop the barrage of images from assaulting his brain. The memory of this breathtakingly beautiful woman brushing her lips across his and smiling against his mouth bloomed sweetly in his thoughts. God, it had felt good to let go of the pain and disappear into her. But it was more than just disappearing.

Charlotte Ames was no distraction. He glanced at the key pressed to the hollow of her neck.

If he wasn't careful, she could be his very undoing.

With each touch, each kiss, and every glorious thrust of his cock, she'd made him feel an emotion that had long been dormant.

The freedom to open himself up to pure bliss.

The kind of feeling he used to have in spades.

But that feeling came with a price.

The joy he'd felt had earned him the title of the world's

biggest sucker. That feeling couldn't last—not for him. In fact, it had blown up his world like a grenade, pulverizing everything in its path. He had to stop fooling himself. Whatever drew him to her had to be ignored.

"You don't have to do this," he said, keeping his voice low as a bitter edge sliced through the statement.

"Do what? Suggest an idea?" she answered, incredulity coating the words.

He hardened his features. "You don't have to twist yourself into a pretzel to try to be what you think I need."

The pink hue of her cheeks deepened. He'd hit a nerve.

"Excuse me?" she bit out.

"I saw you do it over and over again at the bullshit speed date event," he added, deleting the fact that, at the very same bullshit speed date event, he couldn't seem to keep his eyes off her. He'd damn near twisted himself into a pretzel to get close to her. But she didn't need to know that.

She gasped at his harsh words, her mouth opening and closing like a pissed-off flounder, but nothing came out. He was ready to claim victory when she pressed her lips into a hard line and sharpened her expression. And holy shit! Thank God there were no tomato, cucumber, and avocado salads in the vicinity. She looked ready to hurl one at him.

"I'm not twisting myself into anything, Mitch. It was you who told me that you were in trouble with this book project. The back to the beginning idea came to me. And Oscar..." she trailed off, then glanced at the boy. He was still perched in the front seat of the truck with the spatula in his hand.

That spatula.

He swallowed past the lump in his throat. "What about Oscar?" he growled, needing to hold it together. He could not show an ounce of sentiment.

Charlotte's expression softened. "When Oscar pulled the tarp off the truck, he lit up. You could share this with him, Mitch. The food truck book project could be a way to bond with him and keep him connected to his mother."

At the mention of Holly, that red haze of anger returned as his every defense went on high alert. "You don't know anything about her," he growled, his words coming out rough and jagged.

He expected his harsh reply to elicit an equally severe response from her. But she didn't join him on the angry train. Instead, she drank him in with that warm green gaze. And Christ, what he wouldn't have given to spend the rest of his life in a damned stupor, falling deeper and deeper under her spell. She touched his chest, pressing her hand against his hammering heart. "I know that Holly was Oscar's mother. I know she made him hot chocolate and grilled cheese sandwiches. And while I never met her, I think it's safe to say that she loved her son."

He should have known better. Charlotte's true power wasn't her ability to throw salads at people. No, her gift was what she could do with gentle kindness. He inhaled a shaky breath. He should step back and get himself the hell out of Charlotte Ames's orbit. Her touch brought him a comfort he could not allow himself to crave. But he didn't move—not an inch.

"Mitch! Charlotte! Join us! We've got great news," Ines called, cutting short their nanny and hothead huddle. He shoved his hands into his pockets. His fingertips brushed past the heart-shaped lock and every muscle in his body tensed.

Jesus, get a grip, man!

Charlotte dropped her hand from his chest, and instantly, he mourned the loss of their connection.

Forget the stupid lock! Ignore the damned comfort of her touch and get back in the game.

He doubled his efforts to maintain a stony front.

"Mitch," Charlotte whispered with a look of shock on her

face as she pressed up to her tiptoes and peered over his shoulder.

He leaned in. "What?"

She chewed her lip as she focused on whatever the hell was going on behind him.

"Gwen is smiling, or else she's so mad at you she's gone past anger and entered into some sort of loopy delirium," she whispered.

Slowly, he turned toward the women. Each had their cell phone out and was hammering away at light speed. Gwen looked up, and yep, the woman was grinning ear to ear. And yeah, she did have an air of loopy to her.

"Please, join us! Going back to the beginning with the Say Cheese, Louise food truck for a limited run is a fantastic concept. Our marketing folks love it," Gwen whooped—actually whooped.

"It's true," Ines agreed. "People adore a throwback. And a limited-time run of good old Louise is sure to garner loads of publicity. My tech guys are creating new social media accounts for the Say Cheese, Louise reboot, and I've already reached out to a few of the locations where you used to park the truck years ago. They're thrilled, to say the least, about a return visit. You can focus on the lunch crowd. That will give you the evenings with Oscar. It's the best of both worlds, Mitch," she added with a look in her eyes that said, *don't fuck this up.*

"How soon can you schedule a stop?" Gwen asked, still smiling like a lunatic, with her eyes glued to her phone. "We'd like to get things moving as quickly as possible. We've still got a tight timetable."

"Tomorrow! I'm just waiting for confirmation for a location downtown near several businesses," Ines answered brightly.

His gaze ping-ponged between the women.

Tomorrow? This was moving fast—too fast!

"For Christ's sake, slow down!" he exclaimed, drawing on his hotheadedness as he paced across the garage.

"What are you worried about, Mitch? It's a solid concept. We simply need to execute the plan," Gwen remarked.

Sure, it was a solid plan—for her. But there was nothing simple about it. He was the one who'd be doing the work. Not to mention, he hadn't cooked in the food truck since…

He scrubbed his hands down the scruff of his cheeks as competing forces tore at his heart. How the hell was he supposed to set foot in Louise after everything that happened? He observed the bright orange vehicle. He'd chosen the color. He'd even come up with the name. That truck had been an extension of himself until it became a glaring reminder of what he'd lost. After everything had fallen apart, he'd almost gotten rid of her.

Almost.

Could the food truck from his past become his path forward?

"This is your way back, Mitch," Charlotte said gently as if she'd read his mind.

She wasn't wrong.

Still, running a food truck wasn't like flicking on a light switch.

He crossed his arms. "I'll admit, going back to the beginning with Louise is a decent idea. But you don't decide to operate a food truck on a whim. Even if it was for a limited engagement and we're only making the signature sandwich, I need all the ingredients. Arrangements need to be made. Orders have got to be placed weeks in advance. The organic apple butter I use comes from the Applebaum Farm. They're a family-owned operation just north of the city. You can't simply snap your fingers and set off for grilled cheese nirvana without it."

"Oh, but you can!" came a rich vibrato voice with a thick eastern European accent.

"Madelyn?" Charlotte exclaimed in a stunned breath.

Sweet Jesus! Where did she come from?

His jaw dropped as he stared at none other than Madelyn Malone, standing in the doorway to the garage. Who the hell else was going to parachute in on the shitshow that was his life? "What are you doing here?"

The woman smoothed her red scarf, then sauntered in like this was a garden party. "My people are taking care of returning the RV, and I thought I'd drop by and see how you were settling in," she purred, scanning the room. Her gaze lingered on the food truck as the ghost of a grin pulled at the corners of her mouth. "This certainly seems like the place to be. And Gwen, it's so nice to see you—and so soon," she finished, addressing his publisher.

"You know each other?" he asked, beyond befuddled.

"I was a guest at Gwen's niece's wedding," Madelyn answered smoothly.

This lady knew everyone!

"And Ines, what a pleasure it is," Madelyn continued, exchanging air kisses with the woman.

"And I'm Oscar! Say cheese," his son called, taking a picture with his Polaroid camera, then removing the spatula from his back pocket and wielding the utensil like a sword.

Mitch surveyed the scene wide-eyed. His life was getting more surreal by the second.

"It's a pleasure to meet you, young man," Madelyn replied, shaking Oscar's hand before his son skipped off to have an imaginary spatula sword fight near Louise.

Madelyn smiled at the boy, then schooled her features. "Now, what's this about a food truck? Forgive me for eavesdropping. I couldn't help but hear your conversation. Mitch, please explain to me why you can't start tomorrow?"

He blew out an audible breath. "Food," he blathered like an

idiot. Was he the only damn person who understood it was pretty hard to make a signature sandwich without the ingredients?

"What about it?" she tossed back.

Was this happening?

"To make the Louise sandwich, that's the signature sandwich we started out with, I'd need—"

"Plenty of butter, cheddar cheese, that special apple butter from the nice farmer, Dijon mustard, and sourdough bread," Oscar answered, punctuating each ingredient with a swipe of the spatula.

And again, Mitch's jaw dropped. He hadn't even noticed Oscar had drifted back toward the group. But the kid was correct.

"How do you know that?" he pressed.

Oscar continued spatula-fighting his invisible opponent. "Mom used to make them for me. She'd say, *here's Louise*, and then she'd set the sandwich on my plate. And she'd always cut it into—"

"Triangles," he finished, remembering the first time he'd made the Louise back when he was a screwed-up juvenile delinquent.

"Yeah, two triangles," Oscar answered, grinning up at him.

Mitch swallowed hard. He could hear the knife crackling through the freshly toasted bread. But they couldn't start tomorrow. There was too much to prep.

He threw up his hands. "I don't have the ingredients. I'd need to put in an order and check with my suppliers."

"Actually, you have those ingredients here at your home," Madelyn answered with that coy grin of hers.

He respected the woman. She had her nanny match ways, and he got that. But this was cooking, and he was the only chef in the room.

"No, Madelyn, I don't. I think I'd know if I had one hundred pounds of cheddar cheese hanging around my house. A lunch rush can easily go through that much."

She demurely tucked a dark lock of hair threaded with a pronounced silver streak behind her ear. "You do. My people brought it to your place last night. I hope you don't mind."

What was she now—a nanny matchmaker and a cheesemonger?

"Your people brought that much cheddar cheese to my house?" He had to double-check that he'd heard her correctly. This conversation was quickly bordering on bonkers.

"They were on their way here to take care of some finishing touches on Oscar's room. I didn't think it would be a problem to drop off the cheese. You do have a completely empty industrial-sized refrigerator."

He glanced at Charlotte, who shrugged her confusion. At least he wasn't the only one who wasn't able to connect the dots.

"But why would you have that much cheese, and where did you get it?" he pressed.

"From your restaurant, of course," she answered with a wave of her hand as if pilfering a small fortune in dairy products was part of her daily routine.

What the hell?

"You got it from my restaurant?" he shot back.

She nodded as she sauntered past the food truck. "Why, yes! I had dinner there last night. When Ines and I spoke Friday, she mentioned that two guest chefs from Kansas City would be taking over for the next several weeks. So, I decided to head to the kitchen and greet them after my meal. They're lovely, by the way."

"And then they gave you all that cheese and every ingredient to make the Signature Louise sandwich?" he asked. It didn't make sense. There was no way Gabe and Monica would be handing out blocks of cheddar in to-go bags. Surely not one hundred pounds of it!

"Not quite. I overheard your manager telling them that he'd accidentally ordered it—along with extra organic butter, apple butter, and Dijon mustard. There was some talk of putting a sandwich on the menu. You'd told the man to cancel the order, but something glitched, and the items were delivered. I let them know I'd take them off their hands—and make sure that no one got fired over the small computer error," she added, eyeing him closely.

He didn't even have it in him at this point to morph into hothead mode over his manager's ordering mishap. Yep, he'd lost it.

"How much stuff is there?" Charlotte asked.

Good question!

He nodded, grateful that she could think of something to ask because his mind had turned to mush.

Madelyn tapped her chin. "An awful lot! I think the manager had mentioned there was enough for five hundred sandwiches."

"That's *a-lotta-lotta* cheese," Oscar murmured, lowering his voice reverently.

"Well, look at that! The stars have aligned," Gwen announced, sharing a giddy look with Ines.

"I'll confirm tomorrow's appointment," his publicist beamed, texting away.

He shook his head, finding his voice. "Don't confirm anything yet. We're missing an essential piece. Do you know how much bread we'll need? You can't make a grilled cheese sandwich without it."

"A curious thing about the bread," Madelyn mused, walking past Louise.

This was too much. How could there be bread? He had his own recipe.

"You're kidding? Who made my bread?" he asked, incredulity woven through his question.

"Your guest chef, Monica Brandt-Sinclair. She's a gifted baker. She even shared her famous strudel recipe with me," Madelyn answered.

"Did you ask her to make my special sourdough recipe?" he asked. By this point, he wouldn't have been surprised if she also announced that she'd solved the climate crisis and brokered world peace. The woman had an answer for everything!

"Yes, I suggested she make some of your signature sourdough. I figured since you'd be home and you'd need to make school lunches for Oscar, it would be a welcome surprise."

This was more than a surprise.

"How much bread?" he asked. At this point, she could tell him sourdough fairies delivered it, and he'd nod and accept the explanation without a word of dissent.

"I lost count after about fifty loaves. Possibly one hundred— maybe more?" she answered with another cavalier flick of her wrist.

"There's the food you'll need to make the Signature Louise," Ines said, nodding to herself. "Now, we'll need to book a photographer."

"Yes, absolutely, that's imperative," Gwen answered. "We'll want plenty of images to choose from for the book."

"And I can look into hiring someone to take orders while Mitch cooks," Ines continued as the muscles in his chest tightened.

Oh, hell no!

"Stop! Stop!" he exclaimed, waving his arms. "That's where I put my foot down. I choose who I work with. You can't have just anyone hanging around inside a food truck snapping photos. It's close quarters around knives and hot cooktops. And you can't hire just anyone to work the counter. I like my order tickets to be written a certain way. Staffing is my call, or the project is off."

"How long will it take you to hire the help you need?" Gwen asked as her giddy sheen dissolved.

"No time at all," Madelyn answered before he could even open his befuddled trap. "Mitch has got the perfect candidate right here," Madelyn added, wrapping her arm around Charlotte's shoulders.

"Yeah, Dad! Charlotte is a photographer and a nanny," Oscar chimed.

"And a waitress," Madelyn crooned. "She worked at the Crystal Cricket—for, how long, dear, before that unfortunate salad incident?"

"Two and a half years," Charlotte answered. She'd gone white and looked as flabbergasted as he felt as Madelyn plowed on.

"Surely you agree with the choice of Charlotte for your photographer, Mitch. You did hire her to be your son's nanny. You already trust her," the nanny matchmaker finished, emphasizing the word trust as he absorbed the impact of the word.

Trust?

The jarring syllable hung in the air—but the ring of the word didn't burn quite as hot as it usually did.

"You have a business card, don't you, dear?" Madelyn asked, gesturing to Charlotte's tote.

"Yes, I do," Charlotte answered, producing the slim rectangle. "I've also worked as a mermaid, but those skills probably won't be required to work in a food truck. Unless it's an underwater food truck. But who would want a soggy grilled cheese sandwich?" Charlotte gushed nervously. She'd blushed, and it was utterly enchanting.

Madelyn handed Charlotte's card to Gwen.

"What about staffing the front?" Ines remarked.

"I'm sure Charlotte can help with that—at least until Mitch finds someone he deems suitable," Madelyn answered smoothly. "Might I also suggest that you don't charge for the sandwiches? Each time the food truck appears, it's an act of charity—a way to give back to the community."

"I love that," Gwen breathed, nodding furiously. The publisher was nearly foaming at the mouth with excitement.

"That would definitely help improve your image, Mitch," Ines added. "We could highlight the softer side and not the—"

"Hothead," Oscar interrupted through a wide yawn. "Oops, I mean," the boy corrected, then tapped his foot twice.

"Well, Mitch? What do you say?" Madelyn pressed. "It appears you have everything you need right here. I'd call this a most fortunate twist of fate."

That sure as hell was one way to put it!

He wasn't an idiot. He was smart enough to understand that this was the way forward if he wanted to get his career back on track. But in the blink of an eye, this endeavor had become about a lot more than a publicity stunt for a book. The rapid beat of his heart and his hammering pulse spoke to that. He glanced over his shoulder at the Say Cheese, Louise food truck, then looked from Oscar to Charlotte.

He crossed his arms and blew out an exasperated breath. "Okay, we've got our concept for the book. I'm in for the Say Cheese, Louise reboot."

Gwen, Ines, and Madelyn clustered together, clucking like giddy hens. He turned his back to them and studied the food truck. The place had once been like a second home. Awash with competing emotions, he was startled when Charlotte rested her hand on his forearm.

She gave him one of her strawberry sunshine grins. "We can

do this," she said, her voice wrapping him in an invisible warmth.

He nodded.

They could. But it was more than that. And he felt it in his bones. It was a realization that hit him like a wrecking ball.

This endeavor was either going to make him or break him.

THIRTEEN

CHARLOTTE

CHARLOTTE PEERED out of Oscar's window, making sure to stay behind the curtains. The boy's second-floor room looked out onto the circular driveway. Gazing down on pools of light and swaths of inky darkness, she had a bird's-eye view of the fir trees and the smattering of aspens shimmering in the breeze that lined the drive. But she wasn't interested in the landscape.

No, something else had captured her attention.

The nanny match people had taken the RV, but the driveway wasn't empty. She'd casually drifted toward the window to get a look outside at least ten times over the last twenty minutes.

She couldn't help herself.

After they'd said goodbye to Ines, Gwen, and Madelyn, Mitch asked her to help Oscar get ready for bed while he prepped the food truck that now sat parked below Oscar's window. She couldn't help but be curious—and feel a pang of anxiety, or was that excitement? It was still hard to comprehend that her Say Cheese, Louise reboot idea had snowballed into her working as not only his son's nanny but his photographer and his food truck assistant.

She'd be with him all day, every day.

And there he was—carrying a cardboard box into the food truck.

She tried to suppress the dizzying current racing through her body. But it was no use. A surge of energy fluttered in her belly—or was that *below* her belly. She inhaled a steadying breath as her core tightened and her nipples hardened into tight peaks.

"How many times are you going to look out my window, Charlotte?"

She gasped and crossed her arms as Oscar stood in the center of his room, eyeing her closely.

"What do you mean? I'm getting your room ready for bed. I was about to close the curtains," she lied. It was a white lie—no harm done. But that didn't stop her cheeks from heating up.

Stupid redhead tomato reaction!

"Don't close them yet," Oscar said, bounding over in his pajamas. "Is my dad still loading up Louise?"

She looked away, willing her boobs to cooperate. "I wouldn't know. I was admiring the trees," she answered, tightening her hold on her arms.

"Yep, he's still out there," Oscar said. She went to his side as Mitch glanced up at the window.

Oscar waved to the man as she stared down at him. He waved back at his son, then turned his attention to her, and *hello, Tingle City!* She raised her hand and pressed her fingertips to the glass as he stared up at her. It was too dark, and he was too far away for her to read him, but she could sense he was uneasy. The man moved with measured precision. That had to be a chef thing. But there was an undercurrent of apprehension coming off the guy in waves.

She was probably giving off the same energy.

This time last week, he was most likely at the Crystal

Cricket, hotheading away, yelling at sous chefs or berating a line cook, while she was scouring the online want ads for another part-time job between skimming through her photographs, trying to decide which to submit for the Royal College of Art application.

Now, look at them! They were living under the same roof, and they'd slept together!

No, she couldn't think of it like that—even though her friends had made it crystal clear that she'd indeed screwed Mitch's brains out.

No, she couldn't think of it like that, either!

She and Mitch had fallen prey to a momentary lapse in judgment inside of a tent.

Yep, that's what it was.

"Charlotte?" Oscar called.

She peered over her shoulder and found the boy across the room, perched on the bottom bunk.

"How did you get over there? I didn't even hear your foot-steps," she replied, abandoning her post at the window to sit on the edge of Oscar's bed.

He gave her a toothy grin. "It was easy. You don't notice anything when you're looking at my dad."

What?

"That's not true," she answered, gesturing for him to move aside as she pulled down the covers. She had to get ahold of herself! If a six-year-old little boy got that vibe from her, she must be doing an atrocious job at keeping her treacherous libido at bay.

"My dad's the same way," Oscar answered, sliding in beneath the sheets. "When he looks at you, he keeps looking and looking and looking." He relaxed into his pillow. "Maybe it's your freckles."

She reared back. "My freckles?"

Oscar reached out and touched her cheek. "Yeah, the ones right here. My dad must be looking at you so hard because he's trying to count them."

"It could be that," she agreed, smoothing his chestnut-colored hair as the thought of Mitch obsessing over her sprinkling of freckles sent her pulse racing. She did her best to ignore the sensation and stared down at the boy. He had Mitch's eyes, Mitch's smile—when the man smiled—and the same stubborn set of his jaw. It was no wonder these two could butt heads. But there was a sweetness there beneath their furrowed brows. She was certain of that.

"Or maybe," Oscar mused, cutting into her thoughts. "You had a big booger hanging out of your nose, and he couldn't stop himself from looking."

"A booger!" she exclaimed, covering her face with her hand. "Do I have a booger in my nose now?" she asked, cautiously lowering her hand a few inches.

Oscar was in a great position to let her know. Lying on the bed, he had a front-row view of her nostrils. The boy propped onto an elbow, narrowed his gaze, then inspected her face, paying particular attention to her nose. "Nope, I don't see any boogers. But this one time at my old school, the music teacher had a big booger in her nose. It shook every time she breathed like this," Oscar added, wiggling as if he were having a fit beneath the covers.

She couldn't help but chuckle, then smoothed the blanket over Oscar's legs. "Speaking of schools, you've got a big day tomorrow. You get to see your new school and meet new friends."

Oscar's expression darkened, and he pulled the covers over his face. "I got in trouble for fighting at my last school," he admitted, his words muted by the blanket.

She pulled the covers down a couple of inches, revealing his eyes. "What happened? You don't seem like the kind of kid who goes around getting into fights."

Oscar twisted the edge of the blanket. "A bigger kid called me *orphan boy* after my mom died."

There was nothing worse than a bully!

"That wasn't nice of that boy at all. In fact, it was an awful and cruel thing to say. Fighting is never a good thing, Oscar. But in this case, I can understand why that made you so mad," she answered, then smoothed the boy's hair again.

"My mom used to do that to my hair, too," he said, closing his eyes. "She said it had a mind of its own."

"Do you want me to stop?" she asked, her heart breaking for the child.

He shook his head, and they remained quiet as she gently brushed his chestnut locks behind his ear. She thought he'd fallen asleep when he tilted his head and met her gaze.

"Do you think my fighting at school made my mom upset in heaven?" Oscar whispered.

How was she supposed to answer in a way that would give him some peace? She glanced around the room and spied a Polaroid photo on a bookshelf next to the bed. She hadn't remembered seeing it when they'd explored their rooms a few hours ago. Oscar must have had it in his backpack. She reverently picked it up, then showed it to the boy. "Your mom doesn't look like the kind of mom who could stay mad—especially at you. I don't think she'd want you to get into fights. I think she wants you to be happy."

"I miss her a lot," he replied, gazing at the image.

Charlotte swallowed past the lump in her throat, then rested her hand on the covers above his heart. "You'll always have her here."

Oscar rested his little hand on top of her hand. "Have you ever gotten so, so mad that you pushed somebody down?"

She blinked back tears, then exaggerated her features, wanting to shift the mood. She pressed her lips into a tight line, pretending to think hard, then gasped. She'd never gotten into a fight. That was more Harper's department. But she had acted out of anger.

"What is it, Charlotte? What did you do?" Oscar asked, wide-eyed.

She suppressed a laugh. "I once threw a salad at someone."

"You did!" he exclaimed, his eyes twinkling with delight.

Oh no! It was one thing to sympathize with the boy. But the last thing she needed was for him to go to school and start a food fight.

She schooled her features. "Yes, but I shouldn't have done that. The salad looked delicious. Those vegetables didn't deserve to get tossed to the ground."

Oscar giggled. "Who was it? Who did you throw the salad at?"

Her cheeks heated. "Let's just say we both know the person."

"My dad?" Oscar bellowed.

She raised an eyebrow. "Maybe."

"Wow! I've thrown stuff at him before. But never a salad." Oscar's look of wonder transformed into one of curiosity. "Do you have a mom and a dad, Charlotte?"

A heaviness set in as she pasted on a plastic smile. "I do."

"Do they live close by?"

Just breathe and answer the question.

"No, they don't," she answered, hating how it hurt to talk about her parents.

"Do you get to see them a lot?" Oscar continued.

"Not very often," she answered, omitting that it was her parents who showed no interest in spending time with her—the two people who should have loved her but had never made her a priority.

She smoothed Oscar's hair once again as the boy watched her with the same focused intensity as his father when a shiver passed through her. She knew without even looking that she and Oscar weren't alone.

Glancing over her shoulder, she found Mitch standing in the doorway. She held his gaze until Oscar sprang another question.

"Do you get to see them for Christmas and summer break?" he asked.

"No, they're super busy with their own lives," she answered, working to keep up a serene front.

"Time for bed," Mitch said as he entered the room.

She stood. "How long have you been there?"

"Long enough to hear about vegetables," he answered, but there wasn't a biting edge to his tone.

"Do I have to go to school, Dad? I could work for you in the food truck," the boy offered. "I'm good at doing dishes and making grilled cheeses."

"Sorry, kid. You have to go to school."

"Every day?" Oscar pressed.

"Yes, every day."

"Did you go to school every day?" Oscar continued.

Mitch looked away, then cleared his throat. "We're not talking about me. You, Oscar, get to go to a great school called Whitmore."

"And you'll get to meet Phoebe. Remember, I told you about her? You'll be in the same grade," she added, playing along. But she couldn't help but notice that the man had dodged the school attendance question.

Oscar yawned as the day caught up with him, struggling to

keep his eyes open. "Are you done getting the food truck ready?"

"Almost. Just a few more things to load up," Mitch answered.

"I have something for you," Oscar added, twisting his little body beneath the sheets.

Mitch shared a look with her. "For me?"

"For Louise," Oscar answered. He slipped his hand under his pillow, retrieved two Polaroids, then passed them to Mitch. "Can you tape them on the glass with the rest of the pictures?"

She leaned in to get a closer look at the images. One was the photo Oscar had taken today in the garage of her and Mitch with Louise in the background. She stifled a laugh. They appeared as shell-shocked as she'd felt. The other picture was an off-centered selfie Oscar had taken inside the food truck.

"There are no pictures of Charlotte and me in there. I thought you'd want to add us," Oscar explained.

Mitch stared at the images. The man looked lost—utterly lost. "I can do that," he rasped.

Emotion hung heavy in the air—and of course, it would. A cataclysmic shift had engulfed this man's life. It was his son's first night in his home, and he had a nanny sleeping under his roof.

"Let's get you tucked in," she said, taking the lead as she fixed his pillow, only to feel something sharp. "What else is under there?" she asked. He wasn't sleeping with a stick, was he?

Oscar removed the old spatula. "Can I keep it with me?"

"It's not very cuddly," Mitch replied.

Oscar rested the utensil on the pillow as if it were a teddy bear, then patted the worn wooden handle. "I don't mind. I like it. I saw it in a bunch of the pictures in the truck. You used to use it," Oscar finished, followed by another yawn.

"I did—a long time ago," Mitch answered as they watched Oscar drift off to sleep with the spatula resting beside him.

"Can you take me to school in Louise?" Oscar garbled, his sleepy words slurring together.

"Sure, kid. We can do that," Mitch replied as a dreamy smile stretched across Oscar's mouth. The boy's lips parted, and his breathing slowed.

"It looks like he's out for the count," she said, not sure what to do or what to say. It was the first time it had been the two of them since...since they'd made love in the tent.

"You're good with him," Mitch said, his voice barely a whisper.

"It's easy. He's a great kid," she answered. She turned off the lamp, allowing the nightlight near the doorway to provide a gentle pool of golden light. "We should let him sleep, Mitch. He's got a big day tomorrow."

"You could say the same for us," he added.

He was right. Their first day in the food truck was tomorrow. A ripple of anticipation passed through her. Or was it nerves? Or was it excitement?

It didn't matter what emotion was tangled in with her reaction. It was work, and she needed it. He followed her into the darkened hallway and closed Oscar's door. She twisted the hair tie around her wrist as an awkward stretch of silence engulfed the space. What should she do? Say good night and head to her room? Suggest they chat about tomorrow's schedule?

Luckily, Mitch broke the silence.

"I shouldn't have made that comment about you twisting yourself into a pretzel for me," he confessed in the haze of darkness.

"Is that an apology?" she asked, unable to hide the surprise in her voice.

He exhaled a heavy breath. "It's about as close to one as you're going to get with me."

Under the veil of darkness, she smiled. She couldn't help it. "If we're offering up quasi-apologies, I shouldn't have dropped the whole back-to-the-beginning food truck idea in front of your publisher without mentioning it to you first. It just came to me."

He took a step toward her, and her pulse kicked up. "You know it's a good idea. You were there, Charlotte. You saw how Gwen and Ines reacted."

"And don't forget Madelyn. She's the reason you're stuck with me." She was trying to play it off as a joke, but Mitch didn't react—didn't move a muscle.

"Madelyn wasn't wrong," he answered, the low rumble of his words scrambling her brain.

"About what?" she whispered.

"About you, Charlotte, you are perfect." His words floated around her like an embrace.

She closed her eyes, desperate to stop the onslaught of tingles and delicious shivers that took over whenever this man focused his complete attention on her. "I am?" she breathed.

Mitch's entire demeanor stiffened. The energy pulsed between them before the man stepped back, defusing the charge. "For the work. You're the perfect choice to act as my photographer and my assistant in the truck," he clarified, the rigid words coming out in an uneasy tumble.

"That's what I figured you meant," she lied, then nervously twisted the hair tie around her wrist. The poor thing was sure to snap if she kept this up. She worked to clear her thoughts. "Do you need me?" She shook her head. "Do you need anything more from me tonight?" she corrected. And *gah!* It was like she was trying to make this exchange as cringeworthy as possible.

He crossed his arms, then uncrossed them as if he didn't

know quite what to do with the appendages. "If you have a minute, I thought I'd show you around Louise."

"Sure," she exclaimed, infusing ten times too much enthusiasm into the syllable.

Putting aside that she sounded like she'd pounded a case of energy drinks, his suggestion was a good one. This was her job. And as much as she loved eating the food from food trucks, she'd never paid much attention to what was going on inside of them.

"Lead the way," she chirped like an eager cruise director. Luckily, Mitch seemed as off-balance as she felt and didn't comment on her psychotically chipper tone. She followed him down the grand staircase, then out into the night air as the whir of a plane passing overhead slipped into the low hum of nature's nighttime soundtrack.

Mitch looked up as the plane disappeared past the tree line. "Could that be your Mr. Cheesy Forever?" he asked, and she nearly fell over.

FOURTEEN
CHARLOTTE

CHARLOTTE GASPED. Thank God it was dark because the guy would have seen her eyes nearly pop out of their sockets.

"What did you say?" she stammered.

He did that uneasy arm thing where he crossed, then uncrossed his arms. "After all those margaritas, you told me planes make you think of Mr. Cheesy Forever. Why is that? Who is that?"

Curse those potent drinks!

"Well," she began, pacing the length of the truck. "It started when I was thirteen."

"Was it a crush on a movie star or something?" he asked.

She paused, unable to stop herself from smiling. "No, it was more of a crush on two perfect strangers."

He cocked his head to the side. "I don't get it?"

She had to go back to the beginning if she wanted him to understand. And strangely, she did. "My parents divorced when I was little. My dad moved to Kentucky. And for a while, when I was a teenager, I used to fly out there for the holidays. I spent a decent amount of time waiting in airports."

He nodded, giving her space to continue.

She twisted the hair elastic around her wrist. "When I was getting my bags off of the carousel at baggage claim, I saw this guy walk by holding a huge bouquet of red roses and a sign. It was like something out of a movie. I waited there, holding my duffel bag, and watched to see what would happen."

"You were alone?" Mitch pressed.

A sliver of sadness cut through her, but she ignored the pain. "My dad didn't want to pay to park the car at the airport. He said it was too expensive. So, I'd sit on the curb until he got there to pick me up—which wasn't bad unless it was raining or really cold. My visits were an inconvenience to him and his new family. But spending that time in the airport gave me time to observe people and get a look at their inner worlds."

Mitch exuded a heated intensity. She could sense it coming off of him in tumultuous waves.

"What happened at the baggage carousel with Mr. Cheesy Forever?" he asked, keeping his tone even, but there was a slight edge to his words.

She swallowed hard. Mr. Cheesy Forever was the epitome of a dreamy love-obsessed teenager. But she couldn't stop herself. The memory sent a bevy of flitting and flapping butterflies to her belly. "The guy had the biggest smile I'd ever seen stretched across his face. I'll never forget it. But he also looked super nervous. The sign he was holding had, *Will you marry me, Charlotte?* written in big, loopy letters. I watched as he scanned the area for *his* Charlotte. It turned out to be one of the ladies on my flight—another Charlotte. I couldn't stop staring at them. That's when I named the man Mr. Cheesy Forever. It popped into my head, and I couldn't help wondering if one day..." she trailed off.

"If one day, what?" Mitch pressed.

Why did he care?

Her silly heart skipped a beat until another reason for his questioning popped into her head, and the butterflies in her belly disappeared. There was a good chance he wanted to make sure that she wasn't a crackpot who believed boyfriends descended from the wondrous land of Cheesy to propose marriage in public. Still, in Mitch's defense, she had thrown a salad at him, spent an evening with him dressed as a mermaid while completely hammered, and had accused him of kidnapping. The guy had plenty of reasons to want to dig a little deeper into her *psyche* and make sure she wasn't a *psycho*.

She looked up and held his gaze. It was dark, but he wasn't projecting the hotheaded air he'd given off nonstop when she'd waitressed for him at the Crystal Cricket. Quite the opposite. He gave off the vibe of being genuinely interested.

Still, she had to proceed cautiously.

She thought back to the moment in the airport, standing there in the crowd. Bags in hand, most people had stopped to watch the man take a knee and propose to this lucky Charlotte. The scene was cheesy perfection. Pink-cheeked and breathless, the woman cried while saying yes. The couple kissed. People clapped. She'd played the reel of those few minutes in her head so many times it was almost as if she had been the one who'd said yes that day.

But she wasn't. And she wasn't about to disclose that. She'd already said too much.

"What couldn't you stop thinking about?" Mitch repeated, and despite the genuine ring to his tone, she waved him off.

"It's nothing. I was a young girl with silly thoughts." She gestured to the food truck, needing to switch gears. "Can I ask you a question about the signature sandwich?"

Now it was Mitch nodding as if he needed to get back on

track, too. "Yeah, but first things first," he said, opening the back doors. He climbed in, then offered her a hand to join him inside.

She stood in the snug space as Mitch hit a switch and the truck lit up like the Fourth of July.

She gasped. "Wow!"

"Is this your first time on the inside?" he teased, and she welcomed the shift away from her embarrassing explanation of Mr. Cheesy Forever.

She surveyed the space, then ran her fingertips along a large metal sink divided into three parts bolted to the wall beside a much smaller one. "It is. I'm a food truck virgin," she blathered, then cringed.

"A virgin, you say?" Mitch repeated.

Oh no! Oh no, no, no!

"A food truck virgin," she corrected. "Not a virgin-virgin, because...you know, the tent and, you were kind of there when..."

Kind of there?

Was her brain short-circuiting?

"Right! Got it," he blathered, his complexion turning a rosy hue. "I'm the opposite, I guess. Lots of experience—inside a food truck. Cooking inside a food truck. And of course, we've already verified that you're not a virgin-virgin since we..."

This had to stop, or she'd melt into a pool of auburn mortification.

"Yep, I think we've clarified the whole virgin food truck side of things," she replied with a wave of her hand as if she were making a royal decree.

"How about I give you the quick lay of the land since this is your first time...inside of a food truck?" he finished, blessedly getting through the question without dropping another virgin bomb.

"Yes, God, yes! Lay it all out," she exclaimed. And dammit!

She had to take it down a notch. She blew out a slow breath. "Please, continue."

He nodded, doing that weird head shake thing as if he were trying to clear the cobwebs from his brain. He gestured to the stainless-steel interior. "The truck's got a similar setup to the kitchen at the Crystal Cricket, only condensed. He pointed as he spoke. "We've got the fire extinguisher, ventilation over the cooktop, fridge, freezer. Paper supplies are above the window in the bins. The water tanks and the generator are housed below."

She glanced around. "Why are there four sinks?"

Good! She'd asked a question that didn't have the word *virgin* in it.

"The divided one is to wash, rinse, and sanitize. The smaller one with the mirror above it is for us to wash our hands." He tapped a strip above the cooktop. "Order tickets go here."

"Got it," she answered. This was good non-sexual information. She took in the space, then spied a small bin with office supplies and a roll of tape. It reminded her of another totally non-sexual thing they needed to do. "Here," she said, handing him the tape.

He frowned. "Why are you giving me this?"

She scanned the walls, covered in pictures. "For the Polaroids Oscar gave you. You said—"

"Yeah, right," he interrupted, pulling the images from his pocket before gazing at the flurry of photos plastered to the walls as the color drained from his face.

Crap!

"What about here?" she offered, finding a bit of unused real estate near the order window.

Mitch taped the Polaroids to the glass, staring hard at them. It was like he was doing everything in his power not to see the other photos, the old photos of his past life. He stepped back and took in the new additions—the off-center shot of Oscar and the one of her and Mitch with Louise in the background.

"All good," he said in a voice that sounded quite the opposite.

Her gaze flicked from the new Polaroids to an older picture —a picture that, like the others, contained three people. She focused on Holly and the other man. At first glance, this picture looked like the rest. But her eye caught the slight deviation. In this shot, while Mitch was smiling for the camera, the two others in the photo were looking at each other.

And it came together.

"Holly was your girlfriend, and this guy was your best friend. You started Say Cheese, Louise together. Am I right?" she asked.

He turned away from her, clutched the lip of the counter, and dropped his head. "I should have taken the pictures down a long time ago."

"But you didn't," she countered gently.

He straightened, staring ahead at a batch of images. He plucked one from the wall. "I met Holly and Seth when I was seventeen. We started Say Cheese, Louise when we were barely twenty-one. I thought I had everything back then—the girl of my dreams and the best friend who was more like a brother." He set the picture on the counter. "I guess I wouldn't really know. I was an only child. My parents died when I was young. My grandpa Bruce had custody of me, but I pretty much raised myself. What I had with Seth and Holly had felt solid—like what a family ought to be. We were content to happily bust our asses, barely making enough cash to survive when a producer contacted us. They wanted to film our journey starting Say Cheese, Louise. We were so excited. It was a huge opportunity, but it changed everything."

"It made you rich," she offered. "That can't be so bad."

He studied the picture on the counter. "It opened more doors than we could imagine. But after shooting the first season, the show shifted its emphasis from the three of us to me. I didn't think it would be a problem. We were a team. My success was their success. But I was blind to what was happening right in front of me."

An affair. And then, a baby.

"You thought that Oscar was Seth's son," she supplied.

He nodded, looking away.

"How did you find out he was yours?" she asked, her heart breaking for the man.

"Oscar had a bunch of ear infections when he was little. He needed to have tubes put in. Holly and Seth learned that Oscar's blood type was A positive when they did the initial blood work before the procedure. Holly and Seth were both type O."

She took a step toward him. "And you're A positive?"

"Yeah."

"What happened after that?" she continued.

"Seth took off. Last I heard, he was cooking at some resort in Florida. And I offered to help Holly."

"That's why you came back to Colorado," she said, connecting the dots.

"We always—I mean, she liked the mountains. So, I found them a place outside Telluride. And then..." he didn't go on, but she knew this part. Holly passed away, and the responsibility to raise Oscar fell to him.

No wonder the guy blew into Denver three years ago as a raging hothead.

He barked a mirthless laugh.

"What is it, Mitch?" she asked.

"The funny thing is, Ines brought in Madelyn *not* because Holly had died, but because we wanted to give joint custody a try. You know, like having him here on weekends or during the summers. I thought I'd get to ease into being the kid's dad. But here we are."

"Here we are," she repeated, watching him closely.

"That's probably more info than you wanted to hear after only two days on the job as my kid's nanny," he said, his voice a gruff rasp.

"Two days? Is that all it's been?" she exclaimed. But the man wasn't wrong.

"Feels like two weeks," he offered.

"Or two decades," she teased, catching his eye when her stomach growled. She pressed her hands to her belly as another wave of mortification hit.

"I know that sound," he said as the pain in his expression faded and was replaced with a look of purpose. "I'm going to make you the Signature Louise, so you can try it for yourself," he said. He went to the smaller sink, washed his hands, then switched on the cooktop. He moved with a purposeful precision that, to be completely honest, was damned sexy. Opening the refrigerator, he removed a dish of butter and two large plastic bottles—one with *apple butter* written on the side and the other with *Dijon mustard.*

She sucked in a tight breath. "Would you mind making my sandwich without—"

"Without the apple butter and the mustard?" he interrupted, holding up the containers, and she would have sworn she'd heard the hint of amusement in his tone.

She grimaced. "Apple butter and Dijon mustard on a grilled cheese sandwich sounds..." How could she put this delicately? "It sounds..."

"Awful?" he supplied. And there it was—that cocky, slightly hotheaded lilt to his voice that made her head spin.

"Well, yeah," she agreed, watching as the man assembled the tools and ingredients to make her meal.

"To tell you the truth, the first time I made it, I wasn't so sure about it either," he said, falling into a rhythm. All she could do was stand there and watch. In seconds, he had two buttered pieces of bread, a thick slab of cheddar cheese, a scribble of mustard, and a healthy smear of apple butter pressed between the thick sourdough slices. With a spatula, he slid the sandwich onto the grill. It sputtered and popped as hot met cold, and the comforting smell of buttery toasted bread engulfed the space.

She closed her eyes and sighed, inhaling the delectable scent. "That's incredible!"

"And you haven't even taken a bite," he answered with enough snark in his tone to send her pulse racing.

She opened her eyes and found Mitch staring at her.

She raised an eyebrow. "Shouldn't you pay attention to my sandwich? Won't it burn if you lose focus?"

He kept his gaze trained on her. "I could do this in my sleep," he answered, taking the spatula and flipping the grilled cheese over without even looking. The cool butter again crackled against the scorching surface—or maybe that was the air between them.

"Showoff," she teased, fighting the urge to trace the hard angles of his chiseled jawline with her tongue.

"Better than a hothead?" he tossed back with a hint of a smirk. The man was in his element. Cooking in the food truck revealed a side of him she'd never seen.

She leaned against the counter, then spied the order pad. Picking it up, she plucked a pen from the supply bin. "One Signature Louise, Chef," she called, scribbling the order, then slipped the ticket onto the strip.

She might as well get in some practice.

"Order up. One Signature Louise with extra apple butter

and extra Dijon," he called, flipping the entire sandwich onto a cutting board with one flick of his wrist.

Her jaw dropped. "Extra?"

He shrugged off her outrage, an arrogant little movement that had her biting her lip.

This food truck chef was crazy sexy!

Whipping out a knife, he sliced the ooey-gooey cheesy delight into two triangles before sliding the halves onto a paper plate. "I must have read the ticket wrong," he answered. He wasn't smiling. At first glance, he looked like his usual hotheaded self. But his eyes gave him away. They positively glittered with confidence.

And, hello, Tingle Town!

He turned off the stovetop, then handed her the plate. "Take one bite. After that, you won't be able to stop yourself."

Skeptically, she accepted the sandwich. "I don't know about this, Mitch. I'm a pretty cut and dry grilled cheese-only type of girl."

"Are you sure about that?" he countered, his voice kindling the heat between her thighs.

It's a sandwich. Get ahold of yourself, woman!

"Don't think of the components individually. The savory cheese and the sweetness of the apple butter complement each other. The Dijon adds the kick they need to come together," he explained, which made sense, but she still wasn't sure.

"If I hate it, you can't go all hothead on me," she warned, but he wasn't bothered by her ultimatum. In fact, those blue eyes of his darkened with the challenge.

He came closer. "How about this? If you hate it, you can pretend it's a salad and hurl it at me."

This man! Who did he think he was dealing with?

The anticipation sent a shiver down her spine. "Deal," she agreed, then took a bite, and OH MY GOD! She closed her eyes for a few seconds, allowing her tastebuds to take control. The hothead was right. It was the perfect blend of savory, sweet, and tangy. She moaned, not giving a damn who heard her. "It's like a food nirvana," she crooned between bites and sighs. She finished the first triangle like a feasting lioness, then licked the cheese off the tip of her thumb, humming her pleasure.

"Don't do that, Charlotte," Mitch bit out through gritted teeth.

In her food orgy haze, she'd forgotten the man was watching her.

What had gotten into him? Wasn't he the one who was sure that she'd love it?

She froze, her thumb against her lips. "Do what?"

"Make those sounds and lick your fingers," he answered. His rigid body looked as if he was on the brink of coming apart at the seams.

A dizzying, palpable current passed between them that had nothing to do with the ambrosia of a sandwich she'd hoovered in front of the man.

"Why not?" she breathed, her nipples hardening into taut pearls.

A muscle ticked in his jaw. He reminded her of the Big Bad Wolf with his blazing eyes before the vicious creature tried to gobble up Little Red Riding Hood. Except, unlike that red-cloaked gal who hightailed it out of there, this redhead trembled beneath the Big Bad Wolf's devilishly attentive gaze.

He took her plate and set it on the counter. "Because it makes me want to do things to you that I know I shouldn't."

She understood the impulse.

She reached behind and held on to the edge of the small sink, needing to anchor herself, as a titillating thrill rippled through her body. If she was in her right mind, she'd thank him for the sandwich, politely excuse herself, then return—*alone*—to her room.

"What *things* do you want to do to me?" she asked instead, diving headfirst into the pool of desire welling between them.

"I want to taste you again," he answered, caging her in as he had against the RV. So male and so utterly masculine, the possessive posture had her spellbound. But there was also something innately protective about it that heightened her arousal.

"You do?" she breathed, grateful she was still capable of forming words.

He leaned in, then gently outlined the key at the hollow of her neck with the pad of his thumb. "Why does it feel like you've been with me for longer than two days?" he asked as his warm breath caressed her lips.

This she understood as well.

"Because I have been with you. I worked for you for over two years, but you never noticed me," she rasped, tightening her grip on the sink while the hold on her resolve loosened.

"I noticed you, Charlotte," he answered in a low rumble.

"Yeah, when I threw vegetables at you," she whispered, her chest rising and falling with every heated punctuated breath.

"No, it was long before that day," he growled, releasing the key. Slowly, he traced the curve of her cheek before slipping his hand into her hair. He twisted the strands between his fingers. "Somedays, you were the only thing I could see. You and that long red ponytail, surrounded by that intoxicating strawberry sunshine. It nearly drove me insane. All I could do was think about twisting your fiery auburn hair in my hand."

The tantalizing pleasure of being seen by this man scorched her veins. It was almost too much to take. Heart hammering, if he didn't kiss her, she might disintegrate into a million tiny pieces.

His lips skimmed across hers, and she trembled, consumed with raw need.

"What are you waiting for?" she tempted. "You're right here. Take a little bite."

He moved in closer, pinning her between his muscled body and the sink. His rock-hard cock pressed against her, leaving no questions as to his intentions. He wanted her—badly. A delicious thrum of power pulsed through her. She'd never felt so utterly desired. And he wanted *her*—not the version of her who did whatever it took to connect with a guy.

She released a ragged breath when it happened. Mitch's lips met hers as a smile bloomed across his lips.

"I don't want *one little bite*," he replied, his voice intensifying the desire within her.

"What do you want?" she whispered. At this point, she'd trade her beloved Nikon for one kiss from this smiling hothead.

"I want to lick and suck and devour every part of you. I want your taste on my tongue."

Wow!

"That's all?" she teased, and his dirty grin curled into a lusty smirk.

He liked her feisty.

"No, that's not all. I'm going to make you come so hard you won't even remember what goes on the Signature Louise when I'm done with you."

That was hot. But two could play at this.

"That's a tall order, Chef. Especially since it's my new favorite."

"It'll be your second favorite in about thirty seconds," he answered, then ended the excruciating torment as he claimed her mouth in a scorching kiss.

Wrapping her arms around his neck, she melted into the man. His kiss consumed her. Mitch Elliott demanded everything. And she was right there, ready to comply, when that tiny voice in the back of her mind held up a megaphone.

You are sucking face with your boss!

Technically, yes, she was. But this was another exception—like the tent. The emotional onslaught of the day was to blame. This was simply a way to work out that rush of energy.

"After whatever happens in here, we'll keep it professional," she panted as Mitch licked a hot trail from the corner of her mouth to her earlobe. "Like a special menu—one night only event."

"Right, one night only," he agreed, returning to her mouth to run his tongue along her bottom lip. He pulled back. "Do you know what that means?"

Wide-eyed, her body ached for his touch. "What?"

His Big Bad Wolf eyes raked over her. "That means it has to be really good—a blow-your-mind experience."

Double wow!

"I'm good with that," she breathed.

The beast glittered in his gaze as he sank to his knees. Starting at her ankles, he slid his fingertips past her calves, past her thighs, before trailing his hands beneath her skirt. He curved his index fingers around the waistband of her panties and slipped them off in one deliriously sexy whoosh. A feverish shiver vibrated through her, sweet anticipation building, as he lifted her leg and hooked it over his shoulder.

"First course," he said, licking his lips before dipping his head to work her most sensitive place with his magical mouth.

She gasped, clutching the lip of the sink. She was close to ripping the damned thing clean off the wall. But her sexed-up brain didn't care. Mitch gripped her ass, setting a slow, teasing pace. She'd never been one to take, never focused on what got her hot. In fact, to date, her best orgasms had come when she was alone with her vibrator.

Well, until her tent rendezvous with Mitch!

Being with this man was like nothing she'd experienced.

Mitch's lusty growls and dirty moans confirmed he was as into it as she was. He wasn't kidding when he said he wanted to devour her. Just like in the kitchen, when the man put his mind to something, he didn't mess around. With each lick, he was winding her up, revolution by revolution, and had her hovering on the precipice between this world and the next. She rocked her hips, wanting more, so close to meeting her release.

"Patience," he commanded, the hot word tormenting her tight bundle of nerves. "This is to whet your appetite."

This man might kill her with the dirty chef talk!

She held on to the cool metal sink with one hand while tangling her fingers into his hair with the other. Giving in to the hot bliss happening between her thighs, she surrendered to Mitch Elliott's will and his masterful tongue.

Body tingling, her mind whirling, she was right there, ready to let go. But she didn't want to take the plunge without him.

"I think we should skip to dessert," she said between gasps, then glanced at her wrist as a naughty idea took hold. She slipped off the hair tie, then pressed her hand beneath Mitch's chin, guiding him back to his feet. She wasn't this person—this sexually confident siren. But here with him, not worrying about doing the wrong thing or saying something silly, she was free. It wasn't like he wanted to become her Mr. Cheesy Forever. He was her boss. And this one-night-only, special menu sexual escapade would be a one and done. Okay, two and done, counting the tent. But that was all it could be.

With a newfound sense of herself, she turned around and pulled her locks into a high ponytail. "Is this what you used to imagine when you'd think about me?" she purred, swishing her hair as she gripped the sides of the sink. Hinging forward, she brushed her ass against his hard length through his pants when a pang of anxiety rippled in her chest.

Was that too much? Was she overplaying her hand?

She caught sight of him in the little mirror above the sink. The breath caught in her throat when Mitch caught her watching him, and his lips twisted into the dirtiest of grins. If she were wearing panties, the intensity of this man's deliciously menacing demeanor would have absolutely obliterated them. She closed her eyes, listening as he unzipped his pants, her body trembling, oh so eager to feel him thick and rock-hard between her legs.

"There she is," he said. "There's that fiery redhead." He twisted her hair around his fist, then positioned himself at her entrance. Instinctively, she arched her back as he pushed past her delicate folds, sliding his hard length inside her. Everything disappeared, and there they were, caught in a web of irrefutable arousal. She put it to memory, enthralled with the sound of his breath, the heat of his body, the commanding grip at her hip and in her hair. She was at his mercy, but the look in his eyes said that she was the one calling the shots.

"Charlotte," he whispered like a prayer, turning her head, then pressing a whisper-soft kiss to the corner of her mouth.

One would assume because the man spent a decent part of his life behaving like a raging hothead, that he'd make love with that same undercurrent of anger. But again, like in the tent, his touch was firm but tender. He rolled his hips, and the friction between them sizzled and popped. Thrust after beautiful thrust, she submitted to this man while demanding his surrender in return. The ebb and flow of who she was and who she thought she could be converged as everything in her life condensed into this one moment with this enigma of a man.

Inside the truck, surrounded by reminders of his past, he fixated on her. He stared into the mirror, seemingly mesmerized by her every moan and each heated gasp. And she couldn't look away either. The pleasure consumed her. No one had ever looked at her like this—like she made up the totality of their universe. Watching this hulk of a man lose control as he made love to her like he was built for nothing else was not simply intoxicating. It was all-encompassing. It penetrated her heart and her soul.

She straightened, reaching her arms up to touch his face, his beautiful face, as he released her ponytail and slipped his hand between her thighs. Massaging her tight bundle of nerves, he set a decadent pace with his cock, sliding in and out in measured strokes. But his touch was the last straw, and she couldn't hold back. Crying out, the rush of his release filled her as they toppled into orgasmic bliss. She held on to him as the erotic dance played out and waves of pleasure crashed over them. And she couldn't help but stare at him, memorizing his reflection in the mirror as he held her close. Pumping and grinding, they writhed as one body. Were they floating, or were they drowning? She didn't know, and she didn't care. But greedily, she took it all as he ground out every drop of pleasure. Trembling from the exertion, she watched in awe as he smiled at her with a sated, boyish grin that turned her addled mind to absolute mush —and her heart into...

Stop! She couldn't go there!

In the dark of the tent, while she'd sensed his smile, she hadn't seen it. Here, she drank it in, photographing the moment in her mind.

He pressed a kiss below her earlobe. "What do you think? Better than the Signature Louise?" he purred. But his mischievous words couldn't hide the raw honesty in his voice.

"What's the Signature Louise?" she cooed, grinning like a fool.

Could this have been more than sex to him?

Stop!

Thoughts like that would do her no good.

Mitch Elliott was no Mr. Cheesy Forever.

And then, right then and there, she understood that two things were inextricably true.

Number one: Everything in her life paled in comparison to the tingling butterflies she got when she made this man smile.

And number two...

She closed her eyes. Despite the warmth of his body, a chill passed through her as the second realization hit like a rush of arctic air.

She understood what had awoken the angry hothead inside the man. He'd been betrayed in the worst way possible by the two people he'd loved the most. He'd thought they were a family —an unbreakable trio. But Holly and Seth had decimated his ability to trust. It was no wonder the man had locks everywhere, no wonder he hid behind an angry mask. And no wonder he thought the worst of people. It made it easier to endure when they disappointed him—when they left him with nothing.

She caught a glimpse of the Polaroids Oscar had given them taped to the window, and that chill prickling down her spine turned icy cold. What would happen if she got accepted to the Royal College of Art's workshop? It was only for a handful of weeks, but how would he take it?

Should she take Penny's advice and mention the possibility of leaving? Her mind spun until she looked up and caught Mitch watching her. With that sweet, adoring grin stretched across his lips and such ardent tenderness in his eyes, the man took her breath away. She wasn't stupid. She knew very well that he was her boss and the last thing she should be doing is sleeping with him—again! Whatever was going on between them might not be anything more than a tryst. But at this moment, under the intensity of Mitch's complete focus, she couldn't help but wonder if this was how the other Charlotte, the airport Charlotte, felt all the time.

Adored.

Worshipped.

Loved.

She reached up and touched Mitch's cheek, saying nothing as she basked in the glow of his heartbreakingly beautiful smile. She wasn't about to ruin this. There was plenty of time to figure out what to do.

But now, with the scent of sex in the air, the only thing she wanted to do was him.

FIFTEEN

MITCH

"SAY, NEW SCHOOL CHEESE," Charlotte called brightly.

"New school cheese!" Oscar chimed.

Mitch shifted his stance. He wasn't sure what to do with himself while Charlotte snapped pictures of Oscar in front of the sign for Whitmore Country Day Elementary. They'd left early for Oscar's first day, which had been a good call. It had given them some time without groups of children and families descending on the building.

The calm before the storm.

But he couldn't stop the storm of emotions that had him reeling.

"How about one with you and Oscar?" Charlotte suggested. He couldn't miss the hesitant lilt to her words. He didn't blame her. After last night, he barely knew which way was up.

He'd done it again. He'd let his guard down.

Something insane happened to him when Charlotte Ames drank him in with her emerald eyes. The hole in his heart Seth and Holly had left in the aftermath of their betrayal didn't ache when he held her in his arms and disappeared into her strawberry sunshine. Still, he had to keep it together. It was Oscar's first day of school and the first day of the Say Cheese, Louise reboot. He didn't have time to obsess over the woman like an infatuated teenager.

His reputation was on the line. This book deal was his last chance to revive his career.

Why couldn't he get that through his thick head?

That wasn't too hard of a question to answer.

Charlotte's ponytail didn't help him keep his eye on the prize.

With one swish of her auburn locks, he could feel her hair in his fist, sliding between his fingers as his cock worked her sweet center in smooth, rhythmic strokes. He inhaled a tight breath, envisioning her lips parting as she released soft gasps and those dirty little moans that drove him wild. He'd been with plenty of women. But he'd be lying if he said the sex with Charlotte was anything less than the best he'd ever had.

But it was more than sex—more than a physical act. With Charlotte, as he pistoned his hips and let go in a frenzy of pure ecstasy, he'd been reborn, revitalized, made new. Thrilling and terrifying, the only thing he could do was hold on to her.

When they returned to the house, he'd wanted to take her back to his bedroom for round two. Every cell in his body wanted more of her. But once they'd made it upstairs, the sight of Oscar's bedroom door hit them like a blast of icy water.

That space where it was just the two of them vanished as the weight of cold hard reality set in.

He was the boss. She was the nanny. And what the hell would they do if Oscar got up in the middle of the night and found them together? He didn't have to say it. Not a word passed between them in the darkened hallway, but an understanding hung heavy in the air. Silently, she slipped into her room. He didn't even say good night as he'd watched the door close behind her.

The click of the lock said it all. He had to get himself under control when it came to her.

Too bad it was easier said than done.

He'd spent the next hour in the shower, shivering under the cold spray. It was the only thing he could think of to do to get his mind off the curve of her hips or the way she arched into him, taking every inch of his hard length. He'd barely slept. Every time he closed his eyes, he saw her.

"Dad?" Oscar called, pulling him out of his sleep-deprived, Charlotte-induced haze.

"Right! Let's get that picture," he stammered, then joined the boy. Resting his hand on Oscar's shoulder, he peered past Charlotte and glimpsed at the food truck as another barrage of emotions hit.

Say Cheese, Louise was back in his life.

It was just a food truck.

That's what he'd been telling himself this morning. But as much as he tried, he didn't believe it.

Not only was the truck the most poignant reminder of his past. It was now the place—another place—where he'd made love to Charlotte. In those fleeting moments, he'd allowed his walls to come down. And Christ, it had felt good—a welcome reprieve from dwelling in the wasteland of raging anger and prickling resentment.

Still, he hadn't meant for it to happen. But with her, he broke his rules.

For the last seven years, he'd purposely lived a life where he didn't delve into the nitty-gritty of other people's business. The gruff, hothead mask he'd donned had worked at keeping everyone at arm's length until her.

Until Charlotte.

When he glimpsed at the plane, he couldn't help but recall

the wistful expression on her face as she'd stared up at the starry night sky and spoke of Mr. Cheesy Forever.

That's what she wanted—the dreamy, happily ever after Prince Charming.

Maybe he'd fit the bill once. But that wasn't him—not anymore.

He shouldn't have asked her about it. And he sure as hell shouldn't have talked about Holly and Seth's betrayal. But it was so easy with her—so easy to forget the hardened, bitter man he'd become.

"Mitch, will you look at me?" she asked, peeking over the camera.

"What?" he sputtered.

He had to get ahold of himself!

"Could you smile for the picture?" she coaxed.

He frowned. "You want me to smile?"

She chuckled, and it was the sweetest sound. "Yes."

His lips tingled as his body remembered the sensation of the corners of his mouth curving into a euphoric grin as he kissed her. Everything clicked. The noise in his head quieted, and the rage in his veins cooled. It was the first time he'd felt the ease of pure joy in ages.

The ease of pure joy?

What was he? A badass chef or a pansy poet?

He had to cut this out! She worked for him. It was as simple as that.

"Yeah, Dad! If you want to smile, all you have to do is think of something that makes you super-duper happy. And then this will happen to your mouth. Watch," his son instructed. The left side of Oscar's mouth curled, then the right. "See, I'm thinking about grilled cheese sandwiches—like the one you made for my lunch," he finished, grinning ear to ear. He'd never seen his son smile as much as he had since...again, since Charlotte.

"That's a good tip," he rasped, his throat tightening.

What was going on? Was it the stress? Was it the myriad of changes in his life? Why did it feel like he had the emotional stability of a roller coaster?

It was as if he were unraveling.

Staring down at his son, something he should have taken to heart years earlier solidified inside of him. And while he appreciated Oscar's suggestion, he didn't have to think of food to smile.

He had a remarkably amazing son.

At six years old, the kid was rolling with the punches better than he ever could. The tension melted from his body. It was the first time he'd peered down at the boy without a flash of Seth and Holly's betrayal slicing through him.

In the morning light, with the sounds of the sparrows and the click of Charlotte's camera capturing the scene, he saw his son. He saw a child who liked grilled cheese sandwiches, chocolate bars, and sleeping in tents. A curious, precocious boy who dabbled in photography and zipped around with a clunky Polaroid camera hanging from his neck. He gave the boy's shoulder a squeeze, then caught Charlotte observing them. Her expression was the very definition of compassionate tenderness.

She was the catalyst—the buffer that smoothed out not only his rough edges but Oscar's as well. She was the bridge that had brought them together.

"That's it! That's the shot," she said softly, raising the camera. The shutter opened and closed with a mesmerizing series of clicks. He did his best to hide the torrent of emotions raging inside of him when a man's voice caught his attention.

"What do you know! Our chef has another expression besides a perma-frown."

Mitch shook his head. He recognized the voice.

"Welcome to the world of private elementary education,"

Rowen Gale continued, striding up the sidewalk with his fiancée and his niece.

Mitch nodded to the man, then took in the campus. A line of luxury cars had collected in the school's drop-off lane as the rise and fall of children's voices peppered the air. Charlotte and Penny embraced as Oscar scooted in closer to him and stared up at Rowen.

"You must be Oscar. I'm Rowen Gale," the man said, then gestured to his fiancée. "That's Penny, and the little girl with us is my niece, Phoebe. She'll be at Whitmore with you."

Oscar gave the man a weak nod.

"It's so nice to meet you, Oscar," Penny chimed, patting the boy's shoulder. "You're going to love this school."

Oscar nodded again, but he didn't look so sure. While the boy had hooted and whooped with joy as they drove to school in Say Cheese, Louise, his demeanor had shifted with the arrival of Rowen and company. And he didn't have to be crowned parent of the year to notice that the kid was nervous. And he knew what was happening. It was starting to sink in that this was his new life, here in a new town at a new school, surrounded by new people.

He focused on his kid. "You've got this, Oscar."

Oscar swallowed hard, then looked to Charlotte.

"Your dad's right. You're going to rock first grade in Denver," she said, tossing the boy a sly wink.

"Phoebe, why don't you say hello to Oscar?" Penny suggested, smoothing a lock of Phoebe's dark hair. "It's his first day at Whitmore. Mitch, do you know which class Oscar is in?"

He pulled one of the sheets of paper Madelyn had given him from his pocket and unfolded it. "It says he's in Mrs. Bergen's first-grade class. Room 104."

"Look at that, Phoebe!" Rowen exclaimed. "Oscar will be in your class."

The little girl didn't say a thing. She looked from Oscar to the food truck, then pouted. "I saw you get out of that orange truck," Phoebe said to his son as she gestured to Say Cheese, Louise.

"It's my dad's food truck," Oscar answered, lifting his little chin as the boy's hesitation melted away. He had undoubtedly inherited the Elliott gene for putting up a brave front.

Phoebe sized up her uncle with a surly expression. "Why don't we have a food truck, Uncle Row?"

Rowen shifted his stance. "Because I'm a video game developer. We have a Lamborghini, a Land Rover, and a couple of Porsches. And don't forget, we've got a super-yacht in the Caribbean and a plane," the man answered, clearly playing defense with the pint-sized powerhouse.

Phoebe would make one hell of a chef.

He couldn't help but enjoy watching the tech billionaire get his ass handed to him by a six-year-old.

"But we don't have a giant awesome orange food truck," Phoebe countered.

"No, we do not," Rowen sputtered as Penny and Charlotte bit back grins.

The little girl turned to Oscar, and her expression brightened. "I don't know any kids that get dropped off in a food truck. You're going to be the coolest kid at Whitmore. Want to sit by me at lunch?" The girl glanced up at Penny and Rowen, then leaned in toward Oscar and waved him in conspiratorially. "I have a boatload of cookies in my lunchbox I can share with you. I added them when my uncle and Penny were busy getting a book off a high shelf this morning."

Penny and Rowen turned matching shades of scarlet.

"Getting a book off a high shelf?" Charlotte asked with a crease to her brow.

"It was way up there and took quite a bit of effort and time to get it," Penny answered, sharing a panicky look with Rowen. It was the kind of exchange that spoke volumes. God only knew what Rowen and Penny were doing! But he was damned sure it didn't have anything to do with procuring reading material.

Still, while this was the sort of relationship bullshit that used to make him cringe, it didn't grate on him. In fact, he found it entertaining. He glanced at Charlotte. Her gaze flitted over the group before she caught his eye and nodded. A barely perceptible move, but he got the message. Oscar was going to be okay. His son had made a friend.

"I can trade you for the cookies. My dad packed a special grilled cheese sandwich for me. He's a chef. I'll give you half," Oscar announced, holding up his lunchbox like a prizefighter.

"Wow! You have a food truck, and your dad is a chef? That's..." Phoebe tapped her foot twice.

And, oh shit! He forgot that these people were into secret code foot tapping.

Oscar frowned. "Did you tap *hot-head* or something else?"

Phoebe gasped, wide-eyed. "I tapped *awe-some*. How do you know about the taps?"

"Charlotte showed me," Oscar replied with a nonchalant shrug.

"When I get mad, two taps mean butt—" Phoebe began, but Rowen cleared his throat, cutting off the child's explanation.

"We don't say that word out loud, Phoebe," the man chided as his niece rolled her eyes.

And again, watching this sassy little thing take Rowen to task proved to be excellent entertainment.

"In my house, the two taps stand for *hot-head*." Oscar explained, then tapped his foot twice. "That's what Charlotte calls my dad. But he's not really a hothead anymore. I can't even remember the last time he got all red-faced and grouchy," the boy finished, scratching his chin.

The adults chuckled, and Charlotte caught his eye. The connection was there. It was like they were in this child-care quagmire together.

"I see feet tapping. What's the big secret?" came a woman's teasing voice.

"Hi, Harper! Hi, Libby!" Phoebe cried as two women joined them.

He recognized them from when he, along with Landon Paige and Erasmus Cress, had helped Rowen with his insane plan to win back Penny. Rowen had mentioned that the four-some had been friends since kindergarten and basically finished each other's sentences. But something was clearly up with the new arrivals. For starters, donning a wide-brimmed hat, sunglasses, and a scarf that nearly covered her entire face, Harper looked like a starlet going for incognito. Then there was the petite raven-haired Libby. Every other time he'd seen her, she'd seemed pretty mellow. But today, she twitched as if she'd inhaled a few gallons of triple espresso for breakfast.

"What are you two doing here?" Charlotte asked, glancing between the newcomers. "And why are you dressed like you're going undercover, H?"

Harper peeked out from beneath the dark glasses. "First of all, it's nice to see that you aren't on the back of a milk carton, Char."

Charlotte tossed him a quick look, then cringed.

After the phone call on the side of the road with Penny and Rowen, he should have guessed that Charlotte's friends would know about the kidnapping confusion.

"Seriously, Harper, what's going on? You look like the definition of stranger danger," Penny pressed.

"The disguise is necessary. A few of my piano students go to school here. And the last thing I need is to be recognized by one of their parents and get pulled into a convo about

Chop Sticks or little Bobby's prospects for getting into Juilliard."

"And are you okay, Libby?" Charlotte asked, concern marring her features.

"I'm peachy," the woman shrieked, conveying the polar opposite of peachy.

"Are you sure?" Charlotte pressed.

He was wondering the same thing. The chick looked ready to snap. And he knew a thing, or twenty, about that.

"Libbs, honey, Charlotte is right. You don't look as zen-tastic as you usually do," Penny added.

Harper patted the tiny, vibrating woman's shoulder. "Our yoga teacher extraordinaire is having a day."

This lady taught yoga?

Libby's forced grin stretched from deranged prom queen to possible serial killer. "My chi is a little out of whack thanks to a beefcake in the private gym next to the yoga studio. The guy kept dropping zillion-pound barbels while I taught a restorative yoga class. And news flash, there's nothing restorative about incessant banging and clanging," the raven-haired woman answered through gritted teeth.

"Sorry, Libbs, that sounds awful. I'm glad to see you, but what brings you here today?" Charlotte asked.

"I forgot to mention that. I invited them," Penny answered. "I thought we could take you out for coffee after we dropped off the kids."

"Who are those ladies?" Oscar asked, coming to Charlotte's side.

"Where are my manners?" she exclaimed. "These are my friends, Harper Presley and Libby Lamb. Girls, these are my guys, Mitch and Oscar."

My guys.

He'd heard her say it as clear as day. And the part of him,

that sappy part he'd locked away years ago, liked it more than he should.

"*Your guys*," Harper echoed with a curious edge. The dark shades hid her eyes, but he could feel the intensity of the woman's gaze fall on him.

Charlotte blushed. "I mean, this is Mitch Elliott, my boss, and Oscar, the awesome kid I get to nanny for," she corrected, then tousled the boy's hair as the key around her neck dangled from side to side.

"I like your key necklace, Charlotte," Phoebe remarked, pointing to the glinting bit of gold. "Does it open a door or a magic box?"

Charlotte glanced at him. "I'm not sure what it opens."

Oscar's face lit up. "I bet it unlocks my dad's heart."

He could feel the weight of Oscar's observation.

"Your dad has a lock on his heart, Oscar? Is it on the inside or the outside?" Phoebe asked, utterly fascinated as the child checked his body for metal objects.

"No, my dad has an old lock in the shape of a heart," Oscar explained. "Remember, Dad?" the boy continued. "You had it in your pocket when you picked me up."

"Did it work? Did the key open the heart?" Phoebe pressed.

Mitch shifted his stance as Rowen, Penny, Libby, and Harper watched the exchange wide-eyed.

"We haven't tried the key in the lock," Charlotte answered, nervously tucking the key beneath her blouse.

"That's what I'd do. I'd try it in every lock I could find," the little girl quipped, then turned to Oscar. "Do you want to play the foot tap game until we have to line up? You tap a word, and I'll guess. Then I'll tap a word, and you guess," Phoebe offered, blessedly tiring of the key and lock talk. But he could sense Penny, Rowen, Harper, and even the frazzled Libby hadn't moved on so quickly.

"Okay!" Oscar answered as the kids moved a few feet away from the adults, tapping their feet, whispering, and giggling.

"You have a heart-shaped lock, and Charlotte has the key?" Rowen asked with a curious twist to his lips.

Jesus! It did sound a bit bizarro fairy tale-ish.

"It was something Madelyn cooked up. It's nothing," he answered.

But it wasn't nothing. And he knew it. They could try to open it at any time. They were together nonstop. But they hadn't. And he couldn't quite parse out why.

"What do you say, Char? Do you want to treat us to coffee with your fancy nanny credit card?" Harper asked. The woman slid down her shades and pegged him with her gaze. "Charlotte gets one of those, right? Nannyland perks?"

Mitch's hammering pulse slowed as Harper blessedly changed the subject. He regained his bearings. "Yes, that's how it works."

"And a car? The food truck is cool and all, but parallel parking that beast in the city might get rough," the sassy lady continued.

"Yes, there's a nanny car—a Lamborghini Urus. Rowen suggested it."

"You get a Lamborghini, too?" Harper snapped.

This woman was a piece of work!

Charlotte checked her watch. "I promise, we'll get together another time. It's so sweet of you to come by. But I can't do coffee today. Mitch and I have a thing."

"*A thing*," Harper, Penny, and Libby repeated in unison as they narrowed in on him.

Jesus! Charlotte had one hell of a girl gang.

"Charlotte is helping me with my food truck," he stammered, gesturing toward the truck.

"Is she?" Penny chimed.

"Mitch is taking some time away from his restaurant to bring back his food truck for a limited-time run. He's going to write about the experience. And his publisher hired me to take some pictures and help out with orders while he's cooking," Charlotte explained.

So far, so good. That description sounded professional as hell.

"You're one full-service gal," Harper cooed.

"I'm whatever Mitch needs," Charlotte replied, her blush deepening as she reached for the key on the chain and twisted it between her fingers nervously.

And...so much for looking like professionals.

"I bet you are," Harper quipped from beneath the hat, bumping shoulders with Libby, who still looked ready to snap.

"Harper, play nice. I'm sure Charlotte and Mitch have it under control. Charlotte is a fantastic photographer. We know that. You'll be in good hands, Mitch," Penny added.

"What's going on with Mitch's hands?"

Mitch whipped around and found Landon Paige weaving his way past a group of parents. With a ball cap pulled down topped with a hoodie obscuring most of his face, he and Harper looked like two incognito peas in a pod.

"Why are you here?" he asked. *Who else was going to show up?*

Landon gestured over his shoulder. "I'm here with Raz. We were at the gym. And let me tell you—that guy is a beast! You should see what he benches," the man began, then paused and focused on Harper. "I've got to ask. Are you some obscure pop star attempting to hide your identity?"

Oh, Christ!

"Excuse me?" Harper barked.

Landon scanned the parents and children descending upon the school grounds. "I have to worry about that, too. I can barely go anywhere without people asking for my autograph."

"Dude," Rowen chided.

"It happens...sometimes!" Landon exclaimed, then adjusted the hoodie.

This guy!

"What are you doing here, Landon?" he asked.

"Raz had an appointment to speak with the principal, and I offered to drive him here. He's at the door, heading in now," Landon answered, glancing over his shoulder when Libby, who'd barely said a word, gasped as rage flashed in her eyes. The petite woman frowned, then growled something that sounded a lot like the word *beefcake.*

Who even used that word anymore?

Clearly, this chick.

Harper rolled her eyes, then took Libby's arm. "Ms. *No-Namaste-Today* and I are going to take off before she releases a chi-storm and curses the karma of everyone in a fifty-mile radius." She turned to the kids. "Phoebe, Oscar! Be good! And don't put up with any," she said, then tapped twice.

Phoebe saluted, and Oscar followed suit as Charlotte said goodbye to Harper and Libby.

"I better take off, too, and wait in my car," Landon added. "That lady over there in the yellow vest with the sign has looked my way at least three times."

"She's the crossing guard," Rowen countered. "She's watching children cross the street."

"Or she recognizes me," the former heartthrob blurted before taking off for the parking lot when a bell rang out.

"Is it time for school?" Oscar asked.

Phoebe shook her head. "That's the first bell. We have five minutes. This is the time when my teacher usually comes out to tell my uncle about something I did at school," Phoebe answered, then pointed toward the building. "Look, Penny!

Look, Uncle Row! My teacher's coming out, and Mr. Bergen is with her. He must be helping in our classroom."

"Phoebe, what did you do now?" Rowen asked, eyeing the child.

"Hi, Mrs. Bergen! What did I do now?" Phoebe called.

A smiling woman with dark hair and a clipboard accompanied by a tall man joined them. "Nothing at all, Phoebe. I was coming your way to see if this was our new student, Oscar Elliott."

"Yes, ma'am, that's me," his son replied. And damn, look at his kid and those manners.

"I'm Mrs. Bergen. I'm going to be your teacher. We're so happy to have you at Whitmore. We've got lots of great activities coming up."

"Oh no!" Phoebe chimed.

"What is it, Phoebe?" the teacher asked.

"Oscar missed the school ski trip, Mrs. Bergen," the girl lamented.

"But the best is yet to come! We've got the Whitmore Carnival and our week-long class camp trip coming up. I think you picked the perfect time to join our class," the woman countered, smiling at his son like the academic version of Mary Poppins.

"And you're Mitch Elliott, the chef," the man who'd accompanied the teacher said, extending his hand. "I'm Brennen Bergen, Abby's husband. You're the Say Cheese, Louise guy, right? I watched your show and hit up your food truck more times than I can count back in the day."

Mitch shook the man's hand. "Yeah, that's me."

Everyone in Denver knew of the Bergen family. The Bergens owned a mountain sports empire and were involved in many philanthropic pursuits.

"It's nice to meet you, Mitch. My husband saw the food truck and about lost his mind," the teacher added.

"Are you starting it back up?" Brennen pressed.

"For a limited run—a couple of months at most."

A wide grin spread across the man's face. "You'll have to bring it to the Whitmore Carnival. The city agreed to close off a few streets in the Crystal Creek business district for it this year. We've got games and activities lined up, but we could sure use a food truck. I'm on the planning committee for the event. It's only a few weeks away. Can I put you on the list as a vendor?"

"That's a terrific idea!" the teacher agreed.

"Can we do it, Dad?" Oscar asked. "Can we help my new school?"

What was he supposed to say to that?

"We'd be happy to," Charlotte answered for him. "Count us in for the carnival. And let me introduce myself. I'm Charlotte Ames. I'm—"

"Charlotte's my everything," Oscar interrupted, then frowned, thinking hard. "She's more like my dad's everything."

Jesus! First the lock and key business and now this! Could everyone in the city see that something was going on between the hothead chef and the nanny?

"I don't quite understand," Mrs. Bergen replied.

"I'm Oscar's new nanny," Charlotte clarified. "And I'm also assisting Mitch with the food truck."

"And she's a photographer like me," Oscar threw out.

"I wear lots of hats," Charlotte replied as her blush returned.

"It's nice to meet you. I'm sure we'll be seeing a lot of each other. And just a heads-up. You'll want to check Oscar's backpack every day. Today a flyer is going out with information about the end of the year camping trip and the carnival," the woman finished as another bell rang.

"Time for school!" Phoebe exclaimed.

"Phoebe, can you show Oscar where we line up?" Mrs. Bergen asked.

"Come on, Oscar," the girl called, taking his son's hand.

Here goes everything.

They said their goodbyes to Mrs. Bergen and her husband as the kids started toward the playground. They'd barely gone a few yards when Oscar stopped, turned on his heel, then hurried back to him.

"I almost forgot to give you this," the boy said, unzipping his backpack and removing the old spatula. "You'll need this today. Good luck with Louise, Dad."

Mitch stared at the spatula. "Thanks, buddy. Have a great day at school," he rasped as his son enveloped him in a hug.

The breath caught in his throat. Growing up, he hadn't had school days like this. His grandpa wasn't much for affection, and he'd pretty much taken care of himself from the time he was Oscar's age. He wrapped his arms around the boy as the click of Charlotte's camera joined the chorus of children's voices.

"I love you," he said, the words falling from his lips. How had he never said it before?

"I love you, too," the boy answered with a toothy grin, then wiggled out of his embrace to hug Charlotte.

And then Oscar was off, backpack swaying from side to side as he sprinted along with Phoebe toward the mass of children. A million competing emotions welled inside of him when he felt a gentle touch on his arm.

Charlotte.

"I didn't think this would be so hard," she said with a quiver to her voice.

And he got it. These last few days had been so intense, so life-changing. His world had gone from a solitary existence to reviving Say Cheese, Louise with Oscar and Charlotte by his side. The three of them had been together nonstop. It was the most time he'd spent with his son—ever. And the first time in a long time that he'd felt whole.

"I'm glad you're here," he said, his voice barely a whisper. It wasn't a lie. Her smile, her presence, her hand on his arm was what held him together.

"It's crazy, huh—this whole parenting thing," Rowen commented as they watched the children line up and march inside.

"Yeah," he bit out as a chime cut through the air.

"Sorry, that's me," Charlotte said. She pulled her cell from her pocket and stared at the screen. "And our day is about to get crazier."

He frowned. Crazier? How much crazier could it get? "What do you mean?" he pressed.

"We need to go, Mitch. Ines texted. There's a change in plans for the food truck today. The location she'd originally booked had to cancel. She sent a new address for the updated spot. And she says that they want us there immediately. Do you recognize it?" she asked, handing him her phone.

He stared at the address, swallowing hard as another wave of emotion crashed into him. The punches kept coming, the turbulence not letting up a fraction. He turned his attention to the old spatula in his hand, recalling the first time he'd held it as a screwed-up seventeen-year-old.

But there was no turning back now—no hiding from the past.

"Yeah, I know it. But I'm not sure the people at this location are going to be happy to see me."

SIXTEEN

MITCH

FOCUS *on the task at hand, man!*

This is going to be a spot like any other. It's just a location.

Pull up the truck, park the damn thing on the side of the road, cook, repeat.

And do it with the most alluring redhead on the planet by your side.

Dammit! He was screwed.

And it wasn't only the push and pull of his feelings for Charlotte playing tug-of-war with his battered heart. No, it was more than that. If merely a glimpse of Charlotte sent him into an intense simmer, the addition of today's food truck stop kicked up the heat to a fiery inferno on the cusp of boiling over.

He tightened his grip on the steering wheel and tried to focus on the cool breeze coming through the half-opened window. He had to pull himself together. A part of him knew that Ines would try to book the food truck at this location. If he was going back to the beginning, there was only one place to start.

But a pivotal question lingered.

Would he be welcomed back or merely tolerated?

Whatever happened, he'd have to be mentally prepared. But after the morning he'd had, his emotions were blitzed. *Christ!* He'd heard of parents getting misty-eyed when they'd dropped their kid off at school. But not in a million years had he expected the sentimental tsunami that hit when Oscar wrapped his little arms around him.

Up until a handful of days ago, he was a hardened chef. A beast demanding perfection. A monster in the kitchen. A hothead...everywhere! Now he was volunteering to cook at school carnivals. Well, to be fair, that was Charlotte's doing. But when he'd seen the pride on his son's face, there was no way he could turn it down.

What was happening?

And here he was, staring at the road, driving the familiar route. He couldn't even guess the number of times he'd traveled down this street with Seth and Holly, headed *not* for Denver's gleaming buildings and sprawling parks but for the rougher side of town.

Today, he and Charlotte were expected in a grittier part of the city. The location he'd learned the culinary ropes that had led him to stardom.

He could remember the early days of Say Cheese, Louise like they were yesterday.

He'd posted pictures on social media the first time they'd taken the truck to Denver's bustling downtown. He'd thought nothing of it—they hardly had a following—until a producer from a major food network messaged him. Was it dumb luck that his orange grilled cheese truck caught the eye of a flashy TV exec? There were nights when he sat awake staring at the ceiling, wishing he'd never shared those images, chiding himself for responding to the message, and wondering what would have happened if his star hadn't outshined Holly and Seth's.

It was a fool's errand to turn over the questions, night after night. But that didn't stop him.

He reduced his speed as they passed over the railroad tracks, then glanced at the car next to him. A guy was staring at the truck from the passenger side window of a sedan, holding his phone out the window as if he were recording the traffic.

Why would a person do that?

Then he remembered what he was driving.

It wasn't that uncommon for people to gawk at the giant orange beast lumbering through the city. He hit the gas, forgetting the sedan as he concentrated on the road.

He hadn't visited this part of town since he'd made it big. It had been nearly a decade since he'd returned to where it all began. He scanned the neighborhood. It was different now. While a few tents and a smattering of cardboard box homes were still scattered in alleyways, bright murals on the sides of buildings now covered the once graffitied surfaces. Eclectic clothing stores bursting with color, small art galleries, and kitschy coffee shops with mismatched outdoor seating inhabited the once rundown business district. And then he saw it—the building that had served as the location of his punishment and had ended up as the gateway to his salvation.

Well, at one time, he'd thought of it as his salvation.

Block it out. Block it out and cook.

That mantra had worked for the last seven years.

It numbed the pain.

But today, it wasn't doing jack shit for him.

"You might break it if you squeeze any harder," Charlotte said, her voice calling him back.

"Break what?" he stammered, focusing on the road.

"The steering wheel," she replied, and he could hear the concern in her voice.

He slowed the truck, stopping at a red light, then peered at his hands, taking in his white knuckles. He blew out an uneven breath. "I've got a lot on my mind."

"I can tell. You haven't said a word since we left Whitmore. You're tense. And I think I know why."

A pang of anxiety rippled through his chest. There was no way she could know! Yes, he'd dropped the Holly and Seth bomb on her, but he hadn't mentioned this place. He never mentioned this place or the people in it. The world thought Say Cheese, Louise began its journey to stardom in trendy Denver neighborhoods.

It didn't. Not even close.

"Charlotte…" he began, not sure what the hell he was going to say when she raised her hand, silencing him.

"Let's clear the air, Mitch," she said, and he didn't need to look at her to know she also had a lot on her mind. "This reboot of Say Cheese, Louise is important, no, imperative for you and your career. I understand what's on the line. If you're worried about me doing my job, you can stop. I can put what happened between us in the past. I can be your son's nanny, assist with the food truck, and be your photographer. I can keep it professional," she finished with a shaky exhale as if she'd been going over that speech in her head.

One thing was for certain. She was stronger than he was. He could barely go a minute without aching for her touch. But she was right. Today, of all days, he needed to keep his mind sharp.

"Think of it like my camera," she said, glancing at the Nikon in her lap.

The light changed, and he stepped on the gas. "I don't get it. How are we like your camera?"

She held it up and peered at him through the viewfinder. "It's a new frame. A fresh start. The past is the past. From here on out, it's Mitch and Charlotte, the boss and the employee.

The nanny and the hothead," she added, trying to lighten the mood. But as much as he knew she was right, it didn't stop him from remembering when, not even an hour ago, Oscar had deemed her his everything.

"The past that you're describing is barely ten hours ago, Charlotte," he conceded.

She returned her camera to its bag, then slumped into the seat. He glanced over and caught her twisting the key between her fingers. "I know. But every hour with you feels more like a week," she mused.

He understood the sentiment. He'd lived a thousand lives since he caught sight of her dressed as a mermaid at that speed date event.

"It's hard to remember what life was like before..." she trailed off.

"Before what?" he asked, his heart thumping in his chest. His emotions see-sawed so wildly that he barely registered their arrival at the food truck stop. He shifted the truck into park, cut the ignition, then met her gaze.

"Before waking up hungover in an RV in the middle of nowhere. Before there was an us," she finished with the sweetest curve to her lips.

He stared into her eyes as the raw honesty of her words sliced through him.

He never pictured being part of an *us* again. He'd written it off. It had to be that way. But it didn't stop him from unbuckling his seat belt and sliding across the bench seat toward her. He studied the glinting key at her neck.

"The professional version of an *us*, of course," she added on a shaky breath.

"Completely professional," he agreed as the air inside the truck's cab pulsed and crackled with the heat of their attraction. It was undeniable. Her strawberry sunshine scent was everywhere. It called to him as it erased every rational thought from his mind. He drew his fingertips across the hollow of her neck and touched the delicate key. They were back to this place. Back to this secret land of heavenly escape, where the pain that chafed and grated within him dissolved into the beat of his pounding heart. Charlotte trembled beneath his touch, leaning in toward him. Unable to stop himself, he unbuckled her seat belt. She moved closer as if the pull of their magnetism was too much to resist. Her breasts rose and fell with her every breath as she rested her hand on his knee, then tightened her grip, anchoring herself to him. Or maybe it was the reverse, and he was the one desperate for the promise of her safe harbor. And with one smile, this woman demolished his defenses.

"Or we could delay the professionalism—briefly," she offered, her breathy words caressing his lips.

"Yeah," he agreed in a tight rasp. "A postponement before the official professionalism begins."

He didn't know what the hell *official professionalism* was or how it differed from *unofficial professionalism*. He was ninety-nine percent sure he sounded like an absolute imbecile. But the blood in his brain had migrated south thanks to her palm on his thigh and her fingertips digging into his muscled leg. And he sure wasn't firing on all cylinders in the thinking-clearly department while the *getting-down-and-dirty* department had taken the reins.

"I don't understand what's happening," she whispered. "I couldn't stand you a week ago."

He grinned. He couldn't help it. This was her charm—her magic, her raw, unfiltered honesty.

Honesty.

The word floated through his mind like the sun breaking through a bank of storm clouds.

Was she truly someone he could trust with his heart? Was that even possible?

"What about now?" he asked, his voice a low rumble. He rested his hand on top of hers and laced their fingers together. "Do you still want to throw a plate of vegetables at me?"

She studied his face as if she was assessing the composition of a photograph—seeing him, seeing through him, seeing every facet of his being. He drew a tight breath as a delicious tingle worked its way down his spine. There, in the cab of Say Cheese, Louise, she had him, body and soul. And he was powerless against her exquisite allure.

He cupped her face in his hand, breathless as he waited for her reply.

She melted into his touch. "No, I don't want to throw a salad at you, Mitch. All I want now is to—"

"To *not* loiter in front of my building! Perfect, that's what I want, too!" came the prickly voice of a woman he could never forget.

SEVENTEEN

MITCH

"HOLY SHIT!" he exclaimed.

Charlotte gasped as surprise flashed in her eyes. They broke apart like teenagers caught necking beneath the bleachers. Wide-eyed and red-cheeked, she smoothed her skirt as he peered out the half-opened driver's side window and met the gaze of the person who'd changed everything for him.

"I know why you're here, *Mitchell*. Don't try to hide it," the woman began with a surly smirk.

Mitchell.

And double holy shit!

He was about to find out if they were welcome or not. Yes, Ines had booked the spot. But the woman staring him down could have wanted him there to tell him off, just to send him packing the minute she was done lambasting him. In all honesty, that's what he deserved.

And that wasn't the only shitstorm on his plate.

What would have happened had he and Charlotte not been interrupted? He shook his head, working to gain control of himself. He had to be on his A-game.

"And why do you think I'm here, Chef?" he answered,

keeping his tone neutral. But something inside of him awakened at the sound of her crusty voice. Despite not knowing if she was about to kick the side of the truck and tell him to scram, he'd forgotten how much he enjoyed going head-to-head with this ball-buster.

She took a step back and glanced down at her pressed chef's coat with Helping Hands Community Center stitched across the breast pocket. With a flick of her wrist, she tossed the tail of her long silver braid over her shoulder, then stilled. She observed him closely. The lines etched at the corners of her eyes deepened, and she silently evaluated him just as she had the first time they'd met. Last he'd seen her, she was the definition of a take-no-shit chef, and time hadn't changed that. In fact, the woman looked pricklier than ever.

"I'll tell you what you're doing here," she continued. "You came to see for yourself how this cantankerous old gal defies time to keep up her youthful appearance while continuing to prepare impeccable meals for the community."

Relief flooded his system. She was messing with him. This meant, at least for the moment, she wasn't about to send them on their merry way.

"Yes, Chef Louise, that's exactly what I was thinking," he fired off as a warmth wrapped around him, recalling the familiar cadence of their chef and apprentice exchanges.

"Louise?" Charlotte uttered.

He nodded.

"The Louise in Say Cheese, Louise?" she pressed.

"The one and only," Louise remarked.

He glanced at the woman, then nodded to Charlotte. "Yeah, the truck is named after her."

"I hope you're not planning to sit there lollygagging all day," Louise snapped. "When I spoke to Ines this morning and agreed to let you park this orange eyesore in my lot, she said you were going to get off your ass and cook for the community—for free because you're a fancy former TV chef," the woman added with her usual snark. Without missing a beat, she opened the driver's side door and waved them out impatiently. She wasn't mad, though. In fact, he could hear the trace of amusement in her tone. She pointed to the dashboard as he and Charlotte exited the vehicle. "And it appears that you're finally returning that spatula you stole from me."

He swiped the utensil, then closed the door. "You gave it to me, Chef, and you know it."

"I don't give anything away. You earn it with me," she replied with a sly grin.

Wasn't that the truth.

He took in the community center as the memories came flooding back. "I know. I remember."

"And who is this?" Louise asked, eyeing Charlotte.

"I recognize this young lady, Louise!"

He turned to find Louise's husband, Ralph Dagby, ambling toward them. Lanky like a retired basketball player and rarely without a grin, the man moved a little slower than he remembered.

"It's good to see you, Mitch." Ralph shook his hand, then turned his attention to Charlotte. "Well, hello! We meet again."

"You know Mitch's friend?" Louise asked with a crease to her brow and her fist on her hip.

"Remember when I had to head over to the Crystal Creek neighborhood to pick up the donations from the coffee shop? I told you about that woman on the bench."

Louise sucked in a tight breath and cringed. "The one who was looking up at the sky at airplanes and talking to herself? The one you thought might need urgent psychiatric care?" she answered, giving Charlotte a once-over.

"Yep, this is her," Ralph confirmed.

The Dagbys were quite a pair. Decades ago, they'd owned a wildly successful restaurant downtown. But they sold it to open the Helping Hands Shelter and Community Center. Ralph, with his mellow vibe, and Louise, with her gruff, do-it-right or get-out-of-my-kitchen persona, fascinated him. But the one thing the couple did seem to have in common, besides their commitment to each other, was a fierce dedication to helping the community. They'd prided themselves on giving second chances to teens, young adults, and people with special needs who'd run out of options.

Teenagers like him.

Charlotte twisted her camera bag's strap. "I'm Charlotte Ames. It's nice to meet you both. And I can assure you that I'm not in need of urgent psychiatric services at the moment."

Oh, sweet Jesus!

He caught Charlotte's eye as she cringed, embarrassment burning her cheeks. Playfully, he grimaced right back. *And holy shit!* A heady exhilaration pulsed through his veins as the apprehension in her expression faded, and a touch of amusement twinkled in her eyes. He knew this feeling. He understood the powerful pull that came with knowing that comfort could be channeled through the slightest of movements with just a glance or the hint of a smile. It was an intimate exchange, something he hadn't experienced in ages.

"I like her, Mitch," Ralph said, warm grin in place, before a curious look overtook his features as he turned to Charlotte. "Was it Mitch?"

"I'm not sure what you mean?" Charlotte replied.

"The text you mentioned when I found you on that bench. Was Mitch the fella who you hoped had texted? How long had you been waiting to hear back? I think you said six days. Is that right?" Ralph probed.

Charlotte looked from the Dagbys to him, her cheeks

growing pink again. "No, it wasn't Mitch. And the text didn't turn out to be from who I was hoping it would be. But that might have been a blessing in disguise." She swallowed hard. "But that's not important. I'm here because I work for Mitch now. He's just my boss."

Just my boss?

Why did that hurt?

He schooled his features. This was not the time to untangle his feelings for the nanny. "Charlotte is helping care for my son. She's also going to assist with orders while I'm cooking. Plus, she'll be taking some pictures to document the reboot of Say Cheese, Louise for a book I'm working on."

"That's a lot on your plate, Charlotte," Ralph commented, then shared a curious look with Louise.

"I'm happy to help however I can," she replied and resumed twisting the strap of her camera bag.

"You're a photographer?" Ralph continued.

Charlotte brightened. "Yes, that's what I studied in college."

Ralph gestured toward a large mural of the Helping Hands logo. He knew it well—a heart created with multicolored handprints, painted in bright colors on the side of a neighboring building. "Have you been to this part of town recently? It might be right up your alley. It's become an artists' enclave."

"I noticed a few galleries on the drive over," Charlotte answered, excitement woven into her words. "One of my professors from school mentioned that galleries were opening in a new part of town. She must have meant here. Do we have time to look around?"

"Do we have time to look around, Mitchell?" Louise echoed, raising an eyebrow.

"Hold on," he answered, then checked his watch. It was two minutes to ten a.m.

"You've trained him well, Louise," Ralph said through a chuckle, then shared another suspicious look with his wife.

Something was going on.

It might have been a while since he'd spent time with the Dagbys, but he knew this pair well enough to know when they had something up their sleeves.

"I assume you still start serving lunch at ten fifteen. I don't want to get a late start," he answered.

"You would be correct," Louise confirmed.

Charlotte cocked her head to the side. "Why so early?"

Louise released a heavy sigh. The woman might be a badass on the outside, but she was a softie at heart. "Because most of the people who come here for a meal don't have the luxury of eating breakfast," she explained.

"The shelter guests get three squares a day, but for various reasons, people who live on the streets don't always have consistent access to food. We do our best to help," Ralph explained, then played another round of catching his wife's eye. "But we've got a little time. Why don't I take Charlotte around the building and tell her a little bit about what we do here? I can point out a gallery or two along the way."

"I'd love that," Charlotte gushed. "Would you mind if I took a few pictures of the community center and the neighborhood for Mitch's book?"

"Not at all," the man answered.

"You don't mind, do you, Mitch? It's always better to have more shots to choose from," Charlotte asked, pulling her camera from its bag.

"No, go ahead," he said, the words coming out a touch gruffer than he'd expected.

Ralph tossed him a little wink. "You don't have to worry, Mitch. I'll have Charlotte back in a jiffy," he finished before gesturing for her to walk alongside him.

Why the hell would Ralph say that?

"If you stared any harder at that girl, your eyeballs might explode," Louise remarked the second Ralph and Charlotte were out of earshot.

He focused on the old spatula. "I wasn't staring."

"Oh, no? And what were you doing in the truck when you got here? Helping her with her contact lenses?"

He glanced away. "She doesn't wear contact lenses."

"I didn't think so," the chef threw back.

Louise Dagby wasn't one to beat around the bush.

"You knew Charlotte would be with me today, didn't you?"

Louise weighed the question. "Ines might have mentioned you would have someone with you when we spoke. Remember, she and I became friends when she was working on your first reality TV deal. You know, when she asked me *not* to divulge your true connection to this place."

Oh, he remembered.

He fixed his gaze on the entrance to the shelter's kitchen. "Ines was doing her job. People don't look too kindly on juvenile delinquents stealing their cars for parts."

"You and I both know that you had your reasons for doing that, Mitchell," Louise countered.

He shrugged. "The judge didn't think so."

Louise's expression hardened. "Thanks to that judge and the juvenile justice system, your seventeen-year-old ass landed in my kitchen doing mandatory community service and not in some cell."

She wasn't wrong. He was lucky, damned lucky, he'd gotten community service instead of time in juvey. He didn't see it that way at the time. Back then, with his grandfather in hospice care and barely enough money from the old man's pension to cover the rent, stealing cars and selling the parts had filled in the gaps. When the judge sentenced him to community service at the

Helping Hands Community Kitchen, he'd figured he'd do his time making bologna sandwiches for homeless people, then try to find something that paid the bills that wouldn't get him incarcerated. Even back then, he was smart enough to know that it was a whole different ball game when he turned eighteen. He could end up in prison. Instead, he, along with Holly, who'd been caught shoplifting, and Seth, who'd gotten pinched throwing a brick through a store window, showed up for community service.

Three underaged lawbreakers.

And the rest is history—a gut-wrenching history.

"So, what now, Louise? You've got me to yourself. I saw you and Ralph doing that whole eyeball conversation thing. What do you have to say?" He waved her off. "Wait, let me guess. You're disappointed in me. I should have called or emailed. I've been an inconsiderate ass."

The woman's hardened expression softened. "I don't have to yell at you, Mitchell. I could never be harder on you than you are on yourself."

He flinched. "Why do you always call me Mitchell?"

"It's your name, isn't it? It was on the judge's orders. And also, because I don't want you to forget who you are."

He scrubbed his hand down his face. He didn't even know who he was anymore.

"But you're right," she continued. "I did want some time alone with you—not to berate you but to watch you cook. I'm entitled to my namesake sandwich, and the food truck won't prep itself. You cook. I'll observe. Think of it like the old days," the woman answered, heading toward the back of the truck.

He hadn't cooked for Louise in years. He still recalled the first time he, Holly, and Seth had made the Signature Louise sandwich for her. The concept had been his. An organic grocery store had donated a shit-ton of Dijon mustard, and a local apple farmer had sent them tubs of apple butter. Louise wasn't sure how they would incorporate the condiments into the menu before the items expired. But the composition had come to him immediately.

The spark. The gift. His ability to harmoniously integrate different flavors and textures in his culinary creations exploded in a grilled cheese-inspired bang.

Focusing on the task at hand, he opened the door for Louise, helped her inside, then set out prepping the food truck for the lunch rush. The comfort of going through the motions returned. He popped open the order window, grabbed his knives, and methodically laid out his supplies and utensils, concentrating on the order and symmetry of the process.

"I was sorry to hear about Holly. How are you holding up?" Louise asked.

He should have expected she'd bring up Holly's passing.

He maintained a placid front as he went to the sink and washed his hands. "Why would you ask that?"

"Because you loved her. Because she's the mother of your son. I'll have you know that while you set off for greener pastures, Holly kept in touch. She sent me a birthday card every year. It's okay to mourn her loss."

His hardened heart wouldn't have it.

"And Seth?" he asked, spitting out the bitter syllable.

She shrugged. "I know that he cut off all contact with Holly after he found out Oscar wasn't his."

"She chose him," he mumbled, staring at the old spatula lined up with his other supplies.

"She felt terrible, Mitchell. She never wanted to hurt you," Louise shared, lowering her voice.

He flipped on the cooktop. "I wouldn't know. We didn't get into that. We only talked about Oscar. That's all I could manage, and she afforded me that courtesy."

Louise touched the handle of the old spatula. "You bought her a cabin."

He sighed as he finished prepping the ingredients, then started in on slicing a loaf of sourdough. The ridges of the knife's blade might as well have been sawing into his chest. "I'm not that broke kid stealing cars and selling the parts anymore. I've got money, Louise. A lot of money. It was no hardship to buy a place in the mountains. For Christ's sake, I have another cabin outside of Aspen!"

"Fair enough," she tossed back, crossing her arms. "But I've got another question for you."

"It was never like you to hold back," he deadpanned over his shoulder as he tore into another loaf.

"Why this, Mitchell?" Louise prodded, gesturing around the truck. "Why resurrect Louise?"

He set down the knife and gripped the lip of the counter. "Because if I want to get back on TV, I need to rehab my image, and writing a book can do that." He paused, remembering his last meltdown on set. "There was an issue with my anger management. I lost sponsors. My reputation tanked. Producers called me a loose cannon. At least, that's what Ines tells me. I'm sure they'd called me worse things."

Louise's expression darkened, but it wasn't anger or disappointment that graced her features. No, it was almost as if his fall from culinary grace had been a blow to her. "Ralph and I watched you on those shows. We saw the change in you. I understand your desire to stage a comeback. But you didn't answer my question. Tell me, why did you choose to take Say Cheese, Louise out again? I know what it means to you, and I know what you lost."

Agitation prickled through his veins. He took in the stainless-steel wall covered with a myriad of pictures when the shots of Oscar and Charlotte caught his eye. Instantly, the clawing ache subsided. "Charlotte suggested the food truck reboot in front of Ines and my publisher. It just happened. My publisher loved the idea, and there was no turning back," he answered, feeling Louise's hawkish gaze.

"Charlotte had the idea?" she replied.

He buttered two slices of sourdough. Then, with a robotic flick of his wrist, he applied apple butter and Dijon before cutting a thick slice of cheddar and sealing the sandwich with the other piece of bread. Using the old spatula, the Signature Louise hit the cooktop with a familiar pop and sizzle.

"Yeah, she and Oscar went exploring around my property and found the garage with the truck inside. Long story short, I'll be making the Signature Louise all over town for the next couple of months."

"I didn't think you'd kept the old orange beast," Louise remarked, straightening one of the containers of apple butter.

"Yeah, well, maybe I'm not as big of an ass as I appear."

That earned him a bark of a laugh from his mentor.

"What if I told you that I didn't think this *reinventing yourself* was only about getting back on TV or signing deals to sell cheese graters? What if I told you I believe it has a lot to do with Holly and Seth?" Louise challenged.

A muscle ticked in his jaw. He stared out the window, remembering what he'd seen the day everything changed. "Holly is dead, Louise. And Seth fell off the face of the earth. I don't have anything to prove to them."

Louise shook her head. "It doesn't matter if they were here with us or if they'd been gone a decade. This is about you showing them that you deserved your success—that your rise to fame was earned and not a fluke," she shot back.

Jesus! That couldn't be it, could it?

The muscles at the base of his neck tightened as he used the old spatula to flip the sandwich. The pop and sizzle of the cold butter hitting the hot surface filled the stretch of silence.

Louise took a step toward him. "I'm here to tell you that you did earn it. But you lost something along the way, Mitchell. I tasted it when Ralph and I ate at the Crystal Cricket."

What the hell?

His jaw dropped. "When were you at my restaurant? And you're a chef. You know how it works. I have line cooks and sous chefs. How do you even know that I was the one who'd prepared your specific meals?" he barked, but she didn't bite. Instead, the whisper of a grin curved the corners of her mouth.

"We pulled a busboy aside and asked him which dishes you were preparing that evening. We also asked him to personally watch and make sure it was you who'd assembled our order. I believe you scolded him when he bumped into a waitress and a glass broke. Then you fired him. We noticed a scuffle in the back—something with a salad. Then we heard someone yell, *stupid hothead.* It was quite a commotion."

The air grew thick as he plated the Signature Louise sandwich, staring at the golden toasted bread and the bit of cheese bubbling at the edges. Of all the nights to visit his restaurant, Louise and Ralph had to pick that night! Madelyn had been there, too. It was like the universe wanted as many people as possible to witness his hotheaded meltdown.

It was no shocker that he'd been an ass that night. He was an ass every night. But he couldn't change what had happened with the busboy—couldn't go back and right the wrong. He steadied himself. "What did you think of your meal?"

Louise gave a slight shrug. "Technically, it was perfect. But it was missing the one thing that made you stand out above the other cooks."

"And what's that?" he asked through gritted teeth.

"That's for you to figure out," she replied in that damned elusive tone.

"Jesus Christ, Louise!" he hissed.

"Don't worry, Mitchell," she continued. "I have faith in you. You'll find that spark again. The food truck is a start. And this will help, too." She leaned out the order window and waved toward the community center. "Join us in the truck," she called.

Who the hell was she talking to?

He craned his neck, watching as two young men headed their way. They couldn't be much more than seventeen or eighteen years old. Each had on an apron, and one of them looked vaguely familiar.

"What is this, Louise?" he asked, staring at the tall kid with a mop of ash-blond hair beside a short guy with darker features as the pair climbed into the truck.

"It's for Charlotte," she answered, making no damned sense.

"For Charlotte?" he echoed.

"For me?"

He looked out the order window as Charlotte and Ralph stood there peering inside. She looked inside the truck and got a glimpse of the teens. "Erick, is that you?"

"Hey, Charlotte! I never got a chance to thank you for..." the kid trailed off as Mitch put it together.

Sweet Jesus! Erick was the kid he'd chewed out that triggered Charlotte to chuck a salad!

"You work at Helping Hands?" he asked his former busboy.

"Yes, Chef," the kid fired back.

"We hired him after you...terminated his employment," Ralph replied, biting back a grin.

The universe had put him through the wringer today, and it wasn't even lunchtime yet.

His mouth opened and closed like a goldfish—a clueless

goldfish. For the first time in ages, he couldn't think of a damned thing to say.

"When Ines called, I got an idea," Louise said, gesturing to the young men.

"What kind of idea?" he asked, finding his voice.

"Sergio and Erick have been working in the kitchen with me like you used to do."

He studied Sergio's face. "You didn't work at my restaurant, did you?"

A wave of guilt washed over him. He'd fired his fair share of employees without knowing so much as their names.

Sergio shifted his stance. "No, Chef. I'm here doing court-mandated community service. I got caught hot-wiring a car. I'm not proud of it, and I understand if you don't want someone like me working for you."

He held the kid's gaze. "That's how I ended up at Helping Hands."

The man's eyes widened. "Is that true?"

"Yeah, it is."

"You used to steal cars?" Charlotte asked, a strange sort of surprise written all over her face.

He glanced at the teens, then focused on Charlotte. "I did. I made mistakes as a kid, but then I found a better path." He waited for her reaction—waited to see the disappointment in her eyes. But that's not what he got—far from it.

"That's incredible, Mitch!" She beamed. "I had no idea what you'd overcome to get where you are."

A sudden lightness came over him as relief surged through his veins. In the last seventy-two hours, she'd gotten a look at every facet of his life—every secret exposed, every fault of character cracked wide open. And she was still here with such tenderness in her eyes. It took everything he had not to sweep her into his arms and kiss her until he couldn't see straight.

"Sergio and I are working on our GEDs," Erick continued.

"That's excellent," he answered. He had to focus.

"Then we want to apply to culinary school," Sergio finished.

"Sound familiar?" Ralph observed, knowing damned well it was the way he, Holly, and Seth had started out.

"What do you say, Mitch? I spoke with Ines. She shared the list of scheduled stops for the truck so far. Sergio's caseworker has signed off on him getting in his community service by assisting with the food truck."

"And I'm in, too," Erick chimed.

Mitch's jaw damn near hit the pavement. "You want to work for me again?"

The young man lifted his chin. "I want to become a chef, and I want to learn from the best."

"And Erick's survived cooking under Louise's demanding eye," Ralph teased.

But the man wasn't wrong. He'd learned as much under Louise as he'd gotten out of what time he'd spent in culinary school before dropping out to start Say Cheese, Louise.

"I think it's a terrific idea," Charlotte said, those emerald eyes of hers shining with such tenderness it took his breath away.

She was right. It was.

He cleared his throat. It was time to get down to business. He pointed the spatula at the young men. "Do you both know how to prepare the Signature Louise sandwich?"

"Yes, Chef," the teens replied in unison.

"And I know how you like orders to be taken," Erick offered. "I watched the servers at the Crystal Cricket. I saw the tickets. I already showed Serg how to do it. We know what's expected of us."

They were hungry for experience, but he still had to lay down the law.

"You'll learn that cooking in a food truck isn't the same as working in a commercial kitchen. It's a tight space. There are plenty of opportunities to screw up and get hurt. Stand where I tell you to stand. Do what I tell you to do. You'll work in shifts. One with me, prepping and preparing the sandwiches. The other at the window, taking orders."

"Yes, Chef," they exclaimed. He could hear the thread of exhilaration in their voices. He understood it. That was him once, standing under the watchful eye of Louise Dagby.

"Both jobs are important," he continued. "Don't look at working the window as a demotion or as a break. Interacting with the people you cook for is as important as the cooking," he said, then glanced at Louise—the person who'd taught him that it didn't matter who he was cooking for. The woman nodded—barely a perceptible movement. But he caught it. He looked between the teens. "It doesn't matter if it's a guy off the streets or a polished businessman in a three-piece suit. The task is the same. Craft the best possible experience. Food is life. Food is connection."

He wasn't sure when he'd forgotten that or when he'd allowed resentment to swallow him whole. He released a slow breath as a clicking sound peppered the air. He peered over at Charlotte. She snapped another shot, then lowered her Nikon. She didn't say anything. She didn't have to. The warmth in her emerald eyes told him everything he needed to know. She was there for him—there to capture this forgotten part of him.

"Um, Chef, should we start prepping?" Erick asked, cutting into his Charlotte swoon-fest.

She lifted the camera to her eye, and it was time for him to get to work as well.

"Wash up," he ordered. "Erick, you're with me. Sergio, you'll take the window."

"We'll leave you to it," Ralph remarked with an approving nod.

"Not so fast," Louise said, picking up the sandwich he'd made for her. "I need to test the goods first." The woman took a hearty bite, then chewed slowly, taking in the flavors.

There were very few people whose opinions mattered to him when it came to his food. Louise Dagby would always be one of them.

"Well?" he asked, unable to stop himself.

"That thing you lost," she began.

"Yeah?" he rasped.

Louise nodded to herself as she took another bite. "It's coming back."

"And so are the customers," Ralph remarked.

The customers?

He stared out the window as a mass of people descended on the truck.

Erick came to his side. "I probably should have mentioned this earlier, but you're trending on social media."

"How did that happen?" he asked as cars jockeyed for street parking. He turned to Charlotte.

"I haven't posted a thing. Maybe it was Ines or the publisher?" she offered.

"It looks pretty organic. Like it just got posted, then went viral," Erick answered, holding out his phone. "People posted that they saw the food truck at some ritzy school in Denver. Then other people commented, posting the locations they saw it. The hashtag #SayCheeseLouiseIsBack is one of the top twenty tags!"

He recalled the man in the sedan on the way over. He'd barely given the guy a second thought.

"Mitch, it's true!" Charlotte exclaimed, staring at her cell phone. "It's everywhere. Are you ready?"

Was he ready?

His pulse thrummed, but it wasn't out of fear or anger or some crazy desire to prove his demons wrong. His heart beat for her. He was ready because she was there. After all, she was the catalyst for this. He concentrated on the Polaroid of his son as a serene peacefulness set in. The click of the shutter brought him back. Charlotte brought him back. And that spark, that pull, that inexplicable force between them was there, showing him the way.

He schooled his features, then picked up the old spatula. "All right, everyone. Let's make some sandwiches."

CLICK! *Click! Click!*

Charlotte framed the shot. The satisfying sound of the shutter opening and closing permeated the air, fragrant with the heady scent of toasted sourdough bread and melted cheese. She took notice of her position, staying far enough away not to be intrusive but close enough to capture the moment as a reporter from one of the local TV stations interviewed Mitch. At the same time, Sergio and Erick were finishing up with the last of the lunch crowd.

To say that word had gotten out about the return of Say Cheese, Louise was an understatement.

People from all walks of life had shown up, eager for one of Chef Mitch Elliott's mouthwatering creations. It had been a sight to see. But it wasn't the jubilant crowds that had her awestruck. It was Mitch! She'd never seen him like this before. The man was in the zone. Going back and forth between showing the teens the food truck ropes, to speaking with local reporters as they ponied up to the window, to sharing a quick conversation with a patron while simultaneously cooking, Mitch didn't miss a beat.

The line for **Say Cheese, Louise** wrapped around the corner for hours. And true to his word, no matter who he was cooking for, Mitch treated every person with respect as he crafted their artisan grilled cheese.

And not only that! She'd never seen someone make so many sandwiches.

She'd observed him in the kitchen at the Crystal Cricket, but only in flashes. No one dawdled anywhere near the cantankerous man. Orders in. Orders out. And keep your distance from the hothead chef! But that miserable man was nowhere to be found today.

And she'd been there, documenting the transformation. Having Erick and Sergio volunteer to help had been a real godsend. She didn't know how she'd manage both working the window and photographing the event.

Despite only offering the Signature Louise sandwich, there were still those who asked for modifications to their meals. No apple butter. Extra Dijon. Thirty sandwiches for a gallery up the street, hold the cheese.

Yes, they ordered thirty sandwiches with apple butter and Dijon only!

But Mitch didn't bat an eyelash. At the Crystal Cricket, asking the man to modify a dish would send him into a tailspin. But not today. No, the man had even retrieved a set of cookie cutters from a bin tucked way up among the paper goods. She didn't know what he was going to do with them until he handed a little girl a sandwich in the shape of a cat. The child had beamed at the man. Then a toddler whooped with delight when Mitch served him a grilled cheese—no crusts—in the shape of a train. Sandwich after sandwich, his entire demeanor changed as the weight she knew he carried seemed to lighten before her eyes.

And while the lunch rush had blown by in a torrent of activity, one emotion permeated the day.

Joy.

The joy of sharing a meal.

The joy of watching people come together.

The joy of creating.

Artists with clay beneath their nails and smudges of paint on their cheeks, along with people showing up in cars that cost more than most houses, mingled with men and women staying at the shelter.

And that's when it clicked—literally clicked—and she began asking permission to photograph the patrons.

This was the magic of a food truck. An insta-community of individuals enjoying the fruits of Mitch's labors.

She'd become one with the energy. Shot after shot, she disappeared into the scene. And Mitch let her work. Hardly a word had passed between them. But it wasn't like before when the man had gone mute. No, this was different. It was as if he trusted her to capture the spirit of Say Cheese, Louise. And more than that, he gave her free rein and set no limits.

There was no *make sure to get my best side* or *don't you dare take a picture of that sandwich that's burnt on the edges.*

When Sergio had waited too long to flip a row of sandwiches, Mitch didn't blow his top. Instead, the man explained the importance of timing and why it was imperative to coat the sourdough slices evenly with butter. The hothead had morphed into a mentor and a teacher. That didn't mean he'd turned into a pussycat. He was still stern in his direction and exact in his orders, but the words didn't cut. His tone wasn't demeaning.

Throughout the day, she'd lowered her camera and had caught his eye. And heaven help her! If there was anything sexier than watching this man cook, she hadn't seen it.

Their eyes would meet for the briefest of seconds, and a

spark in the pit of her belly would explode into a cacophony of tingles. All things considered, it was really quite a feat that she hadn't dropped her camera or melted into a pool of swooning goo. Despite her raging libido, there was nothing strained or awkward about working in each other's orbits. Somewhere between the first customer ordering a Signature Louise and now, an aura of mutual respect blossomed.

Sure, they'd had rock-your-world sex inside Say Cheese, Louise. She'd never forget that. Not even a pitcher of potent margaritas could erase the delicious memory of his hand in her hair and his thick cock sliding between her thighs. But the conflict she'd seen in his eyes—the second-guessing she knew he was doing because she was doing it, too, didn't hamper the flow and the ease of the day. Regret hadn't reared its ugly head once as he cooked, and she captured the action with her camera.

And of course, she couldn't forget what had happened—or almost happened—when they'd arrived at Helping Hands. Again, she'd been powerless to resist him. Watching the man hug his son and tell him he loved him had given her the kind of feels reserved for bawling her eyes out to a Hallmark movie. A different emotion—a feeling she'd rarely experienced returned when Oscar hugged her.

With Penny, Rowen, and Mitch by her side, she was part of something.

Growing up, she'd left for school on her own and returned to an empty house. She was the after-thought daughter. She performed in school concerts for other kids' moms and dads. She never had anyone to find in the crowd or wave to from the bleachers. Her mom always had excuses—usually a big date she couldn't miss or a new fabulous boyfriend demanding her time.

And her father?

Just like now, the man rarely returned her calls. Making it to a school recital wasn't even a blip on his radar. But this morning, in front of Whitmore snapping picture after picture, she'd experienced a happiness she'd never known. A connection that touched her deeply.

What was she going to do with this rush of emotions? Mitch was still the boss—far less of a hothead. But still her employer.

But she couldn't fool herself or disregard the obvious. Something was there.

That was undeniable.

Whatever it was between them, it couldn't be measured in time. With them, it was moments. She'd lost count of how often he'd glance at her, and the breath would catch in her throat. And every exchange built upon itself. She might have only been his son's nanny for a handful of days, but the torrent of micro-swoon sessions were building up. One after the other, urgent and expectant, inevitable, like storm clouds forming in the distance. Nature taking its course.

Was there any way to stop it? Did she want it to stop?

"Hey, Charlotte? Could we get your help?" Erick called, craning his neck out Say Cheese, Louise's order window.

She nodded, then scanned the square. The line for the food truck had dwindled, and the masses who'd stayed to chat and eat in the shade of the community center's trio of leafy maple trees had dispersed. She took one last picture of Mitch, carefully framing the shot to get the news channel's cameraman in the frame, then jogged over to the truck.

"What's up, guys?"

"We've got class," Erick said, removing his apron.

"Our GED course," Sergio chimed, slinging his apron over his shoulder. "We lost track of time. It starts in fifteen minutes."

"Do you have far to go?" She checked her watch. She and Mitch would have to take off soon as well. They couldn't be late to pick up Oscar from school.

"No, it's down the block at one of the technical college's outreach locations," Erick answered.

"Yeah, if we run, we'll be fine," Sergio added.

"I know Mitch appreciated your help today." She surveyed the interior of the food truck. They'd tidied up, but there were two sandwiches left. "What do you need me to do?" she asked.

"Just get those orders out. Once it started slowing down, we were able to clean up during the lulls. There shouldn't be much left for you and Mitch to do," Erick answered.

She sighed as the high of coming down from a shoot hit her like a...giant orange food truck. "You guys have been great! What a day!" she added, leaning against the counter.

"It's crazy, huh?" Erick replied, gesturing toward Mitch and the news crew.

She chuckled. "He's a little different here in the food truck compared to what he was like at the Crystal Cricket."

"A little?" the kid remarked, clearly biting back a grin.

She couldn't blame the teen for noticing the change. The man had done a one-eighty in the hothead department.

"The chef seems to be in his element here," she replied.

"And you," Sergio added.

"Me?" she repeated.

"Yeah! The guy lights up every time he looks your way," Sergio said over his shoulder as he placed a stack of napkins inside of the paper supply bin.

She felt her cheeks heat, but she didn't want the teens to get the wrong idea. "I don't know about that, Sergio. I caught him smiling more times than I can count, and it wasn't always for me."

"Yeah, dude, you're lucky the guy wasn't in beast mode like he used to be when I bussed tables for him. If you had burned anything at the Crystal Cricket, there's a good chance you wouldn't be standing here to talk about it. The guy used to be a real..." Erick trailed off.

"Hothead," Charlotte supplied with a sly grin.

The kid slapped his leg, grinning. "That's right! That's what you called him after you threw that salad at him," Erick replied, shaking his head. "It was pretty cool of you to stand up for me. You were always nice, Charlotte. But I never had you pegged as a..."

"A hothead, too?" she teased.

"No, a fighter," Erick corrected, his expression growing serious.

A fighter.

Erick's words lingered in her mind. She'd never thought of herself as a fighter. Did she have that spark, that drive? For others, sure. But had she been too timid to reach for the stars for herself?

"What changed with the chef?" Sergio asked.

She pushed away the gnawing thoughts as her heartbeat quickened. She could answer that question. Everything had changed. But this wasn't the time to bask in a Mitch Elliott swoon-fest. She schooled her features. "You guys need to go! I don't want you to be late for your class. Kick some GED prep butt. We'll see you in a few days for the next Say Cheese, Louise stop," she finished, shooing them out of the back of the truck.

Alone, she slipped the camera strap from around her neck and set her Nikon next to the basket of pens, then spied the picture of Oscar taped to the glass.

"Your dad's not so bad," she said, tapping the corner as her gaze slid to the Polaroid of her and Mitch. She stared at her image, zeroing in on her smiling face. "Don't get ahead of yourself with him. He is your boss," she whispered. But that didn't stop the lightness in her chest and the buzz in her veins at the thought of his touch. She studied the walls, covered with the old photos of Mitch, Holly, and Seth. What must that have been like—the moment he learned the woman he loved and the best friend he trusted had betrayed him? Had he hardened his heart right then and there? She knew a thing or two about being let down by those you loved. But there was no time to wallow—no time to give a moment's thought to her parents.

She checked Mitch's position. He was chatting with the reporter as the cameraman loaded up the news van.

She needed to get things wrapped up in the food truck and get out the last two orders. Then they could call day one of the food truck reboot a roaring success.

She washed her hands, exhaling a slow breath, taking this moment to dial down the intensity. Mitch and the teens weren't the only ones who'd gone nonstop. She'd worked her ass off.

Drying her hands, she walked over to where the last two tickets hung and plucked them from the strip.

And holy blast from the not-so-distant past!

Her eyes went wide as she read the names at the top of the tickets.

Something Bryan

Cliff

Forget about slowing down and taking a breather! Her pulse skyrocketed as she stared at the handwriting, and the adrenaline came back with a vengeance. Her mouth grew dry—because, of course, it would at this very moment.

Do not freak out! Do not freak out!

She found her water bottle and chugged a few sips before returning to the tickets.

Something Bryan could mean anything. And there had to be hundreds, perhaps even thousands of Cliffs in the Denver Metro Area.

"It is not your old idiot boss. It is not the douche bag you dated," she murmured.

What were the chances?

Okay! Go time!

Get the orders out, then get on with the day.

She leaned out the order window. "Order up for Something Bryan and Cliff," she called, in a singsong voice, praying two strangers would amble up to the window. It could be two kindly gentlemen who raised chickens and planted trees.

She scanned the square. There were a few people left, but nobody looked her way. A thread of relief wove its way through her pounding heart. The customers could have left. The sandwiches were free. It wasn't like they were stiffing anyone. Maybe this *Something Bryan* and *Cliff* had to get back to work.

"That's me!" called a voice she recognized. A voice that had droned on about BASE jumping, and Cliff, the douche bag, ambled up to the window, followed by...

Oh no!

"My name is *Sutton* Bryan, not *Something* Bryan" her jerk of an old boss corrected in a grating tone as he joined Cliff at the window.

Her heart stopped beating. Okay, it didn't actually stop. But if it continued beating at this accelerated pace, there was a good chance she'd pass out.

Crap! Crap! Crap!

How could she have missed them?

Maybe it wasn't that hard.

She'd been immersed in her work. It wasn't like she was expecting to run into the last two people she ever wanted to see on this earth. The pair must have been waiting just out of her view alongside the truck, a little past the order window. But one thing was undeniably true. This was some next-level crazy karma stuff. Libby, when she was back to her Zen-master self, would be all over this. But that didn't help her now.

Think! Think! Think!

She took another swig of water. Maybe they hadn't seen her. She'd been photographing Mitch across the square. There had to be a way that she could still get out of this without them recognizing her.

"Excuse me? But you got my name wrong," Sutton Bryan snarled, banging on the ledge of the order window.

She gasped at the sound. Whipping around, her jaw dropped as she drank in Sutton Bryan's bulgy-eyed bullfrog expression. Then she slid her gaze to the left.

Could a person die of mortification?

Of all the Cliffs that must live in Denver, why did this Cliff have to be here, smiling like an idiot next to her snarling ex-boss?

What she wouldn't do for a real cliff! She'd happily fling herself off one of those than deal with these two.

"Charlotte, is that you?" Cliff asked, shielding his eyes to get a better look, even though the jerk was standing in the shade.

What the heck had she seen in him?

But he was the least of her problems.

"Charlotte Ames," Sutton Bryan scoffed. "You work at a food truck now? Serves you right after what happened at our last shoot. How pathetic! I knew you'd never make it in photography. And by the way, my mom wants the mermaid tail back. And you better believe we're coming after you if there's any damage to it."

She stood there, mouth hanging open. On a humiliation scale of one to ten, she'd pegged herself at a solid six thousand four hundred and twenty-three.

Dear Universe, you have one hell of a sense of humor! Also... you suck! Hardcore!

"Hey, Charlotte, what are your plans for later? Are you getting off from your food truck job soon?" Cliff asked, shifting his stance. "I was in the neighborhood and saw the sign for free lunch. And look at that! Here you are! And I figured, since last time we went out, I paid. You could pay for this date and then my whole day would be free. Pretty cool, right? So, wanna hang out later?"

"What?" she eked out. "What about your girlfriend?"

Cliff stuffed his hands into his pockets. "Kimberly and I didn't work out. She met some dude at the speed date thing. They skipped town and headed to Cabo together. So, it's your lucky day!"

Lucky day?

How, for even a fraction of a second, could she have thought there was a future with this guy?

The nerve of the creep!

She grabbed the closest thing to her—her water bottle—as a fit of fiery anger roiled in her belly.

"Buddy," Sutton Bryan griped, edging in front of the man in all his spray-tan glory. "*This woman* owes me a mermaid tail."

She stared at the creep. "What are you even doing here, Sutton?"

He cocked his miserable head to the side. "Sutton..."

Oh, for Pete's sake!

"Sutton Bryan, what are you doing here?" she corrected, spitting out his stupid name.

Was it possible to hate this man any more than she already did?

The answer—hell-to-the-yes!

He cleared his throat. "I had an appointment at one of the new galleries down here. I wanted to give them a first look at my newest portfolio," he answered, but without the same swagger and dogged cocky bravado he'd had when he'd rolled up to the counter.

"And? Will your photos be gracing the walls of trendy galleries?" she bit out, surprised she had it in her.

He glanced away. "Nothing is definitive. It's still up in the air. Negotiations are ongoing."

The fire in her belly intensified.

What a load of complete and utter bullshit!

"That's a no, then. You got rejected," she shot back.

Holy cow! Who was this Charlotte? Was she channeling Harper? Had the topsy-turviness of her life pushed her over the edge?

Sutton Bryan puffed up like a bloated orange peacock. "Gloat all you want. No gallery would ever entertain the likes of you and your shit photographs. You honestly owe me for even giving you a shot—even if you did have to dress up like a mermaid."

She narrowed her gaze. There it was—the final straw!

She lifted the water bottle, prepared to launch it at the bloated blatherer when something stopped her—a presence, a calming energy, a magnetic pull she'd recognize anywhere.

Mitch.

"This woman," Mitch began, borrowing Sutton Bryan's words. "Doesn't owe you or anyone anything," he finished, coming to her side.

This humiliation trio just became a two against two quartet.

She glanced at Mitch. He raised an eyebrow mischievously, then scrutinized the water bottle clutched in her hand. He looked from the bottle to the men as if he were assessing the amount of damage it could do to the pricks standing at the order window. Then, casually, as if he hadn't walked in on her about to assault a customer, he gently removed the bottle from her grip. His fingertips brushed against hers, and her pulse hammered as he allowed his thumb to linger, caressing her wrist. In those fleeting seconds, the electricity hummed between them before he gingerly set the bottle onto the counter.

"I've got this," he said, tossing her a sneaky little wink.

"And who are you?" Sutton Bryan barked. "I'd like to speak with the manager. Are you the manager?"

She pressed her lips together in a tight line. Whatever was about to happen, Sutton Moron Bryan had truly asked for it!

Mitch leaned in toward her jackass of an ex-boss. "I'm the guy who decides if you get one of my sandwiches."

"You're the owner?" Sutton Bryan croaked.

Mitch stared the guy down. "Yep."

"Charlotte works for you?"

"She works with me," he growled.

Wow!

This whole white knight plus equality thing was really working for her.

Sutton Bryan scoffed. "Good luck with that, man! Charlotte used to work for me, and I'll have you know that she's a terrible employee and a thief. She took off with a piece of my property—a very important costume my mother made. I fired her ass not even a week ago," the bullfrog snapped like a keyed-up Pomeranian.

Mitch crossed his arms, filling the order window. "Is that so?"

"Yeah, she's the worst! You should fire her before she screws up," he quipped, then wiped a line of sweat from his upper lip.

Mitch nodded. "I'll take your opinion into consideration." He scratched his chin theatrically, then reached for his wallet and pulled a couple of one-hundred-dollar bills out, then slid them across the ledge. "This is for your mom. For the mermaid tail."

"Um, okay!" the bulgy-eyed man stuttered, confusion marring his stupid froggy face as he accepted the cash.

"And I've considered your assessment of Charlotte, and I've got a proposition for you," Mitch continued.

A proposition?

"What's that?" Sutton Bryan croaked.

"I reject your assessment of Charlotte Ames," the man growled. "And if you don't get the hell away from my truck, I will run you over with the damned thing so many times you won't remember that you have two stupid first names. Got that, *Sutton?*"

Her jaw dropped.

That escalated quickly! And while she usually wasn't one for violence. Today, she was totally for Team Escalation!

"You can't say that! I'm the customer, and the customer is always right," Sutton Bryan blathered, taking a step back.

"Do you want to test that theory?" Mitch replied, his voice low and menacing. And OMG! Hearing him talk like that did things to her—tingly, lip-biting, breast-heaving things to her.

The blood drained from Sutton Bryan's face. For a beat, he stood there, frozen like he wasn't sure if Mitch actually threatened him until her hothead chef lunged forward in a quick burst of movement. Sutton Bryan hopped like a—yep, a bullfrog— before screaming his head off and tearing off down the street.

She watched the guy as he turned the corner and disappeared. "That was—"

"About us hanging out later," Cliff said, cutting her off. And holy ex-capades! She'd forgotten the guy was there!

"That won't be happening," Mitch answered for her.

"Why not?" the man stammered.

Had he always been this thick?

Mitch waved the guy to come closer. "Because Charlotte's already got plans with me."

Sweet tingle-mania! This man laying claim to her sent the dirtiest vibration thrumming between her legs. It would be a miracle if she didn't evaporate into the air thanks to the frenzied vibration going on inside of her.

"What about tomorrow?" the idiot Cliff continued.

Mitch glanced at her with the cheekiest of expressions. He liked tormenting her tormentors. And she didn't mind it one bit either.

She sighed dramatically. Two could play at this. "Sorry, Cliff, I'm busy. So very, very busy."

"Oh," the douchebag replied, standing there like his scoop of ice cream had fallen off the cone and onto the hot pavement.

"You heard her," Mitch warned. "Hit the road, Cliff. Charlotte's busy. So very, very busy."

She bit back a grin. While his voice remained low and deadly, she could hear the tinge of amusement.

"What about my fancy grilled cheese? I'm hungry," Cliff mumbled like a distraught toddler.

Mitch slid the plate with the sandwich in front of him. "What about it?" he said, then took a bite.

A BITE!

Cliff finally seemed to be catching on that he wasn't welcome here, nor would he be eating a delicious artisan sandwich. "I better head out," he said as Mitch took another monster-sized bite of the grilled cheese.

It took everything she had not to dissolve into a fit of giggles.

Cliff shifted his stance. "I don't have to run, do I, like that other guy with two names? You won't chase after me with this truck, will you?"

Mitch polished off the sandwich, then pulled the keys from his pocket. "Start her up, Charlotte!" he called as Cliff shrieked, turned on a dime, then hoofed it down the block.

She stared at the goofy man, arms flailing as he hightailed it out of there.

"He's faster than the last guy," Mitch remarked as they observed Cliff catch his toe on a crack in the sidewalk and eat some serious pavement before scrambling to his feet and disappearing into the city. Mitch sighed. "Nope, I take that back. The guy with two names was faster."

She shook her head, pressing her hands to her mouth as she giggled. "I can't lie. It's not so terrible watching you use your hotheaded powers on the bad guys. But aren't you worried? You were pretty rough on them."

"They were pretty rough on you, Charlotte," he answered, his features hardening.

"I get the whole laying it on thick with Sutton Bryan, but how did you know about Cliff?" she asked, watching him closely.

A muscle ticked in his jaw. "This isn't the first time I've seen Cliff."

She put the pieces together.

"The speed date! That's right, you were there! You heard me speaking with Cliff, didn't you?"

"And I heard what he said to you. The guy doesn't deserve you. He doesn't deserve your kindness."

"And my old boss? You're not worried about him going off and telling the world the owner of Say Cheese, Louise threatened him?"

Mitch leaned against the counter. "He had it coming. Both of those tools had it coming. And it was my pleasure to dish it out."

She held his gaze. The man's self-assurance was intoxicating. "I suppose they did," she replied, as that glimmer of mischief returned in his eyes.

"And just as a side note," he began.

"Yes," she purred.

He tapped the water bottle. "Try not to throw things at the customers. I know you have a history of hurling objects at asshats. But try to keep it under control."

"Noted," she answered, smiling at the guy like a besotted

schoolgirl when her phone pinged. She startled, then released a slow breath, getting her bearings. "It's my alarm. I set it to make sure we had plenty of notice before we had to leave to pick up Oscar," she explained, pulling her cell from her back pocket. She tapped the screen, silencing the sound when an email notification flashed. She tapped the email icon as the breath caught in her throat. She could barely believe her eyes.

Sender: Royal College of Art
Application approval and scholarship award

NINETEEN

CHARLOTTE

CHARLOTTE STARED AT THE SCREEN. Had she read it wrong?

No, it was right there in its digital glory—an email from the Royal College of Art. Her pulse had been thrumming for what seemed like days on end. This email sent it into overdrive.

Questions whirled through her head.

How could this email be in her inbox? She'd only applied on Saturday! Granted, the United Kingdom was seven hours ahead. But still! What had they done? Had they opened her application and been so wowed by her photograph of Mitch that they instantly accepted her and offered her a scholarship?

That certainly seemed to be what happened.

Granted, it was an incredible image. Yes, she'd been intoxicated when she'd taken it. Much of that night was blurry, thanks to the booze. But she would never forget what it felt like to frame him in the shot. The vulnerability. The look in his eyes. She'd captured the man behind the hotheaded mask. It was the kind of photo that would make you stop and stare and want more.

That's what good photographers did. Like in Professor

Tran's shots, the true art of photography was to elicit a visceral response that left the observer with questions.

What is the subject thinking?

Is this a normal day for them, or had something extraordinary happened?

She tapped open the email with a trembling finger and scanned the text, picking up bits and pieces.

The committee met today.

Blown away by your submission!

Quite an eye!

Full scholarship.

We can't wait to see you in London.

Please confirm your spot.

It wasn't a mirage or a figment of her imagination. The committee had been wowed. No, more like super-wowed, if that was even a real word.

"Charlotte? What is it?"

At the sound of Mitch's voice, she fumbled with her phone, pawing to close her email like her hands were made of butter.

"It's...um...just a photography thing. A little workshop," she stammered, not exactly sure what to do with this information.

"Just a workshop? Like a continuing education thing?" Mitch asked, watching her closely.

"Yeah, something like that," she confirmed, not quite lying and not quite telling the truth. She flashed him a bright smile, going for casual.

She needed a minute to think. This was huge—crazy, amazing huge! An opportunity of a lifetime!

"Take a sip of water," Mitch said, concern clouding his expression as he handed her the bottle. "I think you're still reeling."

"Reeling?" she repeated, then downed a giant gulp.

"From what just happened—from interacting with those jerks," he finished.

And that's right! The universe had thrown her a whammy with the Cliff Sutton Bryan one-two punch.

"Yeah, that's got to be it," she replied, then took another sip.

"And the photography," Mitch added.

The photography?

"What?" she eked out.

"You've been taking pictures all day. Any time I caught a glimpse of you, you were so focused, so engrossed in your work. I know what that's like. It's exhilarating but exhausting."

Her pounding heart slowed a fraction. There was no way he could have seen the email—and no way he could understand the gravity of what she'd been offered. Should she tell him about London? She could show him the email, and like two grown adults, they could discuss the prospect of her leaving for a couple of weeks. She released a slow breath. "Mitch, I—" she began as he started talking as well.

"Sorry! Go ahead," he said, his cheeks growing pink. A very *non-hotheaded* reaction. It was boyish—sweet and endearing. A heady buzz traveled through her body. And it was because of this man—a man she'd never expected to like. Every day, no, more like every hour, another layer peeled away, and she saw more of him—the truest version of him. The man in the old photographs, looking as if he were on top of the world.

"No, you go first," she said, unable to look away, wrapped in an invisible cocoon made of pure swoon. "You were saying?"

"I need to tell you something, Charlotte," he began, his words infused with tenderness. And the swoon-factor intensified.

"Okay," she breathed.

Between him telling off the creeps in her life, that charming blush, and his gentle tone, he could have started reading the phone book out loud, and she would have been utterly beguiled. But it was more than that. There was something different about him. The sound of her name flowing from his lips made her head spin. Here, alone in the truck, it sounded like poetry.

"You can tell me anything, Mitch."

He smiled—and God, that smile! She was left breathless, staring at his beautiful face.

He looked around the truck. "This was a good day. This was the right place to start."

"Absolutely," she agreed. "You fed a lot of people, got some great press, and I didn't hear you yell at anyone." She suppressed a grin. "You did threaten Sutton Bryan with bodily harm and let Cliff have it, but they don't really count."

"But you do, Charlotte," he said, his voice a low, husky rasp. "You count, and I have you to thank for this."

There it was—the signature Mitch Elliott intensity. He radiated this magnetism that rendered her near speechless. But she couldn't take the credit for today. Mitch, Sergio, and Erick had cooked their asses off. And it was Ralph and Louise Dagby who'd allowed them to park there. She might have been a part of the action, but she hadn't made this day a success.

She shook her head. "You're wrong. This is all you, Mitch. You started Say Cheese, Louise. You're the chef. You got yourself on TV. You worked to build a successful career. And you'll get it back. Whatever you're looking for, whatever you lost. If anyone can get that back, it's you."

She meant every word.

His career might have detoured. But after today, she'd seen what everyone must have seen in the guy the first time he'd cooked inside Say Cheese, Louise.

"But you're the reason I went back to the beginning—the real beginning," he countered. "You were the one who suggested the food truck reboot."

She cocked her head to the side. "Suggested?" she teased, needing to tamp down the intensity. It was almost too much to have him staring at her like that. Like he wanted her body and soul.

Her comment landed as she'd thought it would, and his lips curled into a sly smirk. "I know it's not like me, but I was trying to be polite. The correct description is more like you *ambushed* me in front of my publisher and publicist with the idea. But it was the push I needed," he finished, his expression growing earnest.

"You would have figured out a way forward with the book," she replied.

He took a step toward her. His observant eyes positively smoldered as he gripped the counter, one hand on each side of her. Pinned by his towering, muscular body, her breaths came hard and fast. It was just like when he'd done the same thing against the side of the RV.

"We both know that's not true. I was stuck. I've been stuck for a very long time," he confessed, as his very presence seemed to fill the entire space.

"This seems to be becoming a habit," she said, gazing at him through her eyelashes.

He angled his body toward her. "What's becoming a habit?"

She glanced from side to side, admiring his hands. She must have taken a hundred pictures of them today. Those hands that gripped her hips and tangled in her hair. Those hands that she couldn't stop imagining caressing her breasts and working her most sensitive place. Large and the right amount of rough, a shiver rippled through her recalling what had happened at the sink a few paces away.

"This *caging-me-in* business seems to be becoming a habit," she teased.

He came in even closer. "Maybe it's because I don't want you to go anywhere."

Had it gotten hotter in there? Was the cooktop still on?

No, this was all them—their heat, their electricity.

His words hung in the charged air.

I don't want you to go anywhere.

And what was she supposed to say to that? Oh, by the way, I have an opportunity thousands of miles away across the ocean. No, she couldn't mention it. Not now! Her brain was too scrambled by this man's raw allure.

She twisted the key between her fingers. "It appears that you've got me. My question is, what are you going to do about it?"

This was fun! Tapping into this part of her, the powerful, seductive part of her she'd never known with any other man, made her head spin and her body ache. Mitch's gaze raked over her as he drank her in. It was beyond wrong and beyond intoxicating and clearly beyond her control to resist him.

"How do we always end up like this?" he whispered against the shell of her ear. She hovered there on the precipice, wanting so badly for him to press his lips to her skin while savoring the rush of anticipation.

She released the key and slid her hands up the hard expanse of his chest, relishing the rise and fall of each ridge of defined muscle. She parted her lips, ready to tell this beast of a man that she was ready for round two against the sink when her timer went off again. They pulled apart as the chirping cut through the cheese-scented, sex-fueled charge that pulsed between them.

He looked as dazed as she felt.

"What's that alarm for?" he asked.

She grabbed her phone and silenced the incessant sound. She'd set multiple alarms for Oscar. It was his first day, and she was hellbent on making sure that they weren't late to get him. The last thing he needed was to be the last kid picked up. She knew plenty about that.

"We need to get going. We can't be late to pick up Oscar," she said, finding her voice and recovering the ability to form rational thoughts. She glanced between his hands, still pinning her in place. The guy got the message. He took a step back, then crossed his arms as she smoothed her skirt.

What were they going to do? Bang one out in front of a homeless shelter?

She shook her head, then checked the digital clock above the order window. "Actually, we've got a little time."

Focus!

"I could show you some of the pictures I took today. We could get it on—the work. We could focus on the work of looking at photographs. Because that is part of my job. I take pictures of you and your body. And food. Your body and food," she finished with a resolute nod. She could have ended that statement with a cartwheel, or stuck out her tongue, or blew a series of raspberries. Any of those options would have been less embarrassing than the verbal vomit she'd spewed.

And oh, my God!

Is this what happened to girls who had too many dirty, dirty thoughts? Did their brains simply decay inside of their skulls?

"We don't have time to go over the photos. We should head over to Whitmore. I was on the phone with the school before I came back to the food truck to scare the hell out of your old boss and ex-boyfriend," Mitch said as a cocky edge returned to his voice.

She stared at him as dread welled in her chest. Why was he on the phone with the school? Her thoughts spiraled. "Is Oscar okay? Did something happen? Was he bullied? Did he fall? Did he break his leg?" she rattled off.

He chuckled. "No, none of that happened. Oscar's fine. But wow! You went right to crisis mode pretty fast."

Her jaw dropped. "Yes, I went into crisis mode. Oscar is my..." she trailed off. He's her what? He wasn't hers, but he sort of was. "I'm his nanny," she finished.

"Well, Ms. Nanny, I think you'll like what's about to happen," he said, then opened a small metal door next to the refrigerator. She leaned over to peer inside. It was crammed with extra ingredients—a block of cheese, jars of condiments, a slab of butter, and a few loaves of bread.

She couldn't figure out what was going on. "I thought you guys went through the supplies?"

He closed the metal door. "We used up the food we had for today's lunch rush. But I started packing a hidden stash way back when we first started taking Louise out."

That didn't make sense. "Why? Why not keep everything together?"

A sentimental, almost sad look marred his features. "Back when we started the food truck, it was about making a profit. We'd sell out quickly—sometimes in less than an hour. But once the lunch crowd thinned, we'd get people coming up, asking if there were scraps or burnt sandwiches. They were in search of anything we were throwing out."

"What did you do?"

He sighed and leaned against the counter. "I felt like shit when I had to tell them we were out of everything. These people were hungry and often homeless or living in their cars. So, after that one time, when I didn't have anything to give them, I decided I'd keep a little extra hidden away for just that reason. Seth, Holly, and I barely had two nickels to rub together back then. But those people didn't deserve scraps. Nobody does."

She held her breath, watching the man. It was the first time he'd mentioned his previous food truck partners without looking like he wanted to pound his fist through the wall. He had no idea what he'd done—no idea what a monumental step he'd taken.

"Is everything okay?" he asked.

"Yeah," she replied, smiling up at him. "I get wanting to help. But you're not charging anything. The sign on the window says as much. This is a gift to the city. It doesn't matter who comes up to the window. Everyone eats for free."

He stared at a cluster of photos. "Old habits are hard to break. But I thought of something we could do with the extra today," he finished, turning away from the images and meeting her gaze. "Grab your camera."

Before she could blink, Mitch was prepping the truck to go. He closed the order window, secured several latches, then helped her out of the back.

"Where are we going exactly?" she asked as he opened her door.

"It's a surprise," he answered, sliding into the driver's seat.

A surprise?

"We don't have time for surprises, Mitch. We don't have time to make a pit stop. Especially one where you plan to cook," she exclaimed, then blew out a hot breath. "Don't get me wrong, I love the idea of rolling up and handing out your delicious grilled cheese sandwiches, but—"

"So, you think my food is delicious?" he interrupted as he started the truck, then hit the gas.

This man was infuriating!

She crossed her arms. "Why do you think I endured waitressing for you? The ambiance of the constant hotheadedness? The tips were decent, but the real perk was the thirty seconds you gave your staff to shovel a few bites of the daily special into their mouths."

"Jeez! You can unleash the redheaded hothead when you want to," he remarked, taking a turn.

"Mitch, I'm serious. We can't be late. We have to get to Whitmore on time," she cautioned.

"We're fine. Trust me. This will be a Charlotte-approved activity—not unlike scouring the forest for wood."

Had he lost his ever-loving mind?

"What does that even mean, Mitch? And there better not be any skunks or owls where we're headed," she warned.

"It's Colorado, Charlotte. You'd be hard-pressed to go anywhere that doesn't have at least one of those creatures in the vicinity."

She collapsed into the seat. "What I wouldn't give to be holding an avocado, cucumber, and tomato salad," she mumbled, causing the man next to her to break out into laughter. "Laugh all you want, hothead. Just know, I'm not messing around."

He glanced at her. "I know you're not. I know you mean business. You get a little line between your eyes when you get mad."

She slapped her hand to her forehead. "I do not!"

"You do. It's sort of adorable," he countered.

She sat there, staring at his profile, then slowly lowered her hand. How was she supposed to respond to that? And what was going on with them—besides out-of-this-world sex and a crazy attraction that seemed to intensify with each passing second?

She looked out the window as the school came into view. "How is Whitmore the big surprise?" she asked as he passed the pickup lane and the parking lot. "Are we going to drive around and around the school in circles, searching for someone to feed?"

"Something like that," he said, looking mighty pleased with himself as they pulled up on the far side of the school near the playground. A group of children were seated beneath a leafy oak when one child—*Oscar*—sprang to his feet and waved his hands in the air. The other kids followed suit, jumping and dancing around beneath the tree.

Her gaze bounced from the gaggle of children bouncing in the distance to Mitch. "You're cooking for Oscar's class?"

He tapped his hands on the steering wheel as that endearing hint of a blush colored his cheeks. "Before I threatened Sutton and Cliff with bodily harm, I called the school. I spoke with Oscar's teacher to ask if it would be okay if we stopped by and made them a snack. She thought it was a great idea. None of the children have any allergies. And she said the parents signed some permission form at the beginning of the year saying their kid could participate in snack time. We have enough food in my secret stash for each kid to get half a sandwich."

"You came up with this idea on your own?" She hated that her question came out with such surprise. But she was absolutely blown away.

"I thought Oscar might get a kick out of it. Being the new kid is hard. I'm not so great at the parenting part, but the chef part of me knows what people like."

She stared in awe of this man. "This is really sweet of you, Mitch. He's going to remember you did this for him."

His blush deepened. "I wasn't always a giant, roaring hothead."

A warmth filled her chest. "I'm starting to see that."

She could barely see anything else. Mitch and his world were quickly becoming her world.

She'd learned more about him in the last couple of days than she had in the last two and a half years she'd worked for him at the restaurant. But so much of his anger and awful behavior made sense now.

Of course, he'd demanded perfection in everyone who

worked for him. He didn't know any different because he demanded even more from himself.

He'd become a machine. A hotheaded, perfection-driven machine that, day in and day out, had to prove his worth.

Looking back, it was so clear. The rage and the need to be the best was a shield. But it had disintegrated as if it were made of papier-mâché when he'd learned he was Oscar's father. That had to have been the trigger that caused him to blow his top and lose his status as one of America's favorite prime time chefs. The pain, frustration, and utter agony of being deceived by the people he loved and then learning that he was a father had to have tipped the scales. He couldn't balance the heartache any longer. He couldn't keep it inside. He simply couldn't control the fury. It had taken control.

"I got the idea today when people started showing up with their kids," Mitch continued. "I remembered the cookie cutters. Louise had given them to us along with..."

"That old spatula," she supplied.

He nodded. "Yeah."

It was as if the Mitch Elliott pendulum had swung from hotheaded asshat to compassionate chef and caregiver.

"You're a good dad, Mitch," she said, and she meant it.

He sighed. "I don't know about that. But it's easier to try to be a good parent when you're with me."

His words went right to her heart. But there was no time to swoon or sit there like a glazed doughnut. The cheering children grew louder as Mitch slowed the vehicle and parked. She looped her camera's strap around her neck. It was time to work. She was there to chronicle Mitch's return to his roots. She hadn't even closed the passenger side door before Oscar was at her side.

"Look, Charlotte! Look what I painted at school today," the boy cried, pulling an object from his backpack. She couldn't even see what Oscar was holding in the bustle and bump of children gathering to check out the truck.

"Slow down, Oscar. And take it easy, boys and girls," the teacher said, tapping her clipboard as she addressed the class, oohing and aahing over the giant vehicle.

Charlotte smiled as a little boy high-fived Oscar. "They sure seem excited."

Mrs. Bergen nodded. "They sure are! I had the kids bring their backpacks out with them. I'm dismissing them from here when the bell rings. This should give you a little extra time. I know my husband will be disappointed he missed this. You'll need to be sure to remind Mitch to have plenty of food for the Whitmore Carnival. I'm sure my husband and his brothers will be the first in line. And let me give you this," she added, taking a sheet from her clipboard. "It's the permission slip for the class camping trip. We'll be heading to a spot called the Outdoor Laboratory in Telluride for the last week of school."

Charlotte accepted the paper and scanned the dates. Her gut twisted. Oscar's last day of camp was the first day of the photography workshop. She pushed the thought aside.

"Thank you," she answered, folding the paper and slipping it into her pocket.

"No, thank you! This is such a treat!" the teacher replied, gesturing toward the truck.

"It was Mitch's idea," she answered as Oscar tapped her arm.

"Mrs. Bergen said I could show you my heart," the child chimed, holding out his palm with a shiny, orange ceramic heart glinting in the midday sun. "I painted it the same color as Say Cheese, Louise."

The twist in her gut loosened as she observed Oscar's palm-sized painted heart.

"It's beautiful! Do you mind if I take a picture?" she asked.

"You can take as many pictures as you want," Oscar replied, his proud grin widening. She only got one shot in before Mitch joined them, and the boy pivoted toward his father.

"I painted my heart orange, Dad, like the truck. Now we both have a heart. Mine doesn't have a lock, but it's still pretty awesome because I picked the color by myself," Oscar exclaimed. He shot his arms out, balancing the heart in the palms of his hands as the art project wobbled precariously.

Quickly, Mitch rested his palms beneath his son's hands, steadying them so the ceramic heart wouldn't crash to the ground. Without thinking, she lifted her camera and framed the shot of their hands.

Click! Click!

She checked the screen, assessing the composition.

"Do you want me to take a picture of the three of you?" the teacher offered.

"Sure," Oscar answered for her. "Put your hands in with ours, Charlotte! Right, Dad? We should take a picture with Charlotte's hands, too!"

The man nodded. "Yeah, we should."

"I'm no photographer, but I'm happy to take the picture," the teacher added.

"Okay, thank you," she said, handing the camera over.

"Little, medium, big," Oscar announced, observing their hands. "Charlotte, you're in the middle because you're the medium hand. You can be the glue between Dad and me."

"That works for me," she answered, slipping her hands on top of Mitch's as Oscar rested his hands on hers.

"That looks great!" Mrs. Bergen remarked as the click of the shutter dotted the air.

The three of them stayed like that, hands atop one another, staring at the tiny heart. She knew it would be a good shot. She'd always been drawn to close-ups. Faces, eyes, hands, objects. For her, zooming in on the details always left her wanting more. She framed this shot in her mind, memorizing the shape of their hands, the color of Oscar's pink palms, the glint of the shiny ceramic heart.

Mitch brushed his index finger against the back of her hand. Usually, his touch sent a dizzying current through her body. But this caress was different. Instead of leaving her scatter-brained and breathless, this touch sent a wave of calm through her—a soothing sense of being under this man's protection. And then it hit her. She'd never felt protected by anyone before. Of course, her friends cared for her. Harper would gladly throw down for her at the drop of a hat. But this was different. She looked up to find Mitch staring at her. His gaze brimmed with tenderness.

They were bound together, connected by fate.

"And here's your camera back," the teacher said, her words popping their little hand-tower bubble.

Mitch dropped his hands to his sides, then cleared his throat. "Did you have a good day, Oscar?"

The boy's expression darkened as he glanced at his teacher. "I had a little tummy ache after lunch."

Mrs. Bergen patted Oscar's shoulder. "It seems that Phoebe Gale brought quite a few chocolate chip cookies to school to share at lunchtime."

Oscar nodded emphatically. "Phoebe had to go home early because she puked cookies all over the playground. I only ate four. But she ate eleven of them in under one minute. We timed her with the clock in the cafeteria. But I feel better now. And I'm hungry! Mrs. Bergen says that you're making us a snack," Oscar added, his cheerful countenance returning.

At the boy's mention of snacks, the children went into a six-year-old frenzy, hooting and whooping and launching questions at Mitch, left and right.

Can I drive your truck to the zoo?

Have you ever tried to fill up the truck with caterpillars?

Do caterpillars eat grilled cheese sandwiches?

Do grilled cheese-eating caterpillars turn into grilled cheese-eating butterflies?

Charlotte pressed her hand to her lips, holding back her laughter, as Mitch's eyes grew wide. The children surrounded him, firing off their questions—that seemed to get crazier and more farfetched by the second.

"One, two, three! Eyes on me!" the teacher called as the chatter ceased, and the boys and girls turned to face her like pint-sized soldiers. "I'll get them settled, so you can set up," the woman said, herding the group back toward the oak tree.

"Are you ready for this, Chef?" Charlotte asked as Mitch blew out an audible breath. But the man's look of terror smoothed into one of excitement.

"I think so. I'm actually pumped and a little proud."

"Proud?" she repeated.

"We can't be doing too badly at this parenting thing. At least our kid didn't pound a ton of cookies and throw up at school," Mitch said under his breath, eyes glinting with mischief.

She got the gist of what he was saying. But two words stood out to her.

Our kid.

"I better get started," he said, gesturing toward the truck.

"And I'll ask the teacher if it's okay for me to take some pictures of the class," she said over her shoulder as she headed for the tree.

"Boys and girls, make a straight line in front of the truck, then sit down, crisscross applesauce," the woman instructed.

Charlotte held up her camera. "Is it okay if I take a few pictures of the class interacting with Mitch? I'll try not to get their faces in the shots."

"You can. Our families sign permission forms, allowing us to take photographs at school," the teacher replied as her expression grew pensive. She glanced at the children, who had followed directions, and now sat watching as Mitch popped open the entire side panel of the truck. "Can I speak to you for a minute?" she continued.

Charlotte twisted her camera's strap. "Sure, we can chat. Is everything all right?"

The dreaded *do-you-have-a-minute* teacher question! When she was a girl, she'd heard many a teacher say this to Harper's grandmother.

Mrs. Bergen removed a folded piece of paper from her clipboard. "During our writing time, I asked the children to write a letter to anyone they wanted—real, fictional, dead or alive. Oscar wrote a letter to his mother."

Charlotte nodded, worry flooding her system. They hadn't talked that much about Holly. He had her picture near his bed, and she was ready to listen if he ever wanted to talk. But life had moved so quickly these past few days. There had hardly been a moment to reflect.

"It's noted on his registration documents that she recently passed away," the teacher continued.

"Yes, it happened suddenly. Did Oscar write something that worried you?"

"Quite the opposite, actually. I'd like to share it with you." Mrs. Bergen handed over the sheet of paper. "He's a bright boy. His handwriting and spelling skills are at least a grade above. But it was the content of his letter that made me want to share this with you and his father."

Charlotte unfolded the piece of paper and pored over the boy's words.

Dear Mom,

> *I miss you lots and lots, but I am okay. I like my school. I have a friend in my class. She barfed at recess.*
>
> *I want you to know that you were right. Dad is nice. And I have a Charlotte now. We both like cameras.*
>
> *Love,*
>
> *Oscar*

She touched the spot on the paper where the boy had signed his name as her vision grew glassy. Two competing emotions tore through her. She couldn't help but feel relieved about Oscar's transition to life in Denver. It was everything she'd wanted for the boy—and for Mitch. But tangled in with that relief was a thread of fear over the photography workshop. Would two weeks away hamper Oscar's progress? There was no way to know how he or Mitch would react. It could be fine—no big deal—or it could throw everything off.

"He's a real sweetheart. It looks as if you and his father are doing a great job supporting him through this big shift in his life," Mrs. Bergen commented.

Charlotte looked away to compose herself. "That's reassuring," she answered, handing back the letter.

"Why don't you keep it," the teacher replied, then surveyed a spot on the grass where two wiggly boys sat poking at each other. "I'll let you get back to your photography, so I can get back to making sure these children don't make a ruckus," she added with a wide grin before heading over to quiet the rowdy pair.

Charlotte nodded, then skimmed the letter again, zeroing in on five words.

I have a Charlotte now.

"Who's ready for grilled cheese?" Mitch called. She looked up to find the man, smiling from ear to ear as he spoke to the excited brood of wiggly first graders.

"Me, me, me!" cried the boys and girls.

He looked up from the group and caught her eye. "Then let's do this," he said. There was so much kindness infused into his words, and she felt them settle in her heart.

Let's do this.

She touched the key. Was Mitch talking to her, or was she again getting ahead of herself?

She'd dreamed of being wanted, truly wanted. Is that what this was? Was it the start of something?

What mattered to her?

What was important?

Everything blurred together.

She smiled back at Mitch as thoughts of London drifted away. She'd sort it out later. Lifting her camera, she captured Mitch's expression, basking in the glow of his smile. There would be time to talk—time to figure it out. Because right now, the last thing she wanted to do was jeopardize this sweet slice of heaven she'd found with this former hothead and his darling son.

TWENTY

MITCH

"YOU'LL NEVER BELIEVE THIS, DAD!" Oscar exclaimed, wiggling into his pajama pants. "Phoebe stuffed another cookie into her mouth, and everybody at the lunch table was cheering and clapping. I've never seen a girl do anything like that. It was awesome!"

Mitch chuckled, then handed his son the pajama top. "You've got to be careful with sweets. They're fine in small amounts. But you don't want to go overboard. I'm guessing that it wasn't *so awesome* when Phoebe got sick."

Oscar paused with the top of his head poking out. "It kind of was awesome. She was on the swing next to me, talking and talking and talking. Because that's what she does. Then she stopped talking, and puke was everywhere. In the air, on her clothes, on the swing. I was lucky she didn't throw up my way. She got puke on the sneakers of some older kid on her other side named Grover. He'd pushed a little kid off the swing so he could take it. He kind of deserved to get puked on," the boy finished, lowering his voice.

"Sounds like good old Grover had it coming."

"I hope Phoebe feels better. I don't know how she got so many cookies crammed into her lunchbox," Oscar mused.

Mitch bit back a grin, imagining the ways he could give Rowen shit over the guy's shoddy parenting. But the joke was really on him. Who would have thought that he'd ever feel like he had even the slightest iota of a handle on being a dad? But for the first time in a long time, the endless angry loop playing in his head had quieted.

"Did anything else exciting happen at school? Anything that didn't involve vomit or mean kids named Grover?" he asked as Oscar climbed into the bottom bunk and settled himself under the covers.

The boy beamed. "Yeah! You showed up with Louise! Will you come to my school every day and make snacks?"

He stared at the kid—his son—and met eyes as blue as his. "Probably not every day. But we'll be at the Whitmore Carnival in a few weeks."

Oscar looked away and stared up at the top bunk. He could almost see the gears turning in the kid's head. The boy had something on his mind.

"What about the kids in your class? I got to meet most of them today. They seem all right to me. What do you think?" he asked. Maybe if he kept the boy talking, the kid would share what he was thinking.

Oscar shrugged. "They're pretty nice. I mostly stuck with Phoebe. We talked with our feet during math, and Mrs. Bergen didn't even notice." Oscar paused, then pinned him with his gaze. "Is this what my life is going to be like now?"

Jesus! That was one hell of a pivot.

"What do you mean?" he asked, fumbling.

"The three of us," the boy answered.

There was that word again.

Us.

"Us?" he repeated. That word used to claw at his heart and sour his mood. But not anymore.

"Yeah, you, me, and Charlotte," Oscar continued.

Charlotte.

Charlotte had called them an *us* in the cab of the truck this morning. It seemed like that moment had happened years—not hours ago.

He'd been reeling. Reeling from dropping Oscar off and hearing the boy tell him that he loved him. Reeling from driving the familiar route to Helping Hands. And reeling from the tangle of emotions that kept him from knowing up from down and right from left when it came to the alluring redhead he couldn't quite keep his hands off. And while the attraction between them hadn't let up, today proved that it was more than physical. The click and snap of her camera had woven in with the pop and crackle of the toasting sandwiches like a soothing lullaby, letting him know she was there. Her presence lightened the mental load, allowing him to shed the burden of pain and anger that weighed him down. And let him do what he did best.

Create happiness through food.

With every turn of the spatula, every slice of his knife through a Signature Louise sandwich, and every instruction he rattled off to Erick and Sergio, he returned to himself. It was as if he'd been trapped at the bottom of the ocean, surrounded by a sea of inky black, until Charlotte shined a light—a light that beckoned him to abandon the familiar darkness and swim toward the surface.

To her.

To Oscar.

To the person he once was.

"Dad, is it going to be you, me, and Charlotte together forever?" his son pressed.

How was he supposed to answer that question? He knew how he wanted to answer it.

But the truth was, they were still well within the sixty-day nanny trial period. But he couldn't imagine a day without Charlotte—not anymore. Not since the moment he saw her in the bar.

He pulled Oscar's desk chair over to the side of the boy's bed and sank down, recalling the last few hours. After he'd cooked for Oscar's class, they'd gone home, then headed out into the yard. He and Charlotte had taken turns pushing Oscar on the swing set. They'd zipped through a few games of tag. And when they'd gotten hungry, they'd filed inside. He'd started dinner while Charlotte helped Oscar with his homework.

The routine came naturally.

He'd whipped up spaghetti and meatballs, and they'd eaten at the table, Charlotte to his left and Oscar to his right. He hadn't spoken much, and neither had Charlotte. Instead, they listened as Oscar explained the steps he followed to paint his ceramic heart. And then, after they'd done the dishes together, the boy had asked to play video games on his tablet.

Back at the table, Charlotte brought out her laptop and started scrolling through the images she'd taken today. Oscar sipped on a glass of milk and fought intergalactic space aliens while he jotted down a rough outline for his book.

And here's what was strange about it. There was nothing strange about it. The evening had flowed seamlessly.

"Dad?" Oscar said again.

He nodded to the boy, who observed him carefully.

"I'm your dad, so it will always be you and me. And Charlotte is..."

There were so many ways to finish that statement.

Charlotte is the one person who'd stood up to him in a very long time.

Charlotte is the woman who made him a better father.

Charlotte is the one thing he'd always wanted and never thought he could have again.

"Charlotte is my nanny and your person," Oscar supplied.

"My person?" he repeated, taken aback.

"Yeah, she takes pictures for you. She helps with the food truck, and she makes you happy," Oscar answered.

"How do you know that? How do you know she makes me happy?" he asked, marveling at this smart, intuitive, observant kid. How had he not seen it the minute he'd laid eyes on the boy? Granted, Oscar was a toddler when they first met. But the signs were there. The attentive eyes. The way the boy observed nature. His love of photography. The kid was amazing! And to his detriment, he'd allowed anger and seething resentment to cloud his view of this gifted boy.

"I know because this is what your face does when you see her," Oscar answered, then used his index fingers to mush his lips into one hell of a scary smile.

"I sure hope I don't look like that," he teased, contorting his face to his son's delight. But the kid wasn't wrong. He'd tried to rein in his emotions when it came to the woman. Oscar's observation proved a point. He was beyond controlling what his heart wanted.

Oscar's little body vibrated beneath the covers as his rollicking giggles gave way to a full belly laugh.

The kid's joy was contagious, and he laughed along with his son, soaking in the simple, beautiful pleasure of spending time with the kid. But barely a few seconds had passed before Oscar's mouth widened, and he released a long, gaping yawn.

"What's this funny business? It sounds like a giggle factory in here."

Charlotte.

He turned to find her standing in the doorway—like she'd

always been there. Like she should always be there. She'd twisted her hair into a bun, and a few auburn tendrils framed her face. Barefoot, but still in the skirt and T-shirt she'd worn today, she'd never looked lovelier. His expression softened as he took her in.

"Dad smooshed his face up and looked like he ate a hundred million sour lemons. Show her, Dad," the boy prompted.

"It was something like this," he said, giving her the not-so-goofy version.

"That is a funny face," she replied, entering the room, then cringed. "I'm sorry you had to get Oscar ready for bed. I could have helped you."

He shared a look with his son. "We've got it under control. I didn't want to bother you. You were focused on your work. You didn't even notice when we left the kitchen to go outside and eat dessert."

She gasped. "I missed dessert?"

He hadn't wanted to break her concentration because he'd understood it. He got that she was in the zone, fixated on her photography.

"Yeah, Charlotte, we had popsicles! We ate them outside on the deck."

"How did I miss that?" she exclaimed.

"Easy!" Oscar supplied. "You were staring at your computer so hard I thought your eyes would get stuck like this," Oscar said, then reared his head back as he forced his eyelids to retract. "Your eyes were bigger than that owl's eyes. Remember, the one that snatched the skunk right off the ground and made you run real fast and scream and scream and scream," his son finished, pointing to the Polaroid proof on the bedside table.

"I remember that night," she said, then stilled. "I mean, I remember the animal adventures in the clearing, of course," she finished, her cheeks growing pink as she twisted a lock of auburn hair between her fingers. And he would have bet every-thing he had that she wasn't thinking about the skunk abduction.

He would never forget that night either. When he closed his eyes, he was there with her in his arms. The passion had flowed through him. A hunger so inescapable, it stirred every emotion he'd suppressed.

She sat down on the edge of the bed near Oscar's feet, smoothed her skirt, then patted his leg. "Did you brush your teeth?"

"Yep!"

She leaned in toward the boy. "Really, really, well? Like even got the ones way in the back?"

"Ahh," Oscar opened his mouth, presenting his pearly whites.

"Looks like you are ready for sweet dreams, and I have some news for you, Oscar."

"For me?" the boy chimed.

"Do you remember my friend Penny?" Charlotte began. "She's the lady who's engaged to Phoebe's uncle."

The boy nodded.

"She texted me about Phoebe. She said that Phoebe wants you to know that she'll be back at school tomorrow. And she's glad she didn't vomit on you."

"Yeah, she vomited on Grover instead," Oscar replied as Charlotte sucked in a tight breath.

"Grover?" she repeated.

"Yeah, he's some big kid at my school. He knocked a little kid off the swing next to Phoebe and then took it. And then Phoebe puked on his shoes."

Something quite mischievous glinted in the woman's eyes. "What did Grover look like?"

Oscar scratched his little chin. "Big and frowny," the boy

answered as the whisper of a menacing grin pulled at the corners of Charlotte's mouth.

"That's too bad for Grover," she purred, sounding not at all concerned for the kid. And that's when it hit him. She'd mentioned a Grover at the bar. Grover Cleveland something! It had almost gotten her booted because she'd sounded like such a lunatic.

He studied the alluring redhead, who was doing a damned good job at tamping down her fiery, devilish side when Oscar roared another spectacular yawn.

"Are you and my dad gonna go to bed now?" the boy asked as he blinked slowly, slumber clearly on the kid's horizon.

At the mention of Charlotte and a bed, his mind began cataloging the deliciously dirty things he could do to her in one of those. But he could not think like that. As much as his body ached for this woman, they had to at least try to keep it *officially professional*—or whatever the hell stupid moniker they'd come up with to attempt to label what was going on between them.

Charlotte twisted a lock of her hair as her sly look dissolved into one of panic. "Well, Oscar, your father and I will be going to bed—eventually—in our own beds. That's going to happen for the purpose of sleep. It's science and health, I believe. But I still have some work to do that involves your dad, so we will not be in our own beds alone for a little while." She turned to him. "That is if you have time, Mitch. I have something I'd like to share with you at a table—a table not near a bed."

Christ! Did the nanny need a reboot?

And he thought he was bumbling his way around this whole mind-mushing-tornado-of-emotions business! But after that word salad Charlotte served up, he could see that they were in it together when it came to trying to get a hold on the intense pull between them.

She cleared her throat. "I put together a compilation of

images that I wanted to run by you to get your feedback," she said, then sighed as if she were relieved she'd said something that didn't sound batshit crazy.

He nodded. He could sound *not* batshit crazy, too. "Yeah, that would be...yeah. Compilation, okay," he replied. And winner, winner! He'd taken over as the most batshit-sounding awkward adult in the room.

"Mitch," she whispered.

"Yes?"

"He's asleep," she said softly.

"What?" he asked as the light from Oscar's lamp lit Charlotte in a warm glow. With her hair up, he studied the curve of her neck, taking in her ivory skin.

"Oscar has fallen asleep," she said, slowly—clearly for his benefit. And he appreciated it. His mind might as well be made of the awful *parmesaned-to-the-max* risotto his sous chef had thrown together.

"He does that...at night...as children do...sleep," he replied, immediately wanting to purchase a roll of duct tape and apply the whole damned thing to his mouth.

Why was he acting like a gawky, tongue-tied teenager?

Of course, he knew the answer! She was seated mere inches away from him.

Charlotte patted Oscar's leg one last time, then stood. "My computer and camera are still in the kitchen."

He rose from the chair and walked with her to the door. "Then that's where we can work. The kitchen—where people work on tables."

She cocked her head to the side. "Okay," she answered, probably wondering if he'd blown a gasket and was experiencing the early signs of a stroke. He was beginning to wonder the same thing.

He followed her down the hall to the narrow set of steps

that led to the kitchen and joined her at the table. He settled himself into a chair, then stared at the grainy wood.

Pull yourself together!

He looked up as she scooted her chair toward his, then gathered her laptop, camera, and notebook, then slid into the seat. Her knee bumped his, and they both inhaled a tight breath.

They seemed to have two settings when they were alone.

Let's get it on ASAP mode and middle school dance mode.

"It's easier if we look at the images together," she said, angling the screen between them, and he breathed a sigh of relief.

Work was good. Work would center him.

She leaned forward and gestured to the screen. "The pictures need to tell a story while also allowing the observer to feel like they're a part of the narrative. Does that make sense?"

He caught her eye. "It does."

She released a slow exhale as if she were coming back to herself. "I pulled what I thought were the shots that did that. We want your readers to be on this journey with you," she finished, then tapped the mouse and opened a file. "Go ahead. Scroll through the images."

He nodded, then hit the arrow key. She'd started with the Helping Hands neighborhood. He'd gone through a few shots before stopping on one of a small kitchen—the Helping Hands kitchen. He stared at the photo as the memories flooded back.

"Ralph showed me around the facility. I can take them out if you don't want them."

His gaze moved methodically from the wall of pots and pans to the bank of ovens to the sink where he must have washed a thousand dishes alongside Holly and Seth. He tapped the arrow as a shot of the prep area appeared—the location of where he'd created the Signature Louise.

"It hasn't changed," he remarked, almost able to see the younger, gangly version of himself in the photo.

She nodded. "Helping Hands is one of those places where you can feel that life has been lived inside those walls."

She'd hit the nail on the head with that assessment!

"It is. Louise and Ralph have helped a lot of kids get on the right path in there," he replied, his voice a husk of a rasp. Charlotte didn't say a thing—didn't even move. She let him soak in image after image. Most of them were of him, but not all of them. There were shots of Sergio and Erick watching him cook and photos of Ralph and Louise inside the shelter. Then it shifted to the patrons. People of all colors and creeds clustered together, chatting, laughing, and connecting.

He peered at an image of the line of people that stretched past the community center. "It never feels like it's this many people. I see them one at a time. I know they add up, but in my head, I focus on one customer, one order."

"I can tell," she replied as she evaluated the image. She relaxed into the chair. This wasn't Charlotte, the nervous nanny. This was Charlotte, the confident photographer. And he'd be lying if he said this Charlotte wasn't damned sexy. She pursed her lips, her expression growing pensive. "That was one of my favorite things to catch. People can tell that you want to cook for them." She tapped the arrow and scrolled through three shots of him, demonstrating a technique to Erick. "And you're a different cook in Say Cheese, Louise. There's a flow to how you work, an ease. There's nothing rigid about it."

Rigid was the perfect word to describe what his life had become after he'd learned what Holly and Seth had been doing behind his back. Like a coil, twisting and contracting with each bitter thought, he'd warped himself into the brute of a man he was now. And he'd brought that harsh energy to the Crystal Cricket.

"Rigid, like how it was at the restaurant?" he tossed out, raising an eyebrow.

She held his gaze, unflinching. "Yes, rigid would be a charitable description of your management style at the Crystal Cricket."

It was as if he saw everything anew with fresh eyes. He viewed the remaining images that captured his time with the reporters and then the impromptu pit stop at Whitmore.

"So, what do you think?" she asked as the screen faded to black.

He glanced from the laptop to her camera. "Something's missing."

"Is it something that has to do with cooking?" she asked, opening her notepad. "Would you like me to get more shots of the process of making the sandwiches? I could set up the ingredients to get more of a commercial feel. What I shot today has a photojournalism vibe—like you're right in the mix."

He shook his head. "The style and feel are spot-on."

She picked up the pen that had been sandwiched between the pages of the notebook and tapped the tip to a new page. "Then what's missing?"

He took the pen and notebook from her and set them aside. His gaze slid from the key at the hollow of her neck to her emerald eyes. "You, Charlotte. You're missing."

"Me?" she whispered.

"Yes, you're a part of this. You're the reason for everything. Taking out the food truck again, Oscar, not hating my guts—it's you. You're the spark," he added.

The spark.

He thought back to what Ines and Louise had said to him. He'd lost something. Could he have found it in Charlotte?

She shook her head as that blush he'd come to adore caressed her cheeks. "That's not the job of a photographer."

"Says who?" he shot back.

She chuckled. "All of my photography instructors. I had a conversation with one of my professors—Professor Tran. She's one of the most gifted photographers I've ever met. While photographers are part of the equation, she says that our job is to allow the story to unfold, unfettered and unencumbered by our biases. This is where we uncover the..."

The color drained from her cheeks.

"The what?" he coaxed.

She swallowed. "The truth," she answered as if it hurt to say the words. Eyes shining, she'd never looked more beautiful or more vulnerable.

He picked up her camera. "I think it's time we turn the tables, shake things up, and uncover your truth," he finished, framing her in the shot.

She stared into the camera. "What truth do you want to uncover?"

His finger hovered over the shutter button for a fraction of a second before capturing her image. "Tell me why you chose to study photography?" he said, framing another shot.

She exhaled an audible breath as if a weight had been lifted. "I fell in love with photography at an early age."

"Did your parents get you a camera for your birthday?" he asked, watching her through the viewfinder.

Her bottom lip trembled, but she regained control. "I got my first camera from Harper's grandmother when I was twelve."

"Harper? The crazy one? The big hat and winter scarf chick?" he asked, watching her transform. The darkness in her eyes faded, and the last ounce of whatever was dampening her spirit disappeared. She smiled at him through her lashes as he snapped another picture.

"Yes, that Harper," she answered, stifling a laugh. "We were up in her attic, and I found an old Canon AE-1 camera inside a tattered leather bag. The kind that uses thirty-five-millimeter film—nothing electronic or high tech about it. Harper's grandmother told me I could keep it. There were tons of those little canisters of unused film in the old bag. And I was enamored with it from the start." She stared at a spot beyond his shoulder. "I must have taken hundreds of pictures of Harper, Libby, and Penny that summer. It was the first time I felt in control of what my life looked like," she mused as if she'd fallen back in time.

"What do you mean by that?" he pressed.

"Taking pictures of my friends and my favorite places, and even the night sky filled an empty part of me."

"Just the sky?" he asked.

A sweet smile spread across her lips. "I'd wait, staring into the blackness, hoping to see a shooting star. It might sound silly, but when I'd catch one, it was like it was meant for me—like I was in control of what went into the frame—my frame."

"But not your family?" he asked. He wasn't the biggest family guy either. His parents had passed in a car accident when he was barely four years old. He had no real memories of them. His grandpa had tried to do his best to raise him, but the two had never been close.

He watched her, observing the sadness that clouded her expression as a realization hit. For as much as she knew about him, besides her asshat ex, awful old boss, love of photography, and her lightweight drinking status, he knew very little else about her.

She pressed her lips into a tight line. "I'm an only child. Well, not exactly. I have stepsiblings. My dad has two kids with his new wife. They're in Kentucky. But I don't know them well. I've only seen them a handful of times."

"And your mom?" he continued, finding it hard to believe anyone would turn down time with her.

Charlotte shifted in her seat. "She's quite busy in Florida

with her boyfriends. She seems to have a new one each time we talk, which isn't very often. Like my dad, she doesn't have much time to spend with me. I try to keep in touch with them, but I don't think I fit what they wanted in a daughter," she added, then glanced away as if the reality of that statement sank in. "You probably didn't want to hear all that."

He couldn't stop himself. He snapped another picture. The honesty etched in her expression was too beautiful not to record. "I'm sorry about your family."

"Why would you be sorry?" she asked through a smile that didn't quite reach her eyes.

"Because they sound like jerks, and I was a real jerk to you, too. You don't deserve to be treated like that."

Her expression lightened. "Mitch, you were a real jerk to everyone."

"*Were?*" he tossed back.

"Yeah, *were.* You're not the same person I threw that salad at."

He stared at her as that delicate invisible thread connecting them looped around his heart. He wanted to know more about her—memorize every smile, catalog her every quirk, and see the world as she saw it.

See the world as she saw it?

A rush of euphoria washed over him. That was it. That's where he'd start.

He set the camera on the table, then gazed at the key at the hollow of her neck. "You're right. I'm not the same person. And I need you to do something for me so I can continue on this path."

"Okay," she replied with the tinge of worry to her tone, which he understood.

He did sound a little nuts.

He held her gaze. "It's going to take everything you've got, Charlotte. And I need it now. Right now."

TWENTY-ONE

MITCH

"MITCH, I don't understand? Are you feeling all right?" Charlotte asked, her brow furrowed as she looked him over.

He was acting like he'd been smashed in the head with a hammer, but he couldn't tamp down his excitement. A warmth spread through him just thinking about his plan. "Could you send me every picture you've taken since you've become Oscar's nanny?"

Confusion marred her features. "You want the pictures?"

"I do. I want to see what you see," he explained.

She observed him closely, confusion still clouding her expression. "Why?"

"Because even though you aren't in any of them, you're in all of them. Your honesty, your openness. It's in every shot. It's mesmerizing."

Panic flashed in her eyes, or perhaps he'd thrown her for a loop. But she blinked it away. "You want to see the pictures I've taken since I met Oscar—since the day we went to the cabin in Telluride?"

He couldn't fault her for asking for specifics.

"Yes," he answered.

As a professional photographer, there were surely images she'd taken for clients that she couldn't share. He got that. But if photography was what filled her heart, he wanted, no, needed to see what she saw. Like a scholar hungry for knowledge, he wanted to see this side of her. And that started with the photos she'd taken since she'd become Oscar's nanny.

She shifted in her seat. "Sure, I can email them to you. Do you want them now?"

"Yeah, my email is my first and last name at Crystal Cricket dot com," he answered, fueled by this desire.

She picked up the camera and tapped the display screen.

He watched her work. "Do you still have the old camera? The one from Harper's grandmother?" he asked as the screen lit her face in a white glow.

"I wish. I sold it to an antique shop in Denver a few months ago to pay for a zoom lens for this camera," she replied. "I didn't get as much as I could have because I carved my name on the bottom." A sweet smile pulled at the corners of her mouth. "I wonder about it. You know, who's using it now? Where is it in the world? Seeing it again would really be like going back to the beginning."

Back to the beginning.

There it was again—that phrase that bound them together.

"There are hundreds of images. It might take a few minutes for the email to go through," she said, setting the camera on the table. "But while we have some time, and now that Oscar's asleep, I wanted to show you this." She removed a folded sheet of paper from inside her notebook. "Oscar's teacher gave it to me. It's a letter."

He frowned. "From the teacher? Is there a problem?"

When he was a kid, a note from the school was never a good thing.

"No, it's a letter written by Oscar. It was an assignment.

The kids got to choose to write a letter to anyone. He addressed his to his mom, to Holly."

Holly.

The sound of her name didn't shred his heart the way it used to. But that didn't mean the pain had disappeared. He steadied himself. "Oscar didn't mention a letter."

"He doesn't know that she gave it to me. But I'm glad she did. I think she's keeping a close eye on him with the changes he's been going through in such a short time."

"The information about Holly's death is probably in the file from his school in Telluride," he added.

Charlotte nodded. "I think so."

He focused on the folded sheet of paper as his stomach twisted into knots. "Is it bad?"

"Just read it," she answered, sliding the sheet across the table.

With his heart hammering, he unfolded the page. It was the first time he'd seen his son's handwriting. He concentrated on the carefully formed letters, reading each word as his pounding heart jumped into his throat. "He thinks I'm nice," he read, his voice barely a whisper.

Charlotte nodded.

"I have a Charlotte now," he said, quoting his son.

"That part got me teary, too."

Too?

He wiped at his eyes. He wasn't crying. He didn't cry! "I must have an eyelash in my eye."

Charlotte cocked her head to the side. "In both eyes?"

"It happens," he answered, then cleared the emotion from his throat.

"The teacher wanted us to see that Oscar's doing okay. He misses his mom, which is very normal. But he's getting used to life with you—life with us."

There it was again, the sweet sound of *us*. Charlotte made them an us—a unit. And dare he think it, a family?

He stared at her. "How do you do it?"

She blushed again, and God, he loved when she did that.

"I don't know what you're talking about, Mitch."

"You make it better," he said, leaning in like a moth to the flame.

Her chest heaved as she inhaled a sharp breath. "What do I make better?"

"Me. Everything. Your goodness is everywhere. It touches everything you touch. It brightens the whole damned world. You're sunshine wrapped with an auburn bow, and the closer I get to you, the more of you I want. And I can barely hold myself back." He gripped the side of the table, employing the last of his resolve that kept him from tearing off her clothes and claiming her body in the middle of his kitchen.

She took in his white-knuckled grip. "It's not just you, Mitch. If you haven't noticed, I'm losing my mind over you."

Every muscle in his body tightened. "You are?"

"You heard what I said to Oscar when he asked if we were going to bed, didn't you?"

He nodded. "I did."

"It sounded like the ramblings of a lunatic," she replied, but she was smiling.

He hummed an over-the-top contemplative little sound. "I wouldn't say a lunatic. It was more in the ballpark of someone who'd downed one too many super-charged margaritas, followed by a Jell-O shot chaser while possibly dressed as a mythical marine creature."

She laughed. "You won't let me forget that, will you?"

He dropped the funnyman act. "I can't forget anything when it comes to you, Charlotte." He released his grip on the table and cupped her face gingerly in his hands. His lips hovered a breath above hers—so close to getting what his body so badly craved. She closed her eyes and pressed her palms to his chest as his pulse kicked up. But he stopped himself from taking it any further and pulled back a fraction. "I want to do this the right way with you," he rasped. He was hardly able to believe he'd reined in the beast within. The beast who was two seconds away from making love to her until they couldn't see straight.

"I've kissed you enough to know that you are absolutely doing everything right in that department," she whispered into the sliver of space filled with their heated breaths.

"No, not the kissing part. I want to get the courting part right," he replied, then stilled at his word choice. Courting? His brain must have turned to parmesan risotto mush! Where did he think they were, Victorian London circa 1850?

She opened her eyes and cocked her head to the side. "Courting?"

He dropped his hands, not knowing what the hell to do with his appendages. He felt as settled as one of those damned inflatable tube men with crazy flowing arms. The goofy things that bopped and swayed in the wind in front of sandwich shops and used car dealerships, and that was not the vibe he was going for. He attempted to center himself. "You know, courting. It's the same as wooing."

"You want to woo me?" she asked, enunciating each word.

He frowned. He was tanking in the Casanova department. "When you say it like that, it sounds so—"

She pressed her fingertips to his lips, silencing him. "No, I didn't mean to make it sound negative. I've never been wooed. I think I'd like it."

For the record, *wooing* was a damned silly word. Somebody should come up with a better term because courting sounded ridiculous as well. But it was exactly what she deserved.

"You're okay with wooing?" he asked. He had to make sure.

"Yeah, woo away," she beamed.

Stupid sounding word or not, it was woo time!

He surveyed the kitchen, entirely at a loss. It was woo time, and he had no woo plan.

"I'm a little out of practice—with the wooing," he confessed.

She glanced at Oscar's half-filled glass of milk still on the table, then snapped her fingers. "You and Oscar already had dessert. But I haven't. What about that! We could have a dessert date since I missed it."

Dessert was an excellent suggestion. It had to be one of the wooing cornerstones. And thank God she was firing on all cylinders. This woo business had him grasping at woo straws.

He had to stop thinking and saying all the woo words!

He dusted off his hands. "Dessert it is." Bolting from his seat, the chair skidded across the floor as he sprinted past the island to the freezer. He plucked a popsicle from the shelf, bounded back to the table, then presented her with the frozen treat like a freaking Labrador fetching a stick.

He needed to up his wooing game—and fast! *Woo up? Woo-it to the max?* Damn that stupid word! Except when he looked at her, his wooing reservations disappeared. She gazed at him like he could do no wrong. For Christ's sake, he was an award-winning chef. He was capable of whipping up a perfect soufflé or an intricate tartlet. And what had he given her? A popsicle—and yet, she smiled at him as if he'd handed her the world.

She tore off the paper covering and set it aside next to Oscar's leftover milk. "I got a cherry-flavored one," she said, then—holy hell—she brought the frozen dessert to her mouth, parted her lips, then slid the tip inside. "It's super sweet," she added, then moaned as she sampled the icy treat.

He opened his mouth, thinking words would come out. He

needed to get on upping his woo game. But Charlotte plus a popsicle had rendered him incapable of basic speech.

She licked the shaft. Was that what it was called? Did popsicles have shafts like—

"Mitch, are you okay?" she asked, breaking through his popsicle anatomy predicament.

In his defense, he'd just observed the sexiest woman on the planet suck on the tip of a popsicle. It sure seemed like it happened in slow-motion. And sweet Jesus, he may never recover.

"You're not having one?" she asked, bringing the cock-shaped delight back to her lips.

Did he want to woo her or give himself an exploding erection?

It appeared both events could coincide.

She slid the top of the popsicle across her lips, then licked the cherry-sweet substance. "I feel bad eating this in front of you. You should have one with me," she suggested.

And look at her—talking and using words properly.

"Right. Me. Popsicle. Eat," he replied like a caveman—a caveman with a raging hard-on. He flung his arms as he turned to head to the freezer. With the grace of a bull in a china shop, he knocked over Oscar's glass of milk. Charlotte sprang to her feet. She dropped her popsicle as she gathered her laptop and camera, saving them from the liquid splattered across the table. It doused his shirt, startling him with a cold milky blast.

"Shit!" he hissed, setting the cup upright before peeling off his saturated T-shirt. He scanned the table, making sure the liquid hadn't ruined the camera or the laptop. Then he used his shirt to mop up the mess. "I'm sorry about that," he said, but she didn't reply. She stared at him slack-jawed, her eyes positively devouring his torso.

"The milk," he grunted, holding up his shirt and clearly still in caveman-with-a hard-on mode.

"Uh-huh," she uttered, joining him in Caveman-landia. She pointed to his chest. "Tattoos?"

He studied his exposed skin. "I got them when I was younger. It's a chef thing."

"Uh-huh," she repeated, her gaze raking over him. "They're on your body."

He nodded. "That's usually where they put them."

Was this conversation bordering on insanity, or had they both lost their damn minds?

"About the wooing..." he continued.

Wide-eyed, she shook her head. "Yes, I've been sufficiently wooed."

"You have?" He peered at the partially eaten popsicle, currently melting into a red pool on his kitchen floor. "I didn't know if there was a threshold for it—for the wooing, a woo factor."

Stop with the woos!

"You hit it," she breathed, then launched herself toward him. And holy shit, the nanny could move! His reflexes took over as he dropped the shirt and caught her. Her legs wrapped around his waist, and their bodies came together with a hard smack. She circled his neck with her arms as he gripped her ass. Silently, he thanked the panty gods for making G-string underwear and paid mental homage to whoever designed the miniskirt.

They were genius clothing inventions!

He met her fiery gaze. "We're going with it from here, right? The wooing portion of the evening is—"

"Is over," she finished, her firm tone making it damned clear that she meant business.

And really, who was he to disagree?

"It ended the minute your shirt came off," she added with the dirtiest of smirks as she threaded her fingers into the hair at the nape of his neck.

He met her dirty grin with one of his own. "So, you want me for my body?"

The woman didn't hesitate. "Yes."

"I can live with that," he answered as their lips met in a kiss so steamy it could have melted every popsicle in the entire western hemisphere.

He closed his eyes, dissolving into the caress of her tongue as their mouths explored and tasted. Forget sweet strawberry sunshine. His Charlotte was an explosive cherry bomb. He tightened his grip, sliding one hand into her hair. She gasped as he pulled her in closer, then freed the locks from the messy bun. He ran his tongue along the seam of her lips before pulling back and breaking their kiss.

"What is it?" she asked, not having a clue that she was, without a doubt, a goddess—stunning auburn perfection.

"You. Your eyes, your hair, your everything. You're so beautiful," he whispered.

Was it a cheesy line?

Yeah.

But was it the truth?

Absolutely!

He did a quick survey of the spacious kitchen. And as much as he wanted to take her against every flat surface, it didn't feel right. Each time they'd made love, it had been in a wild, hasty rush of unbridled desire. And while he had nothing against unbridled desire, he hadn't gotten to see her, really see her—lay her down and savor every delicious inch of her body. That was tonight's epiphany. He didn't only want to screw this woman's brains out. He wanted to understand what made her tick, what brought her joy, what made Charlotte Ames the object of his adoration.

"What are you waiting for?" she asked with a teasing lilt to her voice, but he shook his head.

"Not here. Not like this."

Her dreamy expression began to fade. But before a frown could grace her kiss-swollen lips, he shifted her body in his arms. Like a groom ushering his bride across the threshold, he carried her toward the stairwell.

Was he back to *Cheesyville* with this move?

That would be a yes!

But did it return the smile to her face?

Oh, yeah!

A lovely lightness spread through him as Charlotte gasped at being tossed around like a gorgeous sack of potatoes. But when she beamed at him with her shining emerald eyes, he knew this cheeseball maneuver had earned him some serious woo points.

And dammit! There was that word, but he didn't care. This crazy wooing business made her happy. And making her happy sent a rush of adrenaline through his body. It was as if every cell in him was cheering him on.

She giggled, and her breath warmed the crook of his neck. "I thought we agreed the wooing portion of the night was over."

Taking the steps two at a time, he bit back a grin. "If wanting to taste every inch of your body and make you moan my name for hours is considered wooing, then forget calling me hothead. You can now refer to me as Mr. Woo."

She did that adorable thing where she cocked her head to the side as wisps of hair kissed the apples of her cheeks. "Mr. Woo?"

Shit! That sounded a lot sexier in his head.

He cringed, hitting the second floor in record time. "Or we

can ban the woo word. The word woo," he corrected, but there was no time to worry about the woo. He looked from his door on one side of the hallway to hers on the other side. "What do you say? Your place or mine?"

She pressed her hand to her mouth to muffle her amusement. "Who would have thought that mean old hothead Chef Mitch Elliott was actually funny and a romantic to boot?"

"Did you call me old?" he teased.

She gave him a playful shrug. "When I was eight, you were fifteen."

"When you were twenty-one, I was only twenty-eight," he countered.

"Only?" she purred.

Forget this! If being seven years her senior made him a serial wooer and a cradle robber, he was down with that.

"We'll go to my place. The old man gets to decide," he playfully growled against the shell of her ear. He strode toward the door, then stilled. Turning a doorknob while hoisting a tiny redhead proved to be more of a challenge than he'd expected. He shifted her body, trying not to drop her while maintaining a semblance of *woo-ness*.

Stupid woo!

"Need some help, hothead?" she cooed.

He stilled. "We're back to hothead?"

"Fine," she conceded. "Do you need some help, Mr. Woo?"

That wouldn't work!

"Let's stick with hothead. And yeah, I could use an assist," he answered as they both vibrated, holding back their laughter. And Jesus! They were one hell of a pair. He almost dropped her when she leaned over to open the door. But gravity had been kind, and they hadn't crashed to the ground. He nudged the door open with his hip. The hinges creaked their arrival, and they froze, peering down the darkened hall toward Oscar's room.

"We can be quiet," he whispered.

"Very quiet," she mouthed. And hand it to Charlotte for upping the quiet factor. His loud hothead mouth could learn a thing or two. But the moment he set foot in his bedroom, the gravity of the situation set in.

He was a full-time father, and the choices he made impacted his son. "We'll set an alarm to make sure..."

"That we're both where we're supposed to be at eight a.m.," she finished.

"We've got this?" he whispered. He didn't mean for it to come out as a question. Or maybe he did. Perhaps he needed to know that she wanted whatever this was as much as he did.

"We've totally got this," she whispered, then caressed his cheek. Even in the darkened room, lit only by the moonlight, he could see that her expression had grown serious. "But we need to be careful, Mitch. I don't want Oscar to get confused or..."

"Or have to worry about *his Charlotte* and his dad?" he finished, recalling how his son had referred to her in the letter.

I have a Charlotte now.

She stroked his cheek again. "Something like that. He's doing so well. He's off to such a good start at school. I don't want to do anything to jeopardize that."

Neither did he. But the fact that she cared so much about his son made him want her even more. Still, she was right. The kid had been through so much these last few weeks. He could only imagine that it would be damned confusing to learn that his dad was shacking up with his nanny.

But he wasn't *shacking up* with the nanny. He cared for her deeply. And he wanted to protect her and...

And what? Love her? Was that even possible after a handful of days?

Gently, he set her on the bed, then slid his phone from his pocket. "The alarm is set for six—two hours before Oscar wakes up."

"How much time does that give us?" she asked.

He set his phone on the bedside table where the lock Madelyn had given him and Oscar's orange heart sat together. He hadn't expected to see Oscar's creation in his room. His son must have slipped in and put it here.

Charlotte clearly had Oscar's heart, but had she captured his as well? Would the key around her neck unlock not only the physical lock but the lock that kept his heart hidden away?

"Mitch?" she said, and her voice calmed the torrent of emotions welling inside him.

"Yeah?"

"How much time do we have?" she repeated.

"About eight hours," he answered, pulling his gaze from the items on the side table and focusing on the woman in his bed.

"About eight hours," she echoed, leaning back onto her elbows as he drank her in—all creamy skin and delicious curves. "Any ideas on how to pass the time?" she asked with a naughty lilt to her voice.

The raging boner in his pants had quite a few ideas. Luckily, his brain, or maybe it was his heart, still maintained control. "What if, when it's just you and me, you were my Charlotte? All mine."

Damn, he liked the sound of that!

"What if I was?" she tossed back coyly, removing her shirt. "What would you do if I was yours?" she finished, sliding off her skirt and tossing it onto the floor. And God help him! Bathed in the blue light filtering in from the window with her hair cascading past her shoulders, she exuded a radiant beauty men went to war over.

He shrugged off his pants and boxers like they were on fire, then glanced down at his rock-hard cock. "I already told you what I'd do. I want to taste every inch of you," he answered, prowling the length of her body as that pull, that attraction, that thread that formed between them took hold. True to his word, he took his time, tracing a line with his tongue to the apex of her thighs.

"Mitch," she breathed, arching her back as he removed her panties, then ran his tongue across her delicate folds.

"So sweet and all mine." She was like a drug, and he couldn't get enough.

He parted her legs, reaching beneath her to grasp the firm globes of her ass. Taking control of her pleasure, he teased her, licking and sucking, listening in carnal delight as her dirty moans fed his voracious desire.

If there was a heaven, it was right here between Charlotte Ames's thighs.

But his fiery redhead wasn't so keen on letting him run the show.

Between her sharp gasps and gravelly hums, she rocked her hips and threaded her fingers into his hair, setting the pace and switching up the power dynamic.

"Do not stop," she bit out.

He might be the hothead in charge when it came to the kitchen. But in the bedroom, Charlotte had taken over.

And he loved it!

He loved letting her take and take, loved knowing that he was the lucky bastard giving this demanding goddess everything she wanted.

The sound of her breath, the taste of her desire, spoke to him, urging him on. Every touch and each caress sparked electric. But it was the gift of sight that had him truly spellbound. As he teased her most sensitive place and watched as she writhed and bucked, he couldn't pull his gaze away as she came alive beneath him. She might be on the receiving end, but that didn't mean he was missing out. She gave him an erotic show that had his cock weeping, and he wasn't about to stop until he sent her over the edge.

Gasping his name, she turned her head toward the pillow and let go. With her body trembling and her hips pumping, she met her release in a glorious rush of breathy gasps. She twisted her fingers in his hair and pulled. And God help him! He tensed as the delectable bite of pain only got him harder.

He was near delirious when she pushed up onto her elbows and caught him watching her.

"Come here," she beckoned, then reached behind her back and unclasped her bra.

And sweet nanny bliss! When he thought she couldn't be more alluring, she tossed her red halo of hair, then ran her finger between her breasts. He sucked in a tight breath, admiring the utter perfection of a completely naked Charlotte Ames.

"Are you coming?" she purred, and he wasn't about to make her ask twice.

He replied with a wolfish grin. Damn, he liked her feisty! He reveled in her confidence. He met her gaze, then licked his lips, delighting in the taste of her arousal on his tongue.

But this was no time to take a breather.

Sliding his hands up her torso, he paid particular attention to her breasts before peppering her neck with kisses. She rewarded his efforts with a low, sultry sigh that sent a fresh surge of desire pulsing through his veins. Their mouths met, and she welcomed him with a deep kiss that spoke of impassioned yearning and uncontrollable hunger.

She was insatiable!

An impulse he understood well when it came to his feelings for her.

"There's nothing hotter than watching you come," he

growled against her lips as the friction between them pulsed and the air sizzled.

She ran her fingertips down his jawline, past his chin, exploring his neck and shoulders as if she were memorizing the very shape of him. It was as if she wanted to know him by heart, just as he'd wanted to know her. The sensual slide of her soft hands worked their way down to the hard ridges of his abdominal muscles. But she didn't stop there. He gritted his teeth, inhaling a sharp breath when she made it below the belt. She took him into her hand, then stroked her thumb across the head of his weeping cock. Every sensation heightened. Her touch was an electric charge that triggered a pure carnal need to surge through him.

"Lie down," she instructed, releasing him as she guided his body onto the bed, then climbed on top.

"I want to watch you make love to me, and I want you to see me like no one has ever seen me," she whispered. Her words were so raw and so honest. They destroyed whatever was left of the locks and defenses that had once protected his heart.

He drank her in, and this was no longer just about sex. Maybe it never was. In his heart of hearts, he'd known from the moment he saw her at the Crystal Cricket that he wanted her. All of her. But he'd allowed his rage to control him. He'd been so consumed with his anger, he couldn't see what was right in front of him.

But could he take the leap? Could he trust again?

She positioned him at her entrance, then guided him inside. He gripped her waist as she rolled her hips, watching him watch her. Their bodies moved in an exquisite rhythm, slowly building momentum. This wasn't their first time, but something was very different. And then it hit him. He'd never brought a woman into his home, into his bedroom. His home had been his refuge. But in a handful of days, his sanctuary had changed from physical walls and timber to the flesh and blood of two people.

She was his home, and he was a fool if he tried to deny it any longer. It was a revelation that terrified and excited him. But more than that, it was the truth.

"I want you. All of you," he bit out, pistoning his hips as the air grew thick with their heated breaths. She pressed her hands to his chest, riding his cock as her necklace, her key, dangled between them. The metal glinted in the moonlight like a beacon calling out. Her hair framed her face as her luscious breasts rose and fell with each thrust of her hips. The sultry slap of skin meeting skin intensified as animal instinct took over. Every muscle in his body tensed as he made love to her as if it were his sole purpose on this planet. Feverish and on the brink of losing control, he sat up, wrapping her in his steel grip as he pumped his hips. Thrust after delirious thrust, he fell deeper into the sea of desire where she was his anchor. She was his safe haven. Eye to eye, the slap of their bodies and the gasps between them punctuated the air. They were on the precipice, hovering in that impassioned space. And even though it was dark, he could see the brilliance of her green eyes. The image was locked in his heart and imprinted on his soul. His release hit in a relentless blur of color and sensations.

And Charlotte was everywhere.

Her intoxicating scent and her salty-sweet taste consumed him. Their mouths met, and he swallowed her breathy cries as they rode wave after wave of carnal bliss.

"I need you," he whispered against her lips as the intensity of the pleasure rocking his world threatened to tear him apart.

"I'm here. I'm not going anywhere," she answered, her words surrounding him, embracing him, holding him together.

"Good, because this is exactly where I want you," he rasped, his muscles trembling as he came down from the heady rush of pure ecstasy.

In a tangle of sweaty limbs, they collapsed onto the bed. He gathered her into his arms, and she relaxed in his embrace. With her back pressed to his chest, her soft curves melded into his hard angles, and he allowed his hands to explore. He traced the curve of her breasts, then felt the cool metal against her heated skin. The key. He held it, feeling the weight of it, remembering when Madelyn had given him the photo of the necklace.

Could it be that simple? Did Charlotte hold the key to opening the part of him he'd locked away—the part that swore he'd never trust his heart to anyone again?

She hummed a sweet little sigh, and he pressed a kiss to her temple. He knew the answer—his heart knew the answer.

"What if I told you that I never wanted to let you go? Does that sound cheesy?" he asked.

"You know I like cheesy," she answered with a dreamy sigh.

He nodded, his chin brushing across the top of her head. He did. He knew exactly what she wanted.

A Mr. Cheesy Forever.

A quiet peacefulness engulfed the room, and he listened as her breathing grew even just as it had the first night when she'd fallen asleep on his lap. A night where, even in his wildest dreams, he wouldn't have been capable of being anyone's Mr. Cheesy Forever.

But having Charlotte here in his arms was no dream. This was real. And if he played his cards right and kept the hothead at bay, this could be more than real.

As long as he didn't screw it up, this could be forever.

"MOMMY! Daddy! That's the food truck that belongs to Oscar from my class. His dad cooks in it. And he makes the best grilled cheese in the whole wide world!"

Charlotte grinned at the child's comment—a sentiment she'd heard over and over throughout the night. She lifted her camera to her eye, framed the shot of the food truck, making sure to get the twinkling strings of lights in the picture that had been hung for the Whitmore Carnival. With cheerful families dotting the frame and the warm glow from inside the food truck highlighting Mitch, Sergio, and Erick as they served the community a hearty meal, it was the perfect composition—Rockwellian with a modern Denver twist. It was hard to imagine a more picturesque evening in the city.

Several blocks of the Crystal Creek business district were closed off to traffic for the evening to allow the bouncy houses, merchants' tents, and carnival attractions to set up on the street. Groups of people strolled through the maze of children darting this way and that, delighting in cotton candy and Mitch's delectable Signature Louise grilled cheese sandwiches.

She took the shot, then zoomed in and caught Mitch

handing a sandwich to a little girl. She'd seen this scenario play out a multitude of times over the last month. She'd taken hundreds, no, more like thousands of photographs of the man, the truck, Sergio and Erick, and the many customers who were thrilled to pose with Mitch in front of the bright orange Louise. They'd added stops to the food truck's schedule, going out almost every day, in some capacity. And while she'd learned Mitch's rhythm and could anticipate the moment when his lips would curl, and he'd flash that easy grin as he served someone a free meal, it still sent a dizzying current through her body when it happened. The glint in his eyes and how his cheeks grew the slightest bit pink when patrons thanked him touched her every time.

He waved goodbye to the child, but before the next group of customers made their way to the window, he glanced her way. And that's when the butterflies in her belly erupted. Of course, it was her job to take his picture. But they'd hit the pause button quite a few times on the *official professionalism* button. It was as if he could sense when her eyes were on him in a very nonprofessional capacity. His expression changed to that look that was meant for her. A look that said you are utterly and completely mine.

And she was.

Getting hired on as a professional photographer to chronicle the Say Cheese, Louise reboot would have been enough to put her on cloud nine. But there was more—so much more that kept a dreamy grin pasted to her lips and a sweet ache pulsing between her thighs. She'd never known happiness like this. The pieces of her life had fallen into place with Mitch's and Oscar's so seamlessly it was as if they were made for each other.

Their days were filled with food truck stops. Each one was a joyous occasion—a celebration of food where people came together to connect over their shared love of artisan grilled cheese sandwiches. Here, she honed her craft, capturing the hard work inside the truck and the palpable delight outside of it, one shot after the other. And as the news of the food truck reboot made its way around town, the crowds grew, and the media coverage blossomed. Mitch was a natural. Be it chatting with customers or doing a live shot for a local TV station, the man radiated his passion for food. And she was there, soaking it in, becoming one with her subject, and learning the man behind the hothead mask by heart.

But the food truck wasn't the only place Mitch shined.

Despite the time crunch to get a rough draft out, his book was coming along beautifully. A mix of recipes and anecdotes with a heavy emphasis on photography. Mitch was like a machine, working a four-hour lunch shift, then sitting with her as they sifted through the day's shots and brainstormed topics for upcoming chapters.

And they were on the right track. After Mitch had submitted the first three chapters for the editors to review, Gwen's icy demeanor became a thing of the past. Now, when they corresponded with the publisher, the woman's effusive praise amplified with each call. She liked what she saw, and she wasn't shy about sharing her enthusiasm with the culinary community. Sponsors were back knocking on Ines's door and making inquiries into Chef Mitch Elliott's availability. And everyone wanted to get their hands on his next book. The preorders were through the roof. But he hadn't figured out a conclusion, a way to wrap up the narrative. But it would come. She could feel it in her bones.

When they did have a day off, they'd spent it at the Crystal Cricket—as customers. Mitch's friends Monica and Gabe had the whole operation under control. They were a lovely couple, and she'd become fast friends with them. But it also gave her a chance to observe another side of Mitch. She'd photographed the trio talking food and wine and had marveled at Mitch's knowledge and dedication to his craft. He was no longer the one-dimensional angry chef, and everyone at the Crystal Cricket had taken notice.

But the fanfare shifted to the back burner when it came time to pick up Oscar from school. While it was a thrill observing Mitch's transformation from hothead to local hero, nothing beat the moment when the school bell rang, and Oscar burst through the school's doors with Phoebe by his side. Laughing, he'd scan the line of cars, then break out into a wide grin when he spotted Louise. But it wasn't just the joy of seeing the boy acclimating so well to his new life. There was something else that happened in that wisp of a moment. Mitch would look her way, and she'd catch his eye. In that fraction of a second, they shared a silent exchange that said, here comes our favorite six-year-old. We're in this together. And all she could do was smile as the boy ran to them, his backpack swinging from side to side with each stride.

She'd never been part of a family's daily routine. Growing up, when she wasn't with her friends or at school, she was alone. Homework was completed by herself at the kitchen table. Dinner consisted of whatever was in the fridge. There were no games of freeze tag in the backyard, no popsicles on the swing set, no gathering to break bread, no making bubble crowns and bubble beards in the bathtub. With a father she rarely saw and a mother who worked full time then spent her downtime scouring the bars for Mr. Right, it left little time for the mundane moments that proved to be the tiny pieces that fit together to create something extraordinary. Reading together at the kitchen island, taking Polaroids in the park, watching Mitch and Oscar do the dishes—these small moments stacked atop one another were the magic that created a life—a happy life.

And the magic didn't stop once Oscar was fast asleep. Oh,

hell no! But it did turn decidedly less PG and a heck of a lot more *oh, God, please do me!*

The things she and Mitch did with a popsicle behind closed doors were enough to make her blush at even the mention of the frozen treat. But it wasn't just the mind-blowing sex that had her feeling as if she were floating. By nature, Mitch Elliott always ran hot. But with her, between the sheets or against the wall or in her oversized tub, he was positively on fire. The man worshipped at the altar of Charlotte Ames. From the tips of her toes to her auburn hair, not a minute passed when she didn't feel his presence, his intensity. She'd never been the object of anyone's desire. Sure, she'd had boyfriends. But she'd always done the work, twisting herself into what she thought they wanted. Mitch wasn't wrong when he'd accused her of that. But she'd been scared to let any man see the real her. With Mitch, she couldn't hide. They were together morning, noon, and night. He'd kiss her as she drifted off to sleep at night, and she'd wake up to his lips meeting hers in the early morning hours. You'd think that after a few weeks of that, the passion would let up. But it didn't. The desire in Mitch's eyes only intensified.

Adjusting her hold on the camera, she zoomed in closer, and the man, clearly knowing what she was doing, tossed her a sly wink. To be seen by him, truly seen by him, was like basking in a tingly, warm light. Her finger hovered above the shutter button when a voice cut through the murmurs of the carnival crowd.

"How do you get any work done playing googly-eyes with Mitch all day?"

Harper Presley!

Charlotte lowered her camera and glanced to her right. She found not only Harper but also Penny by her side. While Penny looked like a normal human being, H was dressed like she was auditioning for the witness protection program. In a trucker hat pulled low with her long chestnut locks cascading around her face, she was most likely trying to dodge her piano students. Still, a comforting warmth filled her chest at the sight of her girls. She held up the camera. "You guys know that I'm working, and Mitch is my subject."

"Is that what the kids are calling it these days? *Your subject?*" H teased as she leaned in for a hug.

Charlotte tapped the bill of Harper's giant hat. "Have you been discovered? I don't see any children or Whitmore parents chasing after you."

"No, thank God!" Harper replied, scanning the area. "You know how I feel about interacting with my students and families any more than I have to."

Charlotte shared an amused glance with Penny.

"You're taking one for the team tonight, H," Penny teased as Charlotte surveyed her friends, then frowned. While she was happy to see them, these gals should be busy elsewhere at the Whitmore Carnival.

"I thought you were helping Libby over at the kids' yoga tent," she said to H, then turned to Penny. "And you and Rowen are running the gaming station. And you're supposed to keep an eye on Oscar and Phoebe."

"Don't you worry! We decided to take a gaming break," Penny replied, waving her off. "Rowen and the kids are shooting hoops at the basketball shoot-out booth."

Charlotte frowned. "Does Rowen play basketball?"

Penny bit back a grin. "No! And Phoebe and Oscar are pretty much kicking his butt at it."

"Why did you guys leave the video gaming trailer? I thought Rowen had to stay and supervise," Charlotte pressed. Rowen's company, Gale Gaming, had volunteered to supply a state-of-the-art gaming trailer as one of the carnival's attractions.

"Rowen, Landon, and Erasmus are taking turns manning it," Penny answered with a curious lilt to her voice.

"I had no idea Landon and Erasmus were here," Charlotte remarked, searching the street, but it was too packed with people to even see the gaming trailer from where she stood—which raised another series of questions.

She was intrigued with the nanny match foursome Madelyn had put together. It wasn't a stretch to say it was cloaked in a bit of mystery. Here's what she knew. Rowen had Phoebe and Mitch had Oscar, but the guys were notoriously tight-lipped about Erasmus and Landon's situations. She'd figured that they were either fathers or guardians. There had to be kids involved. It was a nanny match service that had brought them together, for Pete's sake! But not even Mitch would share much about the men. And Penny, who was engaged to one of the members, didn't get much more info either.

"Madelyn suggested the guys help out," Penny added with a coy smirk, then her expression grew serious. "I've been thinking a lot about Madelyn these days. There's something familiar about her. Something I can't put my finger on. Like we've met her before."

Charlotte nodded. She'd noticed a strange familiarity as well when the woman ambushed her after the mermaid from hell incident. "I've wondered the same thing, too."

"Madelyn Malone?" Harper repeated skeptically. "Um...the lady is ancient and loaded. So, unless you've been invited to play canasta with a bunch of grannies, who wear flowing scarves and carry purses that cost as much as a year's rent, then I don't think we've met her before this nanny match business started."

Penny nodded. "You could be right. It could be my writer's brain, crafting Madelyn into a character. I already put her in one video game's narrative. She's the perfect muse for that witchy-wise-woman-looking-out-for-you role."

Harper cocked her head to the side. "Um, hello, my blonde

friend! That's pretty much what she is. She hooked you up with a cushy nanny job that bagged you a fiancé, and Char got a…"

"A what, H?" Charlotte pressed, eyeing her friend.

Harper looked her up and down. "Char, you're the definition of walking on sunshine. That Madelyn can make a match. That is, she can match people who can stand children. That woman will never set her sights on me," Harper added, cringing as a gaggle of giggling little girls zoomed past them.

"Hey, H, don't be like that! You like Phoebe and Oscar," Penny countered.

Harper shrugged. "Fine, I can stand two children on this planet."

"What about your work?" Charlotte pressed. "You literally teach children how to play the piano every day. You are steeped in kid-life."

Harper ran her hands down her face. "I know! That damned music major! Little good it did me. I thought I'd be playing in concert halls, not listening to a god-awful rendition of thirty-seven eight-year-olds banging out 'Deck the Halls'," H lamented when a clang rang out, followed by a steady, jarring beat that waffled through the air.

Charlotte scanned the street. "What is that?"

"It's the gong," H answered, shaking her head.

"The gong?" Penny repeated.

"It's for the yoga shit," Harper huffed. "That new studio Libby's teaching at asked her to run a kids' yoga activity here, and they wanted her to bring a gong."

"Could a child be hitting it?" Penny asked, worry coating her words.

"No, I'd bet the last twenty bucks I've got that it's Libby. I thought she would be okay on her own for a while. But I was wrong. I know you two have been busy banging nerds and hotheads, but I should tell you that Libby's not in her right mind," Harper finished as the gong continued to resonate through the night air.

"Are you sure that's not some super angry kid?" Penny pressed, grimacing as the sound intensified.

"It's not a kid. When Libby gets stressed, she loses it with the gong. She was fired from one of the studios for banging the hell out of it," H explained.

Charlotte tried to think back to the last time she'd talked or even texted with Libby. But thanks to her crazy schedule, she'd barely communicated with anyone besides Mitch.

"Are you saying Libby's lost her mind?" she asked.

Harper rubbed the back of her neck. "No, her chi."

"She's lost her chi?" Penny repeated as the clang of the gong grew louder.

Harper released an audible sigh. "Listen, that's what she told me. Some guy has got her off her yoga-master vibe, and she's lost her chi. And her big O, too. She can't...you know...anymore. Not even with a battery-operated device," H whispered as the clanging went on as if a caffeinated toddler had gotten hold of the gong mallet, and the harsh banging cut through the air like a shard of glass.

Penny gasped. "How do you lose that?"

"I don't know. Her Zen is tapped? Her cooch is pooched? I'm not sure what you call it. But she's been a little erratic." H groaned. "All right! I have to go deal with this," she said, then waved over her shoulder as she set off toward the yoga tent.

Charlotte made a mental note to check in with Libbs after the carnival.

"Do you think Libby will be okay?" she asked.

"I hope so, but I'm glad I've got you to myself for a second," Penny replied, her expression growing serious.

Oh no!

"Is everything okay?"

Penny glanced at the food truck, then held her gaze. "I'm just going to say this. I'm the last person to tell you not to get involved with your boss. I mean," she said, then held up her left hand and flashed a monstrosity of a diamond engagement ring. "But I want you to be careful. Don't get me wrong. I can't get over Mitch's transformation. He's like a different person. And it's great to see him with Oscar. But you're my friend, and when you fall, Char, you fall hard. You can lose yourself in a guy, and I don't want you to get hurt."

Charlotte reached out and squeezed her best friend's hand. "I love you for worrying about me but, I'm—"

"Charlotte? Charlotte Ames?" came a voice in the crowd.

A voice she recognized.

Charlotte's eyes went wide as a woman wove her way through the crowd. "Professor, it's so nice to see you. What brings you to the Whitmore Carnival?"

She was trying to play it cool, but a pang of anxiety rippled through her body. This woman reminded her of what she'd been putting off for these last few weeks. She hadn't responded to the acceptance email from The Royal College of Art. It wasn't like she'd purposefully blown them off. She simply didn't know how to respond to the email.

Please, please, please, don't mention the workshop!

"My nephew goes to Whitmore. My sister and brother-in-law are out of town, so I'm on auntie duty this weekend," the woman answered, and Charlotte breathed a sigh of relief. If they could keep it about Whitmore, she might be in the clear.

Regaining her bearings, her gaze ping-ponged between the professor and Penny. "Professor Tran, this is my friend, Penny Fennimore."

"Professor Tran?" Penny repeated as she shook the woman's hand. *Shit!* Penny knew that she'd gone to speak to this very professor about the Royal College of Art workshop. Her stomach did a flip-flop. She hadn't even told her friends she'd been accepted. But not all was lost! Maybe Professor Tran had forgotten about their meeting. It was weeks ago.

"I believe congratulations are in order," the professor continued, beaming at her.

Oh crap! How could she know?

Charlotte's mouth grew dry as her pulse kicked up. And then it hit her. The world of photography academia was a tight-knit group. She should have anticipated that Professor Tran would know someone at the Royal College of Art. But not in a million years did she think the professor would learn of her acceptance into the program. Then again, this might not be about the workshop. Perhaps Professor Tran had seen her working and assumed she'd been hired to photograph the event. Maybe that was why she was offering the kind words.

"I'm not sure I follow. What are the congratulations for?" she asked, playing dumb while doing her best to keep her voice even.

"On your acceptance to the London workshop intensive, of course," the woman chimed.

"Oh," Charlotte squeaked, feeling lightheaded. Was she about to pass out? That would certainly end the conversation. Or she could fake choking. No! What would she choke on— the air?

"A colleague of mine oversees admissions at the Royal College of Art. She saw my name on your application as a reference and shared the good news with me. And you were awarded a full-ride scholarship. I'm so happy for you! It's such an accomplishment."

It was exactly what she'd feared!

Breathe! Breathe! Breathe!

She could feel Penny's eyes on her.

Act normal!

"Yes, it's a real honor," she answered, pasting a grin on her face.

"My colleague emailed a copy of the photo you submitted to me. It's truly breathtaking, Charlotte. Why didn't you share that portrait with me when we met?"

"I took it after I met with you," she answered, her lips ready to split from smiling like a deranged beauty queen.

"My goodness," the professor mused. "It didn't take you long."

"Long to do what?" Charlotte asked.

"To go back and remember why you chose to study photography. Sometimes, all it takes is one spark to tap into your potential," the woman explained.

One spark. That's what it had been—the spark of getting a glimpse of the man behind the hothead.

"Yes, one spark," she answered, breathless, recalling everything about the moment she'd captured on the bench.

"But you haven't let them know if you'll attend. I told my friend it had to be an oversight with your schedule. I've noticed you on the news a few times when they've interviewed the chef from that food truck."

"Me on TV?" Charlotte stammered.

"You weren't the focus of the segment, but you were in the background. I assume you were hired to shoot the limited-time run of the food truck over there," Professor Tran continued. "What a fantastic project for you! I'm delighted to see these opportunities coming your way."

"Yes, it's been hectic," she answered as a cold prickling made its way down her spine.

"That certainly explains why you haven't gotten back to the Royal College of Art. Would you like me to let them know for you? I'm quite close with several of the professors leading the workshop."

This was worse than she could imagine.

"Let them know?" she rasped, a sickness setting in as her belly went topsy-turvy again.

The professor narrowed her gaze. "Yes, Charlotte, this was everything you wanted last we spoke."

"What was everything Charlotte wanted?"

The knot in her belly twisted at the sound of that voice—his voice.

Mitch!

What was he doing here? He should be in the food truck. Her mouth went dry.

He couldn't find out about the workshop—not like this. It would ruin everything!

TWENTY-THREE

CHARLOTTE

CHARLOTTE FROZE, praying a random lightning bolt would strike her to the ground. She examined the sky. And dammit, there wasn't a cloud to be found.

Think! Think! Think!

She chanced a look at Penny—which didn't do a thing to calm her frayed nerves. Her friend flashed her eyes that said, *what the hell, Char?*

But she didn't have time to explain.

And what would she say if she did?

Things are going so well that I didn't want to rock the boat?

That wasn't right. It would be a food truck, not a boat. Oh, what did it matter!

Her heart was ready to pound itself out of her chest. "Hey there, Mitch! This is Professor Tran," she prattled, sounding less like a competent photographer and more like an unhinged game show hostess.

Mitch nodded, then shook the woman's hand. "Yes, Charlotte's mentioned you. She admires your photography."

"And I admire Charlotte's work," the professor replied, studying Mitch's face.

She must recognize Mitch from the photo. That had to be it.

Double, triple, no, quadruple crap!

"Yes, I'm in for the workshop," she blurted, pulling the professor's attention away from Mitch.

"That's great to hear," the professor replied, a little taken aback. "I'm sure they'll be thrilled."

Charlotte peered at the ground. Since the stupid lightning bolt didn't pan out, perhaps a sinkhole could swallow her up. Yes, a sinkhole! They'd have to pause the convo to extract her from the rubble. Yes, the rubble! She needed wreckage and destruction!

Was she losing it?

Her thoughts spiraled.

Yes, it was bad manners to blurt out like that and probably crazy awful karma to wish to be struck by lightning or swallowed by a hole in the ground. But what choice did she have?

She took stock of the people staring at her.

Yes, she should have gotten Mitch's permission to submit his image. But she hadn't expected the committee to accept her into the workshop—let alone get blown away by the portrait! Agreeing she'd attend was her only chance to end this conversation without an act of God and without Mitch getting a whiff of her offer to study abroad. She'd tell him about the opportunity, and she'd apologize for submitting the photo of him without his knowledge. But not like this, and not now.

"Charlotte?" Mitch said gently when a little boy ran up to them.

"Auntie Janine, let's go to the bouncy castle!" the child exclaimed, tugging on the woman's hand.

Charlotte stared at the smiling boy as her skittering pulse slowed. She'd never been so glad to be in the vicinity of a bouncy castle.

"Aunt duty calls! Congratulations, again, Charlotte. I'll be sure to let them know," the professor said, then disappeared into the crowd with her nephew.

"Congratulations?" Mitch repeated, watching her closely.

Act cool.

Charlotte waved him off. "Photography stuff—a little workshop. It's nothing. Why are you out here?" she asked, changing the subject, then checked her watch. "The carnival's got another hour to go." She chanced a look at Penny, who stared at her wide-eyed. And OMG! Between her bff and her boss, this conversation was like juggling hot coals. She gave her friend a minute shake of her head, and Penny pursed her lips. The woman got that she wanted to keep a lid on the workshop. But that didn't mean she liked it.

Penny had been the one who'd encouraged her to tell Mitch about London—and she would. God help her, she would! But when he focused on her like she was the brightest star in the sky, the idea of leaving him and Oscar for two weeks was the last thing she wanted to discuss. Not to mention, those two weeks would overlap with the crunch time for Mitch to finish the rough draft of his book. She could not panic. She'd figure it out. She'd find a way. She'd make it work. She always did.

"There's been a change to the schedule," Mitch said, keeping his tone even. But under the glow of the sparkling lights, she caught a glint in his eyes.

"Is something wrong?" she pressed, praying he hadn't noticed she was on the cusp of begging the universe to wash her away in a flood. Or maybe she could request that a giant bird pluck her from the ground. The lightning and the sinkhole clearly hadn't worked out. And she was quickly running out of creative ways to extract herself from the conversation.

Mitch didn't answer. Instead, he peered past her, then waved. She looked over her shoulder to find Rowen, Phoebe, and Oscar headed their way. "Nothing is wrong. On the contrary, something is about to be very, very right," he added, his voice doing that gravelly thing she loved.

She was ninety-nine percent confident the man didn't have the workshop on his mind. That was a plus, but something was still a bit fishy. Her chef wasn't one for surprises.

"What's going on, Mitch?" she asked, but before the man could reply, the children bounded toward them.

"I get to sleep over at Phoebe's house tonight!" Oscar exclaimed, beaming. "We're going to practice for Outdoor Lab sleepaway camp and sleep on the floor in our sleeping bags. It's a few weeks away, and we need to be ready."

"Isn't that awesome, Penny?" Phoebe chimed. "Uncle Row says that Oscar and I can build a pillow fort and eat cookies all night long."

"It does sound awesome. Everything except eating cookies all night long," Penny replied, raising an eyebrow.

"Phoebe, I didn't agree to the cookie part. And you know the new cookie rule," Rowen chided.

Phoebe kicked the ground. "Sorry, Oscar! We can have two cookies each, *max*. I'm on cookie lockdown," the child lamented.

"That's okay, Phoebe," Oscar answered, undeterred by the cookie limit. "Then you won't throw up everywhere."

"When did this get decided?" Charlotte asked, done with the cookie-vomit talk. She glanced from Rowen to Mitch. The chef was rocking a cat-who-ate-the-canary smirk. And while she was grateful for the shift in the conversation, she was totally in the dark when it came to Oscar sleeping over at Phoebe's place.

"Yeah, we're more than happy to have Oscar spend the night. But when did you make these plans?" Penny asked, eyeing her fiancé.

"Mitch and I worked it out about an hour ago. Mitch has another *engagement* to attend to that could run late. And he needs Charlotte to photograph the *event*," Rowen answered, sharing a look with Mitch.

These two were up to something!

Charlotte observed as Penny cocked her head to the side. Her friend was in the dark, too.

"Why don't you and Phoebe head over to Louise and get a sandwich. I don't think either of you has had dinner yet," Mitch said, ruffling his son's hair.

"Come on, Phoebe! Let's go!" Oscar called as the pair sprinted toward Say Cheese, Louise.

Charlotte stared at the man. The guy had something up his sleeve—something both he and Rowen were keeping close to the vest. But she couldn't tell what it was. "Another event? I didn't see anything else on the schedule—especially tonight," she remarked, looking for answers.

"This came up suddenly," Mitch replied, biting back a grin.

Okay, this was starting to get weird. She parted her lips to express her concern when Erasmus Cress jogged up to the group, his giant body weaving through the crowd.

"Am I late? I just saw your text," the man asked as he slipped his phone into his pocket.

"I thought you were supervising the video game trailer, Raz?" Penny commented.

"Bloody gong going off left and right two tents down," the man answered, his expression hardening. "I told Landon to take over. He was trolling around in the corner, trying not to be *seen*. You know—all those fans looking to bombard him with requests for autographs."

"You're right on time, Raz," Mitch said, clapping the guy on the shoulder. "Do you know what to do?"

Erasmus crossed his muscled arms and surveyed the truck. "I stand inside the food truck. People tell me they want a cheese toastie. Then I tell the blokes cooking to make it," the man answered as his crisp British accent peppered the air.

"It's called a grilled cheese sandwich," Mitch corrected.

The big guy waved him off. "Bullocks! You're not toasting the cheese. You're toasting the bread."

"Raz?" Mitch chided. "I need you to work with me."

Charlotte shook her head, suppressing a grin. If she wasn't so annoyed at being kept in the dark, this exchange between the men would have been absolutely hilarious.

"Fine!" Erasmus conceded. "I'll call it a *grilled cheese. Would you like a grilled cheese where the cheese is not grilled, and the bread is toasted?*"

Charlotte looked from Rowen to Erasmus, then zeroed in on Mitch. "Why are your friends helping you out tonight?"

Mitch's cocksure expression faded a fraction. "Yeah, we're not friends."

"No, we're not mates. Not even close," Erasmus supplied.

"We're just...dudes," Rowen added, then cringed.

"Dudes?" Mitch repeated.

Erasmus grimaced. "What do you mean, we're dudes? We're not surfers. This isn't *hang ten* in California, is it?"

Charlotte shook her head. The whole Three Stooges act needed to end.

"Wait a second, *dudes*! I need to get something straight," she began, eyeing the trio. These men were clucking like hens, and she needed answers. She pegged Mitch with her gaze. "Why are Rowen and Penny taking Oscar for the night? And why is Erasmus helping Erick and Sergio in the truck?"

"I prefer Raz," the muscled man interjected. But she didn't have time to worry about what this beast of a man wanted to be called. She stared him down. And he raised his hands defensively.

"Or Erasmus is fine," he eked out, lowering his voice.

"You're right, mate. She can be quite feisty," he finished, tossing her a wink before jogging over to the food truck.

"Mitch? What are you up to?" she repeated as the hum of a helicopter purred in the distance.

The man looked quite pleased with himself and pointed into the air as the approaching chopper landed on top of a boutique hotel a few blocks down the street. "What I'm up to is waiting for us right there."

"A freaking helicopter! Is this a joke?" she exclaimed as a cocky grin stretched across the man's face.

"No, this is no joke. It's how rich people avoid traffic," Mitch answered, eyes glittering with delight as Rowen nodded in agreement.

Charlotte's gaze bounced from Mitch to the helicopter on the roof of the nearby building when her brain kicked in. She and Mitch were leaving on that mechanical monstrosity sitting atop a six-story hotel. She turned to Penny—the only person she didn't want to throttle. "Make sure Oscar brushes his teeth, especially the ones in the back. And oh no! He doesn't have his pajamas or his toothbrush or his pictures. He needs the picture of his mother. He likes to say good night to her."

Her heart was back to beating like a drum.

They couldn't leave! Not like this!

She turned to her sneaky chef. "Mitch, we can't go. We can't leave Oscar."

"I've got it covered. Rowen knows what to do," he answered, looking more and more pleased with himself by the second.

"Mitch provided us with the code to his security system. We'll stop by and get Oscar's things. Honestly, even without the code, I could have hacked into his system," Rowen assured her— which didn't altogether leave her without some reservations. But at least Oscar would have everything he needed.

She pushed aside Rowen's unsettling hacking comment and

focused on the giant orange truck. "What about Louise? You can't leave her here, can you?" she asked, still unable to believe he'd hired a freaking helicopter to whisk them away.

"Erick and Sergio are going to return it. And Raz volunteered to drop the teens off at their homes after getting Louise back in the garage. It's under control," he replied smoothly.

When had he planned this? She'd watched him all night.

She lifted her chin. She wasn't done with the interrogation. "How did you get a helicopter to come here?"

"I told you. It's a rich person thing," Mitch answered with an unmistakable thread of amusement in his tone.

She glanced at Penny.

Her friend nodded. "Planes, helicopters, boats, houses all over the place. Mitch is right. It kind of is a rich person thing."

Charlotte attempted to regain her bearings. "And us? Are we returning, or is that thing taking us across the globe?" She had to ask. It's not like he'd supplied any information about this event.

Wincing, Rowen inhaled a tight breath. "You would most certainly crash and die if you attempted to pilot a helicopter around the globe."

Charlotte gasped. This night could not include death!

"Honey," Penny whispered, pushing up on her toes to whisper in Rowen's ear. "That's not helping."

Rowen nodded. "Got it. How about this? If you did try to fly a helicopter around the world, your death would most likely be quick and painless and somewhere over the ocean."

"What?" Charlotte stuttered.

Penny gazed at her fiancé. She did like the weirdos. "Let's go check on the kids," she suggested. "And Char," she continued.

"Yes?"

"You'll be fine on the helicopter, and you don't have to

worry about Oscar. He and Phoebe will have a blast. Have fun at the event. It looks like the two of you are going to have plenty of time to talk."

Charlotte nodded, getting the message loud and clear. "Thank you," she replied, holding her friend's gaze.

"Yeah, thank you so much. We owe you," Mitch echoed as Penny and Rowen set off for the food truck, and her little heart fluttered.

We.

She loved the sound of that.

Mitch turned to her, then scanned her from head to toe. "You've got your camera and your camera bag. We're ready."

"Ready for what?" she pressed.

"For tonight," he answered, totally not answering her question and still looking as pleased as punch. He gestured for her to start walking, and reluctantly she fell into step beside him.

"I have a few questions—a few professional questions as your photographer," she began.

"Shoot!" he said, taking her hand in his.

"Let's start with the basics. Are we attending a real event?"

He pondered the question as they strolled down the sidewalk, breaking free of the carnival crowd. "Yes, this is a real event."

She balked. "That's it? That's what you're giving me?"

This was starting to feel like that moment in a horror movie where the crowd starts yelling, *don't go with him! It's a trap!*

"You're not a serial killer doubling as a chef, are you? This isn't how I meet my demise?" she rattled off.

Mitch chuckled, then stroked her palm with his thumb. "We'll be back in Denver bright and early tomorrow morning."

"So, we're spending the night somewhere other than the house?" she asked, not exactly channeling Nancy Drew with that caliber of question, but it would have to do.

"Did you think I rented a helicopter to take us home?" he asked with those stupid blue eyes glinting with delight. He was enjoying this.

"No, of course not!" she shot back.

For the record, the man was acting out of character. Mitch was about the plan, the order, the regimented flow. This impromptu *event* was way out of his wheelhouse. And not only that. It had never been just the two of them. Erick and Sergio were with them most days, and Oscar was with them at night. Yes, he went to bed at eight, which gave them the evenings. But there was always the chance he'd need them during the night. They had to be quiet and careful.

"What can you tell me about this evening?" she asked, changing tack.

"We won't be sleeping at the house," he replied—again giving her nothing.

The loud whirring hum of the helicopter's blades signaled their arrival at the hotel. She stared up as the copter's blinking lights flashed against the night sky.

"You better not be a serial killer," she mumbled under her breath as a doorman waved them inside. They entered the swanky space to find a man in a crisp suit making a beeline toward them through the lobby.

"Ah, Chef Elliott, right this way," he said, ushering them toward the bank of elevators.

"You know him?" she whispered.

"I may or may not have agreed to be a guest chef here for a night," he replied.

"They let you land a helicopter on their building because you said you'd cook for them?"

He gave her that boyish, panty-melter of a grin. "Some days, it doesn't hurt to be famous," he whispered back as the elevator pinged and the doors opened. They entered, but the man in the suit didn't join them.

"The elevator will take you to the top floor. From there, you'll need to take the stairs to the roof. We look forward to chatting with you, Chef."

"My people will be in touch," he answered as the doors closed and the elevator began its ascent.

She studied her mysterious chef. "This feels very cloak and dagger."

"Look at us," he said, lowering his voice as he leaned in for a kiss. "The nanny and the hothead are making a break for it."

She closed her eyes as Mitch's magical mouth sent her body into a wild swirl. She pushed her camera out of the way, allowing her to wrap her arms around his neck. His rock-hard cock pressed against her, and instantly, all she wanted to do was him. She tangled her fingers into the hair at the nape of his neck, panting with desire when a *ping* cut their make-out session short.

"I should have picked a taller building," he said, dusting the corners of her mouth with a kiss.

She peered out of the elevator and spied a small barebones room with concrete walls. A set of cement steps rose from the ground, leading up to a metal door. She untangled her fingers from Mitch's hair, then hit the stop button on the elevator.

Confusion marred his features. "What are you doing? The chopper's waiting."

She pursed her lips. "Listen, I'm relatively sure that this isn't another elaborate kidnapping attempt. But you have to explain this to me. I'm not getting on the helicopter unless you tell me what's going on." She narrowed her gaze. It was time to be that feisty redhead. "And no funny business, mister! I know you tried to scramble my brain with that super sexy kiss. But I've got two functioning brain cells left that aren't ready to jump you right here in this elevator until you talk."

"Every cell in your body except two want to do me? Not bad!" he commented, looking quite pleased with himself.

"Mitch!" she huffed.

"Okay, first of all," he began with a sly grin, "I take issue with calling this *another* kidnapping attempt. I never kidnapped you. You incorrectly assumed you'd been abducted."

She cocked her head to the side and gave him her best stink eye. "I woke up in a camper van. What was I supposed to think?"

"It was a luxury camper van with a grande gourmet coffee and two aspirin waiting for you. That's five-star treatment. Nothing about that screams abduction," he countered in that voice that made him the epitome of a devastatingly handsome SOB. But she wasn't playing.

"Mitch, I'm serious! This isn't like you to plan a surprise."

He cupped her face in his hands and pressed his lips to hers, silencing her inquisition. Again, because this man had a magic mouth, she melted into the kiss, into the warmth of his touch. Deepening their connection, he hummed his satisfaction as he ravished her mouth. The sound went straight to her heart, then proceeded south, setting off a delicious tingle between her thighs.

He pulled back and brushed his thumb across her bottom lip. "We're here because a couple of hours ago, I overheard someone in line talking about a meteor shower tonight, and it got me thinking about you."

"Giant rocks hurling through space made you think of me?" She may only have two brain cells that weren't focused on riding this man's cock all night long. But those two brain cells were still functioning at a level that let her know his response was damned crazy.

"Yeah, I heard meteor shower and thought of you."

"Okay." She chewed her lip. She had heard him correctly.

He twisted a lock of her hair around his finger. "It got me thinking about when you said you liked to photograph the night sky. And how happy it made you if you were lucky enough to capture a shooting star. But it didn't happen very often."

Holy good memory!

This man remembered a random comment she'd made weeks ago! The guys she'd dated in the past couldn't even remember her last name, let alone something as fleeting as a remark she'd made in passing.

Emotion welled in her chest. "It's hard to get a good shot in the city because of the light pollution."

His expression grew tender as he released the lock of her hair. "Now you get it."

She didn't get it. Those two holdout brain cells must have left her high and dry to jump on the *do-this-man* bandwagon. "I don't, Mitch. I don't understand."

"I'm taking you to a place where you'll get the best seat in the house to view and photograph the sky," he explained.

"And where is that?"

He grinned. "My other place in the mountains in Aspen."

She shook her head. "You have another place in the mountains besides Oscar's cabin in Telluride?"

He cupped her face in his hand. "Yeah, I thought I made the whole rich person thing pretty clear. We have ridiculously enormous houses, fancy vehicles, and access to helicopters. You know, cool shit."

He was trying to play it cool and keep it light, but she sensed something vulnerable beneath his cocky chef exterior.

"You're doing this for me?" She had to ask. It was too good to be true.

He gave her a boyish grin. "I mean, I'm trying. You're kind

of putting the kibosh on the romantic surprise element of the night."

She laughed, blinking back tears. "This is more than anyone has ever done for me."

"I want to do more for you, Charlotte." He glanced around the elevator. "I planned on telling you this atop a mountain as meteors soared across the sky, but I can't help myself. I need to say this to you."

"What do you need to say?" she whispered, her pulse racing.

He took her hands in his. "Charlotte Ames, I love you."

Love?

The breath caught in her throat. "You do?"

It was almost too hard to believe. Love was so fleeting in her life. Her friends told her that they loved her, of course. But besides hearing those three words from Penny, Harper, and Libby, she hadn't heard them in ages—not from her parents, not from any boyfriend. But here was this man, this former hothead she'd despised, saying those three beautiful words—to her.

"I do. I love you, Charlotte," he replied, his eyes shining. He observed their joined hands. "You once said that when you saw a shooting star, you liked to think that it was meant for you. But you had it backward."

"What do you mean by that?" she asked.

"You're that star, Charlotte," he whispered, his words floating in the air around them. "And you're meant for me. And you're meant for Oscar. You're the light that connects us. We're meant to be together."

She nodded. It was all she could do through the tears that trailed down her cheeks.

He brushed the tears away. "This time has made me see that I never want to be apart from you."

She shivered as a cold prickle worked its way down her spine, and two words flashed in her mind.

Apart.

London.

Her thoughts spiraled as she stared into his blue eyes, awash with such tenderness it left her breathless...and in love.

He caressed her cheek, then traced his fingertips to the hollow of her neck. Gently, he took the key between his fingers. "You hold the key to my heart. I trust you, Charlotte. I trust you with my son, and with my work, and with my life. What I feel for you isn't like anything I've ever known. I want to give you everything—the stars, the moon, a meteor shower. I want you. And I never want to be without you."

She stared into his eyes. She'd dreamed of a moment like this since she was a girl—since she watched the other Charlotte at the airport dissolve into happy tears when her Mr. Cheesy Forever professed his love.

She swallowed past the lump in her throat. "No one has ever wanted me like this."

"I want you like this," he bit out. "I want you with me. Always."

She ignored the whisper of a chill that prickled along her spine and concentrated on this man—a man who wanted her, who loved her.

Don't ruin this.

This was what she'd always wanted, right? She couldn't bring up London—not when Mitch was filling her heart with words of love.

"I want to be with you—you and Oscar. I love you. I love you both," she said in a tumble of words before there was no more talking, only kissing. She sighed, falling deeper and deeper when a rush of cool air sailed into the elevator's cab.

"Excuse me. Sorry to interrupt."

She and Mitch pulled apart to find a man staring up at the ceiling.

At least the intruder was doing his best to be discrete.

"I'm the helicopter pilot," he said as a blush graced his cheeks.

"Oh, hello," she replied, like running into helicopter pilots was just part of her daily grind.

"I didn't mean to interrupt, but I'm not sure I'm technically allowed to land on this building. So, if you've concluded your business, we should probably get going," he finished, his blush deepening.

Mitch nodded to the guy. "Give us a minute. We'll be right out."

The poor guy shot through the door, and she broke out into giggles.

"How did we forget about the helicopter?"

"It's easy to forget everything when I look into your eyes," he said, then cringed. "Too cheesy?"

"You know I like cheesy," she answered, falling, falling, falling. Hook, line, and sinker.

He leaned in and pressed a kiss below her earlobe. "Are you ready for me to give you the stars, the moon, and a bunch of meteors?"

She glanced at her camera bag and frowned. "I thought of something. I don't have anything packed. I don't have a change of clothes."

His gaze grew positively carnal as he drank her in like the dirtiest of bad boy chefs. "You don't have to worry about clothes. Tonight, you're not going to need them."

MITCH HIT the gas as they cruised down the interstate and passed a large green traffic sign.

Ten miles to Telluride.

They were almost there.

And life had never been sweeter.

He inhaled Charlotte's strawberry sunshine scent, then glanced in the rearview mirror of the Lamborghini Urus and peered at his son in the back. The boy caught his eye in the reflection and smiled.

"We're almost there, aren't we, Dad?" Oscar chimed.

"We are," he answered, hardly able to believe they'd made it to the last week of school. They were on their way to drop Oscar off at the weeklong Outdoor Lab camping excursion with his class. It was quite a way to end the school year. Oscar had been ecstatic and had hardly spoken of anything else over the last two weeks. And even though he'd be sleeping on a bunk bed in one of the campground's cabins, he'd given up sleeping in his bed at home to sleep in the tent in the corner of his room to get in plenty of camping practice. His dedication to preparing for the week was commendable, almost compulsive, and a lot like his father.

Okay, exactly like his father.

They indeed were two regimented peas in a pod.

As little as three months ago, he would have never guessed how much he and Oscar had in common—how similarly they approached life. Then again, he hadn't really seen his son before he'd taken full custody of the boy. No, he'd considered the child Holly's son, and he'd allowed that pain to skew his perception. It had concealed what was right in front of him. He had one amazingly kind and curious little boy.

He did another quick check of his son. The boy unzipped his pack and, lips moving silently, went over its contents for what had to be the fourth or fifth time.

Yep, Oscar was his!

To say that the kid was doing well was an understatement. With good grades and his interests in the food truck and photography blossoming, Oscar Abrams Elliott flourished in his new life.

That's not quite right. It wasn't just Oscar. Both father and son thrived.

And there was one person to thank for it.

Mitch glanced to his right and drank in the reason that the sun shined brighter.

His love.

His Charlotte.

She caught his eye and smiled that smile that was only for him—the one that spoke of nights tangled in each other's arms, blissfully gasping for breath on the cusp of ecstasy. He wanted to reach out and take her hand and thread their fingers together like he did each night when it was the two of them, but he stopped himself. Despite professing their love inside an elevator, they'd agreed to keep their feelings hidden for the time being. It was Charlotte's suggestion. And as much as he wanted to object, it made sense.

Oscar was doing so well, but they agreed that they didn't want to bombard the boy with more change. The plan was to let him know where things stood after camp ended. They'd have the summer to navigate this new life as a trio. But Oscar wasn't Charlotte's only concern. She wasn't just Oscar's nanny. His publisher had a contract with her. He got it. He did. The personal and professional conflicts couldn't be ignored. But that didn't mean he liked it. He'd been counting the days until he could shout his love for her from the rooftop. Still, there was plenty to keep his mind occupied. He'd be wise to focus on the deadline fast approaching. He had a week until he had to submit the complete rough draft. They were close to finishing it, save for one not so small element.

The ending.

Yeah, it hadn't come to him yet.

Night after night, he and Charlotte sifted through her photos, stringing together the book's narrative. She'd organize the images while he wrote. So far, the words had come, and the ideas had flowed.

But he'd hit a roadblock.

Nothing rang true yet for how to end this book.

Granted, it wasn't the typical culinary text. Part cookbook and part memoir, it told the story of Say Cheese, Louise. But it wasn't just about the cooking. He'd revealed himself in the pages—his beginning, the shift from a life of petty crime to working at Helping Hands to the overnight stardom of becoming one of America's most popular chefs. He'd even included Holly and Seth in the story. It wasn't easy, but with Charlotte by his side, it didn't cut quite so close to his heart to revisit the memories of the old days. He'd even inserted his son into the book. That part had come naturally. Thanks to Charlotte's painstaking work to chronicle the reboot, he had dozens upon dozens of pictures of the boy, and images of him cooking with his son dotted the rough draft.

Where would he be without this woman?

He'd be utterly lost without her humor, her talent, her kindness, and the sultry way she'd drop to her knees, unzip his pants, and take him into her mouth. He shifted in his seat, then flicked his gaze from the interstate to her creamy thighs. Last night, he'd kissed a hot trail across her smooth skin before making her come hard against his lips. The mere thought of making this woman writhe in ecstasy got his heart pumping.

"Eyes on the road, Chef," Charlotte murmured with that look that said she knew exactly what he was thinking.

Jesus, he had to get it together! But in his defense, Charlotte Ames in a skirt drove him damn near crazy.

"Right, no ogling the photographer," he answered under his breath.

She glanced at Oscar, still busy with his pack, then leaned across the console and pretended to adjust the air-conditioning. "Not yet."

God help him! He was about to have a solid week alone with her. Yeah, they had to work, but he'd decided on one hard and fast rule: clothing optional. That had worked quite well for them after he'd whisked her away in the helicopter.

"Mitch," she chided.

"Yeah?"

She lowered her gaze below his belt, then pressed her lips together, suppressing a smile as mischief glittered in her eyes. He didn't have to look down to know what she'd discovered. Yep, he was rock-hard, thanks to the gorgeous redhead seated next to him.

"You can't have that when we meet Oscar's class at the camp," she said, unable to bite back a naughty little grin.

"What can't Dad have?" Oscar asked, zipping up his bag.

Mitch cleared his throat. Why did men do that when they had a boner at an inopportune moment? He didn't know. And that should be the least of his concerns. He surveyed his pants. "Camping supplies," he answered, then shifted in his seat.

"What kind of camping supplies are you not supposed to have?" Oscar pressed with a crease to his brow.

Out of the corner of his eye, he could see that Charlotte was barely holding it together.

He observed his crotch and sighed. "A tent," he answered, then started to count each tree they passed to calm himself down. The last thing he wanted to do was drop his kid off with a raging boner.

He could hear the comments now.

Who's that guy with the inappropriate hard-on?

Oh, that's Oscar Elliott's dad.

But honestly, who could blame him? All he had to do was imagine kissing the woman, and boom! Insta-boner! It was amazing he could get anything done with her and that sexy as hell ponytail swishing around.

Focus! Get to the camp—preferably without an erection.

"Charlotte, can I look at your camera to see the picture of the meteors again? I want to look at the one where it looks like the sky is exploding," Oscar called from the back, blessedly dropping the camping supplies line of inquiry.

"Sure, hold on a sec," Charlotte answered as she pulled her Nikon from her camera bag. She peered at the screen, then scrolled through the myriad of photos. "Ah, here it is," she said, passing the camera to Oscar.

"That must have been the coolest night ever!" the boy exclaimed.

But Oscar was wrong.

Labeling that night as the *coolest night ever* wasn't accurate.

It was more like the hottest scorcher of a night ever recorded in human history.

He may have professed his love for Charlotte in an elevator. On a scale of one to ten on places one should make such a proclamation, the six-by-six-foot box wasn't exactly the definition of romance he'd envisioned when he'd gotten the idea to whisk her away for the evening. But thanks to Charlotte's feisty streak and his need to let her know how he felt, that's where it had happened.

But he'd made up for his lacking in the hearts and flowers department.

Big-time.

The truth is, by the time the chopper landed at his place in Aspen, neither had comets on their mind. Between making her call out his name in pure orgasmic bliss on the front porch, in the entryway, and on a bearskin rug in the center of the living room, they'd nearly missed the starry spectacle. By a stroke of luck, the light show started while she was stroking his cock on the second-floor balcony. They'd taken a brief intermission from screwing on every flat surface for Charlotte to grab her camera and capture nature's splendor—and it was pretty awesome. But not as awesome as when he took her over the edge again and again as they spent the night in a state of orgasmic delirium.

"Mitch, there's our exit," Charlotte announced in her nanny voice. "We'll be at the Outdoor Lab site any minute."

That was code for *get your mind out of the-gutter, mister!*

He nodded, resuming his tree count as he exited the interstate, then turned onto a gravel road surrounded by thick foliage.

"Do you think Phoebe's here yet?" Oscar asked.

"We're about to find out," Charlotte answered as the swath of towering evergreens thinned, and they pulled into a parking lot crammed with families unloading backpacks and sleeping bags from luxury SUVs.

"I see her! I see her!" the boy called, bouncing with excitement. "They're right there! Pull in next to them, Dad."

Mitch swallowed hard as he parked the car, then surveyed the Outdoor Lab camp. Nestled on a lake with cabins dotting the landscape and mountains rising in the distance, Outdoor Lab Camp was as picturesque as it gets. Oscar would love it here. He'd be with his teacher, Phoebe, and the other kids from his class. But that didn't stop the twist in his belly from tightening. They'd only left him for one night since Oscar had come to Denver, and the idea of not seeing this kid for a week hit him harder than he'd expected. He looked at Charlotte. She wasn't doing any better than he was. She brushed a tear from her cheek, then exhaled a shaky breath before putting on a brave face.

At least he wasn't the only one getting emotional.

"I'm going to go see Phoebe," Oscar called, swinging open the door and flying out of the car.

"Here we go," Charlotte said, sharing a wobbly smile.

He reached across the console and squeezed her hand. "It'll be okay. No, it'll be better than okay. Oscar will love it here. This place looks terrific."

"Yeah, you're right," she answered, and all he felt was gratitude. He was a damned lucky man to have someone in his life who loved his son as much as he did.

Going into parent mode, he and Charlotte exited the SUV and waved at Penny and Rowen as Oscar and Phoebe vibrated with excitement, skittering between the cars. He pulled a duffel bag and the boy's sleeping bag from the car and listened as the children greeted each other.

"Oscar, guess what?" Phoebe called as Rowen helped the girl put on her backpack.

"What?"

"We flew down in my uncle Row's plane, and then there was a car waiting for us. Did you fly here in a plane?" the girl pressed.

Oscar shrugged. "No, we didn't. We drove down in a Lamborghini."

Mitch shared a look with Charlotte, and the two of them bit back grins.

Kids sure had it rough these days.

"But I got to see license plates from Wyoming, New Mexico, and Texas. I even took a picture of one with my camera," the boy answered, swinging his backpack to one shoulder, then plucking a Polaroid from the front pocket.

"Wow!" Phoebe breathed, gazing at the photo. "You're a really good photographer, Oscar. Let's play the tap game. I'll start. My uncle Row is a," Phoebe said, then tapped her foot twice.

"Phoebe!" Rowen called, exasperation coating the word.

"It's not what you think, Uncle Row. The taps were for *hot nerd.* That's what Penny called you last night when I snuck down the hall to go to the kitchen to get a cookie. I figured you needed to turn on a fan or take a cold shower," the child continued.

Penny and Rowen stood there with looks of sheer mortification.

"Um..." Rowen stuttered.

Luckily, Penny recovered. "Hey, Phoebe, why don't you and Oscar play in the grass while we get your camping supplies?" she suggested as Rowen stood there, slack-jawed.

"Guess what, Phoebe?" Oscar chimed.

"What?"

"My dad has a camping supply he's not supposed to have. Charlotte saw it, and my dad said it was a tent. But that didn't make any sense to me because where would he have a tent driving a car?"

Oh shit! Now it was his and Charlotte's turn to get a beat down from the mortification stick.

"Come on, Oscar," Phoebe said, taking the boy by the hand. "Grown-ups are..." She tapped twice, and the kids broke out into giggles.

"I'm not even going to worry about what my niece called us," Rowen said, regaining his ability to speak. "How about we forget we heard that?"

"Yes!" he called in unison with Charlotte and Penny.

"So," Charlotte began, tucking a notebook into Oscar's duffel. "Why did you fly down?"

God bless this woman for her ability to change the subject.

"It was a last-minute thing," Penny answered.

Rowen nodded. "We need to fly to California for a meeting at Gale Tech as soon as we get Phoebe settled. It was easier to have the plane here and ready to go. I have to meet with my team about an issue with a blob."

"Blob?" Charlotte parroted back.

"Yes, a blob—a binary large object. It's a data term."

Mitch glanced at Charlotte, who smiled and nodded. He did the same. He didn't know what the hell Rowen was talking about. This happened a decent amount, and Penny had shared the nod and smile trick with them. It worked like a charm.

"We'll be back tomorrow. But we wanted to run something by the two of you," Penny added.

"What's up?" Charlotte asked.

"Just to be safe," Rowen's fiancée began, "I added you guys as emergency contacts for Phoebe. Our house manager is on vacation. Otherwise, we would have listed Mrs. Sullivan. I hope you don't mind."

"We don't mind at all. We're happy to help," he answered,

feeling a lightness that was quite intoxicating. He was a *we*—a *we* with Charlotte.

"And we won't be far away," Charlotte added. "Mitch and I are staying the night at his cabin in Telluride before going back to Denver tomorrow." She glanced at him as warmth radiated in her gaze.

Yep, they were going to the cabin!

Initially, he'd balked when she'd suggested the idea. While they had the time—their next food truck stop wasn't for a couple of days—the idea had scared the hell out of him. But she had a good reason to suggest the pit stop. The cabin was filled with pictures of Louise from the old days. She'd seen a few of them when they'd gone to pick up Oscar, and she wanted to go through them for the book. He understood her motivation but knew she hadn't suggested the overnight for purely professional reasons. She hadn't said it explicitly, but he had an inkling that this short overnight was a chance for him to make peace with his past—or at least start the process.

"Yeah, we'll be in Telluride overnight—to work," he added when Phoebe and Oscar returned.

"Is it almost time for camp to start?" Phoebe asked.

"The email said they'd ring a bell when it was time to begin," Rowen answered as Phoebe groaned one hell of a yawn.

"Wow, Phoebe, you're a champion yawner!" Oscar exclaimed.

The little girl nodded. "I didn't sleep much last night because I was so excited for camp. And when I ran into Penny and Uncle Row's room to tell them that it was time to get up, I caught Uncle Row running into the bathroom because Sundays are the day he fixes the sink," Phoebe continued, causing Penny and Rowen to *again* turn beet-red.

Was this parenting? A string of mortifications stretched out until the kids turn eighteen?

"I didn't sleep either," Oscar added.

Holy hell!

"And when I ran into my dad's room to wake him up," Oscar exclaimed in a tumble of words. "The covers on his bed were messy like he'd been wrestling." The boy flailed his arms and kicked wildly. "And then I went to Charlotte's room to see if she was awake. She was lying on top of her bed like she didn't even sleep under the covers."

Busted! Again!

Red-faced, the adults stared at each other, begging the universe *not* to allow the children to connect the dots.

"Kids, why don't you go tap some naughty words in the grass over there," Penny suggested, pointing to a spot next to a rock a good thirty feet away from the cars.

He turned to Rowen and lowered his voice. "You guys are engaged. Why are you still tiptoeing around your sleeping arrangement?"

"Phoebe thinks that Penny is my roommate," he answered in his nerd-tastic robotic tone as Penny's blush deepened.

"Roommates?" Mitch echoed.

Rowen looked away. "Yes, I'm not ready for Phoebe to ask us any questions about the birds and the bees."

Mitch nodded. "I can understand that. I'm not even close to being ready to go there with Oscar."

"Which reminds me," Rowen continued, then zeroed in on Phoebe and Oscar. "I need to talk to you about something."

"Sure, what is it?"

The guy nodded toward the kids, who had taken a seat in the grass with their heads bent over Oscar's pack. "It's great that Phoebe and Oscar are best friends. But I should let you know that my niece won't be dating until she's thirty."

Thirty! What the actual hell?

Mitch's jaw dropped as he observed the children—who were

six years old, chatting and laughing and tapping their feet. And holy shit! Did he have to start worrying about that now? Dating? Relationships? Girls?

"Rowen," Penny chided. "We haven't discussed this."

"It never hurts to be ready," the man stammered. "It's imperative to have protocols in place and be prepared to anticipate any complications in the system."

Penny poked him in the chest. "Oscar and Phoebe are fine. And you might want to rethink your protocols—especially your age requirement."

The man raised an eyebrow. "What makes you say that?"

Penny cocked her head to the side. "I'm not even thirty."

He studied her finger, his glasses slipping as the hint of a grin touched his lips. "Exactly."

Mitch watched the exchange, then met Charlotte's eye. Before she was his, couples' bullshit like this would make him want to lose his lunch. But it wasn't bullshit anymore. He got it. He understood what it was like to have a person, your person. He went over to Oscar's sleeping bag that happened to be right next to Charlotte. "Can you help me with this?" he asked, crouching down, then messing with the tie.

"What do you need help with?" she asked.

He scanned the lot. Penny and Rowen had walked over to the kids, and he had a second alone with his favorite redhead. "I want you to know that I love you, and I'm glad you're here."

Her expression softened. She rested her hand on the sleeping bag mere millimeters from his. "There's nowhere else I'd rather be," she answered, and for a split second, something flashed in her eyes, edging out the warmth. Was it panic, or was she emotional over Oscar leaving for camp?

"Charlotte," he began, wanting to make sure she was all right when a bell rang out.

"Parents, guardians, Whitmore campers! Welcome to Bergen Adventure's Outdoor Laboratory Telluride campsite. If you could join us in the clearing, we'll go over a few instructions."

Rowen, Penny, and the kids joined them at the cars as they gathered the sleeping bags and extra backpacks.

"Let's go stand with our class," Phoebe called when Rowen's phone pinged.

He slipped it out of his pocket, stared at the screen, then frowned.

"What is it?" Penny asked.

"It's the pilot. He says we need to go now if we want to get ahead of some weather that's headed for the coast."

"I can go with Oscar! Mitch and Charlotte can check me in," Phoebe answered.

"Would you mind, Mitch?" Rowen asked. "I've got a lot on my hands with this blob."

Jesus Christ! This nerd!

"Go ahead. We'll get her squared away," he answered, feeling like someone should award him parent of the year. Minus the whole car erection, he was killing it today.

Rowen and Penny said their goodbyes to Phoebe, and then it was the four of them.

"It looks like they've got cabin assignments on that board. Why don't we check it out before the camp directors talk to us?" Charlotte offered.

Phoebe and Oscar sprinted toward the sign.

"Look at us," he gloated.

"I know! It's like we have a clue what we're doing," she beamed. And there it was—the *we* that sent his pulse racing. They joined the kids and found Phoebe in a full-on pout.

"What's wrong?" he asked the child.

"There's a girls' cabin and a boys' cabin," Phoebe seethed.

He glanced at the board. "Yep, that seems to be the case. Is there a problem?"

"I want to sleep next to Oscar. I won't stand for this!" the little girl replied. And holy hell! If this kid wanted to become a chef, she'd be a force to reckon with in the kitchen. He was a grown man, and he was ready to petition the camp to offer co-ed accommodations. Luckily, Oscar stepped in.

"It's okay, Phoebe. We can do every activity together. And I promise to sit next to you for breakfast, lunch, and dinner."

Phoebe hugged her sleeping bag against her chest and huffed an irritated breath. "I guess that'll be okay."

"It'll be great. We'll hardly sleep! There's too much to do!" his son added.

Mitch leaned in toward Charlotte. "I'm not sure Rowen will have to worry about the boys. It might be the boys who have to worry about Phoebe."

Charlotte pressed her hand to her lips to muffle her laughter. "No kidding."

Another bell rang, and they gathered with the other Whitmore families.

"Welcome, everyone! I'm Camden Bergen, and this is my wife, Cadence. We're in charge of the outdoor educational programming."

Mitch caught Oscar's eye. "Bergen?"

"Yeah, that guy is the brother of my teacher's husband," Oscar answered.

"Gotcha," he said as the woman began to speak.

"Parents, keep your phones close by this week. While we don't anticipate any problems, it's helpful to get in touch with you quickly if we have any questions. Now, this is the time to say goodbye. Campers, after you hug your parents, we'd like you to set your things on your bunk, and then we'll meet in the field for a game of capture the flag."

"This is awesome!" Oscar chimed, high-fiving Phoebe.

"All right, Phoebe," Charlotte said, kneeling. "I've got a big hug for you from your uncle and Penny," she finished, wrapping her arms around the child.

He ruffled Oscar's hair. "Have fun, son." He glanced at Rowen's niece. "And keep an eye on her."

Oscar grinned. "I will," he answered, but instead of giggling, the excitement drained from his face.

"What is it, Oscar?"

Maybe the kid was a little more nervous than he'd let on.

Oscar looked up at him with concern in his eyes. "Will you be okay without me, Dad?"

This went right to his heart. His son was worried about him.

"We'll make do," he answered, his voice cracking with emotion.

What would it be like when the kid left for college?

"But we'll miss you, and we'll be thinking about you and all the fun you're going to have," Charlotte said, opening her arms to his son.

His sight grew blurry as he watched the two people he loved most in this world embrace.

Jesus! He was a mess!

"Here, Charlotte, you can keep this with you," Oscar said softly, then reached into his pack and retrieved the orange ceramic heart.

"I'll treasure this and keep it safe," she answered, holding the heart to her chest.

"I brought this one with me. I hope you don't mind, Dad," Oscar said, pulling the old white lock from his pack. "Do you know if Charlotte's key opens it?"

"I don't know." It seemed crazy that they hadn't tried to open the lock. Then again, life had been going at Mach ten from the moment Madelyn stepped into his office and handed it to him. Or maybe he didn't want to know—didn't want to chance that something that felt so right wasn't what unlocked his heart.

The bell rang again, and Oscar looked up at him. "We'll do it when I get home from camp. Love you, Dad! Love you, Charlotte! You guys don't have to worry about me," he called, flinging his arms around them.

"Yeah, Oscar's got me," Phoebe added, flicking a brown braid over her shoulder. "I'll keep him out of trouble."

He nodded to the little girl. And then, they were off, running to join the children gathering in front of the camp directors.

He and Charlotte stood there, waving until the children disappeared down the side of the hill toward the cabins.

"It's just us. What do we do now?" she asked, still pressing the heart to her chest.

He took her hand. "I have an idea. I could use your help."

"With what?" she asked with a coy lilt to her words.

He glanced from Charlotte to the Lamborghini as a deliciously dirty idea took hold. "It's high time we got to the bottom of my issue with camping supplies."

TWENTY-FIVE

MITCH

FEELING like a kid on Christmas morning, Mitch spied the spot he was looking for, slowed the Lamborghini SUV, then pulled over onto the side of the road.

Charlotte watched him closely. "What's your master plan? When you mentioned camping supplies, I assumed that…"

"We would make out in the car like a pair of teenagers because it's just the two of us?" he supplied.

"That would be a yes," she answered, then peered out the window and stilled. "But hold the sexy supply train for a second. Why do I feel like I've been here before?"

He grinned. He couldn't help it as he recalled the melee that had taken place in this very location. "You have been here before. Holly's cabin is down that gravel road," he answered, pointing ahead.

Charlotte took off her seat belt and swiveled around. "Then that's the tree Oscar climbed to pelt us with rocks," she cooed like being bombarded with pebbles was an endearing experience. And maybe it was. Life had changed so drastically since they were last here. His relationship with his son had transformed. And then, of course, there was the woman sitting next to him who revived his battered heart.

"You know what else it is?" she said, then licked her lips.

And hello, car make-out session! His auburn-haired beauty was game for it.

"What?" he asked, drinking her in as her expression grew decidedly dirty.

"It's where I confronted you after you kidnapped me," she purred.

He feigned mock outrage. "I take issue with your characterization of the events that led up to our tête-à-tête on the side of the road. But if you want to get technical, the first time I kidnapped you was after you waltzed into a bar dressed like a mermaid, drank a gallon of margaritas, hoovered a slice of pizza, took my picture, then passed out on a park bench on my lap," he answered, trying to be clever. Still, there it was again—that flash of regret in her eyes.

What was that?

She could be feeling the effects of their goodbye with Oscar. That had to be it. He squeezed her hand. "Hey, it's okay to miss him. I do, too. But he'll be fine—better than fine. He'll have a blast this week, or Phoebe will sneak into the boys' cabin to be with Oscar, and they'll both get thrown out. Either way, I'd say we have at least six hours before anyone from the camp calls us."

Charlotte chuckled, but something still weighed heavily on her heart. He could feel it.

It was time to change tack.

"Why don't you open the glove box. I think you'll like what's in there."

Her expression brightened. "Any hints?" she asked, eyeing the dash.

He shrugged. "It's not a popsicle."

She cocked her head to the side. "Darn, you know how much I like popsicles."

He adjusted himself. Yeah, he knew.

Charlotte pressed the button, and the slim door popped open. "Chocolate!" she cried.

"I put it in there this morning, thinking Oscar might want a treat on the way to camp, then forgot about it."

"What do you want to do with a chocolate bar, Chef?" she asked, her playful tone returning. "Were you planning on whipping up a soufflé in the car?"

He plucked the bar from the glove box, tore open the wrapper, then broke off a piece. "Close your eyes, Charlotte," he said, resurrecting his hothead chef tone.

"Someone is feeling bossy," she answered with a naughty twist to her lips as she complied with his command.

"Someone's camping supplies are available for use," he corrected as he slipped the bite of chocolate into her mouth. Charlotte hummed her satisfaction, and the sound went right to his cock. He unzipped his pants and freed himself from the confines of his khakis. Pumping his hard length, he stroked himself as he concentrated on the beauty next to him.

This was the face he saw in his dreams. This was the face of his future.

She closed her eyes and parted her lips, ready for another bite. But he had something better in mind. Tossing the chocolate bar onto the dashboard, he cupped her face in his hand and kissed her deeply, tasting the sweet chocolate on her tongue. She sighed again, feeding his desire, then pulled back and glanced down.

"That's quite a tent pole. I better help you test your camping supplies. It's always good to make sure everything is in working order," she remarked, wrapping her hand around him. She tightened her grip as she set the pace, working him in slow, sensual strokes, before leaning over and taking him into her mouth.

"Charlotte," he hissed, tilting his head back as this woman sent his senses into overdrive. He tangled his hand into her hair, surrendering to her rhythm, to her touch, to her heated breath. Hovering on the edge, he inhaled a sharp breath. He wasn't about to leave her behind. "Wait, I want you with me," he growled.

She sat up, wiggled in the seat, then slipped off her panties and removed her bra in no time flat.

"You're really good at taking those off in a tight space," he remarked, genuinely impressed.

"It's something I picked up as a former professional mermaid," she answered, then climbed onto his lap.

She straddled him, and the whole situation was hot as hell, but there wasn't much room to move.

"Why don't you shift your left leg forward?" he suggested as Charlotte lifted her right leg and nearly knocked him in the balls.

"Oh, Mitch! Are you okay?" she asked, giggling.

"Let me move the seat back a little," he offered, reaching down and hitting the button that moved the seat up.

"Whoa!" she cried, grimacing as she arched into him.

"Are we bad at this?" he teased.

The mischief in her eyes turned to pure desire. "There's one way to find out." She lowered herself, closing her eyes as she took every inch of him. And it never got old. Making love to this woman got better every time.

He rolled his hips, and she gasped, their bodies coming together as the friction between them went from hot to scorching. What started out as a slow and sensual dance quickened into a furious pump and grind session.

The intoxicating scent of sex engulfed them. In a fury of

breaths and lips and teeth and tongues, he reached between them and massaged her most sensitive place as she rode him, bucking and writhing, owning his pleasure.

The need to hold on to her, to anchor his soul to hers, tore through him. Higher and higher, they reached the peak, and hand in hand, they took the plunge.

Crying out, his voice rough and primal, they met their release, spiraling over the edge into a sea of orgasmic bliss. There was no beginning and no end. Only Charlotte. Only this woman who'd made him whole. He held her close, working her sweet bud as she cried out, surrendering to the passion that burned white-hot. Panting, they clung to each other. It didn't matter that they were screwing each other's brains out in a car. They could be anywhere. But one truth always remained the same.

She was his.

"I love you," he whispered against the shell of her ear. And he did. She'd made him better, stronger. With her by his side, there were no limits.

His fingertips pressed into her soft skin as he explored her thighs, then drew lazy circles around the taut globes of her ass.

"It's like you're photographing me with your hands," she said on a breathy sigh.

He tipped her chin to focus on her beautiful, sated smile. "No, not with my hands, with my heart." He pressed her palm to his chest. "You're here. You're right here," he finished, losing himself in her emerald eyes when a piercing ping ripped through their sex haze.

They stared at each other. And without a word, they came to the same conclusion as to who could be calling.

"Camp!" they cried.

Charlotte scrambled off his lap and reached for her panties

as he looked around wildly. "Do you see my phone? I can hear it. But I can't find it."

She checked the dash. "No, it's not here," she called, then swiped her bra from the back seat. She had that sucker back on before he could blink. But he couldn't figure out why she was adamant about getting dressed and not focused on finding the phone.

"Why are you putting on your clothes?" he asked, checking the cupholders as the cell continued to chime.

"I can't talk to the camp without wearing underwear. What kind of person does that?" she yipped.

"It's a phone call. They can't see you," he answered, continuing his search for the damn phone.

"I get that. But I'll know that I'm not wearing underwear."

Sweet Christ! This wasn't worth debating!

He pulled up his trousers, then felt his phone wedged between the seat and the console. "Found it," he cried, holding it up.

Charlotte snapped it out of his hands. "Fasten your pants," she ordered.

Was she *not* going to answer the call until they both were decent? He wasn't about to ask. Quickly, he made himself presentable, then gestured to his pants.

She looked him over, then frowned. "You got the button but forgot the zipper."

Shit!

He took care of it, nearly catching a nut—and speaking of nuts, this was nuts! "Charlotte, the call!"

"Okay, okay!" she cried, then answered the phone, hitting the speaker icon in a clusterfuck of movements. "Hello, is this about Phoebe Gale or Oscar Elliott? Are they hurt? Are they homesick? We're close. We can come if it's an emergency," she blurted.

"I think we already had an *emergency come*," he said under his breath as she flashed him *cut-it-out* eyes.

"Charlotte, is that you, dear? Are you all right? It's Ines."

The furious beat of his heart slowed as Charlotte crumpled into the seat, coming down from the adrenaline rush.

"Oh, Ines! Thank goodness it's you. We dropped Oscar off at sleepover camp and thought your call might be the camp calling to let us know there was a problem."

"My goodness! You're so out of breath. It's as if I caught you in the throes of—"

"Hey, Ines, it's Mitch," he said, cutting off the woman. While he trusted her with nearly every facet of his life, he hadn't shared his feelings for Charlotte with her yet.

"Good, good! Hello, Mitch! I need to speak with both of you."

"Is there a problem?" he asked.

"Not a problem, per se. I've got Gwen asking about when she'll get the final chapter of the book. The woman is salivating at the mouth. She's loved everything she's seen so far—which is fantastic news for you. But she's a publisher, and she's getting antsy."

The last damn chapter! He and Charlotte had brainstormed a list of possible ways to wrap up the book, but none of them felt right.

He blew out a slow breath. "As my publicist, you can let her know that I'm not in breach of contract. We've got a week left to pull it together," he answered, stealing a glance at Charlotte. She twisted the hem of her skirt and didn't meet his gaze. Could that be what was on her mind—the looming deadline?

"That's what I thought you'd say," Ines replied.

"Anything else?"

"Yes, two items," Ines continued. "There's good news on your numbers front. The old episodes from the Say Cheese,

Louise reality show from back when you started out began streaming in the UK last week. And the ratings are through the roof. They love the three of you across the pond."

The three of them.

He cleared his throat. "I feel like you're buttering me up for something, Ines. Just say it."

She huffed. "Am I that predictable?"

"You're that reliable," he added, softening his tone. "What's the issue?"

"Seth."

Dammit!

The sound of his name was like listening to nails raking down a chalkboard. He tried to ignore the prickling in his veins. "What about him?" he bit back.

"The publishing company's legal department wants us to have him sign a contract affirming that the events described in your book are as you've portrayed them."

Every muscle in his body clenched. "I own the rights to Say Cheese, Louise. It's mine to do with as I please. I paid him a small fortune, so I'd never have to deal with him again."

"I know, I know, Mitch! I'm looking at the contract now. But the publisher wants an extra layer of confirmation that no royalties are due to him since you're writing about Say Cheese, Louise."

He rubbed the knots that snarled at the base of his neck. "Have you spoken to him?"

Silence.

He knew Ines well enough to know she was choosing her words carefully.

"I have."

"And?" he hissed.

Silence again, and the gulf of dead air swallowed the car.

"And he'd like to talk to you," Ines stated, keeping her tone neutral.

Talk?

The bottom dropped out of his stomach as the prickling in his veins shifted to a sharp slash of pain, searing him from the inside out. "No! No way!" he growled.

"Mitch," Ines began, "he says that he—"

"No, Ines! He betrayed me. He broke my trust. You know this. You know everything." He was yelling, his body vibrating. Every cell in his body pulsed as a rush of rage—a sensation he hadn't known in weeks—surged through him.

Charlotte gasped, and he flicked his gaze from the phone to her. The color had drained from her cheeks. The sweet, sex-fueled rosy glow had vanished. She, better than most, knew he could be a damned hothead. But when it came to Seth, he was a viper, seething with venom and ready to strike. He reached out and squeezed her hand, trying to reassure her that this outburst had nothing to do with her. "Ines, Charlotte and I need to go. Tell Gwen she'll get her final chapter on time. And you know what to do about Seth. He's dead to me."

"Oh, Mitch," the woman lamented with a sigh. "All right, I'll be in touch," she added before the line went dead.

Neither he nor Charlotte said a word. He released her hand, started the car, and drove down the gravel drive to the cabin next to the creek. He needed a second to think—to order his thoughts. He hadn't tapped into that blind rage in ages. But it was still there. It festered like a wound that wouldn't heal. He cut the engine and stared at the cozy wooden structure. Surrounded by a sea of green and the San Juan Mountains, it was truly a peaceful sight. But it did nothing to quell the fury that burned beneath his skin.

He tightened his grip on the steering wheel. "I'm sorry, Charlotte. I know I can get intense when it comes to Seth."

"It's okay. I understand," she replied, her voice barely a whisper.

It wasn't okay. It was far from okay because it impacted her. It was in her nature to be quiet. But this silence was different. He closed his eyes and blew out a slow breath, knowing what he had to do, what he had to share with her. He needed her to see it—to view his worst moment, so she could understand. "I want to show you something. Something very few people have seen." He retrieved his cell, tapped the phone's text icon, then scrolled to the video Ines had sent him the day she and Madelyn had entered his office. The footage she'd busted her ass to keep out of the public's eye. He handed Charlotte his phone, and she accepted it into her trembling hands.

"What is this?" she rasped.

A muscle ticked in his jaw as pain laced with humiliation flooded his system. But he had to show her. "It's the worst of me. Hit play."

Her finger hovered over the screen, but before she tapped the icon, she paused. He couldn't read her—he couldn't decipher what was going on inside her head. But he had to share this. She had to see it.

"Go ahead," he coaxed. "Watch it. It's not long."

She tapped play. "It's you," she said, her eyes glued to the screen. "You're...oh, my God, Mitch, you're..."

"Out of control in a blind rage," he finished. It was years ago, but he remembered that moment like it was yesterday. The mess. The destruction. The absolute disarray. It was as if a wrecking ball had done its worst to the TV set. Prepped with fresh vegetables, bursts of red, green, orange, and yellow littered the floor as he flung pots and pans across the set. It was a godsend that he hadn't taken out his knives and a miracle that none of the crew had been injured. But he hadn't seen them. He could only see red and hear Holly's words.

Oscar is your son, Mitch.

With that news, it was as if the scales had been tipped, and the demons he'd kept at bay had broken free.

And these demons were vicious and hellbent on his destruction.

"That recording is what blackballed me in the culinary world. Ines kept it from getting out, but word got around that I was a loose cannon. That minute of footage captured what happened thirty seconds after I got off the phone with Holly."

"When you learned that you were Oscar's father," she supplied.

"Yes," he whispered. His chest tightened as shame set in. "What kind of person acts like that when they learn they have a son?"

Her eyes welled with tears. "I didn't see a man in a blind rage in that video."

"You didn't?" he asked, his voice cracking.

She shook her head. "I saw a man in pain. A man enduring terrible agony. A man who didn't know what to do or who to turn to."

He hung his head. "It was like descending into hell. My whole world spiraled out of control. I had to create chaos to combat the clawing voices in my head. The only thing I could do at that moment was tear down the set, tear down everything that used to bring me joy. I blamed it for bringing me nothing but pain. The TV chef gig had turned into a prison that shackled me to the past. But I'm not that man anymore. And it's because of you."

"Mitch," she whispered, a gut-wrenching sadness coating the word as she brushed a tear from her cheek.

"I didn't mean to make you cry, Charlotte. I showed you that video because I wanted you to know what you've done for me. What you do for me every single day. I'm better with you."

He scanned the contents of her tote and saw the glint of orange from Oscar's ceramic heart. He pulled it from the bag and placed it in her hand. "Oscar and I are both better with you."

She closed her hand around the heart, then peered out the window as another tear trailed down her cheek. "I could do with a little fresh air. Do you mind if I take a short walk?"

He stroked her cheek. "Do you want me to go with you?"

She focused on the cabin. "Why don't you bring our bags inside? I won't be long. It's got to be the emotion from the day catching up with me. I just need a few minutes."

He nodded. "Take your time. There's a dirt path that goes down to the creek. It's a five-minute walk," he said, watching her closely. Yes, he'd dropped some heavy stuff on her, but he'd swear there was something else weighing heavy on her heart.

As if she were sleepwalking, she opened the car door and started for the path. He watched her disappear past a line of leafy aspens, then blew out a slow breath. "Get the bags. Open the cabin. Work on the book's ending," he murmured to himself, relying on order and structure to shift his focus and calm the storm that raged inside of him. He grabbed Charlotte's tote, then exited the car and got their overnight bags from the back. They'd packed light. They'd only planned to spend one night here before heading back to Denver. They had the last two food truck stops scheduled for the coming Tuesday and Thursday. He unlocked the door to the cabin, and the familiar creak of the hinges whined his arrival as a shiver passed through him. Staring into the main room, he half expected Holly to come out from the kitchen to greet him. He swallowed hard. "It's a house," he said when a series of pings emanated from Charlotte's bag.

Shit! Camp!

Would he be like this every time one of their cells rang?

He reached in and accepted the call. "Hello?"

"Yes, is Charlotte Ames available?" came a woman's voice in a crisp British accent.

He set down the bags, then entered the kitchen, searching for some paper and a pencil. "She's not here. But I can take a message."

"Brilliant! My name is Paige Carter. I'm calling from the Royal College of Art regarding the photography workshop."

"The Royal College of Art in London?" he stammered.

"That's the one! Ms. Ames has confirmed that she's attending our workshop, but she hasn't returned our emails regarding her travel plans. As part of her scholarship, her airfare is covered. And with the start of the intensive workshop coming up so soon, I wanted to call and speak with her directly."

"Workshop?" he repeated. He had to remind himself to breathe as it came back to him. The night he'd whisked her away in a helicopter, her professor had mentioned a photography workshop. But Charlotte had downplayed it—like it was some local event—not a huge endeavor that would take her across the ocean.

He swallowed hard. "And what are the dates of the workshop?"

"The two-week intensive begins a week from today. We'd like to arrange her travel as soon as possible," the woman reiterated.

"I see," he answered, and the rage that had permeated every cell in his body flared.

"Might I ask, are you her husband?" the woman continued.

Husband?

"Excuse me?" he bit out.

"I ask because everyone on the selection committee is keen to know the identity of the man in her submission photo. It's a breathtaking shot of a gentleman," the woman explained.

His pulse raced. He had a good idea of the shot she

described. And not because he'd seen it, but because he'd felt the magic in the air when Charlotte had snapped it—that moment with the scent of pizza in the air and tequila on her breath when he knew his life would never be the same. "Is there a truck in the background—a food truck?" he bit out.

"There is! So, you are the man in the photo."

The woman prattled on, but he couldn't hear her over the roar of blood pounding through his ears. "I'll let Charlotte know you called," he blurted, cutting her off, then ended the call.

Thoughts bombarded his mind as he put the pieces together, and his battered heart hardened.

Charlotte had lied to him. She'd deceived him. What was she planning to do—sneak out of the house in the dead of night and hop a flight across the Atlantic Ocean and leave him when he needed her the most?

"Hey," came a voice, Charlotte's voice. She looked better. The color had returned to her cheeks. She took a step toward him, then stopped dead in her tracks. "Did something happen? Did the camp call?"

His gaze bounced from her face to her phone in his hand. He dropped it into her bag like a lump of hot coal. "Did you submit the picture you'd taken of me when we were on the bench that first night to the Royal College of Art for a photography workshop?"

Her lips parted, opening and closing once, then twice before one syllable slipped out. "What?"

"The night that I found you at that speed date event. The night we ate food truck pizza on the bench. You took my picture. Did you use that in an application for a workshop in London?"

"How do you know about that?" she asked, confusion marring her beautiful face.

Red.

All he could see was red.

"They called. They need to speak to you so they can arrange your travel," he spit out, venom infused in his words.

She raised her hands defensively. "I can explain. I was given a scholarship to attend the workshop, and my professor told the committee that I'd agreed to go. Everything happened so quickly. I've wanted to tell you about it, but I couldn't find the right time."

"The right time?" he barked. "It starts in a week! You were going to leave Oscar and me for two weeks. This was supposed to be our time to finish the book. And school ends after camp. We talked about telling Oscar about us as soon as the school year ended. We made plans, fucking promises. But I see now what's been weighing you down. You want to leave me. You want to go."

She stared at the ceiling like she'd expected the justification for her betrayal to be spray-painted in neon colors. "It's not like that. It's not that simple." She met his gaze head-on. "I decided to tell them that I wouldn't attend. I swear, Mitch. That's what I had to work out in my head just now. I needed to figure out a way to tell you."

He gnashed his teeth, damn close to busting a molar. "Just now?" he snapped. "Your professor told them you were coming weeks ago, didn't she? That night at the carnival? But you brushed it off like it was nothing. It never crossed your mind to cancel earlier. Tell me the damned truth, Charlotte!"

"Okay, here's the truth," she said, lifting her chin. "A part of me wanted it. It's an honor to be accepted to the program—let alone earn a full-ride scholarship. I didn't say anything because I thought there was a chance that we'd finish the book early. And then you wouldn't have that on your plate anymore. The workshop is only for two weeks. We could have told Oscar after it ended. It's not an eternity." She paced the length of the room. "I kept running scenarios in my head, trying to see if there was a way to do both."

"No, you lied, Charlotte. You looked me in the eye at the carnival and said that the workshop wasn't important."

"I screwed up. But I never meant for you to find out like this. I didn't want you to think I was like..." she couldn't say it. But he could. The anger pumping through his veins couldn't hold back.

"Like Seth and Holly," he hissed. "The two people I trusted the most, who'd lied and betrayed me."

"Mitch," she breathed.

He closed the distance between them. "Just say it. You want to leave me and go to London."

"No, I want to be with you. I choose you. I love you," she whispered, her eyes glassy with tears.

Did he want to believe her? Of course, he did. Did he want to take her into his arms and kiss her until he'd forgotten his own damned name? Absolutely! But he couldn't.

"I thought you were done acting like that," he replied, stone-faced.

"Done acting like what?" she shot back.

"Like a goddamned pretzel, twisting yourself to please everyone. I don't need liars in my life, Charlotte. I've been there, and I've done that. And I won't be made a fool of again."

The intensity pulsed between them. "I am not a liar. I'm sorry about how you learned about the workshop. But I'm not twisting myself into anything. If I have to choose, I choose you. And I choose Oscar."

"When did you get accepted?" he bit out.

She lifted her hands to rest them on his chest. And that's when he saw it—the orange heart clasped in her hand.

"When?" he shouted as his hotheaded demons got the best of him.

She lowered her hands and took a step back. "I submitted the application the day we picked up Oscar. And I learned I was accepted the following Monday."

He sucked in a tight breath as if he'd been punched in the gut.

"You've known the whole time we've been together. And you didn't say a thing. That makes it even worse. You knew it would hurt me. You knew it all along."

"I love you, Mitch. I never meant to hurt you," she pleaded. "But there's nothing to fight about. I'm not going. I choose you. I choose Oscar. Let's finish your book. Let's put this in the past."

The past?

If he knew one thing about himself, it was that he was incapable of putting betrayal in the past. He pictured the times he'd caught Holly and Seth together. It had seemed innocent, and he'd written it off. Hell, he'd thought he was the luckiest guy on the planet. His girlfriend and his best friend were close. They were a happy trio and business partners. But he hadn't seen what was right in front of him for months before he caught them embracing. And he wasn't about to become that naïve chump again.

"I want to see the picture you submitted," he demanded, lowering his voice. "You didn't send it to me when I asked to see the photos you'd taken since you'd become Oscar's nanny. Jesus Christ! Your ass was saved on a technicality! You'd taken the damn shot the night before you accepted the position. Is that why you never showed it to me?"

He was a fool, a damned fool!

Her pain was palpable, regret written on her face. "I should have shown it to you. And I should have gotten your permission to use it. And for that, I am truly sorry. But I didn't think I had a chance of getting in. I didn't think there was any harm in trying," she confessed as tears stained her cheeks.

"The photo," he repeated, giving her no comfort.

She went to her bag and removed her camera from its case. With trembling hands, she scrolled through the photos. "It's this one," she said, passing him the Nikon.

He stared at his image on the camera's screen. Anyone could see that she'd already captured his heart. The vulnerability in his eyes and the hint of a smile drew him in. He could understand why people wanted to know more about the picture. There was a raw honesty that cut right to the bone. He'd let his guard down. He'd let her in. She'd pierced the walls around his heart, and the picture said that and more. Perhaps he'd thought he could be that person or believed in that instance he could love again. But love and betrayal could not exist together.

He handed her the camera, then stared at the item clenched in her fist—the orange heart.

"I need you to give that to me. It belongs to Oscar," he said, his voice void of emotion.

She stared at the tiny thing. "But he wanted me to keep it for him."

"And you want to abandon him," he shot back through gritted teeth, the hothead taking over. This is where most people backed down, where they skittered off to take cover.

He should have known Charlotte wouldn't flinch.

"Here, take it," she said, handing him the heart. "But I need you to know that I'm not abandoning either of you. Can't you see that, Mitch? I choose you. I don't know how I can make you understand that." Fire blazed in her eyes. That conviction and drive he'd come to love only hurt him more.

He picked up her bags, then threw open the door. Striding to the SUV, he tossed her stuff in the back.

"What are you doing? Talk to me!" She rested her hand on his arm. And Christ, he already missed her touch. But he couldn't give in. He pulled away, then crossed his arms, clenching the heart in his hand.

"You can't change my mind, Charlotte. And that's why you need to leave. Take the car and go."

Her jaw dropped. "What about Oscar and camp? What if something happens?"

He gestured over his shoulder with his chin. "Holly's truck is in the shed. If my son needs me, I'll be there."

"I love your son, and I love you. Stop being such a damned hothead and look at what's in front of you! Yes, I screwed up. But I'm sorry, and I'm here. Don't ruin what we have," she pleaded, her emerald eyes shining.

Her hand went to the key around her neck—the key he'd thought opened his heart. It was a good thing they'd never checked to see if the key opened the lock. It didn't matter. He knew the truth about her. But that didn't mean he had the power to look away. He stared at the glinting bit of gold until the hum of a plane passing overhead caught his attention, and they both looked up as three words echoed in his head.

Mr. Cheesy Forever.

"Go to London. Forget about me and Oscar. And Charlotte," he continued, shattering on the inside. This was killing him, but he had to make a clean break. He had to let the hothead take over.

"Yes," she answered, gaze burning. If there were a salad in the vicinity, she'd sure as hell hurl it at him.

"Good luck finding your Mr. Cheesy Forever. You were never going to find him here," he growled.

But Charlotte didn't back down—not one damn inch.

"If you can't see the remorse in my eyes and the love in my heart for you and for Oscar, then you're right. My Mr. Cheesy Forever isn't here. The only person here is the one who chose to embrace being a hothead over following his heart."

He clamped his mouth closed to keep from pleading with her to stay. He ignored the twinge in his heart, begging him not to let her go. But that was the sap in him—the sucker. His head knew the truth. He was better off alone. Whenever he let anyone in, the results were catastrophic.

He stood there made of ice, his heart as hard as stone. She studied him for a beat, then two as if she were recording this moment, chronicling the end.

"You could have been him," she said, her words piercing the silence. "You don't believe it, but you could have been my Mr. Cheesy Forever. You have everything it takes except the one thing that really matters."

"And what's that?" he snarled.

"Trust—you don't trust yourself with your own heart! I may fall hard and fast, but I know I do it with every piece of myself. I give my whole heart. I'm not perfect. But I know my Mr. Cheesy Forever is out there."

They stared at each other as if this was some emotional showdown. Her gaze cut with a thousand knives, but he didn't budge. He didn't break. She nodded to herself, then released a pained sigh. Her tears had dried, and with one last look, she slipped into the car and disappeared down the drive in a cloud of dust.

TWENTY-SIX

CHARLOTTE SIPPED her latte and listened to the hum of the traffic and the sounds of the Crystal Creek business district opening for the day. Closed signs turned to open as merchants unlocked storefront doors and patrons sailed in and out of the coffee shop up the street. The Colorado sun lit the area in a warm golden glow. With the Rocky Mountains as the backdrop, it was the kind of morning that could inspire one to write a song, pen a poem, or snap a photograph.

That's what she'd been doing these last three days since she'd glanced in the rearview mirror and watched as Mitch's looming form disappeared. From people to wildlife to shots of the city, she'd taken hundreds of pictures. There was no focus to her work, no theme or directive. She simply observed her environment, then captured the moment.

And now she was here, going back to the beginning, perched on the same bench where she'd met Royce and Larissa almost two months ago. The same bench where she'd stared across the street, praying that this would be the day her life changed.

It certainly had. But not in the way she'd expected.

She'd existed in a strange limbo for the last seventy-two hours. Instead of going back to Mitch's place, she'd driven to the bustling part of Crystal Creek and had checked into the same boutique hotel where Mitch had arranged for that helicopter to whisk them away. When she'd pulled up to the glitzy building, she wasn't even sure if she could afford to book a room in their broom closet. But when she'd tapped the banking app on her phone, she'd been rendered speechless.

She was rich—well, rich for her.

Last she'd looked, she had five bucks to her name. Now, thanks to the substantial nanny salary she'd racked up and an enormous retainer fee for her photography work for Gwen's publishing house, she had over thirty thousand dollars in the bank.

She should be walking on sunshine. Without a cloud in the sky, it was certainly the type of morning for it. But her heart wasn't there yet. No, her heart belonged to two people she wasn't sure she'd ever see again. Still, a somber tranquility had taken over when she'd met Mitch's gaze, standing there as she held her ground in front of the cabin.

In those moments, it had become crystal clear.

He loved her, but he also loved holding on to the pain of his past.

She took another sip of her latte. She'd purchased it from the coffee shop that donated part of its proceeds to Helping Hands. They now sold reusable cups with the shelter's logo printed on the side, and that's what she'd bought this morning. She touched the little heart made of handprints and sighed as she shifted on the bench and extended her legs. She leaned back, resting her head on her tote, trying to remember the person she was the last time she was here. She closed her eyes, absorbing the warmth of the sun when a shadow cast down on her.

"Are you all right, miss? Do you need help?" came a soft woman's voice.

Charlotte smiled. She couldn't help it, recalling when Ralph had asked her the exact same thing. She cracked her eyes open and found an elderly couple gazing down at her with furrowed brows. She sat up and smoothed her skirt.

"We can buy you breakfast if you're hungry," the gentleman offered with a tip of his cap.

"Are you homeless, dear?" the woman pressed.

She had to think about that. She certainly couldn't live at Mitch's place after what had transpired, and her apartment was no longer her apartment. The building had turned into a condo, and her unit had probably already been sold. She smiled at the couple, then shrugged. "I guess I am homeless."

"Did you sleep here last night?" the man asked, worry etched on his face.

She chuckled. "No, I didn't. I'm staying in a hotel not far from here. I was just...remembering," she finished.

"Sorry for intruding! We're from a little town in Iowa where we take care of each other," the woman explained.

"Is this your first time in Denver?" Charlotte asked.

The man nodded. "It is! Our son and his family moved out here a few months ago. It's beautiful! Back in Iowa, we sure don't have anything like those to the west," he finished, gesturing toward the mountains.

"Would you mind taking our picture?" the woman asked, slipping a cell phone from her handbag.

"I'd be happy to," she answered, coming to her feet as the woman handed her the phone. She framed the shot, making sure to get the mountains in the background, then tapped the photo button a few times.

Click, click, click!

Be it a cell phone or her Nikon, the sound always brought her comfort.

"There, I took a couple of shots," she said, returning the cell.

"Thank you, young lady. Would you mind us asking another favor?"

"Not at all."

"Where did you get your coffee? I can't make heads or tails of this directions app my grandson put on my phone. I'm not sure we're even headed in the right direction."

"You're on the right track. You don't have far to go. There's a coffee shop about half a block up the street. They're a local company. They donate to an organization that runs a shelter and helps rehabilitate troubled youth. I'm sure they'd appreciate you stopping in."

"Then that's where we're headed," the woman said warmly as her husband offered her his arm, and the pair continued down the sidewalk. She watched them go when another voice, a voice she recognized, brought a smile to her lips.

"I appreciate you advocating for Helping Hands."

She turned and spied Ralph headed her way.

It was déjà vu all over again.

"What are the chances of us meeting here for a second time?" she asked as they embraced.

The lines at the man's eyes crinkled as he chuckled. "Pretty good, actually. I stop by to pick up donations from the coffee shop quite a bit. But I must say, I'm delighted to see you, Charlotte. And I have a message for you."

"What's that?" she asked. Her heart jumped into her throat. Could it be a message from Mitch? She hadn't heard from him. Not a text. Not a call. She didn't even know if he was back in the city. The man had gone silent.

"Louise was going to call you," Ralph began, concern clouding his expression. "She hasn't been able to get ahold of

Mitch. Erick and Sergio told us that he was a no-show yesterday for the food truck stop at the retirement community. The boys tried to text and call him but came up empty-handed as well."

She sank onto the bench. "I was worried that something like this would happen."

Ralph settled himself beside her. "Is he all right?"

Tears welled in her eyes. She hadn't cried since she'd left Mitch. But seeing Ralph opened the flood gates. These last three days, she'd been a ghost. She hadn't answered any of her friends' calls or texts. She'd floated through the city, taking pictures, lost in her photography. It was her one escape. The way to quell the ache in her chest. She inhaled an audible breath as Ralph retrieved a handkerchief from his pocket.

"Here," he said gently, passing it to her.

"I didn't think people carried these around anymore," she replied, patting away the tears on her cheeks.

Ralph offered her a warm smile. "I've been around a while. Old habits die hard."

"They do," she agreed, tears trailing down her cheeks as she pictured the last time she'd seen Mitch. With his hardened facade and searing gaze, he'd reverted to the angry, volatile hothead.

"What happened?" Ralph asked.

"I messed up," she began, resting the handkerchief on her lap. She took the key between her fingers. "I kept something from Mitch that I shouldn't have. I should have been upfront with him, and I wasn't. And then he found out."

"I take it, he didn't find out from you," the man added.

Mitch's face flashed in her mind. She'd known something was wrong the second she'd stepped foot in the kitchen. "Yeah, that's how it happened. I tried to apologize. I wanted to make it right, but he called me a liar. He said I betrayed him." It was as if she were chewing nails as she spoke.

Of course, she was mad at herself. From the moment she'd been accepted to the London workshop, she'd tried to figure out a way to both share the information and soften the blow. But every time she'd even come close to bringing it up, a little voice inside of her head held her back. She didn't want to make waves and jeopardize the happiness she'd found. She'd wanted to be loved for so very long. She'd dreamed of the white knight, gifting her with affection and grand gestures of adoration. She wanted it all—her Mr. Cheesy Forever.

And she'd had it—or at least she thought she'd had it.

He'd professed his love for her.

This man—this famous chef—wanted her. He worshipped her body every night and could make her head spin with one look. She'd fall asleep wrapped in his arms and wake to his kisses.

But whatever they had, it wasn't enough for him.

She could have thrown her camera into the creek and swore she'd never leave him, and it wouldn't have mattered. A realization dawned as she'd stared into his blazing eyes. If it wasn't this workshop, it would be something else. It wasn't that he didn't trust her. He didn't trust himself. He couldn't see forgiveness as a way forward. To him, it was a weakness. It was easier to cling to the pain than to reach out for salvation.

"I've known Mitch since he was seventeen—since his days of hot-wiring cars. Did he tell you about his grandfather?" Ralph asked, bringing her back.

She released the key. "He mentioned that his parents died when he was very young and that his grandfather took him in. But he said they weren't close. He died a little after Mitch turned eighteen. I got the message that once Mitch was an adult, he was on his own."

Ralph sat back and exhaled a slow breath. "That's the barebones version of it. But there's more."

She sat quietly, watching the man as he stilled, seemingly lost in thought.

"I knew Mitch's grandfather—Bruce was his name. I knew Mitch's grandmother, too. They had a tumultuous relationship. She ran off with another man, but Mitch never knew her."

Charlotte swallowed past the lump in her throat. "I had no idea."

Ralph stared ahead. "Mitch doesn't know about that. But when she left Bruce, the man was never the same. He'd closed himself off. By the time Mitch came to live with him, he was a surly husk of a man—bitter until the end. Don't get me wrong. He gave Mitch a roof over his head and three meals a day. He had a meager pension. They got by. But the man had hardened his heart and had no love to give. That type of homelife isn't easy."

Charlotte nodded. She knew that better than anyone.

"When Bruce got sick, Mitch needed to help make ends meet, and that's where he ran into trouble with the law. But there was something about him. He was this hardened, sullen teenager, and then he stepped into Louise's kitchen, and he transformed. The kid pulled you in. His work ethic was second to none. His enthusiasm was pure electricity. The whole kitchen came alive when he cooked."

Charlotte brushed a tear from her cheek. "Yeah, I can agree with you there. Watching him cook is mesmerizing."

Mitch Elliott had been the perfect subject to photograph. And it wasn't only that he might as well be named the world's hottest chef. The man was passionate, enthusiastic, and focused in a maddeningly sexy way that had her ready to ride him like a food truck groupie once the clock struck nine, and they were sure Oscar had fallen asleep. The attraction had been there from the beginning—that breathtaking, all-encompassing thrill.

Even when she'd hated the guy, she couldn't deny the visceral reaction his presence evoked in her.

"So, you can see how Holly and Seth became enamored with him. It's a shame what happened to them."

"What happened to Seth?" she asked. She thought he was living the good life at a resort in Florida.

Ralph leaned forward. "He got into a motorcycle accident last year. We had no idea. We hadn't heard from him in ages. He called Louise last week. I guess Mitch's publisher wanted him to sign some contracts, and it got him thinking about his past. He's fallen on hard times."

"Yeah, Mitch didn't take it well when Ines brought up the subject," she commented, trying to wrap her head around the complexity of her hothead chef and his complicated past.

"I can imagine," Ralph continued. "The three of them share a lot of history. They were so young when reality TV came calling. Then came the overnight success, followed by fame and jealousy. It was hard to watch Mitch turn into the younger version of Bruce after he learned Holly had cheated on him with Seth. But then you entered his life, Charlotte, and he started taking out Say Cheese, Louise again. He opened the door to a part of himself he'd locked away."

"I can't take the credit, Ralph," she answered. "I had the idea to do the food truck reboot. But Mitch made it happen. Mitch is the magic."

Ralph chuckled and shook his head. "That's where you're wrong. Louise believes Mitch found his spark when he found you."

"I don't think I'm the spark," Charlotte confessed.

"No, I'm not saying you are the spark," the man countered.

Ralph had spent much of his life as a social worker, counseling others. And she had the distinct feeling he was dropping breadcrumbs for her. But she couldn't decipher his last comment. "Then what do you mean?"

"I mean several things. You made him want to be better. You showed him another way of life was possible. You helped him face the broken pieces of his past. And you were there to support him when he became a full-time father. You inspired him to seek out what he'd buried deep inside of himself. But here's what I know about Mitch. When he's at a crossroads, he picks a path and forges his way forward, full speed ahead. Sometimes, that path serves him well—like with the cooking and his culinary career. Sometimes, it blinds him from seeing the good things that are right in front of him."

She sat back and exhaled the heavy breath she hadn't realized she'd been holding. "What path do you think he'll choose this time?"

Ralph rested his hand on her shoulder, a fatherly gesture that brought the hint of a grin to her lips. "I can't answer that question. But I can tell you that he loves you, kiddo. Louise and I saw it the first time the two of you pulled up to Helping Hands. Don't give up on him quite yet. I believe he's at a crossroads right now. He could still surprise you."

She picked up the handkerchief and wiped away fresh tears. Were they for her father, a man she wished would offer her wise words of comfort instead of the cold shoulder, or was she scared of the path Mitch would choose? Or was it neither?

What about the choice that was in front of her now—the choice to follow her dreams and attend the workshop? She shook her head, trying to order her spiraling thoughts.

"I have a feeling it's not only Mitch that's weighing heavy on your heart," Ralph added.

She steadied herself. "I have a decision to make. There's an opportunity to attend a photography workshop in London. I have to let them know today if I'll be attending. It's something

I've dreamed of. If I choose to go, I leave in three days. The day it starts is the day Mitch's book is due to his publisher. I'll be leaving him to finish his book alone. Honestly, I don't even know if he wants my help anymore. But this is my crossroads. Any advice from the resident social worker?" she finished, smiling through her tears.

Ralph nodded. "Yes, follow your spark."

"My spark?" she whispered as she stared across the street at Professor Tran's gallery.

"Yes, and sometimes, the answer is right in front of you," Ralph added, coming to his feet. "Good luck, Charlotte. I hope to see you soon."

"Your handkerchief," she said, holding up the cloth.

"Keep it. You've got a good heart. I have a feeling you'll need that handkerchief for happy tears next time."

"Thank you, Ralph," she said, watching the man stroll down the street, when a pack of women staring at their phones nearly ran into the guy. Charlotte eyed the group. That wasn't just any pack of women. It was *her* pack of women—Penny, Harper, and Libby.

With a giant cup in her hand and her cell phone in the other, Harper looked up and shrieked. "She's here! I see her! She's on that bench!"

What the heck was going on with them?

"What are you doing here?" she asked, flabbergasted.

Penny dropped her cell into her purse. "We're sort of tracking your phone."

Charlotte's jaw dropped. "Sort of?"

"Let me help," H said, holding out her cell. "We are *totally* tracking your phone, Char."

"How?" she stammered.

"Penny's hot nerd fiancé hooked us up," Harper added as Penny nodded, looking pleased as punch. "We also had to listen to Rowen's whole spiel on how a bazillion apps are tracking you at any time. So, according to Rowen, we're just one of many who know exactly where you are."

Charlotte stared at the phone. "That's creepy."

"We wouldn't have to resort to being creepy and having my fiancé commit cyber-crimes if you'd answer your phone," Penny replied in a huff, then glared at H. "And Harper thought it would be *fun* if we did it on foot. We've been walking for two hours!"

Charlotte studied the trio. Had her friends lost their minds?

"On foot?" she repeated.

Harper glanced at Libby. "Hey! I thought a little exercise would help Miss Angry Yoga Barbie over here."

Libby tucked a lock of her jet-black hair back into the world's messiest bun, then pointed to her ear. "I can hear you, H. I've lost my chi and my O, not the ability to perceive sound," the woman hissed.

Hissed!

She hadn't heard Libby hiss since they were in Ms. Miliken's kindergarten class, and Libbs had to pretend to be a snake when they were learning how to write the letter *s*.

Charlotte patted the bench. "Sit down," she said as Libby sized up a muscled man walking toward them.

"Sorry to bother you, ladies," the guy began, but before he could say another word, Libby was back in hiss mode.

"You are bothering us, and I doubt you're sorry. We're women who deserve a little respect. We don't want to be disrupted and ogled like female slices of jock-infused beefcake!"

Female slices of jock-infused beefcake?

The man's cheeks burned crimson. "I wanted to check if my phone was on the bench. I misplaced it, and I'm retracing my steps."

"Oh, sorry!" Libby gasped as her cheeks grew pink.

Charlotte eyed her friend, then met the mortified man's gaze. "I've been here for the last hour, and I haven't seen a phone."

"Okay, sorry again," the poor guy blurted, giving Libby one last look before breaking out into a sprint and tearing down the street.

"Sorry, girls, I've been keyed up lately," Libby lamented as the man turned the corner and disappeared.

H handed her the giant cup. "Drink your wheatgrass. I got it with seven pumps of serenity. I don't even know what the hell that means, but it cost a fortune."

Wanting to both laugh and cry, Charlotte surveyed her friends, so grateful to see them as her eyes welled with fresh tears. "I'm sorry I didn't answer your calls. It's like I've been sleepwalking through the last three days."

Her friends clustered around her, settling themselves on the bench. Penny squeezed her hand as H rubbed her back, and Libby offered her a sip from the Serenity Big Gulp.

She waved off the drink. "Mitch found out about the workshop in London."

"Because you told him?" Libby asked.

Charlotte's shoulders slumped. "Because my phone rang, and he answered it. I'm sure he thought it might be the camp calling about Oscar. But it was someone from the Royal College of Art reaching out to book my flight to the UK."

"Char, what happened?" Penny pressed.

"You remember Mitch the Hothead?"

Penny nodded.

"He's back, and he's more hotheaded than ever. He said that I betrayed him—that I lied to him. He told me to leave. So, I drove back to Denver. I've been in a fog, trying to figure out what happens next. But the funny thing is, as much as I miss him and as much as I love him, at that moment when he told me to leave, I was okay. In fact, my heart broke for him."

Harper shook her head. "Char, you've got to stop letting guys do this to you. You give and give, and all they do is take from you."

"No, it's not like that," she countered. "I've been with some real jerks in the past. I'd try to do whatever it took to make it work. But this was different. With Mitch, I came out of it stronger."

"Stronger?" Penny repeated.

It was the truth.

"I love him. I do. But he's the one who's stuck. I don't think it's a conscious effort. It's like he's looking for people to disappoint him. Like he's scared to put his heart on the line and trust in love."

"And what about Oscar?" Penny asked. "Camp ends in a few days."

A knot twisted in her belly at the mention of the boy. "I can't imagine not being in his life. I love him. I love them both."

"What about the workshop? Have you made a decision?" Libby pressed.

She glanced at her phone to check the time. It was nine thirty. That meant it was four thirty in London. "I have thirty minutes to decide. I have to let them know by ten o'clock mountain time. That's five p.m. in London."

"What's your heart telling you to do?" Libby asked.

"I'm not sure," Charlotte replied, staring at her phone, willing the answer to come, when a text from her father flashed on the screen, and she gasped.

"My dad messaged me," she said, hardly able to believe her eyes as she showed her friends.

Dad: We're planning to go on a cruise next week and wanted to see what your schedule looked like.

"Wow, Char! The universe threw a real wrench into your life," Libby said, wide-eyed.

"No kidding," Harper added.

Charlotte stared at the screen, unable to recall the last time her father had invited her to do anything—let alone join his family on a trip! The most he'd done in years was reply to her messages with a thumbs-up. No words—simply a weak acknowledgment. Her mouth grew dry, and she chugged what was left of her coffee. It had gone cold, and a shiver worked its way down her spine.

"How will you reply?" Penny asked.

Charlotte shook her head. "I don't know. But I should at least thank him for thinking of me." Her heart pounding, she hammered out a quick reply.

Charlotte: I'm grateful you'd want to include me on a trip. Thank you for reaching out!

Dots rippled less than a second after she'd hit send. Could this be a new beginning for her and her dad? It had to be a good sign, right?

Wrong.

Dad: Sorry for the confusion. Our usual house sitter is booked. I wanted to see if you could come to Kentucky and take care of the dogs and water the plants while we're gone.

"Oh, Char! I'm sorry, honey," Penny said, reading over her shoulder.

Charlotte scrutinized the reply. If her father had sent this text three months ago, she would have jumped at the opportunity. She would have been elated with the tiniest crumb of attention. She would have already been halfway to Kentucky.

But she wasn't that person anymore.

Her thoughts shifted to Oscar. She pictured his toothy grin —Mitch's grin. The boy had his mother's chestnut-colored hair and his father's piercing blue eyes. And she loved this boy. She loved him the way her father had never loved her. She loved him like he was her own.

A question formed in her mind.

What would Holly want for her son?

The woman had loved the boy fiercely. She could tell from not only the photographs dotting the cabin's refrigerator but from the compassionate, loving boy she'd raised.

What kind of woman would Holly want to influence her son's life? What lessons would she want Oscar to learn?

Charlotte ignored the text and peered across the street at Professor Tran's gallery. And in the morning light, her torrent of thoughts quieted as one truth emerged.

She couldn't say if she and Mitch would find a way to be together. It was up to him to decide if he'd choose a life that centered on the pain of his past or pick the path that led to a future with her. But with him or without him, there was one way forward for her. She'd gone back to the beginning and had emerged clear-eyed. And she knew what lesson she'd want Oscar to learn from her.

The lesson of love. Self-love.

She had to love herself. She couldn't tether her worth to others' opinions. She had to believe in her abilities. And she had to follow her heart. Yes, she loved Mitch. And yes, she wanted to be with him. But real love, the kind she'd want Oscar to know, came from within.

That's the woman Holly would want her to be. She knew it with every fiber of her being.

That woman didn't twist, and she didn't mold herself to another's expectations. That woman embraced her true self. She trusted and thrived in the knowledge that she was enough.

Charlotte took in her friends, the women who had been in her corner since she was five years old.

"I need to pack."

"You're leaving for Kentucky?" Harper blurted, incredulity coating the words.

The old Charlotte would have. But that's not who she was.

"No," she answered. She didn't reply to the man's message with a single word. Clear-eyed and with conviction pumping through her veins, she took a page from her father's playbook—with a little variation. Her finger hovering over the screen, she blew out a steady breath, then tapped the thumbs-*down* icon.

Charlotte Ames was done settling for scraps.

"Then where are you going, Char?" Penny asked as an airplane crossed the sky. Bright white, it soared across the expanse of blue.

There was her message. The plane was the sign.

"I don't need a Mr. Cheesy Forever waiting to greet me at the airport with a sign," she said, studying the sky as the plane disappeared, heading east toward the rising sun. Sure, what she'd witnessed at the baggage claim back when she was a girl was a sweet and heartfelt gesture. But it didn't define how she viewed love anymore.

"Char, are you okay?" Libby asked, moving from the bench to kneel in front of her.

Her friends leaned in, surrounding her with love and support as tears, happy tears, trailed down her cheek. She smiled. Ralph was right. Wiping the happy tears away with his handkerchief, she focused on her friends. "Girls, I'm better than okay. I'm going to London."

TWENTY-SEVEN

MITCH

"DAMMIT! DAMMIT! DAMMIT!"

Mitch stared at the pad of paper, scribbled across the line of text he'd written, then exhaled a tight breath. He was an utter wreck. He closed his eyes and tried to focus on the rush of water as it danced through the rocky creek and the mountain air, rustling the leaves of the aspen trees that dotted the landscape. He'd left the cabin to clear his head. But every time he closed his eyes, he saw her.

Charlotte.

But it wasn't just any image replaying in his mind.

He saw Charlotte's face before she got into the car. And the depth of emotion in her emerald eyes nearly killed him. It wasn't only the grief but the searing disappointment that had ripped apart his very soul.

And there was one person to blame for this living hell.

Himself.

This is what happened when he opened his heart and let someone in. This is why he needed the walls. This pain was the catalyst that transformed him into a seething hothead. Like with Holly and Seth, he hadn't seen it coming. The betrayal had hit him like a one-two punch. It left him gasping and aching in misery just when he believed a life filled with love, *real love*, was within his grasp.

Charlotte was the reason he'd gotten his career back on track, and now she was the reason he'd been holed up in Holly's cabin for the last three days. It was Wednesday. Hell if he knew what time! Probably the afternoon. It wasn't like it mattered. He'd already missed the Tuesday food truck stop and had no plans to make the Thursday stop either. He hadn't showered. He'd barely eaten. His phone rang—almost incessantly—and it pinged with text after text. Erick, Sergio, Louise, Ines, Gwen, Madelyn, Rowen, Raz, Landon—these people wouldn't stop blowing up his phone.

Where are you?

Please call me!

This is important!

If he didn't have to monitor the damned thing for Oscar's camp, he would have thrown his cell into the creek. Of course, it didn't help that he hadn't replied to anyone. But he couldn't. He didn't have any answers. He'd gone back to the beginning, but he didn't know where to go from here.

How did he move forward?

Or, in his case, how would it end?

He stared at the page of crap ideas for his book's final chapter. Nothing gelled. Nothing flowed. He was in a world of shit and spiraling fast. Without Charlotte by his side, he was lost. And what was worse was that she knew he needed her. And still, she'd been poised to leave. With days to go and his career in the balance, he was here, sitting on a rock next to a creek, cursing his very existence.

He reached into his pocket and removed the ceramic orange heart, and his flesh and blood heart shuddered.

How the hell would he explain to Oscar what had happened?

And what would his son do without Charlotte?

He couldn't let his mind go there. The only saving grace was that the kid was at camp, blissfully unaware that *again* another person he'd loved would be gone.

Mitch closed his fist around the heart. He'd been plagued with a tornado of questions. But he kept coming back to one.

Why didn't she tell him the truth about the workshop?

The queries whirled in his mind as a gut-wrenching pain churned in his belly. He opened his hand and stared at the orange ceramic heart. It was as if the object held everything he missed about the woman he couldn't stop thinking about. And God help him, couldn't stop loving.

He gritted his teeth, raised his arm, pulled back, then hurled the heart into the creek. The second it broke the surface, he gasped, comprehending the stupidity of his actions. He kicked off his shoes and sprinted toward the rocky bank. Scaling the muddy incline, he scanned the shallow waters for a flash of bright orange. And thank Christ, he spotted it! He treaded into the cold water, sucking in a tight breath as an icy jolt shocked his system. But the shock was countered by a flood of relief as he plucked the bright orange object from the creek bottom. He pressed the heart to his chest—thinking of Oscar, thinking of Charlotte. Common sense would tell a person to get out of the frigid waters. But he stood there as the creek gurgled around his calves. "What the hell are you doing?" he whispered, drying off the heart with the corner of his shirt when a voice cut through the air.

"It's a lot easier with a fishing pole," a man called.

Startled, Mitch lost his footing on the slick rocks and fell onto his ass. The cool waters saturated his pants. In the melee, he dropped the ceramic heart into the water again, then scrambled to find it again before turning to get a better look at the person who'd snuck up on him.

"What are you doing? Throwing rocks at fish? Are you crazy?" the man pressed.

Mitch had to marinate on that one. *Was he crazy?* That was the question he'd been asking himself for the last seventy-two hours.

"Here, let me give you a hand." The man traversed the creek bank, edging his way down. He was wearing a wide-brimmed hat and overalls, and something was oddly familiar about him.

Mitch shielded his eyes to get a better look. Holy shit! He recognized the guy. "Mr. Applebaum?" he blurted as the gentleman offered him his hand. It had been close to a decade since he'd seen the Colorado apple farmer who also produced the apple butter that he used in the Signature Louise sandwiches.

"Hello, Mitch!" the man exclaimed. "I wasn't expecting to see you here. I'm sorry I snuck up on you," he continued, helping him to his feet.

The men ambled up the side of the creek, and Mitch checked the ceramic heart. It was still intact without a scratch on it—thank God! He dried it with the collar of his shirt, the only part of his clothing that wasn't dripping wet.

"Why are you throwing orange hearts into the creek?" the farmer asked.

And that was the million-dollar question. What was he doing with his heart?

"I honestly don't know what I'm doing," he answered on a weary sigh, then met the old farmer's hazel gaze. "I don't mean to be rude, Mr. Applebaum, but why are you here?"

He picked up a jar from the ground and held it up. "I stopped by to drop off some apple butter for Holly and Oscar."

He looked away, not sure how to break the news. "I'm sorry

to have to tell you this, but Holly passed away a few months ago."

The man pressed his hand to his chest as shock marred his expression. "Dead? She was so young. What happened?"

"She had a stroke. It happened suddenly."

"And how's her boy?" the farmer pressed.

Emotion thickened in Mitch's throat. "He's coping with it."

Mr. Applebaum shook his head. "That's a shame. You hear about young folks passing away, and it makes you want to live every day to the fullest. Can't take anything for granted. She was a lovely lady. She certainly adored her son and always had a kind word for you."

The man wasn't wrong. Still, he was surprised to hear Holly had spoken of him. He'd barely been able to look at her when he'd come to visit Oscar, let alone make idle chitchat. It cut too deep.

"Did you see Holly often? Your farm is quite a ways from here, north of the city, if I remember correctly?" Mr. Applebaum would drop by the community center to donate fresh produce and apple butter from time to time. When he, Seth, and Holly had started Say Cheese, Louise, the man had gifted them with a case of apple butter. Guilt twinged in his chest. He'd been so wrapped up in his pain and anger, he hadn't reached out to the man in years—a man who'd shown them genuine kindness.

"It was always a pleasure visiting with Holly and Oscar. My sister and her family live in Telluride. My wife and I come down a few times a year. We ran into Holly—must have been three years ago. She'd moved here with her boy, and we saw them in town. Oscar is a fan of the apple butter, so I always bring her a few jars whenever we're here. I can't believe she's gone. I'm sorry to hear that."

Mitch nodded. "No one expected it."

"Is Oscar living with you now?" the farmer asked.

"Yes, we live in Denver. But this week, Oscar is at a camp with his school outside Telluride, and I'm here..."

What the hell was he doing here? Licking his wounds? Failing at writing a book? Nursing a broken heart? Allowing the pain in his chest to fester?

"You're throwing your heart into the creek," the farmer supplied with the ghost of a grin.

Mitch peered at the ceramic shape glinting in the late afternoon light. "Yeah, something like that."

"It must be important," the farmer added.

Mitch watched the man closely. "What must be important?"

"That heart."

A slice of silence stretched between them. Mitch studied the heart—the heart his son had painted the same color as the food truck. Then he recalled the heart Oscar had with him at camp—the heart-shaped lock. The lock they were going to try to open with Charlotte's key.

Would he ever get the chance to find out if she truly held the key to his heart?

"I should be on my way," the farmer said, breaking into his thoughts. "My wife's waiting for me in the truck." He held up the jar. "I'll put the apple butter on the porch. But I want to thank you before I go."

Mitch frowned. "Thank me for what?"

"For ordering a substantial amount of apple butter a few months back. Farming isn't the easiest profession. There are ups and downs. That order your restaurant put in helped us make payroll. A late freeze reduced our crop this year, and we had to rely heavily on the apple butter sales."

It hadn't been on purpose. It had been a fluke—an ordering error. But it had turned out to be a most fortunate accident. He studied the man. "How do you do it? How do you live with the uncertainty of not knowing what will happen with your life and livelihood?"

The question fell from his lips as if he'd kept it bottled up for an eternity and couldn't hold it back any longer.

Mr. Applebaum removed his hat and scratched his balding head. "I guess it comes down to trust."

"Trust?" Mitch echoed.

"You've got to trust yourself to make the best decisions you can. It doesn't always work out. We've had years with bad crops, years we couldn't meet the demand, and years we were left with a surplus. It's a labor of love, but there's a decent dose of forgiveness involved, too."

Forgiveness?

Now Mitch was the one scratching his head. "I'm not sure I understand."

"It has a lot to do with what you've got in your hand," the farmer answered.

Mitch stared at the orange heart. "It has to do with this?"

"You've got to know your own heart. You've got to be able to forgive yourself for the missteps, then move on. If you don't do that, your head will be stuck in the past, looking at the old problems instead of finding new ways forward. You have to figure out who you are and what matters. And you certainly don't want to throw away the important things. That's what gets you through the tough times." A horn honked in the distance, and Mr. Applebaum chuckled. "That would be my wife, telling me to get back to the truck and stop dawdling. The older I get, the more I seem to do it," the man added with an easy grin. "It was good to see you, Mitch. Say hello to Oscar for us and take care of that," he finished, gesturing to the heart before heading up the trail toward the cabin.

Mitch stared at the heart as the breeze picked up and goose

bumps broke out on his arms. Barefoot and wet from the waist down, he must look deranged. He slipped the heart into his pocket, peered down at his soaked clothing, then retrieved his shoes and the pad and pen. He slipped on his sneakers, then jotted two items Mr. Applebaum had mentioned on the paper.

Figure out who you are and what matters.

Don't throw away the important things.

But what was important? Christ, he didn't know anymore.

He stared up at the sky as a sleek Learjet passed overhead, descending in altitude as it headed toward the airport. And instantly, his focus shifted to Charlotte and her quest to find her Mr. Cheesy Forever.

Was she right?

Could he have been that person?

He shook his head, working to push the thoughts away when a horn honked. It had to be the Applebaums—maybe they needed something. He headed up the trail and caught sight of an SUV parked in front of the cabin. But it didn't belong to Mr. Applebaum and his wife. This vehicle had the Helping Hands Community Center logo printed on the side, and his jaw dropped when Louise exited the car and Ines got out of the back. "What are you..." he began, then froze when he saw who was in the passenger seat. His heart pounded in his chest as anger flooded his system.

"Good grief! Why are you wet, Mitchell?" Louise asked with her trademark scowl as Ines opened the car's hatch.

He couldn't focus on her. He glared at the man—no, the son of a bitch, who hadn't moved a muscle. For a beat, the men stared at each other. It was as if neither could believe their eyes.

"Why did you bring him here?" he asked through gritted teeth.

With everything he had on his plate, the last thing he needed was this.

"Listen to what Seth has to say. Give him five minutes," Louise answered.

Seth! Hearing the godforsaken syllable sent a prickling tremor through his body.

"How did you even know I was here? No, forget it! It doesn't matter. You won't be staying long," he shot back, setting the paper and pen on the porch next to the apple butter before striding toward the SUV. The car windows were rolled down, and he zeroed in on his former best friend. "Did you come for money? The lawyers from my publisher contacted you, and you came to see how much you could get, am I right?" he hissed.

The rage was as fresh as if he'd just caught the man embracing Holly that damned day when his life turned to shit.

"Mitch!" Ines called, but he ignored her pleas.

"Are you going to get out of the car, or have you decided to sit on your ass all day?" he barked, but Seth didn't say a word.

"Mitch, get out of the way," Ines huffed, exasperation coating her words.

What the hell did she have to be irritated about?

He hadn't asked her to come here, and he certainly didn't request the presence of this bastard of an ex-best friend! He whipped his head in her direction and found the woman maneuvering a wheelchair over the bumpy ground. "Why do you have that?"

"It's for me. And I can answer your question, Mitch," Seth said, holding his gaze. "I will be sitting on my ass. I'll be sitting on my ass all day, every day."

Seth can't walk? Jesus! What happened?

A sliver of bitterness in his heart subsided as the pieces came together, and disbelief edged out the anger. Dumbfounded, he watched as Seth eased himself out of the car and into the chair. It gave him a little time to take in the man he hadn't laid eyes on in years. Seth's blond hair was sprinkled with a few silver strands that glinted in the light. The once muscular man had thinned out, and a long scar cut across his forearm.

"How did this happen, Seth?" He'd hated the man with a passion. He'd spent the last seven years perseverating on the past and feeding the anger within him. But the guy, no matter what he'd done, had still been his friend. And a part of him ached for what the man must have endured.

Seth rested his hands on the chair's back wheels. "I was in a motorcycle accident last year. I was going too fast and lost control. I was in the hospital for six weeks, and when I got out, I left in one of these." He glanced at the polished silver wheel-chair. "It's been rough looking for work. I moved back to Denver a few days ago. I'm living with my sister until I can get back on my…I'd say feet, but wheels seems more appropriate," the man finished with a melancholy twist to his lips.

Mitch cleared his throat. "There are modifications that can be made. It's not impossible to cook in a wheelchair," he blathered. And Jesus, what was wrong with him? That's what he says when he learns his friend had lost the ability to walk?

"How many resorts do you know that would hire a chef in a chair?" Seth countered. "I'm just saying, it hasn't been easy."

The guy was right. The cards were stacked against him. It was a damned shame, too. For all his faults, Seth was an excellent cook. He'd be an asset in any kitchen.

No, he couldn't let his mind go there. Screw this guy!

He crossed his arms. He had to stay strong and maintain his hotheaded front. "Did you come to ask for money? Let me guess. You want part of the proceeds from the book? Well, news flash! There might not be a book. You've come this far for nothing."

"No book?" Ines snapped.

He threw his hands up. "I don't know, Ines! I don't know what the hell will happen." He turned his anger on Seth.

"That's why I need you to say whatever you came here to say, then leave."

"I'm not here because I want your sympathy or your money, Mitch. I'm here because I owe you an apology," the man said, conviction shining in his eyes.

"Fine, you apologized. Now leave," he shot back like a sullen teenager.

"There's more," Seth replied.

Of course, there was!

A muscle ticked in his jaw. "I'm listening," he answered, staring at a point beyond the man's shoulders.

Seth exhaled a slow breath. "I don't want what happened with you, me, and Holly to ruin what you've found with Charlotte."

What the actual fuck!

The breath caught in his throat. He looked from Louise to Ines as the familiar buildup of rage twisted and snarled in his chest. "What have you told him? And what do you think you know about Charlotte and me?"

"Mitchell, it's clear as day that you love her," Louise answered. "And she loves you."

He took a step back. "How would you know that?" he hissed as the muscles at the base of his neck knotted.

"Ralph ran into Charlotte early this morning, and the pair chatted for quite a while," Louise replied.

If he wasn't standing, he would have believed his heart had stopped beating. "Ralph spoke with Charlotte?"

"Yes," Louise answered, her features softening. "When Ralph got back to Helping Hands, Seth had already arrived. He'd surprised me this morning by stopping by unannounced." Louise and Seth shared a knowing look. "We had a lot to talk about. When Ralph joined us, he mentioned he'd spoken to Charlotte and indicated there was some turmoil between the two of you. It made sense to bring Seth into the conversation and tell him about her and what she meant to you and to Oscar."

Mitch ran his hands down the scruff of his face. He didn't have the energy to blow his top over Louise sharing his personal bullshit with Seth. All he cared about was Charlotte and how she was doing. "What did Ralph say about Charlotte? How did she look? Is she okay?"

"No, she's not okay," Louise replied sternly. "She told Ralph that she screwed up and kept something from you. She feels terrible about it. She explained that she tried to apologize and right the wrong. But you called her a liar, and you said she betrayed you."

Yep, that was exactly what he'd done.

He paced in front of the cabin. "She got into a photography workshop in London."

"And?" Louise pressed.

"And it starts at the same time that the book is due to Gwen and when we'd decided we would tell Oscar about our relationship," he replied.

"That's it?" Louise shot back. "That's the reason you're throwing away your happiness—a scheduling issue?"

"It's not that simple. She lied to me," he replied in a tight rasp.

"I doubt her motivation was to hurt you," Louise answered. "In fact, I think she didn't tell you because she wanted to protect you. She didn't want to disappoint you."

He pictured Charlotte's beautiful face. He could hear the little sighs she made early in the morning when she wasn't quite awake. He'd gather her into his arms and inhale her warm, strawberry scent. With her eyes closed, she'd stroke his cheek before falling back to sleep. Completely captivated, he'd watch her, drawing his fingertips along the curve of her neck.

Did he believe that she'd set out to break his heart?

He'd been so sure in his anger and so resolute in his rage that the only choice he had was to tell her to leave.

"I hurt you, Mitch. I hurt you, and I hurt Holly. And for that, I'm sorry," Seth began. "You always burned so brightly. You were the star from the beginning. I know what I did was wrong, but I wanted a little piece of that for myself. I wanted to know what it was like to be adored like Mitch Elliott was. I became bitter, feeling like I was always playing second fiddle to you. I let jealousy guide my path. That, Mitch, is my greatest folly and my greatest regret."

He knew Seth well enough to tell if the man was bull-shitting.

He wasn't.

But that voice in his head, those clawing, skeptical murmurs, wouldn't allow him to believe it.

He hardened his demeanor. "Is that it? Is that your apology? You're not perfect? You got jealous? Anything else to get off your chest?" he shot back, working to keep the emotion out of his voice.

"There is something else," Seth replied, maneuvering his chair over the pebbled drive toward him. "You should know that Holly always loved you. She never stopped."

Mitch shook his head. It was too much to take. "We were friends, Seth! Best friends! Why couldn't you have come to me? I had no idea how you felt. I would have said something to the producers. I didn't intentionally steal the spotlight. I never meant for you to feel like you were in my shadow."

Pain marred Seth's expression. "I know. And that's why I'm here—because I owe it to you. I've watched every show you've done. I've read every book. I saw the guy, my best friend, full of zest and vitality, harden into a shell of a man. And I knew it was my fault. I hated who I'd become. When Holly and I saw

Oscar's blood work and learned I couldn't be his father, I felt relief."

"Why?" Mitch bit out.

Seth exhaled a tight breath. "Because any kid would be lucky to have you as their dad. You have so much to give."

"Jesus, Seth!" he replied, sinking to the ground.

"I need you to hear me, Mitch, not as the guy who stole your girlfriend, but as someone who's been to hell and back. Don't throw away a good thing. Don't turn your back on love. Don't let what I did to you taint the rest of your life."

"Seth is right, Mitch. We're here because we care about you, and we want you to be happy," Ines added when the crunch of wheels on gravel grumbled in the air.

He came to his feet, his focus bouncing between Louise and Ines. "Who the hell else did you invite here?"

Louise craned her neck and stared down the dirt road. "No one," she answered as a mammoth black Suburban with dark-tinted windows came to a screeching halt behind the Helping Hands vehicle.

Was he being investigated by the FBI for being a colossal jerk?

The doors swung open, and Madelyn, Rowen, Raz, and Landon exited the vehicle.

"Did you all drive down to Telluride to yell at me, too?" he asked on a stunned breath.

Rowen adjusted his glasses. "No, we took my plane. Remember, rich people things? We had a car waiting for us there. I would have chartered a helicopter, but there isn't a place to land near the cabin. You should really think about installing a helipad. You know, for your rich friends," the man answered, then cleared his throat.

Oh, for the love of Christ!

"Why are you here?" he pressed, scanning the new arrivals.

"We're here because of Charlotte," Rowen answered.

Mitch cradled his head in his hands. "Yeah, that's why they're here, too. I screwed up." He took in the decent-sized group of people. "Seth Graham, Ines Gordon, and Louise Dagby, this is Madelyn Malone, Rowen Gale, Raz Cress, and Landon Paige," he said, salvaging his manners when a spark of hope ignited in his chest.

Wait a damn second!

He had Charlotte's best friend's fiancé right here.

Penny must know the ins and outs of what was going on with Charlotte. He turned to Rowen. "Has Penny spoken to Charlotte?"

"Yes."

He stared at the guy. "And?"

"Your assessment is correct," Rowen continued. "You must have really screwed up because Charlotte decided to go to London. However, in Charlotte's defense, Penny tells me that Charlotte earned a full-ride scholarship to attend an extremely prestigious photography workshop. In my fiancée's friend Harper's words, you're a giant douche canoe for not being proud of Charlotte's accomplishment."

The anger that had taken over when he'd learned of the workshop had disappeared. In fact, he was proud—damned proud. That crazy chick with the hat and scarf was right on the mark.

"We're here to help you reduce your douche canoe factor and get her back," Landon added.

"Yep, you're a grade-A wanker, Mitch," Raz began. "But you're far less of a...what does Charlotte call him again?" Raz asked, turning to Rowen.

"A hothead," the man supplied.

"Yeah, you're far less of a wanker hothead when you're with

her. And we know you love her, so get over your bullshit and figure out a way to get her back."

Seth stared at the men, wide-eyed. "Are these your friends, Mitch?"

"No, mate, we're not friends," Raz answered as Madelyn eyed the man. "Right, right! We're sort of friends in a forced proximity kind of way."

"Ines texted me, and I gathered the boys to come to check on you," Madelyn answered.

Shit! That's right! Ines and Madelyn were as thick as thieves.

Still, it was quite something that these people had trekked across the state to find him. "You're here for me?"

"Are you just picking up on this, or are you having a moment of introspective self-discovery? Because that shit happens when you least expect it," Rowen remarked. And Mitch couldn't help it. A grin stretched across his face, and he released one hell of a rip-roaring, belly bouncing, full-throated laugh.

Landon shared a look with Madelyn. "Are fits of quasi-psychotic laughter normal in the nanny match process?"

The woman nodded. "Mitch put it together. That's the reaction of a man who's figured out what matters to him."

Holy shit! He had! The nanny matchmaker was right!

He glanced at the pad of paper.

Figure out who you are and what matters.

Don't throw away the important things.

A spine-tingling euphoria passed over him. He got it! He had the answer.

"Rowen, do you know when Charlotte's leaving for London?" he asked, his mind racing.

"Yes."

Mitch ran his hands through his cropped hair. "Jesus Christ, Rowen! I need the dates!"

"Oh, sure! Penny says she's leaving Saturday. My jet is at the airport. We can fly back to Denver, and you can talk to her tonight. You've got plenty of time."

Mitch shook his head. "No, that won't work." He'd seen the look on her face. He knew what she thought of him. She believed that he'd chosen to embrace the hothead. He had to do something on the Mr. Cheesy Forever level if he wanted to prove that he wasn't that hard-hearted, inflexible man anymore.

He needed a plan—something that would knock her socks off.

He surveyed the group as a rush of gratitude left him light-headed. These people had come here for him—to help him. He pictured his grandfather—a miserable man who had soured on life and love. He'd kept himself locked away in the house. And as grateful as he was that Bruce Elliott had taken him in, he couldn't allow that to be his fate—if not for himself, for his son.

He had a choice to make.

For the past seven years, he'd kept his guard up. He'd become the hothead until Charlotte showed him another way. He had to decide who he would be at his very core. He'd either seek out the worst in people, waiting for them to disappoint him, or he'd take the other path and look beyond the black and the white and understand that life wasn't lived in absolutes. He'd either forge a future where the people around him were potential enemies, or he'd employ empathy, tear down his walls, and substitute compassion for callousness.

He removed the orange heart from his pocket as a plan, a crazy-ass plan to win Charlotte back, took hold. "I know how to give Charlotte her Mr. Cheesy Forever."

"Mr. Cheesy, what?" Seth asked.

"I've got this," Rowen replied to the man. "Penny filled me in. Mr. Cheesy Forever is the picture of what Charlotte used to want. But I have to warn you, Mitch. Penny said that's not what

Charlotte wants anymore. Charlotte mentioned that she doesn't need a guy with a sign. I'm a little fuzzy on the sign part."

But Mitch wasn't.

He knew exactly what that meant, and he had an insane idea to win her heart.

"I have a plan to get Charlotte back, but I'll need help to pull it off. A hell of a lot of help. This is big—really big. It spans two continents, and we've got three days to make it happen." He turned to Rowen. "When exactly will Charlotte arrive in London?"

"Sunday at 5:44 p.m. GMT, 10:44 a.m. for us in mountain time zone. Despite my offer to use my plane, she's flying commercial," the man answered. And God bless nerds and their ability to retain and spit out data.

"If your plan has anything to do with the UK, I've got you covered, mate," Raz announced. "I've got connections in London."

"And I have a flat in London if you think you'll be needing lodging in that neck of the woods," Madelyn chimed.

Mitch's pulse raced. This was it! They had one chance to pull off a display of love reserved for cheesy movies.

Cheesy! That was the ticket to her heart.

"Good, good!" Mitch answered, then turned to Seth. "And Seth," he began, then stilled. He didn't see the guy who'd betrayed him. Now, he saw the man who'd been his friend—a man who'd battled his own demons and who'd taken a chance to make amends.

"Yes," his friend answered.

"I can't do this without you. Are you in? I could use your help?"

With his shoulders back and his chin held high, Seth looked like a new man. "You can count on me, Mitch."

And he could. He knew the guy would have his back.

"Is this whole plan prep starting now?" Raz asked.

"Yeah, dude, it is!" he answered. "Don't you feel the momentum of the moment?"

"Right, right! I do. Fight for love, blah, blah, blah. I'm just bloody hungry." Raz gestured to Landon and Rowen. "These blokes dragged me out of the gym and didn't even give me a second to grab a protein shake."

Mitch chuckled. "There's an organic market not far from here that delivers. I'll put in an order and get enough food to make grilled cheese sandwiches. While we wait, I'll fill you all in on the plan."

"You mean cheese toasties," Raz countered with a mischievous glint in his eyes.

"Call it whatever the hell you want!" He went to the cabin's door and held it open. "Come on! We don't have a minute to lose. And Ines," he added, pinning the woman with his gaze.

She raised an eyebrow. "Yes, Mitch?"

"Call Gwen. Tell her I need an extension—just a few days. If what I think is about to happen actually happens, I'll have one hell of an ending for the book."

"On it," the woman replied with a sly grin, slipping her cell from her bag.

He removed the orange heart from his pocket and grinned. With his friends by his side and love, so much love and gratitude in his heart, he was a man on a mission.

A mission to get the girl.

But the clock was ticking. And failure wasn't an option.

It was Mr. Cheesy Forever 2.0 or bust time!

TWENTY-EIGHT
CHARLOTTE

"CHARLOTTE AMES, are you visiting the UK for business or for pleasure?"

Charlotte took in the busy customs area, buzzing with voices and chatter. It was almost six in the evening, London time, and she'd done it. She'd made it to the UK! She tucked a lock of auburn hair behind her ear, then glanced at her camera bag. "I'm here for work. I'm a photographer."

"Is that so?" the customs agent replied, surveying her from behind his wire-rimmed glasses.

"Yes, I'm here for a professional workshop."

She exhaled a grateful breath and grinned. She'd taken the leap.

She'd emailed the admissions clerk at the Royal College of Art and confirmed her spot for the workshop with one caveat. She declined their offer to pay for her airfare. Instead, she'd splurged on herself. With Harper, Libby, and Penny cheering her on, she'd purchased a first-class seat on a direct flight from Denver to London.

And hello, ample legroom!

Between the delicious meals and the seat that reclined into a bed, she'd landed in the historic city rested and raring to go.

"It's being hosted by the Royal College of Art," she added.

"Brilliant! The college isn't far from Chelsea and Kensington Park. Make sure you don't work too hard and get to take in the city. Enjoy your time in London," the man replied, adding the first stamp to her passport.

"I will," she replied. And she meant it. She was ready, so ready to open herself to new possibilities, to reach for the stars. She was nobody's mermaid to push around. She knew her worth. And she understood her heart.

"All right, next," the man called, waving a couple forward as she sailed out of the customs area and headed for the baggage claim.

She studied the swarm of people, absorbing the energy. This was the farthest she'd ever ventured from home. Crisp British accents peppered the air along with snippets of French, German, and a few languages she couldn't quite place as she fell into step with the crowd. She slipped her phone from her bag as she walked, then connected to the airport's Wi-Fi. Texts and emails populated, pinging against the sound of the roller bags grumbling across the airport's shiny tile flooring. Messages from Penny, Libby, and Harper rang out, accompanied by images of the Union Jack flag. She chuckled. Her friends were as excited as she was about this new chapter of her life. She sent them a quick message, letting them know she'd arrived safe and sound, then read the list of new texts, unable to stop herself from hoping Mitch's name would appear.

But there was nothing. Not a text. Not an email. No missed calls.

And that was okay. Yes, she missed him. But a soothing peacefulness had taken over after she'd declined her father's request to water his houseplants. Not to mention, she'd had time to reflect on her conversation with Ralph. The man had cautioned her not to count Mitch out quite yet. Perhaps the man was right. But if Mitch couldn't accept her apology or believe that she'd truly felt remorse, there simply wasn't a path forward for them.

As of this moment, he'd chosen his hotheaded ways over her.

And that's where things stood.

But that didn't mean she'd planned to cut off contact with him entirely.

She had to consider Oscar's feelings and the child's wellbeing.

Somewhere over the Atlantic, she'd decided she'd contact Mitch today once she got settled in London. There was a seven-hour time difference between the UK and Denver. Right about now, Mitch was probably driving down to the campsite to pick up Oscar from Outdoor Lab.

What would Oscar do when he noticed she wasn't there?

She hadn't wanted to disappear from the child's life. At the very least, she hoped Mitch would grant her a call or a video chat with the boy. But it wasn't her decision. As much as she loved Oscar, Mitch was his father. She was simply the nanny—at least for a few more hours. Today was the sixtieth day—the last day of the nanny match trial period. Madelyn would be calling soon to see if this nanny match was the real deal or if the parties wanted to go their separate ways.

Her pulse kicked up at the thought of Madelyn's name flashing on her cell's screen.

She had no idea what she would say when the woman reached out. Then again, maybe Mitch had already told her that they weren't a match. It only took one party to nullify the agreement.

It was surreal. Her life had changed entirely over the past

sixty days. She wasn't the woman who settled for scraps of attention anymore, and she didn't twist herself into a human pretzel for anyone.

Still, the thought of Mitch asking Madelyn to find another nanny candidate sent a ripple of heart-breaking sorrow through her body. She scrolled through her emails again and breathed a small sigh of relief that there was nothing from Madelyn...yet. She exhaled a slow breath as the baggage claim area came into view, and the clump of travelers fanned out to retrieve their luggage. She spied her carousel, recognizing a few people from her flight milling around the edges of the conveyor belt. But she didn't head over.

No, she broke away from the crowd and took a seat.

She needed a moment to soak it in.

She focused on the active area, pulsing with energy. Couples embraced. A little girl skipped toward an older couple with a bouquet of daisies in her hand. And signs. So many signs. There was a cadre of drivers in suits and sunglasses, holding slips of paper with names printed in bold lettering. And then she spied the other types of signs that dotted the lively space. The signs brought a smile to her face. She opened her camera bag and lifted her Nikon to her eye, studying the throng of people holding up poster board and pieces of construction paper.

Welcome home, Melanie!

Hello, Nanna and Poppy!

Daddy, can we get a puppy?

She snapped several photos, capturing the vitality of the people who'd come to greet their loved ones. Young and old, dressed to the nines or sporting yoga pants and flip-flops, some laughing and some crying, the distinctly human element of creating a visceral connection played out before her. There were jovial slaps on the back and the passing over of babies to kiss. She observed a beaming woman jump into a man's arms when she caught a flash of a young boy with chestnut-colored hair dart behind a row of chairs. The breath caught in her throat as she kept him in the viewfinder. But when the child turned around, she didn't see Oscar's toothy grin. Of course, he wouldn't be here. She sighed, blinking back tears. Could it be her heart, her sentimental heart, that hadn't quite given up on a Mr. Cheesy Forever kind of life?

She placed her camera back in its case, then headed toward her baggage carousel. It didn't take long before she spied her suitcase. She'd packed light, and she was grateful she had. The next step was figuring out how to get from the airport to her lodging. Back on her cell, she opened her email and found the message with the address of where she'd be staying. Part of the scholarship came with room and board, and they'd put her up in a rental not far from the school. She scanned the signs, searching for where to hail a taxi, when another sign caught her eye.

Charlotte Ames.

A sign with her name on it.

She scrutinized the letters written in bold orange, then glimpsed the person holding the sign and gasped. "Madelyn Malone!"

The nanny matchmaker slipped the sheet of paper into her handbag, then flung her red scarf over her shoulder before a sly grin pulled at the corners of her lips. "I've always wanted to do that. I considered purchasing one of those hats that drivers wear. But I couldn't find anything that matched my handbag. You know how it goes," the woman finished, brushing a strand of dark hair back into place.

Charlotte's jaw dropped. She had zero knowledge when it came to matching hats and handbags. But that was the least of her concerns. Her mouth opened and closed like a befuddled trout. "You're my driver?" she stuttered.

"Not exactly! My driver is your driver," the woman explained with a nonchalant wave of her hand.

Charlotte's mind spun like an out-of-control carousel. "You have a driver?" she stammered.

Madelyn looked at her as if she'd sprouted rutabagas from her ears. "Obviously, I have a driver, dear. This *is* London."

Welp! That didn't explain anything about this outrageous encounter.

Charlotte stared at the woman. "What are you doing here?"

Madelyn frowned. "We established what I'm doing here. You saw the piece of paper with your name on it. I'm picking you up. I'm your ride."

She got the whole name-on-a-sheet-of-paper thing. But this was insane!

"But why are you picking me up?"

Madelyn peered around the airport. "Because I'm here."

Charlotte was ready to borrow a little hotheadedness from Mitch. This exchange with the nanny match expert bordered on infuriating.

"You live here?" Charlotte shot back, trying to make heads or tails of why Madelyn Malone had left Denver to come to London to pick her up.

"I have homes all over the world," the woman replied.

Charlotte pressed her fingertips to her temples. Was she losing her mind or hallucinating? Maybe it was that second glass of champagne she'd had on the plane, or perhaps she shouldn't have overindulged in the cheese plate they'd presented her with when she'd boarded the plane. But that was hours ago. And holy cheese bonanza! It was the definition of delicious. But whatever it was, something was messing with her brain. She narrowed her gaze. "Madelyn, you're here, now, in London, picking me up from the airport."

There! Direct and to the point.

Madelyn sucked in a tight breath, then cringed. "You're looking a bit frazzled, Charlotte. You need to eat something. I fear you're suffering from jet lag. Let's get dinner. I know the perfect place," the woman offered casually as if Heathrow Airport in London was a totally normal place for the two of them to meet up. For Pete's sake, they were on a different continent!

Charlotte scanned the area.

Who would she meet next, the Easter Bunny?

"Are you expecting someone?" Madelyn asked with that coy twist to her lips.

"No, I just wasn't expecting you," she answered, hating how rude that must sound, but it was the truth.

"Well, isn't this convenient," the woman cooed. "I have a car waiting, and I know the perfect place to eat after a long flight." Madelyn waved over a tall man clad in a dark suit. "Todd, we'd be most appreciative if you could take Charlotte's bag and prepare the car. We'll be dining at the location I mentioned to you earlier."

"Yes, ma'am. Welcome to London, Miss Charlotte," the driver said with a tip of his hat in a rolling British accent.

Madelyn took her arm. "London is one of my favorite cities," she said, guiding her through the sea of people to the waiting BMW like it was totally normal for them to be yucking it up in the UK.

Charlotte examined the luxury car. "This isn't some elaborate abduction, is it?"

Madelyn laughed and shook her head. "You and that strange propensity to think you've been kidnapped. I'm simply taking you to dinner, and I'm sure you'll agree that we have business to discuss."

Here it comes!

Charlotte nodded, her nerves beginning to get the best of her, as she settled herself into the back seat next to the nanny match maven. "You know why I'm here?" she asked as Todd maneuvered the car into the London traffic.

"Yes, Penny tells me you were awarded a prestigious scholarship to attend an intensive photography workshop at the Royal College of Art. That's quite an achievement, dear," Madelyn answered, watching her closely.

"Thank you," she murmured, her mind working overtime.

What else had Penny divulged?

"When did you see Penny?" she asked, crossing then uncrossing her legs and failing at exuding calm.

"I had lunch with your friends. Let's see," the woman pondered. "I always get so thrown off by the time change. It was yesterday. You had already left for the airport. Otherwise, I would have invited you along. I arrived in London before you, because of course, I flew on a private plane."

Multiple houses and private planes—no one could say Madelyn Malone didn't know how to live.

But then Charlotte stilled and replayed the woman's response. She'd said friends—*plural*. And God only knows what Harper said! And Libby, in her chi-less state, could have blurted out a whole host of lunacy.

For what must be the millionth time in the last five minutes, Charlotte's gobsmacked mouth hung open. "You had lunch with Penny, Harper, and Libby?"

Madelyn folded her hands in her lap. "I did. They're such lovely young women. I understand you've been friends for quite a while. You met in kindergarten?"

Charlotte sat back as the muscles in her neck relaxed. Maybe it hadn't been a Charlotte Ames gab-fest. "Yes, I owe a debt of gratitude to our kindergarten teacher. She assigned the four of us to the same table, and here we are twenty years later, still the best of friends."

"Ms. Miliken, correct?" the woman replied.

"Yes, that was her. She was a truly kind and generous woman. Sometimes, I wonder where she is and what she's doing."

"Funny how people can come into your life and change it forever," Madelyn mused, her rich vibrato voice taking on a faraway quality.

Charlotte nodded. "It is."

"Like Mitch and Oscar?" the woman shot back as her gaze slid to the key.

She still had it on. She couldn't bring herself to take it off—couldn't bring herself to believe that she'd never know if it unlocked Mitch's heart. "Have you spoken to Mitch?" she asked, glancing out the window at the sea of cars.

"Yes, I've spoken with Mitch quite extensively over the last couple of days. I take it, you haven't?" Madelyn answered with a distinct lilt to her voice.

This was it—the moment she'd learn if her nannying days were over.

"No...um...well...I..." she began when Madelyn cut off her hemming and hawing.

"You fell in love with him," the woman stated.

Charlotte stared into the nanny match maven's dark eyes. "Yes."

"And?" Madelyn prodded.

"And we had a fight. I didn't tell him about the photography opportunity in London, and he said that I'd betrayed him for keeping the workshop a secret. He said I'd be leaving him when he needed me the most. His book is due to Gwen. He didn't have an ending for it. I know that it was weighing heavy on his heart. If you've spoken to Mitch, I assume you know the rest," she added, recalling his fierce expression and his blue eyes awash with pain and anger.

"Yes, I do," the woman agreed.

Charlotte steadied herself. "Is that why you're here—because it's the final day of the nanny match trial period?"

Madelyn weighed the question. "I guess I am."

What?

"You guess?" she blurted. "I figured you were here to tell me that it's over—that Mitch wants you to find him a new nanny for Oscar."

"What do you want?" the woman countered.

Charlotte shook her head. "I don't understand. I thought if one party wanted to end the nanny match contract, that meant it was over."

"Would you say Mitch and Oscar are your perfect match?" the woman pressed.

Charlotte stared out the window, twisting the key between her fingers. "I couldn't stand Mitch when I worked for him at the Crystal Cricket. I never meant to fall in love with him...with them...with Mitch and Oscar."

"Love is a funny thing. It can find you when you least expect it, but often when you need it the most," Madelyn answered, her words floating in the air like fairy dust.

"Mitch called me a liar. He thinks I betrayed him," she said, her voice barely a whisper. But that was the truth. He'd chosen not to accept her apology. And that's where they'd left it.

"Those are some serious allegations," Madelyn replied, her expression giving nothing away.

Charlotte's mouth grew dry. "I know. Has Mitch told you what he wants?"

Madelyn adjusted her scarf. "He has."

Breathe! Just breathe!

She inhaled a shaky breath. "And?"

The woman craned her neck to glance out the window. "And I see we're getting close to our destination," Madelyn replied with a little clap.

What was going on with Madelyn Malone? She'd gone from somber nanny matcher to giddy schoolgirl. And worse than that, she hadn't answered her question. What had Mitch told her?

Charlotte parted her lips, preparing to demand answers, when the strum of a guitar and the beat of live music caught her attention. She peered out the window and found a line of people curved around the side of a building.

"Is there an outdoor event going on?"

"There certainly is. It's where we'll be enjoying our dinner," Madelyn replied, looking like the cat who ate the canary.

"It must be awfully popular. Is it a new restaurant?" Charlotte probed.

"Something like that," Madelyn answered with her coy grin in place.

The car came to a stop, and the driver hopped out and opened her door. "Enjoy the Signature Charlotte," the man said with a tip of his hat.

The Signature Charlotte?

Madelyn joined her on the sidewalk. "We don't have far to go. Let's stretch our legs, shall we?"

Charlotte observed the line of people. "Shouldn't we get in line?"

"No, these people are waiting on you," the woman answered —again, not making a lick of sense.

"On me? How could they be waiting on me?"

Dumfounded, she stood there, then inhaled the heavenly scent of grilled cheese. The delectable scent she'd been living and breathing for weeks. She studied Madelyn. "What is this? What's going on?"

"What's going on is that we're waiting on some lady named Charlotte to see if we get free cheese toasties," a man standing in line answered.

"Free cheese toasties?" she echoed.

The man scoffed. "Let me guess, you're an American?"

Charlotte cringed. "Yes."

"You call them grilled cheese in the states," the man explained.

She nodded. That's right! That's what Erasmus had called them. She turned to Madelyn as her heart thundered in her chest. "You have to tell me what's going on."

"This is the line for Mr. Cheesy Forever," a teenage girl from the line exclaimed.

Who was she having this conversation with—Madelyn or half of London? And then it hit her, and everything went topsy-turvy. How did people thousands of miles away know about her Mr. Cheesy Forever?

"Where did you hear about Mr. Cheesy Forever?" she asked, eyeing the teen.

The girl shrugged. "Everybody knows about Mr. Cheesy Forever UK," the girl answered as the people in the queue nodded. "It's plastered across social media. It started blowing up this afternoon."

Mr. Cheesy Forever UK started blowing up on social media? What did that even mean?

She gave Madelyn one last look, then set off, her pace quickening as the mouthwatering scent of melted cheese and toasted bread grew stronger. She turned the corner, skidding like one of those hotrods in the *Fast and Furious* movies, ready to break into a full-out sprint when a bank of lights nearly blinded her. She shielded her eyes from the brightness and spied several cameramen. Whatever this was, the media was there to cover it.

Wild-eyed, she surveyed the street, then froze. Parked about ten yards ahead of her sat an orange food truck. But Say Cheese, Louise wasn't painted on the side. No, this truck had Mr. Cheesy Forever written in fire engine red along the vehicle's body. As if she were no longer in control of her body, she moved forward, left foot, right foot, until she caught sight of Erick.

Erick, who should be in Denver!

The young man leaned out the order window and waved to her. She raised her hand as her jaw hit the ground. Beside him was a young woman in a wheelchair buttering slice after slice of bread. She waved to her as well, but she had no idea who this chick was. And then another form appeared, and her heart leaped into her throat.

HOLY HOT CHEF!

It was Mitch!

Charlotte couldn't move. She could barely think.

Could a girl get any more gobsmacked in a day? Probably not!

Mitch caught her eye from the food truck, smiled, then patted the woman in the wheelchair on her shoulder. He leaned in, said something to Erick, then before she could blink, he was striding toward her. The man she feared she might never see again beamed at her, his grin widening with each step.

"Charlotte, you're here," he said as a hush fell over the crowd with only a few whispered words peppering the air.

It's her!

That's got to be the Charlotte.

What do you think she'll say?

Does she hold the key to the chef's heart?

Charlotte ignored the strange whisperings and eyed her hothead chef. "Yes, I'm here. I'm supposed to be here. What are you doing in London?" she blurted.

He looked around. "I'm cooking dinner."

Was everyone going to be cagey with her today?

"In that," she exclaimed, pointing to the truck.

"Yeah, it's a new thing I'm doing. I'm partnering with nonprofit organizations in the US and UK to help troubled teens and people with physical disabilities learn the ropes of running a food truck. We'll teach them the culinary skills they need, set them up with the right equipment, then help them secure loans to start their own food truck small business."

Hello, insta-philanthropy!

He'd rattled off a mouthful.

She took a few unsteady steps forward, taking in the entirety of the food truck. From the shiny paint job to the bold lettering to the gleaming stainless-steel kitchen, it was a sight to see.

"You did this in a week?" she asked, wide-eyed.

Mitch came up beside her. "Actually, we did this in three and a half days."

Three and a half days!

All she'd done in the last three and a half days was take some pictures, board a plane, and gorge on first-class fancy cheese.

"How did you manage to do this?" she asked.

Who was this man? When she'd left him, he'd been an angry hardened hothead. Now he radiated joy.

"It was a team effort," he began. "Rowen got us set up with the tech we needed. Raz connected me with some community centers and organizations that work with adults with physical handicaps in London. Landon hooked us up with a local band. Ines handled the PR and media blitz. Madelyn cut through the red tape to get the permits and licenses we needed here and in the US. And Louise and Seth are overseeing the educational outreach component and running Mr. Cheesy Forever USA."

And there it was! Another mouthful of impressive words.

There was no doubt he'd put together something phenomenal. But one word rang out louder than the others.

"Seth?" she repeated. "Is it the Seth from your past?"

Mitch nodded without an ounce of anguish marring his features. In fact, all she saw reflected in his eyes was gratitude. "Yeah, it's *that* Seth. I'd love to introduce him to you."

A week ago, the man could barely speak his former friend's name without nearly foaming at the mouth in searing anger. If ever there was a sea change in a person, this was it!

She looked around. "Is he here?"

Mitch turned to the food truck, then whistled to get Erick's attention. "Could you send Oscar out with the iPad?"

Tears welled in her eyes. "Oscar's here?"

"Hi, Charlotte! Look, I've got Mr. Cheesy Forever USA right here," the boy chimed, running toward them with his camera bouncing from the strap and his backpack shifting from side to side as he held out his iPad.

She knelt, pushed the camera aside, then wrapped him in her arms. "I missed you. Did you have fun at camp?"

The boy melted into her embrace. "I caught a fish, and I ate s'mores every night, and Phoebe and I built a birdhouse, and I took lots of pictures with my camera."

"That sounds wonderful," she replied, pulling back to stroke his cheek. "I'm so happy to see you, Oscar," she added, swallowing tears of relief.

Oscar's expression dimmed. "I was nervous when Dad picked me up from camp early, and you weren't with him. But then he said he had a big plan. He wanted to do something special for you because he acted like a..." Oscar stilled, then tapped his foot twice. "And he said he really needed my help."

"Did he?" Charlotte answered, glancing at Mitch.

"Here, say hi to Seth, Louise, and Sergio," Oscar chimed, holding up the iPad. "The Mr. Cheesy Forever food trucks are being livestreamed all over the planet. But we can only talk to the people in Denver on my iPad."

All over the planet?

She focused on the video feed featuring another shiny Mr. Cheesy Forever food truck. Sergio, Louise, and a man in a wheelchair waved to her.

"Hey, Charlotte! We're getting ready to serve lunch here in Denver. What do you think of the Mr. Cheesy Forever food trucks? Pretty slick," Sergio remarked.

She pressed her hand to her heart. "I think they're amazing."

"Mr. Cheesy Forever is going to change a lot of people's lives. Mitchell did good. He's worked hard," Louise remarked, staring into the camera.

Charlotte stole another look at the Mr. Cheesy Forever UK food truck, then turned her attention to the media and the throng of people who'd come out. "It sure looks like he has."

"Charlotte, that's my best friend, Seth," Mitch said, pointing to the man in the wheelchair.

"It's nice to meet you, Charlotte. I've heard a lot about you," the man answered.

"It's nice to meet you, too." With tears in her eyes, she turned to Mitch. "What happened between the two of you?"

"I figured out what was important," Mitch answered.

Speechless, she stared at the man.

"Are you ready to try the Signature Charlotte sandwich?" Seth asked from Denver.

"The what?" she stammered, concentrating on the chef. "You named a sandwich after me?"

"Yeah, Dad was the one who named it the Signature Charlotte," Oscar exclaimed. "It's super delicious! I've eaten like six thousand of them since we got here."

Mitch ruffled the boy's hair. "Don't worry, I haven't let him eat six thousand sandwiches."

"I should hope not," she said with a teary chuckle.

Mitch shifted his stance. "I came up with the new sandwich recipe while we were brainstorming how to pull this off. It's super cheesy. It's got cheddar, parmesan, mozzarella, and Gruyere on sourdough with a dash of hot sauce to give it some heat and a dollop of apple butter to tamp down that fire with a little sweetness."

"A little heat and a little sweet?" she repeated, holding his gaze.

"Yeah, like you," he answered, then took her hands into his as he glanced from the food truck to the media, to the iPad, then to the line of people recording them on their phones. "You inspired this, Charlotte. I'm sorry I said those awful things to you. I took, and I took, and I took from you. I was selfish, thinking only of my needs and my career. And when things didn't go exactly as I'd wanted, I lashed out. I resurrected the angry hothead. But now I see that I'm at a crossroads. I've got two choices. The first is to fall back into my old ways, wallow in pain, and cling to old grudges."

"Where does the second path lead?" she asked, breathless.

"If I'm lucky," he began, his eyes shining. "It leads to you."

She sensed the lights pointed their way. She could feel the palpable anticipation of the crowd. But nothing could distract her from Mitch's face.

"The second path takes work," he continued. "This path requires introspection. It forces me to see that I have the power to choose to be better. It's up to me to embrace empathy, kindness, and forgiveness. It's on me to do better, to be better, and to understand that life isn't lived in black or white, but all the colors in between. And it starts by giving back, by opening my heart, and becoming your Mr. Cheesy Forever 2.0."

Tears trailed down her cheeks. "Mr. Cheesy Forever 2.0, huh?"

"It's catchy, don't you think? The perfect name for a grilled cheese food truck," he replied, tears glistening in his eyes.

She released a nervous laugh. "Yeah, it's quite catchy."

Never in a million years would she have guessed that her Mr. Cheesy Forever would become a food truck.

He tightened his hold on her hands. "Charlotte Ames, I've loved you from the moment you hurled a salad at me. You brought me back from a dark place. But it's not your job to make sure I don't revert into being that miserable hothead." He glanced at Oscar, who stood by, beaming up at his father. "It's up to me to be the man you and my son deserve. And I can promise you, I will not disappoint either of you. A very wise person told me not to throw away the things that matter in life. For me, that's you, and that's Oscar. I love you. What do you say? Can I be your Mr. Cheesy Forever 2.0?" he finished. He released her hands, reached into his pocket, then removed the ceramic orange heart. "This is yours. You hold our hearts in your hands."

"And I've got one, too. You can wear this heart on your finger," Oscar added, pulling a sparkling diamond ring from a little pocket in his backpack. The enormous diamond was shaped like a heart—a beautiful, glittering heart.

She pressed her hand to her chest. "Is that what I think it is?"

"Hold on! There's more," Mitch said, then unzipped another pocket on Oscar's backpack and removed a folded-up piece of paper. He took a knee, and Oscar joined him as he unfolded the page.

"I did the writing," Oscar said, giving her his sweet, toothy grin.

She read the sign once, then twice.

Charlotte, will you marry my dad and be my Charlotte forever?

"And Charlotte?" Oscar said, pulling a photo of him and his mother from his pocket.

"Yes," she breathed.

"I think my mom would have liked you a whole, whole lot," the boy added.

"I think I would have liked her a whole, whole lot, too," she answered, smiling through her tears, then met Mitch's gaze.

"If it's not completely obvious, I'm here to tell you that both Elliott men are pretty crazy about you. Will you marry—" Mitch began when Oscar bolted to his feet.

"Wait! We almost forgot the virile lock," the child exclaimed.

"The virile lock?" she questioned.

"*Viral* lock," Mitch corrected, his cheeks growing pink.

"Yeah! Are we eating for free or not?" a man called from the line.

"What is he talking about?" she asked as Mitch's blush intensified.

"That's the twist. It's the reason this whole thing went viral."

"What happened?" she pressed.

Mitch shook his head as a look of disbelief crossed his face. "I wanted to do something that would get your attention—something that helped people."

She took in the crowd gathering around them. "You certainly succeeded."

"We knew we wanted to do something for charity. I was speaking on camera with a local reporter about the Mr. Cheesy Forever when Oscar—"

"When I ran into the room and showed Dad and the TV guy the white lock," the boy interrupted. "Then I said, if Charlotte's key opens your heart, she'll have to forgive you for being a." *Tap-tap.* "And she'll have to marry you. And then she'll be my Charlotte forever and ever, too."

"Somehow, online, it morphed into this. If your key opened my heart, then we were truly meant to be. That's how I'd know I was your Mr. Cheesy Forever," Mitch explained. "And that also seemed to include a lot of people eating the Signature Charlotte sandwich," he finished, gesturing to the crowd.

"That was my idea, too. I said, it'll be a party, and we'll make dinner for London," Oscar added, quite pleased with himself.

"Wow! That's quite a twist!" She unclasped the necklace, then slid the key from the chain and handed it to the boy. "There's one way to find out," she said as the cameramen moved in closer.

"This is the moment. If Charlotte's key opens Chef Mitch Elliott's heart, Charlotte will accept the marriage proposal, and hundreds will dine on free cheese toasties to celebrate," a reporter gushed.

Mitch peered over his shoulder at the bevy of cameras, then leaned in. "I didn't expect this to become such a spectacle."

"I didn't expect to fall in love with a hothead," she countered, biting back a teasing grin.

"A reformed hothead," he corrected with a deliciously cocky grin that made her head spin.

She patted Oscar's shoulder. "There's no turning back now. Go ahead. You do the honors. Let's see if my key opens your father's heart."

She gazed into Mitch's eyes, knowing she'd found her forever.

"Here we go!" Oscar called, doing a great job of hamming it up.

The air grew thick with anticipation. Not a word was uttered as the boy inserted the key.

Click!

"It's in! Are you ready for me to see if Charlotte's key opens my dad's heart?" he called to the bank of cameras.

"Your son might have a future in reality TV," she whispered to Mitch. But the man didn't say anything. He simply gazed into her eyes, shining with the promise of a love that would last a lifetime.

"Three, two, one!" Oscar called. He turned the key in the old lock. With a cranky creak, the shackle released, and the lock sprang open. Oscar held it up like a prizefighter as the crowd roared with hoots and applause.

Mitch slid the ring onto her finger. "The nanny and the hothead are getting hitched!" he called to the cheering crowd.

The applause exploded, and she soaked it all in. The love, the excitement, the palpable joy that permeated every cell in her body. It was like something out of a dream.

"I love you," she said as Mitch gathered her into his arms. And at that moment, she remembered the other Charlotte from the airport. She'd spent years wondering if she'd ever find a love like what she'd witnessed at the baggage claim when she was just a girl.

And now she had her answer—the evidence reflected in Mitch's eyes and in her heart.

"Dad! Charlotte! Say cheese!" Oscar exclaimed, holding up his camera.

Mitch cupped her face in his hands, his lips hovering above hers. "Cheese," he whispered, his breath warm as he closed the distance and sealed this Mr. Cheesy Forever love story with a kiss.

MITCH CROSSED his arms and observed the Crystal Cricket kitchen. It was a quarter past seven, and the dinner rush was in full swing. This used to be the time when he went into hothead mode, barking commands and growling at anyone who dared enter his orbit.

But not anymore.

As much as he loved the rush in the back of the house, he had somewhere else to be tonight.

He clapped his hand on the newly hired executive chef's shoulder. "Stay on top of the tickets. Don't be afraid to let your voice be heard, but practice what you preach. If you demand efficiency from your cooks, you demonstrate the skill."

Seth gave him a cheeky grin. "You sound a hell of a lot like Louise."

"She sure drilled it into our heads," Mitch agreed, gifting the man with an easy grin.

Nearly every facet of his life had changed since the night Charlotte made him the luckiest man on the planet and agreed to marry him. They'd spent two blissful weeks in London. During the day, Charlotte took part in the workshop while he and Oscar took in the sights. Madelyn had kindly allowed them to stay in her luxury flat in Chelsea, which happened to be a short fifteen-minute walk from the Royal College of Art. This fortunate coincidence gave Charlotte the idea to offer up the lodging provided to her by the program to another participant and shack up with him and Oscar.

Everything had fallen into place. He'd *wooed* the hell out of his fiancée. And he couldn't have imagined a more magical city to celebrate their engagement.

With the reruns of his past cooking shows streaming in the UK, he was already a celebrity there. But the Mr. Cheesy Forever proposal, seen by millions around the globe, propelled both himself and Charlotte into the spotlight, and they were treated like royalty.

Tickets to plays, dinner reservations at the hottest restaurants, boat rides on the River Thames, and enough chocolate delights to put Oscar into a sugar coma, London had welcomed them with open arms. They'd even hopped on a train and gotten in a visit with Oscar's Aunt Amy in Paris.

And there was another perk that couldn't be downplayed.

He'd figured out how to bring the book to a close.

Giddy with delight, Gwen had been blown away by the Mr. Cheesy Forever ending he'd crafted for the book—an ending that ushered in a new beginning.

But when it was time to return to Denver, they were ready. With new opportunities coming their way daily, sometimes hourly, the three of them were eager to return home and start the next chapter of their lives. A life that revolved around love, laughter, friendship, and plenty of grilled cheese sandwiches.

Yep, you heard that right. He had friends—real friends who cared about him.

Thanks to the efforts of these good people, he'd gotten the girl, and Mr. Cheesy Forever was an overnight success. Charities and organizations across the US and the UK were lining up to partner with them.

And speaking of good friends, after taking excellent care of the Crystal Cricket, Gabe and Monica returned to their restaurant in Langley Park, Kansas. But working at the Crystal Cricket full time was no longer in the cards for him.

With the demands of running Mr. Cheesy Forever, he needed help with the day-to-day operation of his restaurant.

And he didn't have far to look.

He'd worked out a part-time schedule for himself and put his faith into Seth to run the place by making the man the executive chef of the Crystal Cricket.

They updated the kitchen to accommodate the man's wheelchair. And truth be told, he'd swear the guy was faster on his wheels than he ever was on his feet. Along with promoting a sous chef to head chef position to help shoulder the workload, while the Crystal Cricket belonged to him on paper, he no longer ruled with an iron fist.

He'd gone back to the beginning and emerged with a new perspective. There are no guarantees in this life. He'd spent far too much time insulating himself from others. He'd expected people to fail him. He wore blinders, looking only for the faults in those around him. And this had kept him from experiencing the love and joy that now permeated his life.

And he sure as hell was done with that hothead.

But that didn't mean he'd become a pussycat.

Oh no!

He was still a chef at heart. But he inspired with conviction and dedication, not by berating his staff and throwing tantrums over parmesan. He employed a work ethic that didn't falter, a commitment to his community, and a dogged desire to be the best possible version of himself for Charlotte and Oscar.

But it wasn't only about him anymore. And that's why he was cutting out early this evening.

"Is Oscar staying over at Rowen and Penny's?" Seth asked, following him back to the office.

Sweet anticipation sent a delicious zing through his body. "Yeah, Charlotte's putting the final touches on everything for her first exhibit at the gallery. I figured I'd stop by and give her this," he answered, holding up the box.

"I'm sure she'll love it," Seth answered. It was good to see the guy back in the kitchen, and it was even better to be cooking alongside him.

"Chef?" one of the newly hired waiters called, stepping into the office. "We've got an order for an off-menu item. She says you make her a risotto dish? Her name is—"

"It's Madelyn Malone," Mitch answered, a grin pulling at the corners of his mouth. He owed the woman a debt of gratitude.

Seth nodded. "I know her order. I'll be right out."

"And the pastry chef wanted me to give you this, Chef Elliott," the waiter continued, then handed him a Crystal Cricket to-go bag.

He thanked the kid, then focused on his best friend. "I'm glad you're here, Seth."

Yeah, he was that sappy *I-love-you-man* guy now.

Blame it on his new perspective. He cared about people and wasn't afraid to show it. He'd pegged that part of him as a weakness. He was wrong—dead wrong. Turns out, compassion was his greatest strength.

"Tell Charlotte to break a leg or whatever they say for good luck in the art world," Seth added.

Mitch hung his chef coat on the hook, then glanced around the kitchen, knowing it was in good hands. "Will do," he answered, then headed to the back door.

It was mid-June in Denver. That could mean anything from scorching heat to a late freeze. But the weather gods had blessed the city with mild temperatures. A spring rain had rolled through, and the fragrant geraniums in the hanging flower baskets mingled with the clean scent of the storm. He headed toward the gallery when his phone pinged. He slipped his cell from his pocket, and joy flooded his system when he saw the screen.

A video call from Oscar Elliott.

He accepted the call.

"Hi, Dad," Oscar chimed.

"Hey, Oscar!"

"Hi, Mitch!" Phoebe exclaimed, entering the frame.

"Hey, Phoebe! What's going on, kids?"

He had a feeling he knew.

"I have a cookie question," Phoebe began.

He bit back a grin. "Oh yeah? What kind of cookie question?"

Between the foot tapping and their propensity to inhale chocolate, Phoebe and Oscar were the best of friends.

"Do oatmeal chocolate chip cookies count as cookies?" the little girl pressed, then peered over her shoulder at something out of the frame.

"Rowen and Penny said we could have two cookies each. That's Phoebe's no-puking limit. But we were thinking because they're oatmeal, they're more like breakfast," Oscar explained.

Yep, these two were at it again.

He chuckled. "Oatmeal chocolate chip cookies are still cookies."

"Oscar, let me talk to your dad," Rowen said as Oscar turned the camera, and the man came into the frame. The guy's glasses were crooked, and he looked six stops past exasperated. "I've been trying to explain this to them for the last hour."

Mitch worked to keep it together. "Where's Penny?"

Rowen groaned. "She's writing. I'm holding down the fort."

Mitch glanced up from the screen and crossed the street. "Hang in there, man. And thanks for having Oscar over."

"Have you seen Charlotte yet? Did you give her the present?" Oscar chimed, edging Rowen out as his son returned to the frame.

"I'm working on it. I'm headed to see her now." He held out the phone and panned left and right for Oscar to see the twinkling lights of the downtown Crystal Creek business district.

"Do you think Charlotte would let us have three cookies each?" Phoebe asked as Rowen ran his hands down his face in the background.

"No, sorry, Phoebe. I'm certain Charlotte would agree with the two-cookie policy," he answered.

"What about oatmeal raisin cookies? Those have to be a breakfast food!" Phoebe exclaimed as Rowen took off his glasses and pinched the bridge of his nose.

"Come on, Phoebe! Let's go play dominoes in your room. Bye, Dad! Love you. Tell Charlotte I love her," Oscar added, flashing a toothy grin.

"I will," he answered as the video call ended. He had one great kid. And he owed Holly a debt of gratitude for the love she showered upon the boy. She put every good part of her into Oscar, and for that, he'd be eternally grateful.

He turned the corner, then spied the gallery—the gallery owned by Janine Tran. And the location of professional photographer Charlotte Ames's first exhibit. His pace quickened, but he stilled when he caught a glimpse of her in the center of the space. Her ponytail swished from side to side as she looked between two blown-up photographs. Greedily, he admired his fiancée. This remarkable, talented, sexy as hell woman made his heart sing. And he wasn't her only fan.

Gwen's publishing company had hired her to work with several of their authors and, of course, booked her to work on his next book. And the connections she'd made at the Royal College of Art propelled her career further. Galleries across the US and UK were clamoring to display her photos and celebrate her work. She'd even accepted a job to photograph a wedding in Denver for a couple she'd met while sitting on the bench across the street.

She took a step toward one of the photos, then stopped. It was as if she sensed him watching. She looked over her shoulder, and her serious expression dissolved into a wide grin.

Christ, this never got old! The rush of euphoria at knowing she was his sent his pulse racing.

He jogged the rest of the way, then tried to open the door but found it locked.

She pointed at the closed sign. "Come back tomorrow," she teased, those emerald eyes sparkling.

"Any chance I can get a private showing? I come with gifts," he said, meeting her coy expression with one of his own as he held up the box and the bag.

She rubbed her hands together like one of those over-the-top mad scientists. "Tell me it's something sweet."

His gaze darkened. "It's something very sweet."

With her hand on the lock, she studied him through the glass. "It's against gallery policy to allow anyone besides staff and artists in after hours. But I think we can make an exception for a devastatingly handsome chef who comes bearing sweet treats." He drank in his fiery redhead as the click of the door unlocking sent his desire into overdrive.

She propped open the door, and with the box under his arm and the bag of goodies around his wrist, he scooped her up with his free arm. "Thanks for breaking the rules for me." He pressed a kiss to her petal-soft lips, then gingerly returned her to the ground.

"What do you think?" she asked, gesturing to the crisp white walls adorned with enlarged versions of her photos.

He surveyed the bright room. The exhibit's theme focused on Denver communities. While Charlotte had taken thousands of photos of him cooking in Say Cheese, Louise, she also captured the people and the diversity that made Denver unique. She and Professor Tran had pored over the images and had come up with an exhibition that took his breath away. And seeing the enlarged photographs gracing the walls and fastened to easels in the center of the gallery heightened the experience.

He stared into her emerald eyes. "How did this hothead chef end up with a woman as amazing as you?"

With a mischievous grin, she twisted the key with her left hand. The heart-shaped engagement ring glittered under the gallery lights, and again, he was struck by how lucky he was.

"We have Madelyn to thank. On the night she explained the nannying position, she'd described herself as a facilitator of fate. I'd say she's right."

Charlotte wasn't wrong. Madelyn Malone may have an unconventional approach, but he wouldn't be standing here, beaming at his beautiful fiancée without her.

"Speaking of fate," he began. "I have a gift for you."

"Sweets and a gift?" Charlotte asked, peeking into the bag.

"The sweets are chocolate-covered strawberries, and the gift is a surprise," he answered.

"Gifts and desserts are my favorites," she cooed, pressing a kiss to his cheek. "But first, I want to show you a piece that just arrived." She took his hand and led him toward the back of the gallery.

"Another photograph for the show?" he asked, following her away from the main gallery's bright lights.

"This one is for the entryway to Helping Hands. Louise and Ralph have been so good to us. I want to donate it to them," she answered, leading him into a smaller room adjacent to the gallery. "I had this photograph printed on a large canvas," she explained, then removed a sheet covering a large square that had to be at least eight feet tall by eight feet wide.

He took a step back to absorb the impact of an image of three pairs of hands with an orange heart in the center of the smallest palm. "It's us—you, me, and Oscar."

"Yes, it's the photo Oscar's teacher had taken when you cooked for Oscar's class."

He remembered that day. He'd been so worried about taking Louise out again. Having Charlotte by his side had given him the strength to venture back to his beginning. He focused on the heart. "Louise and Ralph are going to love it," he said, setting the to-go bag on a table in the center of the room. "And now my gift. This is for you," he added, handing her the box.

She jostled it gently. "You know you didn't have to get me a present," she said, then stroked his cheek.

"It's the night before your first exhibit. I wanted to do something special." He eyed the box. "Well, calling it a gift might not be the right word. I'm more of a messenger, returning something that belongs to you."

She cocked her head to the side. "Now you really have me stumped." She set the box on the table, opened the lid, then gasped. "Oh, Mitch! Is this what I think it is?" she asked, her voice barely a whisper.

"There's one way to tell. But fair warning, Oscar and I might have personalized it."

He looked on, and that cocky part of him rocked an internal fist pump.

He was about to become fiancé of the year—maybe even the century.

Carefully, she lifted the old camera from the box, gazing at the item as if she'd been reunited with an old friend.

"Turn it over," he coaxed.

She inspected the bottom of the camera—the camera Harper's grandmother had given her.

"How did you find it?" she pressed, disbelief coating her words.

He wrapped his arm around her shoulders. "I asked Rowen to use his tech skills to scour the city's antique store websites, but we didn't have to go high-tech."

She looked up at him. "You didn't?"

"Penny said she'd remembered going with you to sell it. I called the place, and it was still there. I simply went to the antique shop and got it back for you."

Yeah, he was a damned considerate dude these days.

"This is beyond thoughtful. And I love the little touch you added," she said, her eyes shining as she ran her finger across her name scratched into the bottom with the words *Mitch* and *Oscar* now etched on either side.

"Thank you, Mitch, for this, this life, for Oscar, and for giving me not only a piece of my past but my very own Mr. Cheesy Forever 2.0," she answered, then set the camera back into the box and pinned him with her gaze. "And you're not the only one with gifts. I have a present for you, too."

"You do?"

"I did a little shopping this afternoon. I wanted to find the perfect dress to wear to the exhibit, and I went a little overboard."

He admired what she had on—a pink wrap dress with a bow tied above her hip. Honestly, she could don a paper bag, and he'd have an instant hard-on. "What did you splurge on?" he asked, adjusting his stance. Even the smallest amount of fiancée ogling had his blood supply heading south.

"On this," she answered, untying the bow of the wrap dress and revealing—holy hot lingerie!

Beneath that innocent-looking garment hid the body of one smokin' hot redhead. Clad in scarlet lacy lingerie with curves for miles and breasts quite literally calling to him, his jaw dropped, and his cock took the helm of the USS Mitch Elliott.

"With Oscar spending the night at Rowen and Penny's place, we'll have the house to ourselves. I thought you'd enjoy this little surprise."

His lips parted, but nothing came out. Attempting to produce words while staring at a goddess clad in the tiniest pair of panties that he'd ever seen proved to be a herculean feat. He devoured her body with his gaze. With this level of heat, he wouldn't be surprised if his eyeballs exploded. He stopped at the lace panties that he'd swear were calling out to him to rip them off her body with his teeth.

"I won't be able to make it to the house," he somehow bit out, his brain momentarily connecting with his mouth as he devoured his fiancée with his eyes and his cock went rock-hard in his pants. He slipped the dress off her shoulders and watched it pool around her ankles.

"Do you like your present?" she purred.

He slipped his fingers around the slim lacy band. "This is the best present ever."

She undid his pants and took him into her hand, stroking his hard length. "I can feel your enthusiasm."

"But I have one question," he rasped as he slid his hands down her torso.

She worked him in slow, devastatingly smooth strokes. "Ask away."

He twisted the lace waistband of her panties around his index fingers. "Are there any rules on unwrapping?"

The dirtiest smirk twisted her lips. "It's your present. You decide how you want to open it."

Sweet Christ! This woman!

With a decisive pull and a snap that had him ready to snap, those itty-bitty lacy panties lay in scraps on the floor. Her chest heaved as he lifted her into his arms. She gasped in delight when he pressed her back to the wall, then thrust his cock inside her sweet wet heat. Their joint moans tangled in heated breaths. They didn't have one way of making love. Sometimes it was slow and sensual, and other times, it was frenzied, fast, and dirty.

When Charlotte tangled her fingers into the hair at the nape of his neck, then rocked her hips like the naughtiest of lingerie-clad photographers, he knew this was no time for slow and steady. With one hand gripping her ass and the other wrapped securely around her ponytail, he pistoned his hips, pumping and grinding against her tight bundle of nerves. Their mouths met in a frantic kiss as he shifted her body and adjusted the angle of penetration. He filled her to the hilt, inhaling a sharp breath as she tightened around him. Thrust after thrust, their bodies came together in a delirious need for release. He knew her every gasp and breathy moan. She was close, and so was he. Dialing up his pace, he gave her ponytail a tug, knowing what drove his alluring fiancée over the edge.

"Mitch, yes, harder!" she cried, bucking her hips.

He pulled her in close, instinct taking over. All that existed was Charlotte. Her body. Her breath. Her taste. Her love. Her cries of passion fueled his release, and he let go as they crashed into a rush of ecstasy, hips pumping, bodies writhing.

"I love you," he breathed against the shell of her ear as the heady buzz of making this woman cry out in delirious pleasure coursed through his veins.

As their bodies wound down from the surge of pure bliss,

she rested her head on his shoulder. "Now I know what to get you for Christmas, and your birthday, and Father's Day, and Flag Day, and don't forget Ground Hog Day..." she trailed off as they laughed a rumbly sated sound.

Gingerly, he pulled out and set her down as his phone chimed.

"It could be Oscar. We better check," she said, slipping on her wrap dress.

"You're probably right. There was a debate over oatmeal chocolate chip cookies," he replied, taking a second to watch her.

"Let me guess. Phoebe wanted to know if they counted as cookies?" Charlotte chimed, tying her demure little bow.

He chuckled, fastening his pants, then pulled his cell from the back pocket. He peered at the screen. "This must be an autocorrect error. This text doesn't make sense."

"Why do you say that?" Charlotte asked, coming to his side.

"It's a text from Raz. He says he's been arrested."

It had to be a mistake.

He was about to text the guy back when Charlotte's phone pinged. She slipped her cell from her purse, then pressed her hand to her chest as she stared at the screen. "It's from Libby."

"What's wrong?" he asked.

Had all hell broken loose with their friends?

"She's been arrested, too!" Charlotte exclaimed. "What could they have done? Sure, Libby's been a little on edge these days. But to get arrested? And Libby and Erasmus can't be together, can they? This must be some crazy coincidence or a bizarre misunderstanding."

He was about to agree with his fiancée when he remembered the last time he spoke with Raz. He met Charlotte's gaze. "Oh, no!" he breathed, shaking his head in disbelief.

"What do you mean, *oh no?*" Charlotte pressed.

"I just thought of something."

"What is it?" she asked.

"Raz mentioned Madelyn had found his nanny match."

Charlotte's eyes went wide. "Do you think Madelyn matched Libby with Erasmus? There's no way. She's Miss Yoga Fabulous, and he's a big growly, muscled..."

"Beefcake," he supplied.

"Beefcake," Charlotte repeated, disbelief coating the word. "If it's true, sparks are about to fly. The opposing forces of yin and yang have got nothing on Libby Lamb and Erasmus Cress."

READ THE NEXT BOOK! A cataclysmic karma crash is coming your way in **The Nanny and the Beefcake**, book three in the Nanny Love Match Series.

Hothead fun facts from the author:

The Nanny and the Hothead contains a few crossover cameos. Remember Gabe and Monica, the chefs who filled in for Mitch at the Crystal Cricket? They're part of my **Langley Park Series**. And there are two more cameos! The camp counselors who welcomed Oscar and Phoebe to camp are part of my **Bergen Brothers Series**.

BONUS CHAPTER

MITCH & CHARLOTTE'S CHEESY FARM ADVENTURE

Mitch and Charlotte hit the road and head to the Sperry Dairy in the organic farming town of Elverna, Illinois, to check out the cheese! And you can only imagine what happens when these two enter cheesy bliss! Prepare to laugh, sigh, and swoon! Read it here:

https://BookHip.com/WMZHCKF

Book Three: Man Find

Bergen Brothers: The Complete Series+Bonus Short Story

The Langley Park Series

A suspenseful, sexy second-chance at love series

Book One: The Road Home

Book Two: The Sound of Home

Book Three: The Beginning of Home

Book Four: The Measure of Home

Book Five: The Story of Home

Box Set (Books 1-5 + Bonus Scene)

Own the Eights Series

A delightfully sexy enemies-to-lovers series

Book One: Own the Eights

Book Two: Own the Eights Gets Married

Book Three: Own the Eights Maybe Baby

Box Set (Books 1-3)

STANDALONES

Always Meant for You

A small-town, brother's best friend romance

The Kiss Keeper

A small-town, fake dating romance

Not Your Average Vixen

An enemies-to-lovers super-steamy holiday romance

Sign up for Krista's newsletter to get all the up-to-date Krista Sandor romance news.

Learn more at www.KristaSandor.com

FOOD TRUCK MOCK-UPS & ACKNOWLEDGMENTS

This book wouldn't be possible without the love and support of my husband.

Thank you to Najla Qamber for designing the cover.

Thank you Marla, Carrie, Tera, and Aly.

To my ARC Readers and Book Babes Reader Group, I'm thankful for your love and support. I could not do this without you!

Aren't these mock-ups fun!

ABOUT THE AUTHOR

If there's one thing Krista Sandor knows for sure, it's that romance saved her sanity. After she was diagnosed with Multiple Sclerosis in 2015, her world turned upside down. During those difficult first days, her dear friend sent her a romance novel. That kind gesture provided the escape she needed and ignited her love of the genre. Inspired by strong heroines and happily ever afters, Krista decided to write her own romance series. Today, she is an MS warrior, living life to the fullest. When she's not writing, you can find her running 5Ks with her husband and chasing after their growing boys in Denver, Colorado.

Visit www.KristaSandor.com to sign up for Krista's monthly newsletter.